THE LA[KE]

There was a disturb[ance] [in the]
lake, a bubbling wh[...]
bloody froth. The disturbanc[e ...]
entire lake was in motion, with crimson [...]
waves splashing onto the lakeside.

And, in an explosion of sound, the roc
reappeared. Not the tired and sickened bird that
had sunk beneath the waters, but a young
vibrant, majestic creature from the very depths
of legend. It rose, slowly and majestically,
restored to the prime of its youth.

It seemed a long time afterwards before Diurnan
moved. He walked down the scarred and torn
turf towards the water.

'*Diurnan*?' Maildun demanded.

'The waters renewed the roc's life . . .' He
turned to the captain and his eyes blazed. 'Might
they not renew mine, grant me eternal life?'

Also by Michael Scott

A CELTIC ODYSSEY

Michael Scott

WARNER BOOKS

A Warner Book

First published in Great Britain in 1985 by Sphere Books Ltd
This edition 1992

Copyright © 1985 by Michael Scott

The right of Michael Scott to be identified as
author of this work has been asserted by
him in accordance with the Copyright, Designs
and Patents Act 1988

ISBN 0 7474 1171 9

Printed and bound in Great Britain by
Cox & Wyman Ltd, Reading, Berkshire

Warner Books
A Division of
Little, Brown and Company (UK) Limited
165 Great Dover Street
London SE1 4YA

For Anna, with.
   Courtney, without, and
   Chris.

ACKNOWLEDGEMENTS

A Celtic Odyssey is based on the ancient Irish tale, *Immram Curaig Maileduin* (The Voyage of Mael Duin) which in turn would seem to have been closely modelled on the more famous Voyage of St Brendan the Navigator.

This novel is a faithful recreation of the Voyage of Maildun, based upon the traditional sources.

I would like to express my appreciation to Padraic O'Tailliuir, Padraic O'Conchubhair and Gus MacAmhlaigh for their assistance in obtaining and translating some of the research material. I would also like to thank Chris Ashmore and Paul Kelly for their help.

I speak of the time of the gods,
   I speak of a time of mystery and power,
   a time of awe,
   a time of magic,
   I speak of an elder, lost time.
   Let me speak then of the man born of a woman cloistered in the faith of the White Christ, a man born of her by a petty lordling who took her virginity and her sanity.
   Let me speak of the man who carried his hatred with him like a newly-honed sword, ever ready to strike. Let me speak of the voyage of vengeance that went beyond the world of Men and into the enchanted realms of Faery.
   Let me speak of Maildun . .

PREFACE

I

She screamed aloud as the pain took her again, tearing through her body like a red-hot poker. Her ragged voice echoed off the damp walls of the tiny stone cell set well apart from the main body of the convent. There her screams would not disturb the sisters at their devotions. It would not be seemly if they were to show pity for one of their own number who had found herself with child.

Aife screamed again and then a cold cloth was pressed against her face, more to stifle her cries than to cool her fever-bright cheeks. Shadows moved about on either side of her, and she was dimly aware that they were doing what they could to help her birth this child. The spawn of a rape.

The contractions began again and this time she felt the sudden shifting movement. Her cry turned to a gasp of astonishment, and then strong hands pressed her shoulders down onto the hard wooden boards and a voice, which she dimly recognised as belonging to the Mother Superior, hissed into her ear, 'Push, push now . . . and again . . . again . . . again . . . ah, it comes . . .'

There was a final spasm, and then it was gone, the pain, the pressure, the tearing. The young nun felt herself slipping down into unconsciousness, but she managed to raise herself up onto her elbows and stare down between her upraised legs at the bloody, squalling creature that was being cut free of its fleshy cord.

'What . . . what is it?' Her voice sounded thick and dull in her own ears.

The calloused hands of the Mother Superior pressed against her shoulders, pushing her down onto the rough boards again, and then the hard-eyed woman crossed herself. She glanced quickly at the babe. 'Sister Aife,' she said icily, 'it is a boy. May God have mercy on it – and on your soul!'

1

II

Oilill Agach stumbled backwards over the corpse of his brother and fell to the ground, his battleaxe slipping from suddenly nerveless fingers. He saw the flaxen-haired pirate raise his long-hafted axe high and the chieftain breathed a silent prayer for his soul. There was a low buzzing sound and then the axeman abruptly staggered and fell forward over Oilill, the back of his skull caved in by a stone the size of a pigeon's egg.

Agach remained under the body while the bloody skirmish moved over and past him, back towards the coastal village – his village. He should be there, he knew; the chieftain should be standing fighting side by side with his men, defending their hearthstones and honour from the western reivers. But only a fool would venture back into the village; the pirates had the advantage of numbers, weapons and surprise. He was quite prepared to stay where he was; when the fighting was over, he would allow himself to be discovered lying under the body of his slain enemy. Oilill Agach might be many things, but he was not a fool.

The chieftain lay in the bloody sand-dunes listening to the sounds of slaughter and burning as the westerners plundered his village. For months now they had been raiding along the western coastline of Erin, with the oncoming winter, which the druids foretold would be a hard one, spurring them on. But no one would have expected them to come this far north; they had never done so before. Agach shivered at a sudden thought: had they been sent by the Christ God, or His brown-robed followers, to carry back his severed head? He smiled grimly at the thought; the women followers of the White Christ had neither the power nor the ability to curse him, and although some of the convents were wealthy enough, their beliefs would prevent them from hiring mercenaries to come after him.

It must be nearly a year gone now, but he could still remember the fine features of the brown-robed nun he had taken against her will near the Well of Bridget on the east road. She had cursed him, aye, cursed and screamed and fought with all her might. She had sworn she would see him roast in the flames of Hell. Agach shivered again and made the Sign of Horns with the fingers of his left hand; best not to think of that now, not now when some of the very demons from that pit were raiding his village.

A pall of smoke drifted up the beach and over the dunes, and

2

he wrinkled his nose at the stench of burning flesh. There were more shouts and cries now, but he ignored them all, and only once, when he thought he heard his wife's voice above the others, did he flinch or even contemplate moving.

And then there was silence for a long time, with not even the distant mewling of the gulls to disturb the afternoon quiet.

Oilill awoke from a light doze to find a tall, blond westerner standing over him with a spear levelled at his throat. The chieftain flinched; the bronze point and hardwood shaft were encrusted with dried blood.

'Here's one that both breathes and sleeps,' the westerner said over his shoulder, taking his eyes off the paunchy, balding man on the ground. Oilill used the moment to grasp the spear and twist it away, while kicking out with his other foot, catching the other across the ankle, sending him crashing backwards. The body under which Oilill Agach had been lying had been removed and he came to his feet smoothly, still holding onto the spear. The westerner regained his footing at the same time, his left hand clawing for his dagger. Oilill cracked him across the side of the head with the wooden shaft and then deftly reversed the spear and took him through the throat.

Another reiver came over the dunes towards him, but he lost his footing in the soft, shifting sand and Oilill speared him in the guts as he fell. But the spear-point caught between the stricken westerners ribs and the weapon tore away from Oilill's grasp.

He turned and ran then, hearing the shouts and cries of alarm behind him. He ran as he had never before run in his life, the fear rising like hot bile into his throat. Stones buzzed by his head, and once he staggered as a thrown spear glanced across his shoulder, numbing his left arm down to his fingers. He knew if he fell now they would kill him and the Morrigan's pets would feed on his carcass.

Once away from the treacherous sands the going became easier, the ground firmer. He crashed through a clump of stunted bushes and lay there panting, his thoughts churning. He couldn't just keep on running, he needed . . . sanctuary!

And then he was back on his feet, and running again, but running south this time, doubling back, skirting his burning village. He risked a glance over his shoulder; four of the westerners still followed, their wild hair and beards flowing in the breeze. One, he noticed, had a head tied to his belt by the hair.

He was now on the southern side of the village, close to where the priest and his followers had built their tiny church. He came over an incline and the church was before him, and although Oilill had always thought that the stone building with its wood and turf roof looked hideous, at that moment it looked·like a palace. He ran across the hard-packed earth and staggered through the small arched doorway, slamming it shut behind him. He lay with his back against the wooden door as spear-butts and sword-hilts battered against it.

'Sanctuary!' he shouted, his breath coming in burning gasps. 'Sanctuary; I claim the sanctuary of the House of God.'

There was a silence and then a short barking laugh, rough and harsh like an animal's cough, broke the spell. Oilill felt the sobbing breath catch in his throat, and his fear froze into a solid knot in the base of his stomach when he heard the sound.

'You are no believer in the White Christ, Oilill Agach. You and I follow the Old Faith; we honour the old ways – come forth now and you may fight me in a fair and honourable combat.'

'How can I trust the word of a pirate?' Oilill shouted.

The barking laugh came again. 'You know me, headman; I am Archu, the Hound of Slaughter; you know I am a man of my word.' There was a pause, as if the speaker were gasping for breath, and then the voice came again, adding in a different tone, 'I presume you too are an honourable man, Oilill Agach. I choose to believe that you did indeed lie stunned beneath my man back on the beach; I choose to believe that you were not taking the coward's path and seeking to escape by feigning death. Come forth now and fight me.'

Oilill held his hands in front of his face and waited for the trembling to stop. He breathed deeply, willing his heart to slow its pounding. Aye, he might be a coward, but he had also fought and taken heads in battle . . . and he knew when to run and when to fight. But for all his battle experience, he had never before experienced the bowel-loosening knot of fear he felt now, as he crouched behind a flimsy wooden door while Archu, the reiver from Leics, called battle-challenge outside.

There were no windows in the tiny church, but enough light seeped in through the tight-packed stones for him to see the heavy wooden cross on the stone altar. He made a quick dash down the church for it and then back down the aisle to lean against the door where he examined it carefully. It was plain and unadorned, shaped not unlike a sword and, although blunt, its weight felt good in his hand: it would make a good club.

Oilill moved away from the door and pressed himself against

the wall, the cross upraised in his left hand. It had been quiet outside for a little time now and he was beginning to wonder what the reivers were planning when the door creaked open on its leather hinges. Sunlight shafted across the floor, and he could hear the men moving restlessly outside and once he thought he heard Archu's rough voice issuing whispered commands.

The door creaked open a little more, its warped boards scraping across the rough earthen floor, and then a slight figure stepped into the light. Oilill struck, using his full strength to drive the heavy wooden cross into the other's face. There was a sodden crunch of bone, and bright blood spurted from nose and mouth as the figure toppled backwards, leaving only a wood and leather sandal behind him.

Oilill slammed the door shut and leaned against it, the sudden realisation of what he had done just beginning to sink in: the western reivers did not wear sandals!

'Agach, you lying whoreson bastard!' Archu's ragged voice was almost incomprehensible with rage. 'You claim the sanctuary of the House of the New God, and yet you strike one of its priests . . .' The door shifted suddenly as something thudded solidly into it. Oilill dug his heels into the hard-packed earth and pushed back, but slowly it was pushed inexorably inwards.

Oilill Agach threw himself away from the door, and two of the westerners tumbled into the darkened church. The wooden shaft of the cross crushed one skull and snapped another's spine, before the world exploded into fragments of light and pain for the petty chieftain.

He awoke to find himself lying on his back tied to a cold stone slab in a darkened building. There was no feeling in his arms and legs and his range of vision was limited to a few blackened rafters and dark sods of turf above his head. He was unable to sit up, but, by twisting his head towards the light, he found he could make out an arched doorway. He realised then that he was tied to the altar in the church of Dooncloyne.

Metal clinked on his right-hand side and then the scarred face of Archu moved into his range of vision. Oilill saw only the reiver's eyes – and they were cold and hard, like tiny polished pebbles.

'There was a time when I would have thought that you did indeed lie stunned on that beach.' The westerner's voice was harsh and laboured, and the livid scar across his throat shifted and moved like a second mouth. 'I have heard the name of Oilill Agach spoken of with honour, and if I heard aught to the contrary I ignored it, thinking it the pratings of a petty-minded man. It seems I was mistaken.' The westerner touched his scarred throat and then fingered his cropped beard. 'But I see before me a man who sought sanctuary in the church of the New God, and who then used the holy symbol of that faith to kill.' Archu paused again for breath. 'I do not think you are an honourable man, Oilill Agach,' he spat out. He turned and walked away, his footsteps leaden on the hard-packed earth.

Oilill struggled frantically, but he had been securely tied down with dampened leather thongs, which only tightened as they dried: short of a knife there was no way for him to get free.

And then he smelt the rank odour of burning turf.

The fire quickly ate through the summer-dried turf and wooden spars, and by the time the westerners had returned to their beached craft, the roof had fallen in and Oilill's screams had ceased.

CHAPTER ONE

The heavy banks of fog shifted and swirled and four horsemen appeared suddenly on the winding path that led up to the convent. A young novice, nodding over her beads above the gate, started with fright and quickly crossed herself. Her hand went immediately to the bell rope and then she paused. She squinted down into the morning mists. She could only see four riders; men by the shape and height of them, closely wrapped in heavy cloaks of blues and greens. One of them lifted his head and stared up at the squat-walled building before him and the novice caught the gleam of gold about his throat: nobles.

The young woman waited until she was sure that they were alone before running lightly down the steps to the main gate. She pulled back the little grille and peered out. Her breath suddenly caught in her throat and she stifled a scream. The four riders were much closer than she had expected and they loomed before the convent gate like giants.

One of them rode forward and rapped with the butt of a tall hunting spear on the wooden gate. The sound boomed out dully on the morning air, the heavy mist muting the noise but it was loud enough to bring most of the convent from their cells and devotions.

The novice hung back, afraid either to open the gate or to tell the riders to be off, wishing the Mother Superior was there. And then gravel crunched as the older woman appeared, her face set in grim lines. She glared at the younger woman before ramming back the bar and jerking the gate open.

She stood in the gateway like a warrior, tall and straight and proud, wearing her simple rough woollen robe as if it were a hide-and-metal jerkin.

One of the riders leaned across the head of his mount and pushed back the hood of his travelling cloak, his copper hair striking colour into the drab morning. 'A good day to you, Reverend Mother,' he said politely, his speech and accent betraying his education. 'This is the Convent of the Mother of Jesus?' he asked.

7

The Mother Superior nodded and crossed herself at the holy name. 'It is, by the grace of God. What do you want here?' she demanded rudely.

The rider edged his horse closer to the stern-faced nun. She could see now that he was quite a young man, with a long, thin face dominated by a pair of hard green eyes. 'I have come to speak with one of your nuns.'

'Impossible,' she said flatly and stepped back, preparing to shut the gate.

The young man urged his horse forward, using its bulk to force the nun back, filling the gateway. He smiled easily, showing his teeth like a hunting dog, but the smile never touched his eyes. 'I have been riding for four days, Reverend Mother,' he said softly, 'I will not be put off.'

Baine had been Mother Superior of the Convent of the Mother of Jesus for close on twenty-five years. She had seen many things, and was old enough to remember the great druidical sacrifices when the country was still predominantly pagan. She could still remember the days when women were but little better than slaves, with little or no rights or power. But since she became head of the order she had grown used to getting her own way; her every command was carried out without question. It was not something she was proud of – for that was sinful – it was just a fact. And so, as she stood inside the gates of her convent on that cold and foggy autumn morning and stared up into the unsmiling, hard green eyes of the young nobleman, she felt – for the first time in many, many years – a touch of cold fear.

She opened her mouth to protest, but the young man raised his hand, and so sharp and clear was her image of him, she could see the sword-weals across his palm and fingers. 'I have come to speak with my mother,' he hissed softly, 'and I will not allow you to stop me.'

Baine crossed herself unconsciously, and her dim grey eyes opened in horror. 'I don't know what . . .' she began.

The young man's calloused hand closed into a fist. 'Don't even think about lying to me, Reverend Mother,' he said, and his very lack of expression frightened the woman even more than if he had shouted at her. 'I have come to see my mother, Aife, who was a young nun in your convent when she bore me.' He saw the woman's eyes harden and the lines about her mouth tighten, and he continued. 'Don't try to tell me that she's not here, or that she's dead, because I intend to search.'

'You cannot,' she whispered, 'the king . . .'

8

'I am – *was* – fostered in the king's dun,' he snapped. 'The king's sons are my foster-brothers.' He tilted his head towards the three silent riders.

'And you are?' Baine asked eventually.

'I am Maildun,' he said simply.

The small herb garden set apart from the convent was chill and the damp bit up through Maildun's boots. The air was tart and fresh with the odours of the many herbs and plants. A thin film of dew covered everything, touching them with silver, bejewelling the spider webs.

Maildun made his way down the gravelled path towards the south wall, his footsteps crunching softly on the sandy gravel. Outwardly he appeared calm and at ease, his rather plain features impassive, but inwardly he seethed and churned with new and strange emotions. He was about to meet his mother and yet, barely five short days ago, he had thought himself an orphan.

There was a dry, hacking cough and a shape moved against the high wall ahead of him, the dark homespun robe hard to distinguish against the earthen colours. Maildun stopped, his heart hammering; he hadn't felt this frightened since he had taken his first head in battle.

He schooled his breathing and waited until his heart throbbed less violently before stepping forward, dragging his boots in the gravel, deliberately making a noise so he would not startle the nun . . . his mother.

The woman started and spun around, staring at him in amazement and horror. Maildun belatedly realised that this was certainly the first time she had ever seen a man other than a priest within the convent walls.

'Don't be alarmed,' he began, immediately realising how lame that sounded. 'There is nothing to be afraid of. I won't harm you,' he continued quickly, seeing the expression of fear that had come into the woman's eyes. 'Aife . . . ?' he whispered then.

She nodded and then her lips formed a word that plumed on the chill morning air, even though she didn't speak it aloud. She crossed herself and shook her head, repeating the word again and again until it eventually sounded from her lips, 'Agach . . . Agach . . . *Agach*?'

'I am Maildun,' he said quickly, frightened now by the strange, bright light in the woman's eyes. 'Maildun,' he repeated, as she continued saying the one word over and over again.

9

'Agach . . . Agach . . . Agach . . . Agach . . .'

He took a step towards her. She raised her hands, fingers curled into claws, and bared her teeth like a wild animal. Spittle drooled from the corner of her mouth and her eyes were quite mad.

There was a crunch of gravel behind him and Maildun spun around, his hand automatically falling to his sword-hilt. It was Baine, the Mother Superior. She looked at Aife and crossed herself. 'You would not have believed me if I had told you,' she said quietly.

Maildun looked over at the woman with the mad, bright eyes and the snarling expression. 'How . . . how long has she been like this?' he asked finally.

'She has grown progressively worse over the last few years,' Baine said. 'She was never quite right . . . afterwards, but in the beginning she was quite lucid.' She looked across at the younger woman. 'I blame myself; I lacked charity and understanding at the time. Every day I pray for forgiveness,' she said fiercely. 'Every day,' she insisted. She shook her head sadly. 'But I shall pay for my sins in the next life, I know.'

Maildun looked over at his mother again, and he felt tears sting his eyes — the first tears he had shed since he had fallen from a chariot when he was ten and cracked a rib. He could see that his mother had once been a very beautiful woman. Although what wisps of hair escaped from beneath her cowl were grey, there were enough chestnut strands amongst them to know what the original colour had been. Her face was long and still retained tokens of its former beauty; her eyes, like his own, were emerald — piercing and arresting.

'Can she speak,' Maildun asked.

Baine shook her head. 'On the bad nights she screams and howls, and she cries out words then — terrible words — but she rarely speaks now, and even then it is usually a name . . .'

'Agach?'

Baine glanced at him. 'You know?' she accused.

'She . . . she said it when she saw me.'

'Ah,' the Reverend Mother nodded, 'you must bear some resemblance to your father.' She looked up at the young man. 'Aye, that was his name: Agach, Oilill Agach of the tribe of Owenacht.' She almost spat. 'And I hope to see him in Hell some day.'

'My father?' Maildun repeated dully.

The old woman nodded. 'Your father. Come, walk with me,

and I'll tell you of your father and mother, Maildun, son of Agach and Aife.' She turned away and walked quickly from the herb garden.

Maildun lingered a few moments more, looking for a last time on the mother he had never known, feeling the pain and rage well up inside him like a berserker's battle fury. He bowed to her then, as a lesser noble to a queen, and then he walked away without once looking back.

Baine was waiting for him beyond the herb garden, near the kitchens. She pointed the way and he followed her without a word, unwilling to break the silence.

The old nun led him through the grounds of the convent, past the large church and oratory, which had been built by the nuns themselves, past the tiny stone cells they slept in, and then down to the well. It was deserted at this hour, since most of the convent were already at their morning devotions. Baine leaned against the low stone wall and stared down the dark length of the well; Maildun hung back uncertainly, suddenly feeling ill at ease with the older woman.

Baine looked around and stared at him for a few moments before asking, 'What *do* you know of your parents and birthing?'

He looked up slowly and shook his head. 'Nothing.'

'Then why did you come here?' she demanded.

The young man smiled slightly. 'Until some five days ago, I thought I was an orphan fostered in the king's dun. And then I chanced to beat some petty lordling's son at *fidchell* and he, in temper, demanded to know what right I, having neither title nor lineage, had to associate with royalty.' Maildun shrugged. 'I broke his teeth for him, and then I spoke to my foster-mother, Queen Digde, and it was she who told me that my mother was Aife, her step-sister, who had been cloistered while still very young.'

Baine nodded. 'That is true. Your mother was – is – Aife, stepsister to the present queen, and by that you have a perfect right to be fostered with the king's sons.'

'My father . . .?' Maildun asked.

'Your father,' Baine continued in a different tone, 'was Oilill Agach. I did not discover that until later, and by that time it was too late . . .'

'Too late . . .?'

The old nun held up her hand, and continued. 'Your father,' she spat, 'raped your mother while she was on a pilgrimage to one of the holy places in the west.' Baine crossed herself quickly. 'He was a village chieftain, married with two daughters who would have been around your mother's age at the time. His honour was accounted dubious, and it was said that he raided his neighbours for cattle and sheep, but, of course, nothing was ever proven, else he would have been slain out of hand for the thief that he undoubtedly was. He professed to follow the ways of Christ . . .' Her voice trailed away.

Maildun felt the bitterness well up within him, and then the cold rage took hold of him again. He swallowed hard, fixing his attention firmly on the rough stones of the well, engraving the countless tiny cracks and imperfections, the glittering crystals and bright mosses into his memory. He had come from knowing nothing about his parents to knowing too much too quickly.

Baine continued in a flat, emotionless voice. 'In her shame, your mother carried you for almost the full nine months in secret. We knew nothing until the birth pangs started. We were harsh with her; we thought that she had broken her vows of chastity, and the full story didn't come out until later.' The old nun breathed deeply and hurried on. 'She had you sent for fostering to her stepsister and left your naming to her. It was Digde who told me the full story.'

'And my father?' Maildun asked woodenly.

Baine glanced up at him with a curious look in her eyes. 'When I discovered the truth, I sent my brothers to find him . . .'

Maildun looked up in surprise.

'I asked them to bring me back his head,' she said flatly. She smiled at Maildun's expression. 'She was in my charge; you might almost say that she was my daughter. And I failed her. I may have lived within these walls for more years than even I can remember, but I am still woman enough to feel the pain and degradation that she must have felt.'

'Did they bring it back?' Maildun asked, his knuckles tightening about his sword-hilt.

Baine shook her head. 'Raiders had attacked the village, and put everyone to the sword.' She smiled crookedly. 'It must have happened just about the same time your mother gave birth to you. God's retribution,' she said softly.

'Did they find the body? Had Oilill Agach been slain?'

She shrugged. 'I don't know. My brothers told me that there were no heads to bring back, for the raiders had taken them. I do not know whether your father still lives. Why?' she asked suddenly.

The young man turned away, and his reply drifted back over his shoulder. 'I would like to know.'

Baine stood by the well and watched him. She could almost feel his sickness, his loathing, his anger. 'Wait,' she called, and hurried after him.

Maildun paused by the high wall and stood with his back to her. She stopped a little way from him, suddenly unsure what to say. 'What will you do?' she asked suddenly.

'Find him.'

'Who?'

'My father.' He said the word slowly, almost as if he found it difficult to shape the sound.

'And then?' she whispered.

He turned round and looked into her eyes. His face was closed and tight, and his eyes were hard, bright and terribly reminiscent of his mother's mad gaze. 'And then I'll kill him,' he said calmly.

CHAPTER TWO

The druid lived in a small, evil-smelling cave at the foot of the jagged wall of cliffs that guard Erin's western shoreline. Although the cave was above the high-water mark, it was still rank with the stench of the sea, and its mouth was encrusted with shellfish and hung with strands of weed.

Maildun paused by the opening, holding his breath against the miasma that wafted past him. His three foster-brothers stood at the foot of the thin, winding pathway that led up to the cave, their weapons drawn, waiting for him.

'Nessan,' Maildun called again, shouting above the pounding of the breakers that foamed along the rough beach behind and beneath him. There was no answer, and he was about to turn away when there was a sudden flare of light from the interior of the cave and a tendril of acrid smoke drifted out – followed, almost immediately, by a small, wizened man with streaming eyes and a hacking cough. He staggered past Maildun and stumbled blindly down the pathway to the beach. Colga, Maildun's eldest foster-brother, put out his hand to stop him, but the old man deftly twisted out of the way and loped down to the water's edge, where he threw himself flat on the stones and allowed the frothing waves to wash in over his head.

Maildun slithered down the path and stood with Colga, Gussan and Ruarc, his foster-brothers, while the old man lay prone on the beach. From behind he presented a comical figure, with his thin, filthy legs poking out from beneath a robe that had once been white, but which was now the colour of burnt grass.

'Nessan?' Maildun asked as the old man sat up, shaking dry his straggling grey hair and beard. He turned around, blinking short-sightedly at the four armed men.

'I am Nessan, the druid,' he said, without preamble, in a voice that was surprisingly strong and vibrant.

'We know . . .' Maildun began.

The druid smiled toothlessly and held up his wizened hand. 'I know you do; I was merely reminding you, lest you forget to show me the respect due to one of my class.'

14

Colga, the eldest of the four, with strands of grey already in his hair, nodded in understanding. When he had not yet come to manhood, he had yearned to follow the white-robed teachers, but his father had explained the rights of kingship to him and forbidden it, but he still remembered enough to place both fists to his forehead and bow in respect. His brothers and Maildun followed suit.

The druid nodded in satisfaction and then he chuckled. 'I haven't had someone do that to me since . . . well, for a long time,' he said conversationally. He stood up, squeezing water from the hem of his robe, and then walked up to the four men. The old druid stared up into their faces, studying each in turn: Colga, with his broad, flat face, and twice-broken nose, light brown eyes and pleasant expression; Gussan, very like his brother, except that his features were sharper and harder, a warrior who excelled in all things except in the use of a sling- shot and spear throwing, for his distance sight was poor, and Ruarc, the youngest of the three brothers, the smallest, topping the druid by barely a head, and with the features and bone structure of a woman. He had neither the strength nor speed for weapon-work, but he made up for it with his ability with the sling, and he once said – and proved that it was no idle boast – that if he could see it, he could hit it.

Nessan finally came to Maildun. The old man stood for a long time looking up into the sharp features of the warrior with the hard, cold eyes. Maildun squirmed uncomfortably; he felt as if his very soul were being stripped away, layer by layer, by this foul-smelling old man with his filthy robe and his dancing, piercing eyes.

The druid nodded slowly, and his expression changed subtly, but only Maildun saw the shadow of fear that flickered behind his eyes. Nessan smiled abruptly and turned away. 'Come, come, you must hunger and thirst if you have come all this way to see me.' He turned away from them and walked quickly up the beach and ran up the track that led to his cave. 'Oh, I remember when I was a young man, I was always hungry and thirsty . . .'

The four men followed him, Colga leading and with Maildun to the rear. He stood for a moment at the mouth of the cave, listening to his foster-brothers' footsteps echoing off the stone. The druid's change of expression had both frightened and disturbed him with its intensity. The druid feared him, that was plain enough – but why? And then another thought struck him: did the druid fear him – or did he fear *for* him? He shivered and

15

pulled his cloak round his shoulders, and then he ducked down into the cave mouth.

The four warriors had ridden south and west since they had left the convent two days ago. They had stopped briefly near the village and church of Dooncloyne, where Oilill Agach had been chieftain, and, while the village had been rebuilt, the church remained a ruin. Maildun had questioned the few remaining villagers about their former chieftain, but they were either unable or unwilling to tell him anything, other than that which he already knew: that the village had been pillaged and burned some two-and-twenty years previously and everyone neither fit nor young enough to be taken as slaves had been put to the sword. However, Maildun did discover that Oilill Agach's corpse had never been discovered, although he should have died defending his village. But it was possible – although unlikely – that he had been taken by the raiders.

Leaving the village, they had continued on south, for Gussan had heard tell of a famous druid, whose knowledge of hidden things was supposedly unbounded, and who was reputed to possess the *Sight*. They had taken the great western road then, looking for Nessan the druid.

The interior of the cave was surprisingly clean, with most of the foul odour coming from a cooking pot suspended over a glowing fire close to the entrance. The four warriors had to crawl along the narrow, twisting opening, but once through this the cave opened out into a tall rounded chamber. The walls had been washed with a coating of white and spiralling designs had been painted onto them in various earths and pigments. The floor was covered with pelts, mostly seal, but some wolf, boar and elk. Neatly piled in one corner were bundles of dried herbs and grasses, and more were suspended from the high ceiling. On the other side of the room, casually covered with a badly-cured pelt, some pieces of gold and bronze winked in the dull light.

Nessan moved about the chamber lighting small pots of oil, gradually flooding the cave with warm, muted light. He then pulled off the ragged tunic he wore and dragged a long, white woollen robe over his head. He turned and indicated that his guests could sit, and then rummanged amongst his supplies looking for a flagon of mead.

Colga cleared his throat and spoke to break the lengthening silence. 'I've never heard tell of a druid living in a cave before,' he said.

Nessan grunted, as he attempted to pry the seal from an ancient, squat-bellied, stone crock.

'In fact, I've never heard of a druid living by the sea before,' he continued, a flush spreading up his broad face, while his two brothers grinned at him. Maildun sat a little apart from the others, near to the entrance, carefully watching the druid, not joining in their banter.

'I am not like other druids,' Nessan said sharply, as he returned with the opened crock of what might once have been mead. He handed the jug to Gussan and then produced a bone comb, which he ran through his tangled hair and beard. In his long white robe, with the golden sickle of the priesthood on his woven belt, he looked more like a druid, although neither his attitude nor manner were typical of a priest of the Old Faith.

'Now . . .' He settled himself down on a pile of ancient pelts and looked from man to man, the fingers of his left hand playing with his streaked beard. He waited until Maildun had wet his lips with the mead and passed it back to his foster-brother. 'Now, would you like to tell me why you're here?'

'Don't you know?' Gussan asked, his obvious surprise taking any real insult from the question.

Nessan folded his hands on his lap and rocked back and forth with silent laughter. 'Of course I know; you don't think I'd invite four armed men into my cave if I didn't already know of them . . .?'

'Then what *do* you know of us?' Maildun asked suddenly.

'Ah,' the old man smiled, 'I know a little . . .'

'Enough of these games, old man,' Maildun snapped. Colga leaned across and put his hand on his foster-brother's arm, his fingers biting painfully into the flesh. The older man looked over at the druid.

'You must forgive him, his mind is unsettled by ill news . . .'

Nessan nodded in understanding and then he sighed. 'Enough of this then. I came here to these wild and inhospitable shores to escape people – people like you – and the many requests they made upon me.' He saw the expression in Maildun's eyes and he smiled bitterly. 'Hear me out, Maildun, son of Oilill Agach, and I will come to the reason behind this.'

Maildun started when he heard the druid using his father's name, and he opened his mouth to question him, but then he nodded briefly and leaned back against the cold stone wall.

'You need to be hard and uncaring if you have the *Sight*,' Nessan continued. 'Many of those who profess to possess it

17

don't, of course, and indeed there are few enough trained druids who do have the gift of the gods. I do. I can see – imperfectly sometimes, and then betimes with great clarity – glimpses of the future, the past and, every now and again, into the very soul of a man.' The druids flat, grey eyes drifted across Maildun's face, and then they clouded and his voice altered slightly as he suddenly looked into a different time. 'I came here because I could not bear the pain I inflicted on others. Oh, I didn't do it deliberately, nor did I take any pleasure in it; but I often told them what they did not wish to hear, what they didn't want to know. There is a certain security in ignorance. And I, in my own ignorance, would shatter theirs.'

'What do you see for me, druid?' Maildun suddenly hissed.

Nessan's gaze drifted back and he looked at the tall, thin young man with the hard, intense gaze. He shook his head slowly, pity showing in his eyes. 'It would be better for you if you were to go back with your foster-brothers and forget that you ever had a father.'

'I cannot!'

'You could, if you so wished it. But, of course, you don't. You will try to take revenge on your father for the crime that was committed before you were even born; a crime that led to your birthing.' He smiled grimly. 'There is no reason behind it, but I suppose if you thought about it you might not be able to find a coherent reason for it yourself.'

'I want his head,' Maildun said with icy calmness.

'A barbaric custom,' the druid said pleasantly, 'and surely sinful for a professed follower of the Christ God.'

'I want him,' Maildun said slowly and distinctly, leaning forward so that the wan light washed his face in yellow and darkened his eyes, giving it a sickly cast. 'I will have his head – even if I have to follow him to the gates of Hell to claim it. I swear it.'

'Then you are a very foolish young man,' Nessan said quietly, leaning forward so that his face was barely a knife's length from Maildun's.

'I want him, druid,' Maildun repeated, his voice high and tight. 'And with or without your help I will have him.'

The druid nodded slowly, and he continued in a tired, resigned voice. 'If you cannot be dissuaded then . . . ?'

'I cannot.'

Nessan shook his head, and leaned back against the wall, the shadows cast by the oil lamps running down his face like tears. 'I can tell you nothing about your father . . .' he began, and then jabbed an accusing finger at Maildun when he started to protest. 'Hear me out, boy!' he snapped. 'On the day that you were born, your father's village was raided by pirates from Leics. They razed the village and slew as many of the unusable inhabitants as they could find.' He paused and then added, 'I do not know what happened to your father on that day.' He closed his eyes. 'I can see him running; I can see him killing – but then there is nothing. I do not know.'

'The pirates, would they know?'

'You would have to ask them to find out, wouldn't you? They were led by a man called Archu; he leads them still and, although they are not as active as they once were, they are still wont to raid the lonelier villages and forts along the coast. He is called the Hound of Slaughter – and with good reason.'

'How will I know him?'

'He has the laugh of an animal.'

Maildun leaned forward eagerly. 'And where will I find this Archu?'

The druid inclined his head to one side. 'To the west and south of here there is an island. It is dominated by a large fort: you will find him there.'

'Would he know what had happened to my father?'

'What will you do if you find your father is already dead?' Nessan countered.

Maildun looked confused. 'I . . . I don't know; kill his slayer, I suppose,' he said in surprise. He stood suddenly. 'We'll go now. I thank you for your hospitality, druid . . .'

Nessan smiled up at the young man. 'And tell me; just what will you do now?'

Maildun frowned. 'I will put together a small raiding party, hire a couple of currachs, and visit this pirate in his den.'

Nessan shook his head. 'I am afraid that that is not the way of it.' He stood slowly, pressing his hands into the small of his back and grimacing. 'If you are determined to seek Archu, then you must build a new ship, long enough and strong enough to hold thirty men.'

'I will not,' Maildun snapped, colour rising to his face.

'You will,' Nessan said calmly, 'or I will lay bonds of *geasa* on you to do so.' Maildun paled; *geasa* would compell him to follow the druid's instructions, or else suffer the consequence of the usually fatal curse. And although a baptised follower of the Christ, the customs and beliefs of his heritage still held him in thrall. 'I will build the boat then,' he said sullenly, 'if that is what you command. But that means I will not find Archu this year.'

'You have waited this long,' Nessan said calmly, 'another year won't kill you. And you have a lot to complete in that year. Come,' he said suddenly, 'Let us walk on the beach, the air is fresher and cooler there.'

The small, aged druid led them from the cave and down onto the beach. The sun was sinking into the west, and the chill evening water was awash with its blood. The sand hissed softly with each lapping wave and their feet sank slightly into the yielding surface.

'Your craft must be constructed of newly-hewn wood,' Nessan said suddenly, continuing where he had left off. 'The sail cloth must be freshly woven, even the very nails in the boards must be newly forged.'

'Why?' Maildun demanded.

'Because yours will be a maiden voyage, and you will travel into waters that do not wash onto Erin's shores.' Maildun laughed rudely, but Nessan continued calmly. 'You have sworn to seek your father at the gates of Hell; words lightly spoken, but words which may not be recalled. You will travel beyond the seas you know into strange and frightening waters, and you must ensure that you take only the best. Let your weapons be newly forged of the purest iron, let your bows be of fresh wood and your arrows newly fletched.' The druid stopped and faced the young man. The setting sun behind him threw his face into shadow, but his eyes remained glittering harshly, brooking no comments. 'Your vessel will be sheathed with a triple covering of tanned and seasoned hide, and you must ensure you take a sufficient quantity with you for repairs.'

'In the name of all the gods,' Maildun murmured, 'you make it sound as if I'm sailing to the very edge of the world.'

Nessan smiled happily, his small, round face crinkling around the eyes and lips. 'Aye, it does. Now the crew. You must take thrice times ten men, and three others – and no more. That number is fixed; you must leave Erin's shore with no more and no less. The thirty men you may pick yourself, and I'm sure that you will find there will be many only too glad to accompany you on this venture. The other three will be Germane, the southern navigator, and Diurnan Lenkard, the northerner, who will act as your first mate, and both of whom are known to you. The other . . .' He paused.

'The other . . . ?' Maildun prompted.

The aged druid turned and looking into the setting sun. A line of clouds on the horizon had been touched with pink and gold, and the sky itself had faded to an imperial purple. 'He will come,' he said softly. 'He is a man, and more and less than a mortal man.'

Maildun gritted his teeth in frustration. 'You speak in riddles, druid. How will I know this man?'

Nessan waited until the tide had retreated and the stones stopped rattling before he replied. 'He has but one hand, and in the place of his left is a curious silver hook, the like of which you have never seen before nor will you ever see again. He is a bard, and men call him Paedur.'

Maildun shook his head. 'I have not heard of him. Where is he from, and why must he accompany us?'

'He is reputed to be from the east – and beyond – but he is your only hope of ever returning from this foolhardy voyage.' The druid turned away suddenly, leaving Maildun standing alone as the tide washed in over his boots.

Gussan stopped the druid at the foot of the track that led up to his cave. 'His father is dead, isn't he?' he asked quietly.

Nessan nodded briefly. 'He is; Archu slew him.'

Gussan nodded towards the tall figure of his foster-brother. 'Why didn't you tell him?' he asked.

'He doesn't want to know that.'

Gussan considered and then he nodded. 'I don't suppose he does. He has been a changed man since he discovered his mother and father.' He looked down at the druid. 'Is this voyage necessary?'

'It's necessary.' The druid was about to brush past, but then he stopped with his foot on the bottom step. 'A word of warning, warrior. Do not go with him on this voyage. His path and yours should part at this point.'

'But it's only a raiding party.'

Nessan shook his head. 'No, it's more than that, much more. Accompany him – and you will not return,' he warned. 'The same holds true for your brothers.'

'And what of Maildun,' Gussan called as the druid ran lightly up the path. 'Will he return?'

The druid paused at the mouth of the cave. 'That is for the gods to decide,' he said with a terrible finality.

CHAPTER THREE

Maildun closed his eyes and leaned back against the smooth boulder. It was still warm from the afternoon sun and he could feel the heat seeping through his leather jerkin and into his taut muscles, relaxing them.

On the beach below the final preparations were being made to his ship, the *Avenger*. He had named it much against his foster-brothers' and Nessan's advice, who maintained that it would anger the gods and bring ill luck on what already seemed to be an ill-omened voyage.

Maildun had remained adamant.

The sun had recently dipped into the waves, and the sky and sea were still reddened with its death-blood. There were camp fires winking on the shadowed beach, and the smell of wood and seaweed drifted up to him, the mixture of odours sparking images behind his eyes: of a village of wood and straw burning, the stench mingling with the crispness of the salt air. He shook his head, clearing the images and concentrated on the scene below.

It was six months and more now since he and his foster-brothers had first visited the half-mad druid, and in that time everything seemed to move at an almost frightening speed. His foster-father, the king, not fully understanding what was happening, but relying on his son's good sense, had sent his shipwrights and sailmakers, with their supplies and their servants, to the wild western coast. Smiths and armourers had followed, and from the very earliest days the sounds of ringing metal and the odour of burnt ores had stained the air, as they worked to fashion new swords, shields, spears, arrows and knives, all in accordance with the druid's instructions that everything brought on board the ship should be fresh and newly made. The queen had sent her sewing women and their servants with bundles of cloths and hides, and each of the thirty-two men had been fitted out with a completely new outfit which they would wear when the longship cast off.

Men had come, of course, and that had been one of the most

difficult choices for the young man to make: to pick only thirty from the huge number that had assembled. Rumours had spread about the voyage, and comparisons were being made to the legendary voyage of the Ui Corrai, and the equally legendary voyage of Saint Brendan, and the fabulous stories about the mythical land of Tir na nOg – the shining, golden paradise to the west of Erin – were told and retold, and soon it was whispered that Maildun was actually going in search of the mythical Land of the Ever Young.

In the end Maildun had left the choosing of the crew to his two old friends who had come at his summoning: Germane, who was called the Navigator, a small, swarthy southerner from the land of the Romans, where the sun burned the colour from the sky and the seed from the ground, and Diurnan Lenkard, a blond, blue-eyed barbarian from the ancient forests of Gaul.

But of the bard, the third member of the crew that the druid had promised would come, there was no sign.

A chill wind whipped in off the sea and swept down the beach, sending sparks spiralling upwards into the heavens. Maildun watched them idly as they drifted past his face, and he suddenly felt an intense loneliness. As he watched the sparks die away against the purple sky, he painfully realised that he was alone in the world, totally alone. Even his foster-brothers – his companions for as long as he could remember – seemed distant and almost strangers now. Nothing mattered now but the voyage and vengance.

And what of the voyage?

Why was he undertaking what promised to be more than just a quick raid? Was it because this Archu represented the last link with his family? Did he really care what had happened to his father, whether he lived or died . . . ?

He watched the last spark die, and found he didn't have the answers. The druid had said that it was his destiny; that the woof and warp of his life had been set and that this was part of the greater pattern. Maildun smiled grimly; was he running to or from that destiny?

Only time would tell.

Gussan and Ruarc raced down the beach towards the growing sounds of disturbance. It was almost full night now, but though the sky was clear the moon had not yet risen, and the only illumination came from the fires behind them and the guttering torch before them. They heard the shout again, and Gussan recognised the voice of one of the men who had been detailed to guard the horses.

It might possibly be horse thieves. Since they had set up camp several months ago, they had caught a few thieves, mostly local people attempting to steal food or weapons, but – after making an example of a few – the last few weeks had been quiet.

The two brothers ran into the circle of light cast by the torch, their weapons drawn, and found both guards lying on the ground. The two guards had stopped a stranger making his way through the horse pens. Taking him for a thief, one of the men had struck at him with the butt of his spear, but the stranger had countered the blow with the flat of his hand and then struck the guard in the chest, sending him reeling back as if he had been thrown. In the brief scuffle that followed, the stranger overcame the guards with almost casual ease, and was standing quietly above the two men, leaning on a spear, waiting for the brothers.

Gussan and Ruarc circled the stranger, watching him carefully, wary of a trap. He was taller than either of them and wrapped entirely in a long, dark cloak of some coarse hair that shimmered in the torchlight. His face was long and thin, not unlike Maildun's, and his eyes were sharp and intense . . . and wrong, Ruarc realised. For a single moment he thought that the stranger was blind, but then he saw how his gaze shifted from man to man.

The stranger smiled at Ruarc, the dancing torchlight colouring his eyes, and then Ruarc realised what had disturbed him about them: they reflected the torchlight like mirrors.

'Who are you?' Gussan demanded.

'I am Paedur,' the stranger said, his voice rich and powerful. He allowed the cloak to fall back from his chest, and crossed his arms in a curious form of salute. Ruarc gasped aloud, for the stranger's left hand was missing and in its place was a fabulously curved silver hook. It was almost a complete half-circle, and the torchlight touched and burned in the runes incised into the metal. Ruarc saw it as a thing of beauty, a strange example of the silversmith's craft; Gussan saw it as a weapon: the tip was wickedly pointed and he was sure the curve of the blade was razor-sharp.

Ruarc bowed slightly. 'We have been expecting you, Paedur. You are the bard?'

The tall stranger nodded. 'I am.' He stepped past the brothers, moving like a shadow, without a sound. Once beyond the light of the torch, he melted into the night. 'Wait,' Gussan said, his

24

sword darting out to bar the stranger's path. There was a flicker of metal and pinpoints of light sparked on the night air, and then Gussan's sword was deftly twisted from his grasp. He stood dazed, staring stupidly at the weapon which throbbed in the sands close to his feet. The bard turned and, with only his face faintly visible against the night, raised his hook. His teeth flashed in a humourless smile. 'Never raise a weapon to me,' he said softly, and then turned away and continued on down the beach.

Maildun slowly became aware of the growing silence on the beach below him. From his vantage spot he could see the flickering points of torchlight bobbing down the darkened beach towards him. The low murmuring and occasional shouts, coupled with snatches of song, had faded, and now the silence was broken only by the hiss of the sea and the flapping of the wind.

Pebbles rattled on the rocks beneath his seat and then Gussan called up to him, his voice sounding strained and tense. 'Maildun, I think you should come down,' he called.

'Why? What's wrong?' He began to edge away from the lip of the boulder, his hand automatically loosening his knife in its sheath. Something was wrong.

'Your crew is complete, Maildun, son of Oilill Agach.' The chilling voice stopped Maildun in his tracks. It was strong, vibrant and powerful; a trained voice used to command. It drew him to the edge of the stone and he peered down. The faces on the beach below were but pale ovals against the night, and indistinguishable – all except one, and that stood out as if it were illuminated. Maildun looked down into the unblinking, colourless eyes and felt his world shifting, as if he already stood on the deck of the *Avenger* in a rough sea. He automatically crossed himself, and then made the Sign of Horns with the fingers of his left hand; surely this was a *bocanach* – a demon?

The powerfully commanding voice spoke again, and Maildun felt the spell that had bound him fall away. 'I am Paedur, the bard. It is my duty to sail with you,' he said, and then he turned away and was lost in the night.

Dawn touched the skies in the east, lightening them to grey, and the hard points of the stars had paled, although in the west they still glittered sharply. Against the smoke-grey light of the dawn, the hazy shape of the *Avenger* stood out against the paling sky. Its single sail was furled, and the ropes and stays hung slack, flapping and cracking in the gusting wind.

The *Avenger* was unusal in many respects; it was longer and

25

broader than any other ship of the time ever constructed in Erin, and was unusually high both in the stern and bow. Diurnan Lenkard had suggested that they appease the savage sea demons by carving their likeness on the bow, and so now a snarling dragon figurehead glared towards the open sea. The ship was of a wood-and-hide construction, and in this case the hides used had been of the best quality and of triple thickness. They had been daubed with a gummy, resinous mixture which ensured that they remained waterproof.

The supplies, salted meat, dried bread, water and mead, were stored in the stern, while the newly forged weapons and armour had been placed under guard in the bow.

All was in readiness.

As the first rays of the sun touched the horizon, tipping the grey clouds with pink and gold, washing the sombre colours from the morning, the crew began to assemble on the beach. They were nearly all tall, young men, most of them no older than five-and-twenty summers. In the main they were also second sons, with no inheritance and nothing to lose on a voyage into the unknown, eager for the adventure and their share of the spoils. They had come from all over Erin, drawn by the whispered stories and growing rumours, and in the end over two hundred men had to be turned away, for Maildun, with Diurnan and Germane, had only chosen those men who were personally known to them, companions who could be trusted.

The sun was moving up beyond the edge of the cliffs when Maildun and his three foster-brothers appeared from the druid's cave. In the still morning air Maildun's angry voice carried clearly.

'You cannot accompany me; I cannot – will not – allow it.'

'You cannot stop us,' Gussan said quickly.

'You are not coming with me – and that is final!' Maildun lengthened his stride and walked through the groups of waiting men. He nodded to Germane and Diurnan, and his close friend Aedan, and acknowledged the bard with a flicker of his eyes. He stopped at the water's edge and then turned to face his crew.

For the first time he felt a quiver of unease. He could justify what he was doing: he was seeking his father or his father's slayer, but could he justify putting the lives of these men – men he either knew from childhood, or had come to know and admire in the last few months – at risk? He had said as much to Nessan the previous night, but all the old man would say was, 'They follow their paths, you follow yours, and if those paths cross, then so be it.'

He had prepared a brief speech, but now, standing in the shallows with the chill dawn water lapping around his booted feet, he suddenly forgot all that he was about to say, and merely turned and clambered aboard. Then the crew, abruptly silent now with the imminent departure, followed him.

There was a brief flurry of confusion as the crew settled into their appointed places, and then the oars rattled in their locks and came to life like so many insect legs. Diurnan, the first mate, called the beat, and the oars rose in unison; a beat, and they dipped – and the *Avenger* surged forward.

Colga, Gussan and Ruarc stood on the beach watching the ship move away. They looked at each other, and then, without a word they began to strip off their weapons and heavy jewellery. As one they ran into the shallows and then threw themselves forward and began to strike out for the retreating craft.

In the stern of the *Avenger*, Maildun's lips tightened as he saw the three heads break the surface of the water in the ship's wake. 'Increase the beat,' he called over his shoulder to Diurnan. The northerner hesitated a moment, but then shrugged and called a beat and a half.

'If you don't take them on board then they will surely drown.' The bard's voice was casual and almost disinterested.

'If I do then they will surely die,' Maildun snapped. 'It is the druid's prophecy.'

'Is their love for you not more important?' Paedur asked and turned away.

Maildun stood by the rail, stung by the bard's parting remark, watching the three heads slip further and further away. Smacking his fist into the rail, he turned away and called down to the first mate. 'Stop the beat, Diurnan; hold us steady.' He turned aside to Aedan. 'Lower one of the small currachs; pick them up.'

Maildun watched the small, round craft being lowered into the water, an ominous feeling settling into his stomach. They were still in sight of Erin's shore and the druid's cave, and already they had broken one of his commands. It boded ill for the coming voyage.

CHAPTER FOUR

The longship slipped out of the heavy mist, its lights doused and its sail furled. Its muffled oars barely broke the surface of the waves, silently edging the craft in towards the shore.

Maildun gripped the horns of the snarling figurehead and leaned forward, straining to make out the voices that drifted out across the waves. They were muffled and indistinct, but the sounds of the language were neither Irish nor Welsh, nor the bastard tongue of the easterners from the land beyond Alba. A harsh, coughing laugh suddenly broke through the mist, shattering the relative silence.

Maildun stiffened, his knuckles tightening on the figurehead. 'It's him,' he hissed through gritted teeth.

'Are you sure?'

Maildun didn't move, the bard's sudden query chilling him to the bone. 'I'm sure,' he said at last. 'Nessan told me there would be one with the laugh of an animal.'

'Archu, the Hound of Slaughter?'

Maildun climbed down from the tall figurehead and stood beside the shadowy figure. 'How do you know?' he asked.

Cloth rustled and the half-circle of the bard's hook glinted in the night. 'I know,' he said simply.

Maildun shrugged, leaving his questions unanswered. There would be time enough for them later; time enough for many things.

'We will move in,' he said. 'Give the order, if you will, bard.'

Paedur moved swiftly and silently along the deck, confidently wending his way through the men, supplies and weapons that cluttered the boards. He moved in absolute darkness. He spoke briefly with the navigator, who then whistled twice in the call of the sea-bird – the order to ship oars – and the craft drifted in towards the shore on the tide. The crew saw to their weapons and lined the rails – waiting.

The mist parted before them like shredded cloth, and just as quickly closed in behind. They were close enough now to smell the land odour, and to hear the voices clearly. A bard was

28

declaiming one of the Setanta's feats in a rich, if slightly cracked, voice. '. . . And then the boy drove the ball down the hound's throat, killing it instantly, and then Culain, the Smith . . .' A sudden cry shattered the night. Immediately, dark figures moved before the dancing flame of firelight high on the beach, and it was abruptly doused. The *Avenger* was close enough for the crew to smell the stink of wet wood and hear the hissing of the waves of the beach.

'Who goes there . . . ?' The voice was rough, the words slightly blurred, as if the speaker's throat had once been damaged.

Maildun's hand closed around a light throwing spear. Its head was of whalebone and barbed: it could only be cut from the flesh or pushed through a wound. He dropped to one knee, squinting into the night, trying to locate the exact position of the voice.

'Who goes there?'

The young man braced himself, and drew back his arm. 'I am Maildun, son of Oilill Agach of the tribe of Ninius,' he shouted.

There was a brief silence and then the raw voice shouted back. 'Maildun, son of Oilill Agach. I never knew he had a son.' There was an audible gasp for air and then the voice called out again, but sounding cracked and strained. 'What do you seek, Maildun, son of Oilill?'

'I seek my father, or his whereabouts.' He had the location of the voice now; ahead and a little to his right.

Archu's laughter was like an animal's coughing roar, harsh and grating. 'Your father burns in the Hell of the Christians, and believe me, boy, no man more deserved it.'

'You killed my father . . .' Maildun began, and then a body smashed into his back, throwing him to the deck. Something whistled over his head and thudded into the mast behind him. 'Down,' the bard commanded, but the captain threw off his hand, pushed himself to his feet and flung the spear towards the sound of Archu's voice. He heard the hard, bone head of the spear shatter against a stone, and a muttered yelp as someone scrambled for cover. 'I have come for you, Archu,' he called.

The harsh, animal-like laughter mocked him. 'Let me tell you how your father died, Maildun, son of Oilill Agach of the tribe of Ninius.' There was a liquid sound of drawing breath, and then the taunting continued. 'He died tied to the altar of your Christian god. First I cut his veins as we did when we sacrificed lifeblood to the earth, and then I burned the church over his head. His screams were music in my ears, Maildun, son of Oilill...'

Maildun shouted aloud and threw spear after spear blindly, until the bard knocked him to the deck again, and Diurnan held him down.

A rain of spears and stones clattered onto the deck, rattling off shields and helms, but occasionally finding a softer target. A stone struck Maildun across the shoulder, numbing his arm, the pain bringing him back to his senses; another bounced of the deck before his face and a third struck sparks from Diurnan's breastplate. Someone near the bow screamed – a long gurgling cry – and fell into the water. He thrashed about loudly, but the sound was abruptly silenced.

'Something is happening on the beach,' the bard said urgently, leaning forward over the side of the craft, staring intently towards the shore.

'Let me up,' Maildun demanded, struggling to his knees, having convinced Diurnan that he had regained the use of his senses. He looked towards the shore but could see nothing, and wondered briefly at the bard's ability to see in the dark.

'They're falling back towards the base of the cliffs,' Paedur murmured, almost to himself. 'There are caves . . . one is coming forward – an old man, his hair and beard are unkempt, and his eyes have the light of madness in them. He is a wizard,' he snapped.

A tiny emerald light suddenly sprang up on the beach. It darted about for a few heartbeats before settling down, and then it rapidly grew into a large, pulsating ball, outlining the pebbled beach and incoming waves in a ghastly light. They could all hear the chanting now, the aged voice calling forth in the Old Tongue, the language of the Tuatha De Danann, calling down the Pagan Gods and their servants, the Elementals. Another voice joined the first, and this time the language was that of the Men of Mil, the harshly guttural sounds contrasting sharply with the smooth liquidity of the older speech.

'A woman – no more than a girl – has joined the wizard, she is calling down the female elements, water and air, while he calls down the male principals, earth and fire . . .' The bard's voice trailed off and he swore softly to himself in a hissing alien tongue. When he looked back at Maildun and Diurnan, the green light from the beach had touched his face, turning his eyes to emerald chips of stone. His voice was terribly calm. 'You must prepare yourselves,' he said. And then he raised his head and shouted in his trained voice, 'Everyone to the deck; tie yourselves down.'

The green light on the beach continued to grow, and now it began to pulse with an insistent beat that matched the ebb and flow of the tide. The damp night air came alive with suppressed power. Tendrils of fire ran along the mast of the *Avenger* and clung briefly to the sailors' weapons. The captain could see the hook that hung in place of the bard's left hand quite clearly in the witch light, and the sinuous runes etched into the silver metal seemed to writhe with a life all their own.

The wizard's voice rose, and the woman sang counterpoint to it, and then a new note entered their terrifying duet: command. Paedur plucked a spear from the deck and pressed it into Maildun's hands. 'The Elementals are very close now; if they materialise, then we are lost.' He pointed with his hook. 'Aim to the right of centre of that globe of fire; the wizard lurks there.'

Maildun hefted the spear in his hand, gauging the weight of the weapon and the distance. Ruarc should be here, he thought – with his sling he would be able to pick off individuals on the beach. He closed his eyes, breathed deeply and then opened them again. He squinted into the throbbing light; he could just make out the two figures behind it, standing erect with their arms raised in invocation. The figure closest to the fire would be the wizard . . . Maildun drew back his arm and threw.

But, even as the spear found its mark, and the figure fell with a hideous gurgle, the emerald ball of light drew in upon itself, and disappeared, leaving nothing behind but dancing after-images burnt into the retina. For a long, tense moment nothing happened.

And then the wind struck the *Avenger* like a fist, almost overturning the sturdy longship. Luckily the sail had been furled or it would have been torn to shreds, and the mast with it, but as it was, anything not tied down was immediately swept away.

The sudden lurching caught Maildun unawares and sent him reeling forward, against the side of the craft. His hands slipped on the wet wood and his nails scored long grooves against the sides. Another blow struck the craft, sending him over the side, leaving him hanging on by his damp fingers. He heard a muted rumbling and risked a terrified glance over his shoulder. A huge wave was building up, heading directly for the ship. He felt himself slipping, his legs thrashed in the water, one hand came free, leaving him dangling by the fingertips . . .

And then the bard's hook sliced into the thick leather collar of

31

his jerkin. It caught, holding him, and Paedur hauled him aboard as easily as if he were lifting a child, instead of a full-grown man weighted down by clothing and weapons.

The storm struck in all its raw fury. Huge waves broke over the bow of the craft and foamed along the decks, scouring them clean, painting the polished boards with silver phosphorescence. Lightning flared across the lowering skies, and pale blue fox-fire etched the mast into the night, or sparked from metal with the sound of angry insects. A tiny ball of coalesced lightning formed at the tip of the mast and slowly, almost gently, it rolled down onto the deck. It was about the size of a man's head and it seemed to be twisting and turning in on itself as it moved to and fro. One man reached out for it with his sword, and the bard's shouted warning went unheard as the ball almost leaped across the deck, dancing up along the sword and onto the man's metal helm in a shower of sparks and fire. There was a stench of burning and, when the ball drifted away, the sailor's face had been burnt almost beyond recognition, and the metal of his helm had melted into the flesh.

Paedur pulled Maildun's dagger from his belt and threw it point first into the deck, close to the ball-lightning. It immediately spun and danced over to it, fastening on the metal like a hungry beast, sparking, crackling angrily, and then rolling away, leaving it a smouldering slag.

'Draw it to me,' the bard called urgently to Diurnan, 'use your knife . . .'

The blond northerner nodded. He had seen the demon fire before, he knew what it could do to a craft. He drew his dagger and threw it underhand, sending it into the deck close to the bard, and then his second knife landed almost at the bard's booted foot. Diurnan touched the amulet that hung about his neck and prayed to his wild northern gods that the bard knew what he was doing.

The ball arched across to the knife, reducing it, in a matter of heartbeats, to useless metal, and then skipped across to the second knife and fed again. And then the bard reached out with his left arm, with his hook . . .

The ball-lightning came to the metal like a hawk to its master. It hung, almost poised, on the tip of the hook, sizzling and crackling, and then it began to dissipate. The runes in the metal burned and glowed as if the lightning were being absorbed into the hook. One by one they winked out like stars.

Hail abruptly lashed across the decks, the stones large, sharp

32

and cutting, bruising skin and drawing blood. The mariners prayed to the New God, the Christ, or turned in despair to the older, wilder gods of their fathers to save them now. They clung to the decks, unaware and uncaring where the wind and waves took them, and only the bard braved the elements to rise from the deck and stare out over the side, trying to catch sight of land. Once, when the storm whipped aside the clouds, revealing the stars shining hard and sharp in the night, he studied them carefully, and found that they were not the stars he expected to find.

The longship sustained a terrible beating, and its timbers groaned and cried aloud like a live thing – and if one was to believe the tales of mariners – perhaps it was. But Nessan's advice – to build it of seasoned wood and cover it with tanned and seasoned hides of triple thickness – bore fruit, and she rode out the pounding waves.

The sorcerous storm lasted most of the night, and it was only with the coming of the dawn that the wind fell and the waves calmed somewhat. Just before sunrise the clouds finally broke and a chill breeze sent them scudding across the heavens towards the north.

Maildun crawled out from under a coil of rope and pushed himself to his feet. He was stiff and bruised, encrusted with dried salt and blood that had run from a long gash in his cheek where a sliver of wood had cut him. He stretched and groaned aloud as his muscles cracked in protest. Something fluttered at the edge of his vision and he spun round, his hand falling to his empty knife sheath.

Paedur moved away from the mast, his colourless eyes dancing in amusement. 'I did not mean to startle you,' he said gently.

The captain shrugged in embarrassment. 'I thought I was the first to awaken . . .' He looked at the bodies sprawled about the deck, tied to oar benches or to swords and knives driven deep into the boards. Some were beginning to move, but there were others who – from their unnatural positions – would never face another dawn.

Paedur stood by the rail and looked out across the waves, his usually hard expression softening. To the east the sky was touched with pink and salmon, the high clouds tinged with fire and warm gold. The sea beneath was hard and flat, reflecting like polished metal in the sunlight. Maildun stood back and looked at the bard. The wan light flowed off his cowled fur cloak like oil off water, and Maildun, who had hunted most of Erin's furred

33

animals, found he couldn't identify the pelt. As he moved, colour rippled down it and the tiny, grey-tipped, black hairs assumed strange and arcane patterns. Paedur glanced over his shoulder at the captain. 'If what you see in me interests you,' he said quietly, 'then I think you will find the coming months astonishing.' He turned away and nodded towards the sunrise. 'There's always something special about a sunrise. It is instructive to remember that it has happened since the dawn of time and that it will continue until this world is no more.'

Maildun patted his torn cheek with the back of his sleeve. He brushed a lock of curling red hair from his forehead and then rubbed the heels of both palms into his eyes. 'I've never been so glad to greet the dawn,' he said wearily.

Germane, the navigator, limped up and joined them. A slim, dark southerner, he grinned up at the captain with his customary good humour, and nodded briefly to Paedur. 'What a storm; I've never seen anything like it in all my seafaring days.'

'The wizard was slain just as he completed his enchantment. His death released a sudden explosion of energy which fuelled the spell.' The bard cleaned his hook absently on the hem of his grey-black cloak. 'We're lucky the Elementals fed on that and didn't materialise to feed on us.'

Maildun shivered in the chill morning air. He ran his fingers through his salt-stiffened hair. 'And just where are we now?' he wondered.

Germane squinted into the east and then turned to stare into the west, to where a few remaining stars still lingered. He frowned in puzzlement. 'I . . . I don't know; these stars seem to be unknown to me.' He turned to the bard. 'Do you recognise any?'

Paedur glanced up at the sky in the west. He hesitated before turning back to the navigator. 'Some seem vaguely familiar, but it is impossible to tell now, the patterns are lost. We must wait for the night.' He shrugged, dismissing the subject. 'We can do nothing but wait.'

Germane nodded and turned back to Maildun. 'He is right; there's nothing we can do until nightfall. We may be able to recognise the stars then.'

'And if not?'

Germane hesitated. 'Then we're lost.'

Maildun gripped the navigator's arm. 'We cannot be lost; we didn't sail more than a day's voyage from Erin before we came upon Archu's island.'

34

'Tir na nOg lies just off Erin's shore,' Paedur reminded him gently, 'and yet only a few come to it.' He paused and added, in a voice that was little more than a whisper, 'And that is because it lies in a different realm.'

'What realm?' Maildun demanded.

'It would take too long to explain,' the bard said, turning away.

'Tell me!'

'Later. I think you should see to your crew, captain.' The bard turned away and made his way slowly down the length of the craft, rousing the crew, helping men to their feet, tending to their wounds.

Germane watched him for a while, something about the tall, dark-clad figure stirring almost forgotten memories. He worried at the thought, like a dog shaking a rat, but it refused to come. There was something about the bard that he felt he should know . . . He shrugged, dismissing the thought for the moment. He turned back to Maildun and was surprised to find him staring meditatively at the strange figure. 'What is it about him?' he asked the captain.

Maildun shook his head slowly. 'I don't know. But something about him troubles me.' He glanced across at the navigator. 'I feel I've been used, Germane. Nessan knew what would happen, and now we have the bard, who seems unsurprised by the turn of events.

'Almost as if he were expecting them,' Germane added.

'Almost.'

CHAPTER FIVE

It was late afternoon when the island was sighted on the horizon. On the bard's advice, the *Avenger* had sailed into the west, with the morning sun and the wind at their backs. As the day passed, and all traces of the storm vanished, the sea grew flat and soon only the slightest breeze ruffled the sail. They had been becalmed several times, and Maildun had ordered the men to the oars twice, when they had remained motionless for an unusual length of time.

Around noon a thick, black cloud had formed on the horizon. And, since its shape was not that of a storm cloud, the *Avenger* had shifted direction slightly and headed towards what might be an island. Shortly afterwards a huge cone, spitting fire and heavy dust-laden smoke, rose from the sea. As they neared the island they could see that one side of it was scarred and blackened where the lava flow had burned through the vegetation. Germane advised the captain to drop anchor while they were still some distance from the land, since he did not wish to risk the craft in unknown waters with night drawing in.

With the *Avenger* rocking gently on the waves, a hundred or so lengths distant from the shore, Maildun stood by the figurehead staring towards the island, watching night fall over it. When he could see no more, he turned away and walked down the length of the ship, calling for Diurnan, Germane and Paedur. He stood in the stern waiting for them to join him, staring down into the waves lapping easily against the heavily tarred sides of the craft, tiny phosphorescent bubbles rising from the ebon depths, exploding on the surface like tiny stars.

When Germane and Diurnan had joined him and the bard had silently drifted into the group, Maildun nodded up towards the heavens. 'Do you recognize any of them?' he asked casually, aware now that something was terribly wrong. There were no volcanic islands off Erin's coasts.

The slim navigator studied the stars in silence. The sky was ablaze with luminescent sheets of light sweeping away to the south in a gauzy spiral. Strange configurations glittered in the

36

heavens to the north, and the stars burned with an unusually sharp, crystal hardness. He shook his head. 'They are all unfamiliar to me,' he said softly.

The captain turned to Paedur. 'And you?'

The bard ran his hook down the light stubble on his cheek as he stared into the skies. The stars were reflected like points of silver fire in his colourless eyes. 'The sorcerous storm has tossed us far; we have passed beyond the bounds of your . . . our world. We are in the Shadowland.'

'I find your jests in poor taste, bard,' Maildun snapped.

Paedur turned on him, his hueless eyes glittering strangely. 'I do not jest,' he said flatly.

The tense silence was broken by Diurnan. 'Where are we then?' he asked in his harsh northern accent, 'for I do not recognize these stars. How close are we to home?'

The bard looked up into the purple skies. 'Close,' he whispered, 'very close.' He pointed skywards with his hook. 'Look, the Sword and Shield.' He then traced a line west and south from the Shield stars. 'And there is the Mace and Axe just rising. There,' he pointed almost above the ship's mast towards a curiously distinct configuration, 'is the Greve and Helm.'

'But I don't know those stars,' Germane protested.

'But that one?' Paedur asked, pointing into the northern sky.

Germane studied it for a moment, and then he gasped. 'The Pole Star!'

'Aye, the Pole Star. And it can only be found in those Shadowlands which lie closest to your homeland.'

'Which means?' Germane asked.

'Which means that this can only be the Island Sea.'

'Bard,' Diurnan said gruffly, 'I've sailed these waters since my father first took me with him, and I no more than five or six winters, and I've never heard of the Island Sea.'

Paedur hitched his dark cloak higher on his shoulders. The cloak seemed to absorb the light and he became one with the night. 'But surely you have often heard stories of the mythical isles – those islands that appear briefly and then disappear back into the sea mists? You have heard of Tir na nOg, the Isles of the Blest, the Happy Isles, Hy Brazil, Lyonesse?'

The northerner nodded. 'I've heard of them, and many more besides.'

'I've even seen some of them,' Germane said. 'I've sailed past islands and lands that were on no charts I've known.'

The bard nodded. 'They are but the shadows of the worlds

that are close to yours; images from those other planes that drift across to yours.'

'And you're saying that we've drifted away from Erin and through to one of these other worlds,' Maildun asked, in a flat, emotionless voice.

The bard nodded.

'Is there anything we can do?'

'We can do nothing but sail on.'

'Could we not go back; retrace our steps?' Diurnan asked.

Paedur shook his head, the movement barely visible in the darkness. 'We are trapped here. I have neither the power nor the ability to pull us back. But this is a world rich in Power – this is a place where the magic of your world still lingers. This is a place similar to where the Tuatha De Danann went when they left your world in ancient times. There must be someone here who can use that Power to throw us back across the worlds.' The bard finished abruptly. He bowed briefly to the small group and then stepped back and disappeared into the night.

Diurnan and Germane stood with the Captain looking up into the heavens for a while, and then the northerner bade Maildun a good-night, and made to move away. But before he left, the captain gripped his shoulder and whispered urgently to him and Germane, 'Say nothing of this to the crew. When the time for telling comes, I will do it myself.'

The navigator nodded towards the alien stars. 'They're not fools; they'll know soon enough, if they haven't already guessed.'

Maildun nodded. 'I know . . . I know. But say nothing for the present.'

They both nodded and moved away.

When they had left, Ruarc joined his foster-brother by the rail. It was the first time they had spoken since he and his brothers had been hauled out of the sea, and he felt uneasy in Maildun's presence.

His foster-brother leaned over the rail and stared down into the water, seemingly oblivious of the other's presence. Tiny splashes of light coloured the bubbles in the ship's wake, and Maildun wondered briefly what caused them. 'You know,' he said almost to himself, and so softly that Ruarc had to bend over to hear him, 'if I were a superstitious man, I might believe that my loyal foster-brothers had brought this on me because they did not heed the druid's warning.'

'I think you know, Maildun,' Ruarc said, equally quietly, 'that this was ordained for you. The druid knew what was going to happen. Did he not say that yours would be a maiden voyage into strange waters . . .'

Maildun nodded wearily. 'I know. I know. I just wish you hadn't come. I have lost a mother and a father; I have no wish to lose my brothers.'

'It was our decision,' Ruarc reminded him.

Maildun turned away. 'That doesn't help me,' he said softly.

Germane brought the *Avenger* in to shore on the tide at first light. He used the oarsmen to bring her round a jagged line of reefs that almost completely enclosed a small semi-circular harbour, and then ordered the oars shipped about ten lengths from the shore and the anchor dropped.

Seen close to, the island presented a curious contrast. On one side, the violent volcanic activity had burned away all signs of growth, leaving nothing but black ash in its wake, while on the other, rank, almost tropical vegetation came down to the edge of the golden sanded beach. A thin strip of sand bordered the trees, and it was enclosed on both sides by a tall line of ragged cliffs, which in turn were almost completely hidden beneath the abundant growth. Breakers rolled in onto the smooth beach, stranding scores of tiny silver fish which flopped briefly and then lay still, but, aside from this, there was no other sign of life on the island. No birds flew through the dark trees, nor called in the fresh morning air, no small animals scurried through the undergrowth and, for all its appearance of life and growth, the island might have been dead.

Diurnan Lenkard joined Germane at the tiller as the blond northerner was strapping on his large, double-headed battleaxe.

'Expecting trouble?'

Diurnan grunted. 'That damned bard again.' He spat into the sea. 'He hints that there might be trouble and that it would be as well to go armed as if for battle.' He stared into the navigator's dark eyes. 'I tell you, he is a demon; he knows far more about this voyage and this place than he pretends.'

'I know. I've noticed something else about him: I've never seen him eat or drink – and no matter what time of the night I'm on watch, he's always prowling about.'

'It's unnatural,' Diurnan agreed. 'If I had my way, I'd have him overboard.' He glanced down the ship at the bard, who was leaning across the figurehead staring intently towards the island. 'He also seems to have some sort of hold over the captain; it's getting so as he can't make a move without consulting that hooked devil.'

'But don't forget,' Germane said, lowering his voice, conscious of the stares they were getting from the curious crewmen, 'he does seem to be the only one who knows where we are and where we're going. He might just be our only hope of ever returning home.'

Maildun appeared from his quarters clad in leather leggings and jerkin. He was strapping his longsword over his left shoulder. Aedan, his companion, handed him his gauntlets, which he pulled on before accepting a long, thin knife which he slipped into his boot. Diurnan joined him and they stood quietly while two burly crewmen, both armed with spears and axes, let down a small round currach on the port side. While they slid down the ropes into the boat, Maildun turned back and shouted up to Germane. 'If we have not returned by noon, continue on. Try to make land where there is civilization; let the bard guide you.' He raised his right hand in a brief salute and then, gripping the rope in both hands, slid down into the gently rocking boat. The crew cast off the ropes and the rolling waves swept up the hide boat and carried it in towards the shore.

Germane joined Paedur by the figurehead, and they stood in silence watching the small, frail-seeming craft bobbing on the waters. Germane glanced across at the bard. The sunlight did little to dispel the shadows that clustered about him. The light ran in liquid ripples down his strange cloak, and the Bardic Sigil high on his left shoulder burned against the dark cloth like quicksilver. His delicate, long-fingered hand traced the scales of the dragon-prow and, not for the first time, Germane wondered how he had lost his left hand. Paedur blinked slowly, almost deliberately, and his large eyes took on the colour and consistency of eggshells as they followed the progress of the currach.

Abruptly, his gaze swivelled onto the navigator and he smiled strangely. 'Why do you fear me?' he asked softly.

'I do not fear you,' Germane said, startled.

'All men fear what they do not know. You do not know who – or what – I am, and thus you fear me. You fear the influence I may be having on Maildun, and perhaps you think I am one of the demons from your Hell-fire religion.'

'I am not a follower of the New God,' Germane said softly, glancing over his shoulder to make sure that none of the crew were listening. 'I am a follower of the Old Faith.' He said it proudly, almost defiantly, as if daring the bard to mock or scoff.

40

Paedur nodded slowly. 'I too am a follower of the old ways.'

Germane raised his fine eyebrows in surprise.

The bard laughed grimly. 'Yes, I too follow an Old Faith, but my faith and yours differ greatly. It is the principle that we worship that is the same.'

'I would have thought you one of those godless men, one of those who eschew the worship of gods.'

'No man is above the worship of the gods. Without men and the faith of men, the gods cease to exist. The days of the Greek and Roman pantheons are drawing to a close; the gods of the Babylonians and Egyptians have passed into legend. But remember, without the gods the world of men would surely crumble.' He suddenly pointed with his hook. 'They have reached the shore.'

Maildun leaped from the currach and splashed through the shallows and up onto the beach. The drying bodies of countless tiny silver fish steamed in the early morning air, making footing treacherous and dusting his boots with shimmering scales. He stood just above the low-water mark and waited for the northerner to join him.

They had come ashore a little to one side of the enticing beach and before them stretched the cliffs, which were almost lost behind the luxuriant vegetation. Tendrils of green drifted down over the edge of the cliffs and every nook and crevice was ablaze with brilliantly coloured flowers. The cliffs were dotted with caves of varying heights and sizes, ranging from smaller than a man to one which it would have been possible to march four abreast through.

Maildun gestured with his gloved fist. 'What do you make of it?'

The huge northerner unhitched his battleaxe and slipped its thong onto his wrist. 'There's something about it . . .' he said, feeling a chill tingle on the nape of his neck. He sniffed the fresh morning air, coughed as pumice tickled his throat, and tried again. The captain breathed deeply and then he caught it too: a curious, sharp, acrid odour.

They made their way up the smooth beach towards the largest of the caves. They had almost reached it when they heard a sound – a low, muted crackling or chirping – which was all the more distinctive for being the first sound of life they had heard on the isle. The odour was stronger now and seemed to be coming from the cave mouth.

'Perhaps the volcano . . .' Maildun suggested, but he knew that the odour was not from the volcano and he slid his sword free. Diurnan poked through the piles of debris heaped at the mouth of the cave. It consisted of gleaming bones, most of them animal, but the few that were human looked ancient, and were mingled with stripped branches and smooth stones.

The cave was inhabited – but by what?

Something glinted yellow in the light and Maildun bent to pluck it from beneath a bleached skull. It was a heavy gold torc, and it had been shorn in two by a blow from . . . from what? He held it up to the light; the cut was not sharp and clean as from an axe or sword, and its edges were ragged and torn.

A shadow fell across him.

Maildun moved instinctively, throwing himself backwards, bringing his sword up before him in a two-handed grip. And he found himself looking into the face of a nightmare. A hugely bloated head set on a slender neck was crowned by two snake-like feelers and almost completely taken up by two massive, sickle-shaped mandibles. The long, obscene body was pinched together into two parts and there were six legs.

The creature hesitated, its feelers waving to and fro, and then it abruptly darted forward. Maildun lunged to one side, crashing into Diurnan, sending him sprawling and then they both rolled away in different directions. A long pincher stabbed into the ground between the two men as the creature moved with terrifying speed. They both came to their feet at the same time and attacked the creature simultaneously. The captain's long-sword sliced through the armour-like carapace, and thick, reeking ichor spat and hissed onto the sands. The northerner's axe sheared through one of the hind legs and the creature fell to one side, chittering in a high-pitched squeal that passed beyond human hearing. It thrashed about, its legs waving frantically as Diurnan hacked at it, and Maildun attacked it from its blind side, concentrating on its sensitive feelers and deadly pincers. The air was fouled with the reek of its blood and the stench of acid was overpowering.

Maildun, his sword clutched in both hands, finally separated the head from the rest of its body, and then staggered back, gasping, his throat raw and his eyes streaming. 'Leave it, Diurnan.' He hawked and spat the foul taste from his mouth. He rubbed his watering eyes with the heel of his hand and looked at the dismembered creature once more . . . and he suddenly recognized it.

42

It was an ant.

An ant taller and broader than a tall fighting horse. He backed away in amazement, and stumbled on the shattered remains of the creature's mandibles, and then he suddenly knew what had shorn through the golden torc. Still dazed, he looked around for it and saw it glinting in the sand where he had dropped it when the creature had attacked. Maildun plunged his sword hilt deep into the sand to clean it and walked slowly over to pick up the lump of metal. He was stooping down when a shadow moved in the mouth of the cave and another ant – even bigger than the first – ventured out, its antennae waving. The captain screamed a warning, grabbed his sword and ran.

The giant ants streamed down the beach, their long legs tapping the stones like sticks, their antennae weaving, testing the air, reading the message of blood and acid.

The two crewmen who had accompanied Maildun and Diurnan came running when they heard the captain's shout. They stopped and stared in horror at the creatures that were now pouring down the beach. Diurnan shouted and waved them on, and they turned and ran back towards the currach. Maildun and Diurnan passed them, fear lending them speed, and the northerner reached the small craft first. He heaved it out into the shallows and pushed it into the oncoming waves before throwing himself into it.

Suddenly, one of the sailors fell heavily on the scale-slick stones and his cry of pain brought the ants' feelers swivelling in his direction. He staggered to his feet, but then fell back with a groan as his leg buckled under him.

Meanwhile, his companion had reached the rocking currach and had been hauled aboard by Diurnan.

Maildun turned back and ran up the beach to the fallen man. He sheathed his sword and dragged him to his feet, but the man screamed in pain and went limp in Maildun's arms. The captain laid him down on the sand and probed his leg, his long fingers finding the break in the shin bone and the dislocated ankle. His rough probing brought the man back to his senses, and his wild eyes flickered past Maildun to the giant ants which were nearer now, their bitter sweet stench almost overpowering. 'Kill me,' he begged.

Maildun glanced over his shoulder and shook his head. He crouched down, bending almost double and then heaved the man over his shoulder. Ignoring his screams and cries, Maildun staggered down the beach.

Diurnan swore by all his wild northern gods and threw himself back into the water, his battleaxe in one hand and a long throwing spear in the other. He slipped once and almost fell on the slick stones, and then he was pounding up the beach towards Maildun and his burden. He reached them just as the first of the ants approached. Diurnan rammed the spear into the base of one of the creature's feelers, and scalding liquid jetted from the wound, splattering his face and hair. He vomited with the stench and taste, but jabbed the spear blindly again and again. There was a terrible squeal and then something struck him low in the stomach, sending him crashing backwards, and he fell and rolled with the direction of the beach, finally splashing into the shallows.

Maildun felt the man on his back jump as something struck him and then Diurnan was beside him, jabbing with his spear. He saw the northerner covered in the creature's gore, saw him strike out blindly at it, saw it crash to the ground, a foreleg striking him, sending him rolling away.

Maildun dropped his burden and, dragging his sword free, swung it, without looking, in a tight arc that severed the questing feelers of another of the filthy creatures. The ant staggered back into yet another, and Maildun hacked at its forelegs, bringing it down. A second ant attacked the first, its pincers closing in a vice-like grip about its head, and the creature's frenzy gave Maildun a moment's respite.

'Kill me now,' the crewman begged. His eyes were wide and there was a thin line of yellow froth on his lips. Maildun bent over to pick him up, but the man pushed his hand away and then twisted to one side so that the captain could see the long rent across his shoulder blades where the ant must have struck him. 'Don't let them take me.'

Maildun finally nodded and, placing the point of his sword against the man's breast, pushed. The crippled sailor stiffened and fell back onto the smooth beach, now slick with blood and gore.

Maildun splashed into the shallows and dragged Diurnan to his feet and together they struck out for the currach.

The atmosphere aboard the *Avenger* was tense when the small currach returned with the three men, and the crew were angry and sullen. They had elected Aedan, Maildun's boyhood friend, as spokesman, and he stepped forward and confronted Maildun and Diurnan as soon as they had been hauled aboard.

'We want to know where we are,' he stated flatly, folding his

44

massive arms across his chest. 'There is no island like that off Erin's coasts, and no creatures like those this side of Hell.'

Maildun stood wearily by the rail, feeling his muscles relax as the tension drained away. His throat was raw with thirst and there was a savage pounding in his head from the acrid stench that pervaded his clothes and hair. He felt a brief twinge of sympathy for Diurnan; what must he be feeling now, covered in the evil muck?

He swallowed hard, wincing with his raw throat. 'To begin with, I must tell you that I do not know where we are,' he said, his voice hoarse and ragged. 'But, it seems likely that we have sailed away from Erin's shores into what the bard calls a "Shadowland".'

An angry, frightened murmur ran through the crew and some crossed themselves or made the Sign of Horns.

The captain nodded slowly. 'It does not please me either,' he said. 'However, you are all volunteers; you all came of your own free will, for adventure and spoils. Well, you're getting that adventure now, and as for spoils, perhaps they will come later.' He shrugged and looked up into the clear blue sky. 'We are in the hands of God.'

Aedan stepped forward, his eyes slitted. 'Well that's not good enough, is it?'

Maildun breathed deeply, clearing his head of the lingering fumes of acid, feeling the subtle change in the crews attitude. If this was not settled now, he would have a mutiny on his hands – and the voyage not even properly started. He looked around the men, forcing each one to meet his eyes, trying to gauge how they would react, and who would side with him if it actually came to a fight. He saw Gussan, Colga and Ruarc move a little apart from the main body of the men, saw the battle light in Gussan's eyes and noted the leather sling idly twirling on his younger foster-brother's wrist. He saw Germane move away from the fig-urehead, rubbing the blade of a flame-edged knife against his leggings. He looked around but could see no sign of Paedur and he felt vaguely disappointed; he had thought he might side with him, but the bard owed him nothing, and he had no right to expect anything in return.

He stepped forward until he was face to face with Aedan. He saw the man tense and knew it would take very little for him to attack now. 'Why are you doing this, Aedan?' he asked softly. 'I thought we were friends . . . and perhaps more than friends. Do you not trust me?'

45

'It is not a matter of trust, Maildun, it is . . .' His voice trailed away and he looked over his shoulder for support, but his crewmates were loath to meet his eyes. 'What of Conn?' he demanded, jerking his head back towards the island.

'We can only pray for his spirit,' Maildun said wearily.

'Is that all? We demand that those devil creatures be slain . . .' His stance changed and now his hand was resting on the hilt of the knife in his belt.

'You are in no position to demand anything!' Paedur pushed his way through the men and shouldered Maildun out of the way.

Aedan laughed contemptuously. 'Stay out of this, hook-hand; it doesn't concern you.'

'Oh, but it does.' The bard smiled easily, but without humour. 'And now, return to your duties.' He turned his back on the man and began to push his way through the bemused crew.

Aedan slid his knife free and leaped for the bard in one fluid movement. But Paedur turned and took the descending knife on his hook, and his right hand caught his attacker across the throat. Aedan gagged and went down on his knees, and the bard cracked him across the side of the head with the flat of his hook. The man's eyes rolled upwards and he went limp. Paedur turned on his heel and walked away.

There was a moment's stunned silence. It had all happened so quickly; they had been prepared for violence – indeed, it had been almost necessary to relieve the tension – but they had certainly expected nothing like this.

Diurnan waded into the crewmen then, bellowing orders, and his filthy appearance and rancid odour did more to dispel the men than his sheer size. Aedan was hauled away to sleep off the blow the bard had given him and the remainder of the crew drifted back to their various duties.

Maildun joined the bard by the rail close to the bow. His gloved hands clenched and unclenched about the rail. Behind them Germane gave the orders and the sail was hoisted; it billowed and cracked, and the *Avenger* lurched underway, taking a course that would lead her around the island, but continuing on into the west.

Maildun stared at the receding island, and then, without taking his eyes from it, he spoke to the bard, his voice chill and hard. 'You ever do that to me again, and I'll have you thrown overboard,' he warned.

'It was necessary,' Paedur said mildly.

'*Necessary*!' Maildun spat. 'He was my . . . friend, my crew-man; mine to deal with as I wished. If I am to keep the respect of this crew, I cannot allow someone to fight my battles for me.' He paused and added in a quieter voice. 'What's more, you have made a dangerous enemy, not only of that man, but of his cronies amongst the crew.'

'Maildun,' the bard said gently. 'I am not for one moment suggesting that you are not a brave and valiant fighter. I saw how you returned for that man on the island. But consider; you had fought the giant ants, so were you in any condition to fight a bigger, fresher man?' He raised his hook as Maildun was about to answer. 'If I had not intervened, you would have been forced to fight and kill or be killed. As it is, neither has happened and you are the captain of an undivided ship.' The bard nodded and turned away. Behind him, Maildun stood by the rail and watched the volcanic cone of the island pour hot ash into the clear blue skies.

CHAPTER SIX

The day wore on, and the sun, rising towards the zenith, turned the water into a metallic bowl, and washed the colour from the sky. The heat grew intense and the breeze from the east was straight from the ovens of Hell.

Diurnan, Germane and Maildun conferred quietly in the supply room with Pol, one of the older men, who had assumed the duties of cook, and, on his advice, the captain ordered a quantity of unsalted meat thrown overboard, for fear that it had become tainted in the heat. Almost immediately a sharp, black fin appeared in the ship's wake, gliding swiftly through the sparkling waters. The sea was briefly disturbed where the meat floated and then it was gone in a welter of white foam.

Maildun and Germane leaned over the side of the ship and stared down at the dim shape in the water. 'It must be huge,' the navigator said, 'look at the size of that fin.'

Diurnan joined them. He had taken the precaution of placing a guard over the water supplies; they didn't know when they would sight land again and be able to refill their water casks. He spat at the fin. 'It must have paced us from the island. I've seen such creatures do so for days on end, scavaging the offal and waste thrown overboard.'

'If anyone falls overboard, they won't have a chance,' Maildun commented. 'Do we kill it?'

'If we kill it,' the northerner said, 'the blood will only draw more of its kind.'

'And they are not so easily killed,' Germane reminded him.

In the late afternoon it was joined by another – even bigger – shark. The newcomer must have been almost half the length of the *Avenger*. Its massive fin sliced through the water like a scythe, and it rose up once, displaying a cavernous mouth filled with needle-pointed, triangular teeth, and regarded the craft with dead, soulless eyes.

Maildun gave the order to distribute the weapons as the creature rose for a second time, and he then had the oars shipped.

There was no chance that they could outrun the huge shark, and he feared it might attack the oars in its battle frenzy.

The *Avenger* glided to a halt and rocked on the waves. The sail rippled in the feather-light breeze, but no amount of tacking could catch an air current. The crew gathered nervously on the port side and watched the two fins cut through the waves barely two oar lengths away. Suddenly they changed direction and began to move purposely towards the craft.

'They're going to attack,' Maildun called, pulling his sword free. 'Make ready. Archers, as soon as they come in range. Ruarc,' he called to his brother, 'use your sling; place your shots below and before the fin. Gussan, try to gaff it with the boar-spear if it comes too close . . .'

'They won't attack,' Paedur said quietly, joining the captain at the rail. His thin lips curled into a smile as he looked at the captain's drawn sword. 'and what are you going to do with that?'

Maildun glanced at the huge fin slicing through the metallic waves, and then at the sword in his hand: compared to the size of the shark it was little more than a needle. He shrugged. 'If I could get in one good blow . . .'

'Pray that it never gets close enough for you to get in that one good blow.'

The sharks veered off at the last possible moment. One of the creatures had two shafts projecting from its back, and Ruarc had bounced a stone the size of a hen's egg off the other's skull, but without any obvious effect. They reappeared on the starboard side of the ship and once more cleaved through the water towards the *Avenger*.

'Move back,' Paedur commanded urgently, 'they're going to attack now.'

Maildun hurriedly backed away, but the bard stood by the rail and raised both arms to the metallic skies. The fingers of his right hand were splayed and slightly clawed, as if he sought to clutch something, and the hook that took the place of his left hand was but a semi-circle of blinding light in the harsh afternoon sunlight. Paedur called aloud in a hoarse, croaking tongue, totally unlike his own, and indeed totally different from any tongue either Germane or Diurnan, who were well travelled, had ever heard. The raw sounds hung on the still air, and seemed to vibrate upon the sparkling water.

Abruptly, the atmosphere became charged with power. Writhing lines of fox-fire ran along the bard's hook, gathered briefly at the tip and then discharged into the water – directly in the path of the shark. Lines of incandescent force danced along the waves, spitting and crackling, and the huge creature was flung into the air. The shark writhed in agony as the lines of force encased and surrounded it; tendrils of dark, oily smoke issued from its gaping mouth and gills, and as it fell back into the water it seemed to explode outwards in a bloody mass of steaming entrails and gristle, which had been seared and blackened from within.

Paedur staggered and fell back, and Maildun caught him as he fell. His thin face was pale and sweat glistened on his forehead and cheeks, and his eyes had rolled in his head leaving only the whites showing. The captain gently eased the bard to the deck, while behind him Diurnan ordered out the oars and began to call the beat. The *Avenger* shuddered and then, as the oarsmen caught their rhythm, it slid smoothly forward, leaving the oily black smudge smouldering on the bloody water with the smaller creature circling it patiently.

Paedur regained consciousness late in the evening, just as the lookout sighted the second island. It rose from the sea in a smooth, rounded hump, rather like the *duns* of the Tuatha De Danann in their native Erin. However, as they neared it, they could see that the mountainside rose upwards in a series of regular steps.

The bard joined Maildun and Germane by the figurehead. The navigator was squinting into the distance, his hand shading his eyes from the last rays of the setting sun. 'The mountain has been terraced, worked by the hand of man – although I can see no sign of habitation,' he added.

'Man had no hand in that isle,' Paedur said hoarsely. He looked pale and tired, and his eyes were sunken into deep hollows, making his face look even more skull-like than usual. He pointed with his hook. 'Look again; if you can see the terraces from this distance, then consider what size they must be and then look again at the vegetation.'

As they neared the isle, they saw that the terraces were like cliffs and the distances between one and the next were very great. Lush greenery rose from them – small trees and ornamental bushes carefully worked and shaped into the likeness of a hundred beasts both mythical and factual. Bushes of different hues and leaf patterns had been carefully placed side by side to give the appearance of feathers or hide, and some of the creatures looked amazingly lifelike.

The wind, which had sprung up just before sunset, blew from the island and carried the heavy, cloying perfumes of a thousand flowers in full bloom, and brought with it the gentle susurration of the branches and leaves in motion, like a resting army whispering urgently together.

Seed pods floated by. One touched the snarling figurehead and burst in an explosion of foaming white dust motes. The navigator reached out and caught one as it wafted past. He held it up to the waning light and examined it; it was a curiously regular, star-shaped nut, stark white except for thin, dark blue veins which encircled it. It was almost weightless and trailed four long, feather-like strands beneath it.

Paedur glanced across at the navigator and his eyes widened. He lunged across and, with the point of his hook, flicked the seed pod from Germane's hand. The navigator gasped in pain, thinking the bard had cut him, but when he looked at his palm, he found the mark of the star-seed etched into the flesh.

'It would have burned right through,' Paedur explained. His hook flashed in the wan light and sliced another in half as it floated by; it fell into the sea and disappeared in a hiss of steam. 'The seeds generate their own heat . . .' Paedur began, and then a pod touched the heavy leather sail and burst. The tiny star-seeds quickly ate through the leather and fell away in tiny meteors onto the deck where they continued to burn. Diurnan threw himself down onto the deck and impaled the burning seeds with the point of his knife and carefully flicked them overboard.

Three crewmen attempted to furl the burning sail, while the others milled about, scraping away the burning seeds that now seemed to cling to every portion of the deck.

'Cut the sail,' Germane shouted, 'cut out the burning portion.' He swore in his own dialect as no one moved to obey. 'Diurnan – the sail, cut it.' He pointed upwards to the sail which was beginning to hang in flaming tatters. Diurnan nodded and, grasping the lower spar of the mast, heaved himself upwards. His knife sliced through the heavy, oiled leather, cutting out an irregular patch that was burning furiously. He moved up the mast, methodically cutting out the burning sections, dropping them down onto the deck below where they were quickly thrown overboard. The lookout suddenly screamed and fell past him, his arms and torso enveloped in flames. His fall ended in a sickening crunch on the deck below.

Diurnan ducked as another star-seed drifted lazily past his head. He was almost at the top of the mast now, where a portion of the sail and a patch of the mast itself were burning fiercely. A pod must have struck the lookout directly, he reasoned, surveying the wreckage of the unfortunate's perch. The stench of burning leather was sickening and heavy wreaths of smoke coiled about his head. He closed his streaming eyes and hacked blindly; he felt his knife bite into the leather and drag. The skin on his hands and arms began to blister and he could smell his own singed hair. His knife caught and he dragged it free, almost losing his balance as it came out suddenly. His arms windmilled as he sought to catch his balance; his nails dug into wood and leather, slipped, and then caught with a shoulder-wrenching pull. But his knife had fallen quivering to the deck below.

Diurnan backed down slowly, his bare feet moving carefully along the grooves in the mast. Above him the unchecked fire was now spreading rapidly, eating through the leather, threatening to destroy the mast. He heard a shout below, someone calling his name. He looked down and saw the bard, a short-hafted battleaxe clutched in his hand. He mouthed words that were lost in the crackle of fire and began to twirl the axe by its thong. The northerner suddenly understood what the bard was saying and what he was attempting to do, and he felt his blood run ice-cold along his veins. He pressed himself to the mast and froze, only his lips moving in a silent prayer to his wild northern gods.

Paedur swung the axe until it was but a smooth blur, and then he abruptly released it at the apex of its spin . . . it buzzed through the air and bit into the wood above Diurnan's head. The northerner slowly opened his eyes and stared in disbelief at the still vibrating axe just above him. He shook splinters from his blond hair and then pushed himself back up the mast. Wrenching the axe free almost cost him his perch, it was embedded that deeply. He moved on up to his original position and then swung the short axe again and again, tearing ragged lumps from the leather, hacking through the burning section of the mast. Scraps of flaming leather drifted lazily to the decks below. And then, suddenly splintering, the topmost section of the mast snapped and plunged downwards.

Diurnan screamed aloud as flaming splinters tore into his bare back as it fell past, laying open the skin from his shoulders to his hips. The *Avenger* swayed beneath him and his vision blurred. His hand slipped and the axe fell from its thong to bite deep into the deck and slowly, one by one, the fingers of his left hand came away from the blood-smeared mast. Numbness crept upwards through his legs . . .

52

Maildun caught the lower spar and pulled himself onto it, and then moved quickly up the scarred mast, his booted feet slipping on the wood. He reached Diurnan just as his grip gave way, and the captain held him with one hand while the other maintained a vice-like grip on the mast. But now he was stuck; he couldn't move downwards with his burden.

There was the scrape of metal on wood and then Gussan and Colga joined him, and between the three of them they managed to bring the northerner back down to the deck, where Germane and Paedur took him from their grasp.

They laid him face down on the deck and examined his back. Long, jagged splinters stood out from the wound like needles and there were dark, angry patches of burned and charred flesh where the leather from the sail had stuck and burned.

Maildun knelt beside them, his eyes narrowing at the mass of raw flesh. He reached out to pluck one of the long splinters from between Diurnan's shoulder-blades, but the bard caught his hand and pushed it away. 'Don't touch it,' he commanded. 'If you want him to live, that is,' he added.

'What will you do?' Maildun asked. 'What can you do – what can anyone do?' he murmured bitterly. 'I doubt that he will ever walk erect again: he will never be able to straighten his back when – if – it heals.'

'If you touch him now, then he will never walk again,' Paedur said quietly. 'Attend to your ship, captain; I will see what I can do.' He looked up at the skies, and the faint, unfamiliar stars already beginning to appear. 'We should drop anchor here – you would be very foolish to continue on in these waters at night.'

'I had no intention of doing so,' Maildun snapped.

The bard nodded in the swiftly gathering dusk. Already his features were fading and the shadows seemed to gather more closely about him. 'Boil some fresh water and bring me blankets and spirits.'

Germane stood up and moved away, leaving Maildun alone with the bard. 'Why?' he asked softly, looking at the terrible destruction of his friend's back.

'You mustn't blame yourself. I have told you before; you follow your path, he follows his. There is no choice in the matter.'

'Have I ever had a choice? I feel as if I'm a puppet, pulled hither and yon as if on strings.' He leaned across Diurnan and hissed into the bard's face. 'But who pulls the strings, eh? Tell me that.'

Paedur's teeth flashed in a sudden smile. 'You really don't want to know.'

The night was warm and close and overhead the stars glittered in the skies; strange configurations wheeled across the heavens, some vaguely familiar, others totally alien.

Germane stood by the snarling figurehead with the bard. Behind them the deck was ablaze with lights, whilst in the centre, beside the mast, a low fire smouldered on an upturned shield. Diurnan lay beside it, where they had left him, and Maildun knelt by his side.

'The water is nearly ready,' the navigator said quietly. He turned to face the bard. 'Will he live?'

Paedur hitched his long, furred cloak higher on his thin shoulders, and pulled the cowl up. Only his eyes remained visible, hard points of light glittering amber-gold in the reflections of the torches. 'Perhaps.'

The silence between them dragged on and then the navigator said, 'The seeds have disappeared.'

'The offshore winds have dropped for the night. But they will spring up again with the coming of the dawn.' His head moved, rustling against the cloth of his hood, and Germane felt his gaze on him. 'As a navigator you should know that.'

'I have never sailed these seas before, but you, you know this world,' he stated flatly.

'I know many worlds.'

'Then why are we here? What has brought us to this accursed place,' Germane demanded, his voice low and angry. He watched the bard shift his position, saw the reflected light vanish from his colourless eyes, saw them take up the reflections from the stars. 'Hate and desire for revenge brought us to this world; one man's desire for vengeance. And here we shall remain until that desire has been appeased. Many men go into the Shadowlands – few return.'

'Are there many worlds . . . many Shadowlands?' the navigator asked in a whisper.

The bard's voice grew distant and his head tilted as he stared into another time, another place. 'There are many, many Shadowlands. Some men know of in myth and legends, but there are others which are completely unimaginable. Some things, however, never change: there is always violence and death, there is always love and hate.' He pointed upwards with his hand. 'The stars may change, the lands may be different, the beasts strange

54

and frightening – but one thing remains the same: man, the greatest beast of all. And he never changes; he remains in all his shame and glory.' Cloth rustled as the bard shrugged. 'Such is the way of things.' There was a pause and then the tone of his voice changed. 'The water is ready now.'

Maildun stood as the bard and Germane joined him. 'He is feverish and fluid is beginning to seep from his back.'

Paedur knelt by the still body of the northerner. Germane brought a steaming bowl of water and placed it beside the fire, and then returned a few moments later with an earthen bottle of raw spirits and a freshly washed cloth. Paedur sank his hand into the steaming water and then had Maildun dry it for him on the cloth. He then passed his hook through the flames of the fire, until the metal glowed a dull cherry red, before plunging it into the bowl of water, most of which immediately steamed away.

And then, with infinite care, he began to pick the splinters from Diurnan's back, and cut away the charred and brittle flesh with his hook. The northerner twitched and jumped as each jagged splinter of wood was removed and groaned aloud as Paedur peeled back the skin before cutting it away.

When all the splinters had been removed and the burnt flesh removed, Paedur asked Maildun, Germane, Ruarc and Gussan to hold the northerner's arms and legs. He then commenced to wash the wound with a mixture of hot water and spirit. Diurnan screamed. His eyes snapped open and he cried aloud in his guttural northern tongue. He thrashed about, raving and calling for his savage northern gods, and the four men were hard pressed to hold him down.

Paedur balled the sodden cloth and tossed it aside. He then moved back and extended his left arm, and passed the gleaming curved hook over the raw flesh, barely touching the skin. He called aloud in a smooth, hissing whisper – and the hook blazed into sudden incandescent life. The intricate runes worked into the metal began to coil and flow like serpents. They hung lingering on the air when the bard moved the hook, and tiny tendrils of blue smoke writhed over the weeping flesh. And as the bard drew his hook down the first mate's back in an arcane pattern, the wounds visibly closed leaving the flesh unmarked and unscarred.

Maildun drew back in shocked disbelief, crossing himself while his hand fell to the dagger tucked into his boot. The bard glanced at him, and the captain suddenly felt the hilt of the knife grow uncomfortable warm.

55

The crew moved away as the bard stood and gathered his cloak about his shoulders. 'Wrap him warmly in blankets. He will awake refreshed and well in the morning.' He stepped back out of the circle of firelight and disappeared into the shadows.

Maildun and Germane knelt by the northerner and examined his back. It was perfectly smooth and clear, and even an old scar, which Diurnan had had upon his left shoulder since his youth, was gone. Germane ran his fingers down the flesh, and it was smooth and silken. His eyes met the captain's only to find the fear and confusion he himself felt mirrored there. Together they lifted the still body and carried it to the captain's small cabin, where they laid him down on the long box-like bed. Maildun poured them both a drink from a small, crystal-stoppered, earthen jug.

'What is he?' he asked suddenly.

The navigator shook his head. 'I don't know,' he said sincerely, 'but I doubt that he is a man.'

CHAPTER SEVEN

As the first rays of the sun broke through the massed cloud banks that huddled on the horizon, the island came abruptly and raucously alive. A huge multitude of varicoloured birds rose from the trees and ornamental bushes. Their cawing and screaming filled the air, drowning out the eternal noises of the sea and the creak of the ship, and they turned the island into a mass of pulsating colours as they rose and fell. They wheeled over the island initially and then some broke away from the flock and came winging towards the ship, flying low over the smooth water.

Maildun strapped on his sword and ordered the crew to arm themselves. This time he would take no chances; he had learned a valuable lesson the previous day with the star-seeds – nothing on this world could be trusted. Paedur joined him as the captain settled his longsword across his back, with the hilt projecting over his left shoulder. He nodded briefly and then pointed towards the brightly-plumed birds. 'Are they dangerous?'

The bard shrugged. 'All beasts are dangerous if they are attacked.' He paused and stared intently at the birds, which were closer now. 'Have your men lay down their weapons and cover all the metal they can find, daub it with grease or fat; but cover it and quickly.'

'Why?' Maildun asked.

'*Do it!*'

The captain pulled off his sword and wrapped it in his cloak and passed the order onto Germane, who carried it down the ship.

Diurnan joined them. The huge northerner was fully recovered from his wound, and although he had attempted to express his thanks to the bard, Paedur had brushed them aside with a brusqueness that had vaguely angered him. Moreover, Diurnan's thanks were tempered by the knowledge that he had been cured by sorcery and he felt vaguely tainted, as if a slug had crawled across his flesh leaving a shining silver slime on his skin. He glanced across at the bard, who was standing by the

57

figurehead, the cowl of his cloak covering his head, his hand tucked into the sleeve and his hook hidden in the folds of the other. He might not be human, Diurnan thought, but he was vulnerable, and the northerner vowed to find out where.

The birds descended on the *Avenger*, their lustrous plumage burning vividly on the early morning sun, their hard, flat eyes cold and as sharp as their polished beaks and claws. Some were familiar sea-birds: gulls and gannets, albatrosses and cormorants, but there were others, large, hook-beaked, long-taloned birds with brilliant metallic plumage which rasped unpleasantly as they moved, and which seemed to regard the men with more than avian intelligence. They perched in the fire-scarred rigging, whilst others strutted long-legged on the deck, pecking at the casks and coiled ropes or the oarsmen's benches. The crew remained still and silent, unwilling to move and draw the creatures's attention to themselves.

One bird swooped down and alighted on a small bronze dagger that a crewman had left embedded in a bench. Its first attempt to pull it free failed and it rose with an angry cawing, before swooping down and tearing it out with the second attempt. More and more of the large birds alighted on the ship, silently lining the rails, clutching the rigging or the spars, regarding the frightened crew with flat, slitted eyes.

Maildun put his mouth to Diurnan's ear and whispered, 'If they attack us now, we'll stand no chance without weapons.'

The first mate nodded almost imperceptibly and began to edge towards the tall figure of the bard. Almost as one the birds' heads swivelled in his direction. One crept forward and struck the deck almost by his foot with a taloned claw, gouging a long tear in the hard, polished wood. Diurnan froze, his heart pounding. If that bird should move again, he was going to snap it scrawny neck with one kick, and the consequences be damned . . .

But now the birds seemed distracted. They had become totally silent, and even the soft clucking deep in their throats had ceased. And then, faint in the distance, though clear and distinct, came a shrill cawing. The birds moved again, and this time their claws tapped the decks and spars with determined ferocity, tearing and gouging the wood, and the birds clinging to the rigging and sail began slowly and methodically to tear them to shreds.

Maildun touched Diurnan and nodded to one of the large oars. The northerner nodded slowly. If they didn't do something the creatures would rip the ship to pieces.

A bird darted forward and pecked at a crewman. He yelped with fright and pain and stumbled backwards, a long gash in his forearm. All movement ceased as the creatures turned to look in his direction. They tensed.

The bard turned suddenly, his left arm raised high, the sickle-like hook blazing in the morning light. The sight of the shining metal seemed to enflame the birds and they rose in a single mass and encircled the bard, screaming and cawing. One swooped, claws extended to clutch the metal, but Paedur's arm seemed only to twitch and the silver hook sliced through the bird, shearing off a wing. It screamed in a voice that was almost human and fell in a slow spiral towards the waves – only to be torn to pieces by others of its flock before it reached the water.

Paedur then etched a pattern in the air, and the crew of the *Avenger*, felt the cold wind of sorcery touch them. The bard called aloud in the Old Tongue of the Tuatha De Danann, 'Begone!'

The birds fell back, screaming angrily, their metallic feathers ruffled and splayed, their claws still extended, ready to rend and tear. Fights broke out amongst them and a score of the creatures fell into the waves in flurries of blood and plumage. But slowly, inexorably, the main body of the flock were drawn back to the terraced isle. Paedur remained by the figurehead, still with his left arm extended, willing the creatures away from the ship. The fresh morning air was now tainted with sharp, acrid, copper-and-blood stench of sorcery, and every man felt the hair on his arms and at the nape of his neck rise and crackle with the strength of it. The birds settled back into the trees, disturbing others, which rose in vivid flashes of colour, and then settled down again, complaining bitterly. Gradually silence fell over the island, and the only sounds were the rustling of the trees and bushes.

Paedur dropped his arm with a sigh of exhaustion.

Maildun and Germane joined him. Paedur nodded at the sun. 'The wind will take up again soon, and then the seeds will come; we must be downwind by then.' He turned away, his features pinched and tight, his eyes leaden. He clutched his left arm, and even the metallic sheen on his hook seemed muted and dulled. 'There is a storm brewing,' he said, glancing back over his shoulder, 'it would be better if we make harbour. There is another island half a day's sailing beyond that.' He nodded towards the Island of Birds.

*

It was late in the afternoon when they dropped anchor in a small natural bay on the fourth island's south side. This isle was smaller than the others, being little more than a single mountain rising out from the sea. It too bore evidence of volcanic activity, but the cone was old and had collapsed in on itself, and the slopes were covered with lush greenery. However, as they neared the island and the broad sandy beach, they began to realise that it seemed to be totally devoid of life; no birds circled through the skies, no creatures moved rustling through the rich undergrowth, nor warmed themselves on the flat stone that bordered the waves and, save for the whispering of the wind, the isle was totally silent.

As the afternoon drifted into evening, the storm which had been brewing since the dawn broke. The rain came down in a solid sheet, shattering the surface of the sea, churning the beach into soft mud, flattening the vegetation and shrouding the top of the mountain in a grey mantle of cloud. The crew of the *Avenger* huddled under oiled leather sheets, drinking and storytelling, swearing at the unnatural weather, whilst an unlucky few stood watch or swept the worst of the pooling water overboard.

Germane, Diurnan and Paedur were squeezed into the captain's cabin. A smoking oil lamp sent flickers of yellow light about the tiny room, casting crazy, dancing shadows on the sloping walls. Germane sat on the low bunk, beside Maildun, while Diurnan crouched on his haunches with his back against the wall. The bard sat with his back to the door, the light dancing off the Bardic Sigil on his left shoulder, deepening his sallow skin to parchment yellow.

Maildun filled his own goblet and passed the flask around, and both Germane and Diurnan filled their own cups with the frothing mead before handing it back to the captain. The bard had refused the drink. Maildun drank quickly and leaned forward, the torchlight turning his fiery red hair to deep bronze and ruddy gold. 'I've asked you here for a reason,' he began hesitantly. 'I began this voyage in search of my father's murderers and some answers. I lived for years thinking myself an orphan. If I thought about my parents, I assumed them to be dead but closely related to the king. And then I traced my mother . . .' He stopped and drank again, aware of the rawness in his voice. 'She was – *is* – a nun. She was a newly-professed nun when my father raped her . . .'

Germane swore in a hushed whisper, while Diurnan merely grimaced, his face betraying the pain he felt for his friend.

60

'My mother is . . . insane. She has been so since my father took her against her will.' He drank again, and quickly refilled his glass. 'I wanted him dead, and now that I know that he is dead, I want revenge on his murderers, and yet I know that they've never done anything to me.'

'Might you not be taking revenge on your father through them?' Paedur asked quietly.

'Aye,' Maildun nodded, 'be that as it may . . .' He looked into his glass and shook his head. 'I'm sorry, I've rambled from the point, this drink speaks, not I.' He swallowed hard and rubbed the heel of his hand against his eyes. 'Well then, I began this voyage in search of my father or his murderers, but it's become much more than that now. I should have known,' he added with a wry smile, 'the druid said as much, and the instructions he gave me for the building of this craft were much more than one would normally get from a country druid to a minor lordling.' He grinned. 'In fact, he as much as told me . . . However, Paedur tells us that we have sailed beyond the boundaries of our own world into a Shadowland, and from what we've seen, we can only believe him.' He swallowed the remainder of the drink and caught the bard looking at him through amber slitted eyes. He looked directly across at him. 'What I want to know is where we are, and where we're going.' He jabbed a finger in the bard's direction. 'And I want to know your place in all this.'

'I think we would all like to know that,' Diurnan said quietly, feeling a cold chill walk up his spine. He hitched himself up against the wall, his face impassive, his eyes alert behind the rim of his cup.

'I don't know for certain where we are,' Paedur said slowly. 'I need to see at least one more island before I can be certain; perhaps in the morning . . . ?'

'But you said that this was the Island Sea; you knew these islands were dangerous, and you knew of the dangers,' Maildun accused. 'You knew we would find this island, for example.'

Paedur smiled, his eyes golden in the light. 'I am a bard – whether you choose to believe it or not – and I merely heeded the legends.'

'What legends?' the navigator asked.

'The legends which tell of the kingdoms which border your world, which tell of a sky filled with stars that are unknown to man, of a sky that burns brightly even at the dark of the moon. And the legends which speak of the Island Sea – or the Sea of Many Islands . . .'

Diurnan sat up suddenly. 'I've heard of those. I've heard the skalds in my own land tell of the Broken Land, and the Sea of Islands that lay far to the west of Ogygia. Some of my race even went in search of them.'

The bard nodded. 'Ogygia is one of the ancient names for Erin. The legend is almost universal, and I have come across it, and variations of it, countless times in my travels.' Paedur hesitated while lightning flashed across the sky, outlining the door in lines of stark white. However, the worst of the storm had passed them by and when the thunder came much later, it was far to the north.

The bard leaned against the door of the cabin and his hard, colourless eyes glazed as he stared into the lamp light. His voice deepened and took on a resonant, vibrant tone – the speaking voice of a professional bard.

'In the time of the First Men, when the world was but newly formed and the gods walked as men, there was but one continent. It was a vast land mass enclosing nearly all the northern globe. But at this time the world was unsettled and still bubbled and seethed. The land rose and fell, mountains formed and re-formed, deep valleys were cut into the earth, mighty seas were created, destroyed and then recreated as lakes. And gradually the world as it is today was formed.

'The central core of the first great northern continent remained untouched in the midst of the rapidly cooling seas that surrounded it. And whereas the elements and upheavals had destroyed the traces of civilisation on the newly formed surrounding islands, the old order remained untouched and unsullied. And this was the Prime Land. Huge cities rose on its chalk-white cliffs, glittering jewels that blazed in a sun that was still new, and, like all young creatures, still violent. The first metal was forged in that land, the first glass was blown. It was there that the masons, the carpenters, the builders and architects first perfected their crafts. The philosophers and theologians first described the chaos and then ordered it, suiting it to their needs and the magicians fashioned their creatures on that land.

'The First Folk, however, grew bored with their lot. They had everything, they wanted for nothing, and so they turned more and more inwards. Inbreeding created creatures that were neither man nor beast, and some of the gods lay with men, and their offspring – although incredibly powerful – were neither men nor gods. The First Folk took the roiling chaos, fashioned it to their needs and whims, and thus were the hybrids formed.

'But their workings with the stuff of chaos eventually destroyed them. One man, the son of a mortal maid and a god, tapped a huge vault beneath the continent – a vast cavern of natural, raw power. He drew from it again and again in his fashioning. His creatures and creations grew more and more extravagant and outrageous; he brought myth to life and made the legends walk. From bone and tissue he brought forth again the great lizards that walked the world before the First Man, and he would often set them against each other in a huge arena he had constructed in a day and a night for that very purpose.

'But little did this magician know that the stuff he worked with was the very binding of the continent, and eventually, when he had completed the fashioning of a huge, floating island zoo, what remained of that force dissipated, and the continent staggered under the onslaught of the forces of nature. Chaos returned to its natural form or, as happened in many cases, assumed new and totally different forms. The continent broke up and vast tracts of it sank beneath the boiling waves. Much of the remainder succumbed to the inexorable pounding of the waves, and is no more. But what does remain – a little more than thirty singular remnants of the Prime Continent, populated by the last of their fashionings and the later products of nature – swims in a vast ocean. And this is the Island Sea.

'And when the Prime Continent sank it created ripples in the Void, and thus were the Shadowlands formed: echoes separated from each other by little more than a blink and a heartbeat, accessible by little more than an idle thought, a wish or a dream.

'Your world is a Shadowland; this is the Prime Land.'

Silence settled on the tiny, cramped cabin when the bard finished and the strange light faded from his eyes.

'Truly?' Maildun whispered eventually. 'We are sailing this Island Sea of legend?'

Paedur nodded and when he spoke his voice was slightly cracked and ragged. 'I believe so.'

'But why?'

'As a lesson?' the bard suggested.

'Or a warning,' Germane added softly.

'And you, bard, why are you here?' Diurnan asked.

The bard smiled wanly. 'I am your guide, your protector, and mayhap your doom.'

'Tell me, Paedur,' Germane asked quietly, 'what was the name of the magician who ultimately destroyed the Prime Land?'

The bard shrugged, his fur cloak rustling in the shadows that had gathered, now that the oil in the lamp had run low. 'He has many names in many places, but the one that appears most frequently is *tLanteco Astis*.'

CHAPTER EIGHT

Germane notched an arrow as he followed the bard up the gently sloping beach. Behind them, Gussan and two of the crew filled the ship's water casks from a small fresh-water spring that came trickling down from a cleft between two upright stones and disappeared into the sands.

The sun had not yet risen and the sea-mists lay heavily on the beach and water, shrouding the *Avenger* in wreaths of gauze, and the morning twilight blurred the outlines of the trees and shrubs that bordered the beach. The island was alive with the steady trickling of water and the almost metallic plinking of droplets as they slid off branches and leaves. The air was vibrantly fresh; the storm the previous night having washed it clean, soaking into the dry earth and stimulating the buried shoots into life. The damp-earth smell and the scent of greenery overrode the ever-present tang of the salt sea.

Germane breathed deeply, tasting the air like wine. A mariner for most of his life, actually born aboard a ship at sea, and with salt in his lungs for as long as he could remember, he found the rich, earthy smell of freshly turned soil almost overpowering . . . The navigator blinked and shook his head, breaking the spell. He turned and caught sight of the bard cresting a rise a little way ahead of him, and lengthened his stride to catch up with him. He had no wish to be lost on this isle – and certainly no wish to be left alone. It had been a mistake for him to come over, he knew, but the captain had insisted that the water casks should be filled before they ventured further on the Island Sea, and had thought it prudent to do so before whatever creature of horror inhabiting the island came awake.

'But what happens if it's a night creature, and not yet asleep?' Germane had wondered.

'Then you had better hope it fed well last night, because you're going ashore.' Maildun had smiled cheerfully and clapped him on the shoulder.

'Me! What for?'

The captain had taken him to the starboard bow and pointed

up to the low mountain that dominated the island. 'Climb it,' he commanded. 'Find out where we are in relation to . . . to anywhere. Look for any land mass that might be Erin.'

'But why? We have the bard . . .'

'For that very reason!'

'And on my own?' Germane had stood back and shaken his head. 'I navigate on sea, I do not climb mountains,' he had stated emphatically.

'Well then, there is a first time for everything. I want to know where we are, and where we're going.'

'I'm not going on my own!'

Maildun had paused and then grinned wolfishly. 'Then the bard will accompany you.'

'Dry land makes me ill,' Germane had complained.

The captain nodded absently, but his eyes were on the island. 'Go now; I want you both off the isle by sunrise. It may look uninhabited, but I've no wish to test that impression.'

Germane caught up with Paedur. 'Does anything live in those caves?' he asked, gesturing to a row of dark openings in the base of the mountain.

The bard shook his head. 'There is grass growing in the cave mouths and stretching back into the caves themselves; nothing has lived there for a long time.'

The navigator relaxed and lowered his bow. 'Does anything live on this island?' he wondered.

The bard pointed into the undergrowth with his hook. 'Something has made those runs; a large, heavy animal.' He paused and sniffed the air. 'And not too long ago either,' he added.

Germane's grip tightened on the polished horn of the bow. 'Are you sure?' he asked, his voice dropping to a whisper.

Paedur glanced back over his shoulder and smiled briefly. 'I'm sure.'

They continued on, moving through long grass now that they had left the sand-dunes, and then taking a rough track that wound its way up along the side of the low cliffs. The plant life grew taller and wilder, and soon the stench of rotting vegetation and the humidity of the air – even at that early hour – were almost unbearable. They crossed a small stream, which Germane made the mistake of walking in – only to discover that it was scalding hot, but at least it explained the unnatural warmth. The forest they were moving through now was deathly silent and soon even the eternal sound of the sea had faded into silence.

Germane staggered up the trail, painfully conscious that he was completely out of condition, and that too many months of easy living, fine food and wines had given him a slight paunch for which he was now paying the price. He stumbled against a broad, flat stone and sat down.

'A moment, if you please,' he wheezed.

Paedur shrugged and joined him on the broad stone. Germane leaned back and closed his eyes, feeling the muscles in his thighs and calves jumping and twitching and the painful thump of his heart in his chest. He sat up suddenly and looked at the bard. 'You're not even winded,' he accused.

The bard rubbed the sole of his boot in the dust. 'Perhaps I'm more used to it than you,' he said, 'and then again, I have climbed bigger mountains.'

'Where?' the navigator asked suddenly.

The bard pushed back his hood with his hook and looked quizzically at the smaller man. 'Why do you wish to know?' he asked.

Germane coloured. 'I'm sorry; I've no right to ask. I'm just curious.' He smiled briefly. 'Call it professional interest.'

Paedur laughed heartily, the sound shockingly loud in the unnatural quiet of the dripping forest. 'Professional interest, eh? Tell me,' he said suddenly, 'How many lands have you visited?'

Germane considered and then shrugged. 'I don't know. In my youth I came overland from the south – I must have crossed a score of lands until I reached a village in Gaul. From there I sailed with a crew of pirates who were returning to their northern homelands; that's where I met Diurnan Lenkard. The following summer I sailed south with him when he went reiving along the coasts of Pictland, Alba and Erin and across into Gaul again. We were caught by an early winter and we were forced to spend it in Erin, and that's where I met Maildun. I've sailed around the coast of Erin, north to south and north again, explored even its most desolate bays, visited its most deserted islands and even navigated to the upper reaches of the Sinann.' He looked across at the bard. 'Is that enough?'

Paedur nodded. 'Aye, I suppose it is. Have you ever wondered what lies beyond the horizon though?' he asked quietly.

Germane sighed and nodded. 'Once. In my youth it was my ambition to explore this entire world. I was going to take my father's boat and, with my brothers for a crew, I was going to navigate to the very edge of the world, and chart the strange lands that are supposed to cling to the world's edge. I swore I was going to stand on the highest mountains on one of those islands and watch the sun come spinning up from under the great waterfall where the ocean spills down into the Void.' He sighed again. 'But that was many years ago, and I was a younger man then.'

Paedur shook his head sadly. 'You amaze me. You are an intelligent man, you have travelled extensively, and yet you refuse to face the evidence that your world . . .'

'"*Your world*",' Germane broke in suddenly, 'you speak as if *my* world were not *yours* also.'

The navigator was suddenly conscious how silent the island was, and he was abruptly aware that he was alone on a deserted island, far from his friends, with someone who not only awed him, but also terrified him.

The bard rubbed his right hand against his cloak, raising and flattening the pale-tipped hairs. He ran his fingers through his grey-flecked hair and shook it in the slight breeze and then eased himself to his feet. 'Perhaps it is not,' he said quietly. He moved away and then turned back to the navigator. 'What would you say if I told you that your world is round?'

Germane stared at him blankly.

Paedur pointed into the heavens. 'Look above you. The stars are the mirrors of this world – oh, they may be distorted betimes, but they are mirrors nonetheless.'

'Not round,' Germane cried in horror, 'surely that is impossible'

Paedur reached forward and grabbed the navigator's arm above the elbow and yanked him to his feet. He dragged him up along the track and, as they came above the vegetation and the tops of the trees, he stopped and pointed out over the little forest towards the sea.

'Tell me; what do you see . . . ?' he demanded.

Germane squinted into the wan morning light. 'The sea, the tinge of the dawn on the horizon . . .'

'And the horizon; what do you notice about that?'

'I don't understand,' Germane said weakly.

'Its shape man, what of its shape?' the bard persisted.

'It . . . it curves.'

'In every direction?'

Germane nodded.

Paedur spun the bemused navigator around and pointed up into the heavens. 'And the stars, what is their shape?'

'Round.'

'And the sun?' he pressed, 'and the moon when it is full?'

'Round also.'

Paedur stared down into the navigator's face, and Germane felt his will being drained away by the bard's colourless eyes. 'And what would that lead you to believe?'

'That . . . that this world is round also?' Germane whispered.

Paedur loosened his grip, and Germane went staggering backwards. The bard smiled coldly. 'Very good. I would consider it an invaluable lesson for a navigator to discover that the world he walks is round.' He turned away, and his chill, slightly amused voice drifted back over his shoulder. 'At least you may rest assured that you will never fall off the edge.'

The track up the mountainside was steeper than it had looked from the deck of the *Avenger*, and both men quickly realised that there was no possible way for them to obey Maildun's command to return by sunrise. They had the choice therefore of continuing onwards or returning to the ship.

They choose to continue on.

It was close to mid-morning by the time they reached the highest point of the mountain. The latter half of their journey had been along a track that led upwards through a barren, blasted rockface. The mountain had once been volcanic, but it had been many hundreds of years since it had last given voice, and the cone had long since collapsed in on itself, leaving a jagged spur rising up into the heavens like a long, accusing finger.

Paedur and Germane stood at the base of the pinnacle and stared out over the sea. In the distance to the east they could see a chain of small islands. The midday sun touched some of them with brilliant fire, sending vibrant colours dancing on the pure morning air, which was obviously vegetation in motion, while others, the barren isles, remained dark and shadowed. A pall of smoke hung over some of the further isles.

Paedur pointed with his hook. 'You can trace the line of the mountain range of which these islands are but the tips. When the Prime Land sank beneath the waves in three days and three nights, nearly everything was destroyed. The seas rolled in and cleansed the lands of almost every living thing, and only those who had fled to the mountains survived. Of course many of those died in the following days and months as they fell victims to hunger, thirst, the elements or *tLanteco Astis*' animals. Soon, only the beasts survived.'

'What about this isle?' Germane asked.

Paedur shaded his eyes with his right hand and stared down over the island spread below them. Without turning his head, he continued in the same tone of voice. 'Oh, it is inhabited. The creature has been following us ever since we came ashore.' His right hand flew out and caught Germane's shoulder in a vice-like grip. 'It would be unwise to move now. It is watching us.'

'What are we going to do?' Germane whispered urgently.

'Do? We do nothing. We merely plot the *Avenger's* course.' He pointed again with his hook. 'If we continue to sail into the setting sun – therefore following the line of the isles which runs east to west – we should eventually reach that gate through which we entered this world.'

Germane casually nocked an arrow. 'How sure are you that it will still be open?'

'Archu's pet druid rent the very fabric of the worlds with his spell; it is a wound that will not heal quickly. The alternative is for us to find a magician powerful enough to will us back to Erin . . .'

'Bard,' Germane said urgently, 'are you sure we're being watched?'

Paedur glanced across at the navigator. 'Quite sure. Behind you and to your left in that last clump of stones in the shadow of those stunted trees. Turn slowly and casually.'

Germane walked a little way down the track and turned as if to ask the bard a question. He scanned the stones Paedur had indicated, but there was nothing there. He slowly ambled over to them, his every sense alert, knowing it would take less than a heartbeat to pull and loose an arrow, knowing that it took even less time to die. He bent and examined the ground around the stones, and hissed in astonishment. The earth was flat and dry, but something with large, splay-taloned claws had stood there and had been heavy enough to leave an impression in the baked ground.

Paedur's screamed warning sent him rolling backwards, away from the stones. The creature crashed onto the ground where he had been standing barely a heartbeat before, but its hind talons glanced off his leggings, slicing through the tough leather as if it were silk.

Germane rolled to his knees and loosed off an arrow blindly, and scrabbled in his quiver for another. And then he saw the creature. He froze.

It was as big as a horse, which it vaguely resembled, and stood taller than Diurnan, who was the tallest man Germane knew. It

70

was a uniform dun colour, and while its features, mane and tail were equine, its legs were those of a large, shaggy hound, and it had the feet and claws of some great bird of prey. Its lemon-yellow cat's eyes sparkled with unnatural intelligence and its gaze caught and compelled his, and he began to experience a vague uneasiness somewhere at the back of his mind. Images rose unbidden from his subconscious and frightening emotions crawled forth from their hidden lairs. The navigator attempted to move away, but his body seemed leaden, almost as if it belonged to someone else.

And then he felt it – the cold slither of an alien, completely unhuman presence in his mind. Slowly, and with a tacky persistence, it insinuated itself into the inner recesses of his mind, controlling, commanding and ultimately consuming. Germane, although immobile, was alert and fully aware of what was happening to him. He felt the control of his limbs go first, and the bow and arrow dropped to the ground at the same time as his legs gave way and he fell forward heavily.

It was with a curious sense of detachment that he saw Paedur approach the creature, moving slowly as if in a dream. He saw the bard gather himself like a great hunting cat and launch himself onto the creature's back, saw the silver hook bite deeply into its throat. A thick, emerald ichor gushed from the severed jugular, and where it splashed onto the bare earth the soil bubbled and seethed. The bard's hook rose again, the point ripping through one eye, and then Germane felt the pain lance through his own face. It felt as if the top of his head were being ripped off. He screamed; a long agonised, woman-like scream that threatened to destroy his throat. And then icy blackness engulfed him.

The stench awoke him. He came awake to find the bard holding him face down over the reeking carcass of the slaughtered horse-creature. He coughed and gagged and Paedur hauled him to his feet.

'How do you feel?'

'Sick.'

The bard laughed grimly. 'Count yourself lucky that you still have feelings. The Kapall would have drained you dry of all feeling, emotions and memories, and left you a husk into which it would have poured its own vile essence . . .' The bard's head snapped up. 'Come on, something's coming.' Supporting the navigator with one arm, Paedur hurried down the rough track. Germane bravely attempted to match the gruelling pace, but his legs still felt weak and shaky, and he could still taste the foul odour of the Kapall.

They crashed through the undergrowth, heedless now of the need for silence, conscious only of the need to be away from the isle, and with only one objective: to reach the ship.

They were almost free of the wood when they heard the screaming coming from the beach. Paedur dragged Germane along the track and then pushed him in the direction of the cliffs. 'Go to the caves; choose one with an entrance that is too small to allow the creatures space to enter.' The bard then set off down the track at a run, his furred cloak flapping behind him like a pair of huge wings.

Paedur burst down onto the beach – and into an abattoir. The shattered and bloody corpes of the two crewmen lay strewn about the beach, reeking and steaming in the midday sun, and a huge Kapall had Gussan backed up against a large granite boulder. His face was lined and drawn, and sweat ran in rivulets down his broad frame as he attempted to fight the creature's insidious probing. Suddenly, he sagged against the boulder, and his sword and knife fell in the sand by his feet.

He shivered violently and clutched his head and fell to his knees. The Kapall moved in for the kill.

Paedur's flying leap carried him almost twenty paces onto the horse-creatures back. It reared up on its hind legs, its talons tearing the air before Gussan's blank face, as it attempted to throw the bard off. But Paedur had a firm hold in its thick mane and he rode out the creature's bucking. The point of his hook tore into the Kapall's throat, but missed the vein and only enraged the creature further. It screamed, a long, blood-curdling shriek that tore at the nerves and set the teeth on edge. And then it fell to the ground and rolled over. Paedur leaped free and threw himself to one side as the creature tried to crush him, but as he came to his feet, he slipped on the bloody sand and fell heavily.

The creature's front claw lashed out, striking directly for Paedur's chest, but he caught it on his hook and twisted it away. The Kapall's huge, slab-like teeth snapped across the hook, capturing it. The bard swore and then spoke a word and the hook blazed with incandescent light – which sent the creature reeling backwards, screaming with fright and rage and pain. But the wash of power staggered the bard and he slumped back onto the sand.

And then Germane was by his side. He shook the bard savagely. 'Another comes.'

They took the semi-conscious Gussan between them and

splashed down into the shallows, leaving their own small boat and striking out directly for the *Avenger*. The cold water revived Gussan somewhat, but he still moved as if in a dream. The lookout aboard the ship spotted them, and they heard clearly his shout of alarm, and the splash of a currach being dropped into the water.

The Kapall that galloped down onto the beach was larger than the two they had already seen. It was the female of the species; its mane and tail were a delicate azure, and its long talons a darker shade of blue – although they were now stained with dried, crusted blood. It screamed aloud and began to tear at the earth as it spotted the three men making good their escape.

The dazed and wounded male wandered across its path and the female struck out blindly, its curved talons disembowelling it, the second blow crushing its skull with terrifying ease.

Arrows began to hiss through the air as those in the approaching currach opened fire on the creature. One struck the Kapall a glancing blow across the hindquarters, enraging it even further. It reared up on its hind legs and pawed the air, and from the distance it took on a vaguely human appearance.

The currach reached the three men in the water and eager hands hauled them aboard. The bard clambered into the craft of his own accord, his metal hook ringing hollowly on the stretched hide. He shook water from his dark hair and snatched a spear from one of the crew.

The Kapall screamed again, and one of the men fell forward in the currach, his ears and nose pumping blood.

Bracing himself, the bard drew back his arm and threw the heavy hunting spear.

Germane shook his head slightly. 'You'll never hit it . . .'

The spear took the creature directly through the mouth.

'. . . at this distance.'

CHAPTER NINE

Over the next few hours the weather deteriorated. Heavy clouds rolled in from the north, bringing rain and ice with them, and a chill wind whipped up the waves into angry white horses. The *Avenger* wallowed in the cross-currents, the sail hanging slack and useless one moment, and filled and billowing the next. The oars couldn't be used.

The storm had risen once they had passed beyond the waters of the Kapalls' Island, blowing up with such swiftness and ferocity that it could only have been sorcerous. With the onset of the storm the night had closed in rapidly.

Paedur stood by the figurehead with Maildun. Both men were wrapped in their cloaks, and from the distance they might almost have been taken as part of the ship. Paedur scraped his hook off the wooden rail, rubbing away the thin patina of ice that coated it. 'I think it is time you told the crew,' he said abruptly.

Maildun nodded, the movement lost in the darkness. 'I know. I've heard the talk . . .'

'They know that we've passed into another realm, but they're under the impression that you know where we're going, and what we're looking for. Their trust in you will also lead them to blame you for anything that should go wrong. I think you should tell them that you know as little about this voyage as they do.' The bard paused and then added softly. 'And you'll have to tell them soon, otherwise you'll have a mutiny on your hands.'

'In the morning perhaps.'

'That might just be too late; we'll sight land before dawn.'

'You're sure?'

Paedur laughed softly. 'Why do so few people trust me? Yes, I'm sure.'

'Another island?'

'Of course,' Paedur agreed. 'But this time you must not land any men on shore.'

'We need water,' Maildun reminded him. 'Gussan left the waterskin back on the last island.' He paused, and then added.

74

'He disobeyed my orders and went in search of you and Germane.'

'Gussan almost left his life and soul behind on that island,' Paedur said softly.

'Aye,' Maildun said wearily. He turned and faced the bard, his face a dim oval against the darker cloth of his cloak. 'I'm sorry. I . . . I just wonder if this was all worth it. I'm losing my crew at every step of the journey. We've been tossed beyond our own world into this cursed Shadowland, and there seems little chance of returning to our own world and even less chance of finding my father's murderers . . .'

'You are a follower of the Christ God,' Paedur said gently, a statement more than a question.

Maildun nodded. 'Aye, my foster-mother had me baptised into the New Religion, apparently in deference to my mother's calling. My foster-mother, the queen, still followed the Old Faith. Many of the nobles do, but pay lip service to the New Religion. Why?' he asked, finding the sudden change in conversation disturbing.

'I thought that the followers of your god believed that at the moments of deepest despair you were closest to your god, and then he would come the more easily to your prayers.'

Maildun laughed uneasily, and then crossed himself self-consciously. 'I doubt if He watches over this world.'

'If you believe, then he is there. Faith lends substance,' he added reverently, almost as if he were repeating an incantation or prayer.

'And you, Paedur, what gods do you follow?' Maildun asked.

'Yours, but by a different name,' the bard said, turning away.

The lookout spotted the island just before sunrise. The weather seemed to be clearing, and the wind and rain had lessened, but a heavy sea-mist still clung to the land, wreathing it in thick gauze, rolling across the waves like tumbling weed.

Germane brought the *Avenger* in as close to the shore as possible and dropped anchor. The mist here was almost impenetrable, soaking up all sound, so that even the crash of the waves on the beach was strangely muted. Even though the wind was onshore, the mist carried within it the heavy, dank odour of rotting vegetation, and a faintly carrion smell of something long dead.

Maildun drew Paedur to one side and spoke to him urgently. 'I've just checked the supplies with Pol, the cook. We cannot afford to bypass this island; we need water badly. I have to send someone ashore.'

Paedur caught his wrist and squeezed it with surprising strength. 'You cannot,' he hissed. He nodded into the east. 'It's almost sunrise – it's much too late; we'll have to sail around the island and wait until nightfall.'

'Impossible,' Maildun said firmly. 'I want to be well away from these cursed isles by nightfall. I would prefer to drift in the open sea at night.'

The bard shrugged and released his hold. 'I have warned you,' he said, 'on your head be it.'

The small currach had almost reached the beach when they heard a low rumble in the east. And, although the noise resembled thunder, it was not the sound of another storm brewing. The currach was barely visible throught the mist, and it bobbed in the shallows, connected by a long rope to the *Avenger*. The rumble came again, closer this time. The two frightened crewmen in the small boat began to haul themselves back to the ship, when the captain appeared at the rail and waved them on.

Diurnan joined the bard by the starboard rail. Paedur was staring into the rising sun, shading his eyes, which reflected the red and orange glow, with his hand. 'They're coming,' he said in a whisper.

The northerner squinted into the east, but the mist that clung to the waves obscured his view and he could only see the hazy outline of the crimson ball of the rising sun.

'I can see nothing,' he confessed.

The bard smiled bleakly. 'Count yourself lucky then.' He glanced back across the sea. 'But they're coming.' He pointed with his hook, which glistened with tiny droplets of moisture, which brought the runes engraved on the metal to quivering life.

'But there's nothing there,' Diurnan insisted.

Paedur described an arcane sign in the damp air with the point of his hook. The northerner's vision blurred and his eyes stung and watered. He shook his head and wiped the moisture from his eyes – and, when he looked across the waves again, he saw them . . .

Huge shadows raced across the sea: giant men riding even larger mounts. The horses' hooves struck the crest of each wave, dashing it to white froth. Their riders were neither men nor gods, nor were they demons, but something of all three. The water boiled as they approached the island and the giants' voices boomed across the morning skies. Each rider seemed to be urging on his mount to even greater speed, racing against the others. One of the great horned creatures stumbled and fell against one of the jagged rocks in the mouth of the bay. Diurnan saw its rider impaled on the rock writhing in agony, whilst its life-blood stained the water green, but the remainder of the crew of the *Avenger* only saw a huge wave erupt in savage, frothing fury against the rock.

The giants raced up the beach onto the island and disappeared into the interior. A hoof struck the small currach amidships, shattering its stout hide, killing both crewmen outright, and Maildun and his crew could only watch, horrified, as the boat was shattered seemingly against a submerged rock.

Paedur grabbed Maildun by the shoulder and spun him round. 'We must be gone, now,' he insisted.

The captain shrugged off the bard's grip. 'We need water!'

Diurnan joined them. His face was drawn and his hands were shaking. 'Let us leave now,' he said tightly.

'You too?' Maildun snapped. 'This is my ship – and I will command it as I see fit. That' – he gestured at the shattered remains of the small currach, which was now being cast up onto the beach – 'was an unfortunate accident. We need water – we must have fresh water, for I will not risk madness by having my crew drink salt sea-water. And you,' he jabbed Diurnan in the centre of his broad chest, 'and Germane will go ashore and fill the casks . . .'

'That is madness,' Paedur snapped. 'Beyond the horizon, barely a day's journey, is an isle that is suited to your every need, and yet you are going to risk two of your most valuable men . . .'

Maildun's eyes narrowed and his voice took on a dangerous edge. 'I have listened to your advice, bard, but I will not take orders from you. Take care now, lest you push me too far.'

Paedur backed off, his right hand coming across his chest and touching the Bardic Sigil high on his left shoulder, and he bowed. 'Of course. It is not my place to interfere with the destiny of any man; you are free to do as you wish.'

Diurnan looked across at the bard in surprise; it seemed to him as if Paedur had backed down from a confrontation. Even Maildun seemed somewhat surprised, perhaps expecting more resistance.

Maildun turned back to the first mate. 'Get Germane then, and arm yourselves.'

The bard stood back as Diurnan brushed past him. He could

sense the northerner's confusion; he had expected Paedur to fight the captain, and Diurnan knew that the bard had enough influence – and, if it came to it, the actual power – to change Maildun's mind. But instead he had backed off and left the captain to do his will – even though it meant sending more men to almost certain death.

Paedur watched impassively as the currach was lowered into the water and shoved away from the *Avenger*. It wallowed briefly, before Diurnan took up the oars and struck out strongly for the shore, while Germane knelt in the small, round craft with a nocked bow. The mist closed in around them as they neared the beach, cutting them off from the ship. Paedur waited until his sensitive hearing caught the crunch of gravel and then he raised his left arm, the curved hook glittering in the damp morning air, and etched a blessing after them. He glanced over to his left and found Maildun looking at him, a strange expression on his face, but whether it was fear or loathing, even the bard, with all his strange powers, could not guess. His lips curled in a smile, and his eyes mirrored the grey of the morning. 'Let us pray that we have not sent them to their deaths,' he said, pulling up the deep cowl of his cloak.

Maildun shook his head and turned away.

When the first stones rattled off the underside of the small craft, Diurnan leaped into the chill water and hauled the boat up the rocky beach.

The *Avenger* had disappeared behind the shifting, writhing banks of mist and only the vaguest suggestion of the main mast and the snarling figurehead could be distinguished. The rocky beach soon levelled out into a broad, flat green that stretched off into the misty distance. Diurnan and Germane walked slowly up it, looking for any signs of life, and especially any signs of a freshwater spring. Germane stopped suddenly and pointed down by his feet. 'What do you make of that?' he asked in a whisper, his voice as tense as a bowstring.

The northerner looked down. Cut into the green sward by their feet were the curved, regular imprints of horses' hooves, but they were easily ten times the size of any hoof mark either man had ever seen before.

Diurnan looked uneasily over his shoulder. 'I know what they are, I even know what made them; I've seen them. The bard briefly enabled me to see through the fog . . .'

'See what?'

'Demons; demons on demon mounts – great horned and tusked beasts with manes of glittering silver and eyes of fire.' His voice shook and he swallowed hard before continuing. 'The riders were Loki's creatures: horned like their mounts, their flesh like a lizard's, scaled and shining, and their hair like fire . . .'

'Did they sink the first boat?' Germane whispered.

The northerner silently handed the navigator a piece of stiffened leather that he had picked up on the beach. It was part of the currach's hull, and it was neatly shorn through in a half-circle.

Germane gazed out at the shifting fog banks that writhed over the smooth sea. 'I wonder if they can see us?' He traced the probable path of the demon horsemen across the waves, their path intercepting that of the currach, up the beach and on past him into the mist. 'You know,' he answered his own question, 'I don't think so. Surely they would have destroyed the *Avenger* if they had seen it?'

Diurnan nodded. 'I don't think they even saw the currach. And remember, the bard had to grant me the sight to see them; surely that might also work in reverse, and they might not be able to see us naturally?'

'Also, they would not be expecting anyone in these waters,' Germane added.

They continued moving cautiously inland. On the soft, green earth there was evidence aplenty of the demon steeds' passing, and even small trees had been uprooted and bushes trampled, stones lay shattered to powder on the ground or pressed deep into the turf. The tracks led on into the interior of the island in an almost straight line. And once they were away from the sea, the mist thinned and disappeared in patches, increasing visibility, but also increasing their own chances of being seen. They crested a slight rise and saw what they first thought to be another bank of mist, but, as they watched, they saw it was a rising cloud of shifting dust, in which shadows spun and twisted in the midst of the disturbance.

Germane and Diurnan crept nearer. The ground now trembled beneath their feet and the very air seemed to vibrate with the noise of the demon horsemen. They heard snatches of conversation and sudden cries drifted across the plain, and the language was a slightly hissing, sibilant version of Old Irish.

'. . . on the roan . . .'

'. . . no, the black, observe the black . . .'

'I will wager the . . .'

'Doubled.'

'Done.'

'By the Blood of Christ, what are they wagering on?' Germane exclaimed.

The northerner shook his head. 'I don't know, and I don't think I want to know, nor do I think it is wise to call upon any god by name in the midst of demons. Let's go.' He crept backwards from the concealment of the bushes and then swore briefly as his knee hit something hard and unyielding. It was embedded in the sward and his knee had struck one of the uprights. The northerner gripped the curved piece of metal and pulled, and it came loose with a liquid sucking.

Germane looked over his shoulder. 'What is it?'

Diurnan held it up to the morning light. It was a large piece of curved metal, with a series of regular holes set at intervals in the sides. He shook his head.

The navigator also shook his head, and then comprehension dawned in his dark eyes. He laughed shakily. 'Don't you see? It's a horseshoe!'

Diurnan looked at the semi-circle of metal that could encircle a man's thigh, and then slung it over his shoulder. 'For luck,' he said. 'Come on, I don't want to meet its owner.'

'They were demons on demon mounts,' Germane said, sipping scalding mead in the captain's cabin later that same evening.

Diurnan smiled in the wavering light, his teeth startling white against the dusk and his weatherbeaten face. 'And they seemed to be wagering on the outcome,' he added.

'What were they wagering?' Maildun wondered. He looked over at the shadowy figure of the bard standing by the door. 'Have you any idea?'

Paedur shrugged and adjusted his cloak with the point of his hook, the metal running liquid amber in the light of the oil lantern. 'It would seem likely that they were wagering the worship of their followers,' he said quietly.

Maildun shook his head. 'I don't understand.'

The bard leaned back against the heavy wooden door frame, and his voice deepened and took on the same resonant tone they had heard before: the voice of a trained bard. 'Both the gods and demons in all the planes of existence – the Shadowlands – need the worship of their followers to survive. The more people who worship them, the stronger they become. Why is it that the powers of Light and Dark are constantly vying for the attention of man? Because they need the worship of man. Faith lends substance, and without faith – belief – there can be no substance, no existence, for the deities and demons.

'Where do you think all the old gods go to? Where are the gods of your great-grandfathers, the shapeless, formless creations that were born out of man's first gropings into the unknown? Where have they gone? And remember, the gods never truly die.

'But as man loses faith, so too does the god lose his powers and strength, until he eventually becomes as a mortal man – but still retains his immortality. All the gods that have ever been exist still. Oh, there are some now that are but shadows haunting fanes and temples, but others are still powerful entities. To survive they need worship. That was the coin of your demons.' The bards voice quivered and the fire died from his eyes as he blinked.

'And what will happen to those gods when the Day of Judgement comes?' Maildun asked, a little thickly, for he had been drinking heavily from the small earthen bottle by his side.

'On the day when this creation draws to a close, all the gods that have ever been will come again – and then man will pay dearly for the gods he has worshipped . . .' The bard's voice trailed off and his eyes burned redly in the light.

'Ragnarok,' Diurnan said uneasily, his hand shaping the Sign of Horns automatically. 'The Coming of Fenris and the Serpent.'

Paedur nodded. 'The gods will exact their own retribution on their followers.'

'But not Our Lord Jesus Christ,' Maildun objected, his eyes darting. 'He is not like that; He preached peace, innocence and love.'

The bard nodded. 'I know. I knew him briefly before his end. But even he had begun to grow disillusioned with mankind about that time, and the world of man had tainted some of his power.' The bard sighed with regret. 'But even so, his presence and strength were incredible; he could have ruled this world had he so wished.'

The captain rose suddenly, his knife sliding free from its sheath in the top of his boot with a dry rasp. His face glowed ruddy in the light and was set in hard lines, and his eyes, though bloodshot, were cold and unyielding. 'You mock us, bard,' he spat, his words sounding thick and slurred. 'You mock us and defile the memory of the Christ. You claim to have met the Lord Jesus, and yet He died on this world hundreds of years ago. You are a liar, bard, and a bad liar at that.' He staggered slightly, and the point of his dagger snapped up and flickered in front of Paedur's face. The bard didn't flinch and his reflective eyes continued to regard the captain with something akin to amusement.

'You are drunk, Maildun,' he said softly.

The captain took an unsteady step closer. 'I've a good mind to cut your lying tongue from your head . . .'

Diurnan came to his feet in one fluid movement. His right hand shot out and enclosed the captain's wrist in a vice-like grip. Maildun grunted in pain, and turned his rage upon the northerner. 'You too? Is this mutiny? Are you going to side with this . . . this . . . lying heretic . . . ?' He spat at Paedur's feet.

Diurnan exerted a little more pressure and the knife fell from the captain's hand and embedded itself point first in the floor. The northerner shook Maildun as if he were a child and then backhanded him across the face, sending him sprawling against the bunk. 'Control yourself,' he snapped. 'Have you taken leave of your senses?'

Maildun levered himself up against the curved cabin wall and pushed himself to his feet. His eyes were bright and feverish, and his breath came in great laboured gasps. His tongue darted out and licked away the blood that oozed from his split lip. His right hand came out with a second dagger from a sheath on the back of his belt. He held the blade before him, the point tilted slightly upwards, allowing it to catch the light and reflect into the northerner's troubled eyes. And then he suddenly flipped the knife, caught it by the blade and threw it in one smooth action.

The bronze blade glinted blood-red in the light, as it flew across the short length of the cabin towards Diurnan. The northerner stumbled backwards, but knowing that he could not possibly hope to evade the blade at such close quarters. And then the bard's left arm shot out, and his hook struck the knife in midair with a ringing, musical tone, and sent it thudding into the deck beside its companion.

The captain growled like an animal and launched himself at the bard, but Germane, still seated on the long bunk, shot out his foot and hooked the captain's feet from under him, sending him crashing to the deck. Diurnan dropped on him, and pinioned his arms. Maildun fought and writhed and screamed like a wild creature – or a man possessed.

Paedur stopped and touched the point of his hook against the captain's head. Maildun shuddered and went limp.

Diurnan looked over at the bard. 'What's wrong with him?

He's not the sort of man who succumbs easily to drink.' He moved off the prone body and straightened his arms. 'It's unnatural.'

Paedur knelt and carefully examined the unconscious man. Maildun's breathing was shallow and rapid and his pulse was racing. He then pushed back one eyelid and examined his eyes, and even Germane, sitting on the bunk behind Paedur, could see that the pupil was shrunken to a pinpoint.

The bard rose from the body and examined the glass from which Maildun had been drinking. It was a simple goblet of rough glass, inset with irregularly hewn chunks of semi-precious stones, a gift to his foster-father from one of the dark-skinned southern traders. In the bottom of the glass the dregs of liquor still swirled. Paedur rolled the contents around and breathed in the aroma, and he tilted his head back and tasted the liquid with the tip of his tongue. He grimaced and spat.

'There's something in it?' Diurnan asked.

'A poison?' Germane said, reaching for the bottle on the deck beside the bunk.

'Of sorts.' The bard dipped his fingers into the liquid and rubbed it between them. He set the glass down carefully. 'Someone has introduced the crushed flowers of the violet-horned poppy into this.' He took the heavy stone bottle from Germane's hands and breathed its aroma. 'Aaah, a trace lingers.'

'I've heard of the flower,' Germane said, 'it grows freely in my country. But what does it have to do with Maildun's behaviour?'

'The crushed flowers of this plant, once they have been boiled into a syrup and added to a drink, produce strange dreams. It can make men think themselves gods; they believe they have the power to fly, to rule the world, to do anything they wish. On the other hand . . .' Paedur nodded down at the captain. 'It can turn harmless men into crazed killers.'

'But why did he attack you?' Diurnan asked, stooping down to lever Maildun's knives from the deck.

'Because I touched on a subject very close to him.'

'His faith,' Germane breathed.

Paedur nodded.

'And yet,' Germane went on, 'he is usually the most tolerant of men. As long as a man keeps his beliefs to himself and does not try to force them on others, Maildun does not interfere.'

'I doubt if he has ever had his senses interfered with by poppy juice before,' the bard said wryly.

Diurnan stood up, towering over the bard. 'Aye, and that begs the question: who poisoned his ale?'

Paedur nodded. 'A bad business. The dose is potentially lethal; it could have burned out his mind as easily as a flame chars a moth.' He ran his fingers through his thick black hair. 'It's certainly one of the crew and someone reasonably close to him.' He looked over at Germane. 'Do you know of any of them addicted to the weed, or indeed to strong drink?'

Germane shook his head slowly. 'Not to my knowledge. They're all fond of their drink – find me a sailor who isn't. But I've never caught any of them using any weed, or chewing those toadstools that are supposed to bring visions.'

'Do any of the crew behave strangely off duty, are they overly aggressive or withdrawn?' the bard persisted.

Germane frowned and shook his head. He looked at Diurnan who shrugged his massive shoulders.

'Have you ever caught any of them sleeping on duty? Do you know if anyone aboard has stained lips or fingertips, or discoloured eyes. Did you ever see one whose eyes had grown huge or tiny . . .'

'Wait.' The northerner raised his hand. He frowned, trying to capture something which had flashed across his mind. 'Wait. One of the crew has discoloured eyes; the whites are tinged with yellow.'

'Who?' Paedur demanded.

Germane looked up suddenly. 'Aedan,' he said in understanding. 'And a close friend of the captain's; they have been so for many years.'

'He is the one I fought yesterday?'

Diurnan nodded. 'Aye, the same.'

'Yellowed eyes are not in themselves conclusive evidence,' the bard said. 'However, he might bear watching.' He lifted the bottle again. 'Perhaps he intended the drink for me,' he suggested.

'It is unlikely,' Diurnan said. 'Most of the crew are aware of your . . . unwillingness to eat or drink with us . . .'

The bard smiled. 'A matter of religion and custom,' he remarked quietly.

'Aye,' Diurnan said, sounding unconvinced, 'however, I don't think Aedan would be that subtle: a knife in the dark would be more his way. Moreover, this bottle is from Maildun's personal supply.'

'It was intended for the captain then,' Germane said coldly.

'Perhaps we should talk to this Aedan?' A slim stiletto blade suddenly appeared in his hand.

Paedur shook his head. 'Not yet. We have no evidence. It might also be instructive to discover why he wishes to harm the captain.'

'Perhaps he hoped he would attack you,' Germane suggested.

Paedur smiled grimly. 'Perhaps.'

Maildun suddenly groaned and his eyes flickered open. He attempted to push himself to his feet, shaking his head from side to side. The bard stooped and hauled him up with surprising ease. He half-carried him to the small cot and pushed him down onto it. 'Lie still,' he commanded.

Maildun mumbled something and then his eyes rolled in his head and he lapsed back into unconsciousness. His facial muscles began to twitch, and beads of sweat appeared at his hairline and ran down into his beard.

Paedur placed his hand on the captain's brow and whispered an incantation in the Old Tongue of the De Danann. Maildun sighed deeply and then lay still, his chest rising and falling in easy sleep.

The bard stood and then ushered Germane and Diurnan outside. After the closeness of the tiny cabin, the air was fresh and chill, heavy with damp and salt, and touched with the odour of vegetation. The *Avenger* rocked on a gentle swell, the only sounds the lapping of the waves against the leather sides of the craft and the rattling of the rigging. Germane and Diurnan followed the bard to the starboard rail. There was no visible movement on the deck, save for the lone figure of the tillerman standing tall in the stern of the craft, shapeless in a thick, heavy cloak.

'Maildun will awake in a few hours,' Paedur said in a whisper. 'He should be alert and refreshed, but his memory of this night will be confused. We should,' he added, 'have sighted land by then.'

'What will we do about Aedan?' Germane asked softly.

'We will do nothing for the moment – let Maildun decide on a course of action; the threat was directed against him, and it is his ship.'

Diurnan nodded, agreeing with the bard. It went contrary to his way of thinking – he would have tossed Aedan overboard without a second thought – but he respected the bard's judgement. He leaned against the ship's rail and stared into the east, breathing in the air, testing the wind. 'A fine day, I'll wager,' he said.

The bard nodded agreement. 'Aye, a fine day, and one you will not easily forget, even in this world!'

CHAPTER TEN

The first light of dawn revealed a new island which was very different from any other they had so far encountered. At first they thought it must lie at some distance, but as the *Avenger* slipped through the gentle swells towards the isle, and it grew only slightly larger, they realised that it was tiny, certainly no bigger than an outcropping of stone in the water. But what made it all the more remarkable was the small, ornate fort of gleaming white stone that almost entirely covered it.

The building was a miniature version of some great palace. It was built from small blocks of polished white stone, cunningly fitted together in the manner of the ancients. Several bricks had been removed from the walls some time after it had been built, and ornate, gilded frames inserted, which were then glazed with thick, polished horn.

The main and, as far they could see, the only door, was missing and at high tide the sea must wash into the hallway. A single tall tower rose in the centre of the courtyard that lay beyond the missing gate.

Germane and Diurnan stood by the figurehead watching the first rays of the morning sun strike fire from the tiny crystals set in the white stone, so that the whole wall scintillated and sparkled like a huge jewel, and rippled with the changing colours of dawn and sunrise.

A shadow fell across the mismatched pair as the bard joined them. His strangely reflective eyes sparkled with tiny spots of light against the deeper blue of the sea and sky.

Germane nodded towards the isle. 'Land, as you promised. It seems inhabited.'

The bard shaded his eyes with his hand and then pointed across the waves with his hook. 'It is. That is the Palace of Solitude,' he said, his voice low and wistful. 'It has a counterpart in every Shadowland; places of peace and untroubled beauty set apart.'

'There is none in our world,' Germane said.

'Indeed there is,' Paedur said quickly, 'more than one in fact.

The great stone henges in both Alba and Gaul were once sanctuaries of peace, and the Hill of Tara in Banba, now Erin, once held a similar henge.'

'I have visited the standing circle in the land of the Britons,' Diurnan said, 'but it was nothing like that,' He pointed towards the shining palace on the island.

'You did but look at the outward appearance. You should have looked deeper, felt the atmosphere that such places have.'

'But it is a holy place, sacred to the druids – it reeks of their sanctity, and now the followers of the Christ have built a chapel for their own use on the Tor.'

'It was a sacred place before the white-robed ones used it.' The bard's eyes glazed as he stared at the shining stones of the palace. 'The circles and lines of stone are the last remnants of the First Race that walked this world before the advent of man. When they knew that their time was drawing to a close, they set aside certain places and fashioned them into doorways between the worlds; places where the fabric between the Shadowlands was stretched to the limit. They departed through these doorways to the Shadowlands – but the doorways remain.' The risen sun struck fire from the gilded roof of the single tower, and the bard's eyes blazed with the light.

'But man, in his ignorance, built his palaces and holy places about these doorways.'

'Why?' Germane asked.

Paedur's attention snapped back to the navigator. He shrugged. 'Oh, they are places of great peace and calm; since they are neither in this world nor in the next, and they absorb little of either. And perhaps man, with some distant memory, remembers that the gods once walked through these gateways, promising to return.'

Diurnan leaned across and touched the bard's arm. 'Maildun.'

Paedur glanced over his shoulder in time to see the captain emerge from his cabin. He looked pale and his eyes were sunken and red-rimmed. He paused by the doorway, his chest heaving as he breathed in great gasps of the fresh morning air, and then he slowly walked across the deck and joined the trio by the rail. He leaned across it and spat into the clear water, and then he ran his hands through his hair and raked his fingers through his beard. His voice, when he spoke, was cracked and raw, barely above a whisper. 'What happened last night?' he demanded.

'What do you remember?' Paedur asked softly.

Maildun glanced over at him. The sun was behind the bard

and the captain had to squint against the glare. 'I remember . . . little,' he said slowly. 'There might have been a fight, or it could have been a dream. What little I do remember was mostly a dream,' he added hesitantly.

'There was a fight,' Paedur said. 'You tried to kill me.'

Maildun closed his eyes briefly and shook his head. 'It was not a dream then,' he said, almost to himself.

'You were poisoned,' Germane said quickly, 'a drug introduced into your drink.'

Maildun looked up, his expression hardening, his mouth drawing into a thin, cruel line. 'Poisoned?' He looked from the navigator to the bard.

Paedur nodded. 'It is as Germane said; a drug, almost guaranteed to rouse you to anger, was added to your drink.'

'Who?' Maildun whispered.

'*Reefs!*' There was a pause and then the lookout called out again, 'Reefs off the starboard bow.'

Germane and Diurnan moved quickly up the starboard rail of the *Avenger*, towards the bow. They could see the water foaming white over the covered stones, stones which could rip the underside from the craft in an instant, leaving them helpless and stranded in these dangerous, enchanted waters.

Germane leaned out over the rail, his sharp eyes vainly looking for any gap in the frothing disturbance that seemed to encircle the isle. He shouted over his shoulder at Diurnan, 'Ask the lookout if he can see a break in the rocks – I can't.'

The northerner repeated the question. There was a pause and then the lookout cried out that rocks swept around the isle as far as he could see in both directions.

'Change course then,' Germane snapped. 'Oars and sail. We'll try to go around.' He spat into the water and swore at the shining white fort on the nearing isle. 'I should have guessed that such a sweetmeat would be but bait,' he raged in his own tongue.

Diurnan laughed grimly, not understanding the words, but reading the meaning clearly. Death held no fear for him; he had grown up with it, played in its shadow, fought by its side and nearly embraced it more than once. And now his only regret was that there would be no skald to make a lay of this voyage and his death.

The wind caught the huge leather sail, cracking it open with a snap, and the craft heeled in the water, wallowing unsteadily as it fought the wind and current. But then the oars dipped once in unison, and then again, pulling it strongly away from the approaching island.

Maildun stood by the ship's rail and watched the island beginning to recede. He turned to the bard, who was standing a little apart from him. 'Is there any way we could land?'

'There is; but there is no reason to land.'

'It looks peaceful enough . . .' Maildun mused.

'Aye; so do most traps.'

'It is a trap then?'

The bard shook his head. 'Not really. If there is a trap, it is only of the most subtle kind – and it lies within whomever lands on the isle.' He pointed with his hook. 'It is the Palace of Solitude, a place of perfect peace and tranquillity. If you were to land there, you might not want to return.'

Maildun grimaced. 'Then it is a trap!'

'Only if you make it so,' Paedur agreed.

As the morning wore on towards noon, the heat became unbearable. The sky was washed of all colour, leaving a shining, copper-metal bowl overhead, and the water reflected back the brilliance with an almost painful intensity. The breeze that had come up with the dawn had died in the early morning, and soon the *Avenger* and her crew floated on a sea that almost steamed with the heat, and even the pitch that caulked the boards began to bubble, and the stench only added to the mixture of odours that pervaded the craft: sweat, salt-tang and rotten fruit.

The crew moved about the decks performing their tasks woodenly, and with an almost sullen defiance, and even the bard, who usually seemed impervious to the extremes of temperature, doffed his heavy cloak, although he still retained his leather jerkin and breeks.

In the latter half of the morning Diurnan put the men to the oars, in an effort to break the lethargy that had claimed them, and he called the beat while Germane stood to the tiller and guided the longship arrow-straight into the west.

However, just as the sun passed the zenith, when the crew were beginning to mutter, and the oar strokes were becoming ragged, the lookout cried 'land', and the men set to again with a better will. Paedur mounted the platform beside Germane and began to chant an old Viking sea-shanty. Diurnan took up the response and soon the entire crew were bellowing the responses to the bard's shouted queries:

'What shall we do this spring day?'

> *'Go a-reiving, a-reiving, oh!'*
> 'Whither a-reiving?'
> *'South and east, to greener land!'*
> 'And what shall we take?'
> *'Booty and slaves!'*
> 'How shall we take it?'
> *'By fire and sword!'*
> 'And if we should fall?'
> *'Then we'll fall happily!'*

The new island was a mass of living green. Row upon row of neatly tended trees marched down to the smooth beach in long, straight lines. An errant gust of wind carried the almost palatable odour of fresh growth, greenery and . . . something else.

Germane handed the tiller over to Ruarc, who had shown a surprising interest, in the stars in particular, and in navigating in general. The slim southerner tilted his head to one side and breathed in the odour again; there was something haunting about it, something which reminded him of his youth in the vineyards of Italia.

'Familiar, eh?' Diurnan asked, leaving off the beat, and allowing the crew to rest on their oars. The current had taken the craft now and was slowly drawing it in towards the shore.

'I can't place it,' Germane said slowly. 'but there's something about it . . .'

Maildun turned round as they joined him near the prow below the figurehead. His eyes were bright and there was an excited flush on his cheeks. 'I think we're home,' he said quickly. '*Apples!* Those are apple trees; surely there are no apple trees in this cursed Shadowland?'

Germane suddenly placed the rich odour; it was similar to the smell of the vineyards in full bloom: the rich, heavy, almost intoxicating smell of fresh fruit.

'There are apples in this Shadowland, I'm afraid,' Paedur said quietly, coming up behind the trio. 'It is one of the few fruits common to all the Shadowlands. It is one of the fruits common to nearly all legends. Did not Eve tempt Adam with an apple in the Garden of Eden; did not Hercules labour to carry off the Golden Apples in the Garden of the Hesperides; and did the sons of Tureen of your own race not steal three of the apples from the same garden as part of their venge-payment to Lugh?' He shook his head briefly. 'We still have a long voyage ahead of us before we return to Erin's green shores.'

Maildun turned round and, leaning on the rail, stared over at the island. They were close enough to it now to hear the wind sighing through the laden branches and to see the irridescent flashes of colour as the fruit twisted slowly on the gnarled branches. The scent of fresh fruit was almost overpowering.

'Can we land?' the captain asked eventually.

The bard shook his head. 'I would advise against it,' he said. 'It's guardians and gardeners are not human. It is their eternal task to keep the trees fresh and in bloom, and to ensure that no pest or blight interferes with them.' He paused and smiled briefly. 'They might consider man a pest or a blight.'

'Is the fruit edible?' Diurnan asked, swallowing hard.

Paedur nodded.

The tall northerner shaded his eyes and stared across at the isle. 'We need fresh fruit,' he mused. 'Perhaps it would be possible to harvest some of the fruit without landing on the isle. What do you think?' he asked Germane. 'Can you bring the ship in close enough?'

The navigator considered and then shook his head. 'I've no idea of the currents in these waters, and I'm certainly not bringing the *Avenger* in that close to the shore. Take a currach.'

Diurnan smiled. 'I though you might say that.' He turned to Maildun. 'What do you think, captain?'

'What?' Maildun turned round, his eyes puzzled and vacant.

Diurnan glanced at the bard before answering. 'Can we take a currach and pluck some of those apples? We're low on fresh fruit.'

'Oh. Aye.' He waved his hand and turned back to the island.

Diurnan moved away with Germane and the bard. They stood by the mast and looked back towards the captain. He was still standing by the rail, leaning forward, his expression lost in concentration as he stared intently across towards the island.

'What's wrong with him?' Diurnan asked.

'Perhaps some of the drug still lingers,' Germane suggested.

The bard shook his head. 'Neither,' he said softly. 'He is merely enthralled by the beauty and mystery of the place. I have seen that happen before, but usually only to lonely, frightened men; only to the lost souls.'

'Is Maildun then a lost soul?' the northerner wondered.

The bard glanced at him. 'I think a man who sets sail upon a voyage of revenge, for something which happened before he was born, is indeed a lost soul.'

Diurnan looked back at the captain and nodded. 'I've seen

such men before,' he said. 'They usually have little respect for themselves – and even less for others. They are dangerous, deadly people.'

'So is Maildun,' the bard said.

The small, round currach rocked unsteadily as Diurnan stood up in the centre of the craft. 'Hold it steady now,' he commanded, as he hoisted up a spear and attempted to knock down some fruit. His first swing missed and he nearly toppled into the smooth water. As it was, all he succeeded in doing was to send a few leaves fluttering onto the surface. He was about to try again when he noticed a pale, almost translucent shape drift up from the sea-bed – which was barely a sword-length beneath the flat-bottomed craft – and engulf the leaves. Without a sound, and with hardly a ripple, they disappeared down into the water.

Diurnan knelt in the currach again and ordered the two crewmen to lift their broad-paddled oars. He then tore a corner off the edge of his undershirt and dropped it into the water. It floated for a few moments and then the pale, amorphous blob rose up again, engulfed the piece of cloth and pulled it down. Diurnan watched it settle down on the seabed in a shower of sand, and then, as he continued to search, he suddenly saw that the whole sea-bed was covered with a vast undulating mass of the creatures. Some of them were tinged with pink, others with green and blue, some were regular, while others had long strands and tendrils depending from them.

On an impulse, he dipped the blade of his spear into the water and moved it about. Almost immediately a score of the fleshy creatures detached from the sea-bed and rose up like huge gelatinous bubbles. One swallowed the blade of the spear – and then exploded in a frenzy of thrashing as the razor-sharp edge sliced through it. It sank down in a welter of pale pink fluids, and the other creatures followed it down, gradually enfolding it as it fell.

Diurnan stood unsteadily in the currach. He had recognised the creatures: they were common to nearly every water he had sailed upon, and were a species of inedible sea flower, or plant, or fish, no one quite knew what. He also knew that they could sting – sometimes fatally. He had no illusions about what would happen if he tumbled overboard. He swore at the bard; he might also have sworn that Loki's pawn knew about these creatures – he knew almost everything else about this voyage. And then he shrugged; he should have guessed it himself. An island like this

93

was too good a prize to be unguarded . . . and, thinking of guards, where were the guardians and gardeners that the bard had spoken of? He reached up with the spear and lopped off an apple-laden branch, and decided he didn't want to know.

The small currach moved slowly along the shore, with the *Avenger* pacing it a little distance away in deeper water. The small boat soon took on the appearance of a moving bush, as the amount of branches, leaves and twigs accumulated. Diurnan had forbidden the crewmen to throw them overboard, lest the creatures rise en masse and possibly even attempt to suck down the currach.

Diurnan had almost finished, when he heard a sound within the forest of apple trees. It began as a low, plaintive keening, such as the women of Erin made upon the death of a loved one or a warrior in battle. This sound was full of pain and torment, the cry of the dreaded *banshee*. He had heard a cry like it once before; on one of his early raids a companion, who was certainly not much older than himself, which would have been around fourteen summers then, had taken a blunt spear through the stomach. He had lain there for most of the battle crying and holding himself, watching his life flow away, not really feeling the pain, but only the sorrow, the loss of his life.

And this sound was very similar.

He caught a glimpse of movement through the trees from the corner of his eye, but when he looked full at it, it was gone. But for a brief moment he thought he had seen a woman. He shook his head; he had been too long asea. But . . .

Diurnan ordered the two men to bring the currach about and row towards the *Avenger*.

The apples were pronounced safe by the bard and one was distributed to each member of the crew, while the remainder were stored away. The rotten fruit and leaves were tossed overboard, and then the men lined the rails, watching the water turn to jelly as the creatures rose and cleansed the surface of everything. Some of the men sported with the creatures, attempting to hit them with their apple cores.

Only Diurnan and the bard refused the apples. Paedur because he didn't eat in public, and Diurnan . . . Diurnan didn't know why he refused the fruit. After all, he had risked life and limb to get them, but something prevented him from eating them.

He wandered down the ship looking for the bard. He found him sitting beneath the main mast, staring across at the island.

Diurnan sat down beside him. 'For a moment I thought you had gone like Maildun, when I found you staring so intently over there,' he began.

Paedur grinned. 'Such things no longer have any power over me,' he said softly. 'The captain was lured by the peace of that place, and once he had basked in its reflection for a while, he returned to his usual gruff, ill-humoured self.'

'Aye,' Diurnan agreed. 'Tell me,' he asked, coming directly to the point which was troubling him, 'are those apples safe to eat?'

Paedur looked sidelong at the northerner. 'They are; why do you ask?'

Diurnan shrugged. 'Just curious.'

The bard tapped him on the arm with his hook, sending a slight shiver up along the nerves. 'Now, that I don't believe. Tell me why you asked.' There was a definite tone of command in his voice.

The northerner squirmed uncomfortably. A man of action, he was unused and unable to formulate his thoughts and feelings into words easily. 'I just felt . . .' he began. 'I heard something,' he said at last.

The bard nodded encouragingly.

'I heard a keening, a cry of pain, of anguish, and once I thought I saw something – a young woman – in the trees.'

'And?'

'And nothing. I just wondered . . .' He rounded on the bard. 'Tell me,' he demanded, 'just who – what – are the guardians of that isle?'

Paedur stood suddenly, coming to his feet in one fluid movement. With the onset of dusk, he began to lose definition and become one with the night. 'Have you ever heard of dryads?' he asked.

CHAPTER ELEVEN

A thick fog closed in with evening, reducing visibility almost completely and dulling all sound, until even the eternal slapping of the waves against the side of the craft was muted and distant. A thin film of moisture covered everything, and the crew huddled beneath their leather cloaks and cursed the weather. Someone attempted a song, but the lone voice sounded so lost and forlorn, and the fog so robbed it of every nuance, that it was soon dropped and silence once again settled on the craft.

The *Avenger* drifted on the waves, lost on a grey sea on a grey world. Germane, who found he could not sleep, hunched over the figurehead, with a long spear in his hand, occasionally probing the mists ahead, terrified of rocks or reefs. He had once been on a merchantman coming through the Pillars of Hercules in a fog such as this. They had struck rocks three times that night, and each time he thought he was going to die, as the craft lurched and settled even lower in the chill water. There was something absolutely terrifying about sailing on a fog-shrouded sea, with neither sight nor sound for guides.

He heard a chink of metal behind him and he turned, expecting to find the bard, who never seemed to sleep, or at least Diurnan, who had no fear of fogs. But there was no-one there, and he was about to turn back when he saw an indistinct shape – vaguely manlike – moving not five paces away from him. Germane felt a cold knot of fear settle into the pit of his stomach. His own people told stories, which he had also heard on his travels, about the creatures of the deep: fish-like men with scales and talons, who sometimes crept from the waves in a thick fog and decimated ships, butchering the sailors and feeding their bodies to the waves. He had come upon such a craft off the coast of Tyre, drifting crewless and abandoned, with no signs of a struggle and with all the cargo intact.

Germane pressed himself back against the figurehead and strained to make out the shape. It was difficult in the shifting, twisting strands of fog, but he thought he saw the figure move to the side of the craft and then he heard a muted splash. He immediately came to the conclusion that a body had been dropped overboard. The shape moved past him and, almost without thinking, he struck at it with the spear he held in his hand. It was little more than a throwing Javelin, and he felt it slide along something hard and unyielding – scales! – and then sink into flesh. He found his voice then and shouted aloud, but the fog blanketed the sound and he realised that it sounded pitifully weak. The shape turned and flowed towards him. Metal winked. Germane realised he didn't have enough room to use the spear again and dropped it, pulling his long stiletto free just as the creature fell onto him. He felt something sear his shoulder and down along his arm, as he struck upwards with his knife, aiming it in towards the creature's breast. The knife sank home, and he heard a muffled whimper – but this was a man's cry!

The figure slumped against him, entangling his arms in the cloak which he was wearing, and Germane suddenly realised he was holding a dead man. Another shape moved out of the fog towards him, and he saw the long length of metal coming in towards his head before he heard the whistling of the blade. It bit deeply into the wood, barely a finger-span above his head, and he heard the man grunt as he tugged it free. Germane heaved the dead man from his arms and pushed him towards the second figure. He shouted again, and was aware that there seemed to be movement further down the deck. The sword came towards him again, trailing wisps of fog behind it like a sword of fire, and took a slice from the figurehead's scales.

A lantern bobbed amidships and a voice called out in query. The second figure paused and Germane took the opportunity to throw himself to the deck. He realised that the other man was having just as much difficulty seeing him. He saw the shape turn, the sword a dull length of greyness against the darker fog, and then he melted away into the night and was gone.

Germane was slowly coming to his feet when an ice-cold blade was placed against the cheekbone. 'Up now, and slowly. Let's have a look at you.'

Germane straightened up, and light the colour of sour milk shone on his face from an oil lamp. He grinned at Diurnan's surprise, and then he blinked as he felt the craft spin under his feet, and for the first time felt the burning sensation on his arm. He touched it with his hand and felt his fingers come away sticky. He staggered forward and Diurnan caught him as he fell. 'There's a body . . . somewhere . . . and another lives . . . something in the sea . . .'

The dead crewman was named Corran. He had been a close friend of Ruarc, but even he could not explain what he had been doing moving about the ship at that late hour, and why he had attacked the navigator.

The reason why became apparent later on the following morning when the rations were about to be divided. Pol, the cook, came to Maildun and told him quietly that most of the salted meat was gone, and the stored apples they had picked up the previous day had been cut up or ground into pulp. There was now barely enough food to keep the crew for two days. Maildun ordered him to say nothing, and to distribute the morning rations as usual, and then he went to find the bard.

Paedur stood aside and allowed Dirunan to tie up the bandage on Germane's arm. The wound wasn't serious; Corran had managed to dig his knife into the navigator's shoulder as he fell, and then the knife had been dragged down along the upper arm. The bard had washed the wound and treated it with a salve, but his single hand prevented him from tying an effective knot.

Maildun joined them. He waited until Diurnan helped Germane to his feet and then walked away. The three men followed him. The captain paused by the figurehead and examined the sword cuts. He rubbed his thumb against the tears in the wood and then, with thumb and forefinger, pulled some strands of Germane's dark brown hair from the wood.

The navigator absently felt the top of his head. He hadn't realised the first blow had been that close.

The fog had lifted somewhat with the onset of morning. The sun was high in the sky, but was only distinguishable as a harsh white spot against the grey-white clouds. Visibility was still down to about twenty paces in any one direction, but, every now and again, a stray gust of wind pushed through the fog, swirling and shaping it into patterns, and seemed to promise a clear noon.

Maildun turned around and, leaning back against the figurehead, folded his arms. He forced himself to smile and then said casually to the three men, 'Someone has destroyed most of our supplies. What you saw last night, Germane, was someone dumping our meat overboard.' He stretched and then ran his fingers through his red hair and beard, combing out the tangles. 'We are – I'm sure – being watched by Corran's companion or companions, so let them assume we are not discussing anything of importance.'

Germane nodded briefly, and then he too smiled broadly, as if the captain had just made a joke. Diurnan grinned, but it was a forced rictus.

'Do you not think it is time we discovered the identity of this person or persons?' the bard suggested gently.

'Aye,' the northerner nodded, 'and when we find out, we'll feed him – piece by piece – to the sharks.'

'I would also like to find out why,' Paedur continued.

Germane looked up. 'That has me puzzled also.' He turned to Maildun. 'All the crew are companions of your youth, are they not?'

Maildun nodded. 'Either mine or my brothers',' he said. 'The only stranger here is Paedur.' He turned to look at the bard.

'I think Paedur has proven that he is with us,' Diurnan said quietly.

Maildun nodded. 'I never meant otherwise. I am merely stating a fact. I have known, or my brothers have known, all these men since our youth. And they are all to be trusted.'

'Obviously not,' Paedur said softly. 'Are you sure none of them has any cause to hate you?'

'None that I know of.'

'Any boyhood enemies?' the bard persisted.

'None that I can remember, and certainly none on this voyage.'

'What about the youth who told you about your parentage?' the bard asked, his voice dropping to a whisper.

Maildun froze, the smile on his face hardening to a grimace. 'What do you know about that?' he asked harshly, his voice rising. Beads of perspiration appeared on his forehead, and his eyes took on a curious gleam.

The bard smiled, showing his even, white teeth. His reflective eyes were a dull grey this morning, the colour of muted fog, and his face had taken on something of a mask-like quality. 'You must remember that I am not a man, not as you would label such things. I know . . . what I know.' He smiled again, and this time with genuine sympathy. 'It would not be wise to probe too deeply into what I am. All you need to know is that my path lies with yours, and that I will do what I can to assist you. Now tell me, what of that youth?'

Maildun breathed deeply. There was a lump in his throat and another in the pit of his stomach. He was sure if he spoke he would be sick, physically sick. He could remember with absolute clarity that evening when he had been told that he was of no lineage, no family, no past; that he was an illegitimate nothing.

He rubbed his knuckles reflectively. He could still feel Demman's teeth splintering under his fist.

'Maildun?'

The bard's voice brought him back to the present. He breathed deeply again, and then he sighed. 'He is not on board, if that is what you are thinking; nor, to the best of my knowledge, are any of his companions. But you would have to ask Ruarc that; he was of his age and background.'

'What about Aedan?' Diurnan asked.

Maildun glanced at him sharply. 'What about Aedan?' he demanded.

Diurnan was taken aback by the captain's sudden intensity. He looked at Paedur and Germane for assistance.

'We think Aedan may be the one who drugged your ale,' Germane explained cautiously, wary of the captains' humour.

'How do you come to that conclusion?' Maildun asked coldly.

Germane looked at the bard, and Maildun followed his gaze.

'His eyes are yellowed and discoloured in the manner of a poppy user,' the bard said softly, watching the captain intently. Something about his manner aroused his interest and he determined to push on. 'What is it about this Aedan that interests you so?'

'I have no interest in Aedan,' Maildun said quickly.

The bard's colourless eyes became hooded. 'None?'

Maildun's arm shot out, his fingers curling for the bard's throat. Paedur caught his hand, the fingers of his right hand lacing through the captain's. He continued smiling as he squeezed. 'When you have but one hand,' he said, 'you must make it do the work of two, make it as strong as two.' He dropped Maildun's hand, and the captain held it out stiffly, working the fingers which were pale and numb. The bard's grip was inhumanly strong.

'I do not think you realise the seriousness of your situation,' Paedur said. 'You have one dead crewman, another' – he nodded to Germane's bandaged arm – 'wounded. Food has been destroyed, and your ale was drugged. That would suggest that someone on board this vessel does not like you. Now, at the moment there has been no direct attempt – discounting the drugging of the ale – on your life, but I think that it is only a matter of time.' Paedur's eyes seemed to grow in his head as he stared at Maildun. 'Now, what is your connection with Aedan?'

'There is nothing . . .' Maildun began.

'*Lovers!*' Diurnan said suddenly, in his blunt manner. 'Aye, look, he colours. They have been lovers.' He grinned at the captain. 'Oh, it's nothing to be ashamed of, lad; I've had one or two myself on the longer voyages when there was nothing else to do.'

The captain grimaced. 'It was a long time ago. We were still boys.' He turned round and stared out to sea. 'I think there is land ahead,' he said woodenly.

'There is,' the bard agreed, 'but let us settle this first. What disagreement did you have with Aedan, and was it serious enough to make him want to kill you?'

Maildun turned round again, with a curiously lost expression on his face. 'No . . .' He shook his head. 'I don't know.' He breathed deeply. 'We were friends, boyhood friends . . . and more,' he added. 'We fought when he discovered that I had no background, and that I was not related to the king in any way. When I resolved to set out on this voyage, I asked him to accompany me. He agreed, he seemed almost eager to do so. And then he discovered you were coming.' Maildun turned to Germane, who looked at him with astonishment.

'Me!'

'Aye. Aedan thinks that, because of your looks and features and your nationality, which accepts male lovers as easily as female, you and I were . . .' He shrugged again.

'He is now trying to destroy you,' Diurnan said. He looked at the bard. 'Should I kill him?'

'No!' Maildun stepped forward and his hand rested on the hilt of his dagger. 'No, I forbid it. This is still my ship – and I'll kill any man who flaunts my authority.'

Diurnan grinned with genuine good humour. 'And will you kill me Maildun? Do you think you could?'

'Enough of this,' Paedur snapped. 'We are facing a definite threat to our continued existence and this voyage, and your time would be better spent neutralising – if not removing – that threat.' He rounded on Maildun and jabbed a stiffened forefinger into his chest. 'You may talk to Aedan. Do it now before he manages to kill you, or, indeed, kill us all. If I do not find his answer to my satisfaction . . .'

'If you do not find his answer to your satisfaction!' Maildun roared. 'You! And just who do you think you are?' he demanded.

Paedur smiled coldly. 'I think you forget that I alone can guide you through this Shadowland back to Erin. Without me you are lost, doomed to sail the Island Sea for all eternity. I think you fool yourself if you honestly think you are the captain of this ship.' He looked past Maildun and turned to Germane. 'Bring us in towards the beach; we'll send a currach ashore for water.'

Germane hesitated, looking from Maildun to the bard and then back to Maildun. The bard glanced sidelong at him. 'Until your captain comes to his senses and realises that we cannot afford sentiment on this voyage, I am taking over. When he has reached a satisfactory conclusion with regard to Aedan, then he can regain control of his ship. Go about your duties, navigator.'

Germane looked at Diurnan. The northerner stroked his jaw, a smile playing at the corners of his mouth. He nodded to Germane. 'Do as he says; I've a mind to return to my homeland some day.' He turned back to the bard. 'I will support you as long as you keep your word. If you break it, then I will kill you.' He then turned to Maildun, whose complexion was now as red as his hair and beard. The veins in his temple and neck were clearly visible and his large hands clenched and opened convulsively. 'I am your friend, Maildun, but I was a sailor long before I knew you. I recognise the need for a strong captain and, while you blind yourself to the threat that Aedan presents, you cannot be such. Destroy this man, and I will follow you again.'

Maildun seemed about to speak, and he opened and closed his mouth several times. He suddenly brushed past them and strode down the deck towards one of the currachs that was stored near the stern. He paused once and beckoned one of the men to him, and together they set about making the small craft ready to go ashore.

The bard looked at Diurnan, his eyebrows raised in a question.

'Aedan,' Diurnan said quietly.

The island stank. The foul odour hung over it in an almost unbearable miasma, blending with the remaining tendrils of fog, coating everything with a liquid scum.

Maildun gagged as the currach neared the shore. The wind coming off the island carried the stench, blanketing the ever-present smell of the sea. He dipped the edge of his cloak into the water and held it across his mouth. Aedan rested on the oars and did the same, wiping the scum from his face.

Maildun stood in the small, sturdy craft and then staggered as it scraped the sands. He jumped into the shallows and helped Aedan pull the boat up along the sandy beach. He lifted a broad-bladed hunting spear from the bottom of the currach and waited until Aedan had slung the waterskins over his shoulder, and they set off up the beach.

They walked in silence for a while, the stench making conversation difficult, and then Aedan stumbled over the first skull. It was brittle and yellow with age, but enough of it remained to distinguish it as belonging to a horse. There was a perfectly round, fist-sized hole in the back of the skull, and most of the snout had been sheared off; there was no sign of the remainder of the skeleton.

Aedan looked round nervously, and then back at Maildun. 'Perhaps we should go back; whatever killed this might be still alive.'

Maildun shook his head curtly. 'We need water. We need food too, if we can find any; someone has been tampering with our supplies.' He watched Aedan carefully, but he showed no surprise – but perhaps that was, in itself, an indication of his guilt. Would an innocent man not have said something? The captain pointed up the beach towards a cleft in the low cliffs. 'We'll try through there.'

They passed more bones as they progressed higher up the beach. Generally the remains were shattered and seemed ancient. They saw a horse's spine which had been sheared in two, and the hindquarters of another which had an almost circular hole driven through it.

Maildun raised his hand and stopped. He heard Aedan drawing his knife, and then he realised that it was the only sound he had heard on the island, other than their own laboured breathing. No birds sang, no insects moved through the air, nothing stirred the undergrowth – there was total, absolute silence. He moved forward quietly, feeling the silence beginning to oppress him. Where was the animal life? What had killed the horses?

'Let's go back,' Aedan said tightly, 'we'll get water on the next island.' Maildun realised that his companion's teeth were chattering with fear.

'We go on,' he said quietly.

'No!' Aedan dropped the waterskins and stepped back, as Maildun turned round. His face was pale and tight with fear, and the knife in his hand was trembling.

Maildun leaned on his spear. He looked first at the waterskins and then at Aedan. 'Pick them up,' he said wearily.

'I'm not going any further. We don't know what's up there.' He nodded towards the cliffs.

'We need water,' Maildun said patiently, his voice low and soft. 'Come now, I'm a little tired of your humours and tempers.

103

Pick up those skins!' he suddenly shouted, lashing out with the spear, knocking Aedan's knife from his hand.

The dark-haired crewman yelped with fright and clutched his numbed fingers. He glared at the captain with unveiled hatred. 'How dare you,' he spat. 'You, who are nothing, without family, without honour, without lineage. How dare you raise a weapon to a nobleman's son.'

Maildun smiled sadly. 'Do you hate me so much Aedan?' he asked. 'Do you hate me enough to try and destroy me?' He struck out again suddenly, sweeping Aedan's feet from under him. He fell heavily and Maildun placed the point of his spear against his throat. 'Do you hate me enough to kill me?'

Aedan looked up at the tall, red-haired young man standing over him, and the look in Maildun's eyes frightened him. 'I despise you,' he said finally, 'you and your foreign catamite.'

'I thought you loved me' Maildun said softly.

Aedan opened his mouth to reply and then his eyes widened and he screamed – a high-pitched scream of absolute terror. Maildun threw himself forward, over Aedan's prone body, rolled to his feet and came up with his spear levelled.

The horse – if it could be called a horse – was long and low, close to the ground, and with an extra set of legs set midway on its stomach. Its head was roughly equine, but its snout was almost completely circular, and rimmed with wickedly barbed, triangular teeth, giving it a snake-like appearance. Its body was patched with a light covering of short dun hair, but its legs were bare and looked slightly scaled. It crouched before Aedan, its head oscillating slightly from side to side, its cat-like eyes regarding him unblinkingly.

Aedan attempted to scramble backwards, but the creature lurched towards him, its round snout striking hard into the sole of his boot. Aedan was speechless with fear, but his eyes were wide and pleading.

The captain stepped back deliberately, and then watched dispassionately as the creature lunged for Aedan again, this time striking for his leg. The terrified young man barely managed to twitch to one side, and the flattened head thumped into the ground. He kicked out at it and then scrambled to his feet and began to run. The creature struck again, lightning fast, taking him low in the leg, punching right through flesh and bone with its razor-sharp teeth.

Aedan screamed and then vomited with pain. 'Maildun, for the love of God . . .'

104

Maildun nodded once. 'For the love of God,' he said, and then drove his spear through Aedan's heart, impaling him on the ground. He turned and ran then, and soon the only sounds on the island were a sickening crunching and cracking as the creature fed.

Paedur, Diurnan and Germane were waiting for him when he reached the *Avenger*. They passed no comment on his haggard expression, nor on Aedan's absence, nor on the missing spear.

Maildun waited until the currach had been hauled aboard and then quietly told the silent, waiting crew. 'Aedan was slain by a horse-like creature on the island. He died bravely; pray for his soul.' He turned away and was about to brush past the bard, but then stopped. 'Whither now?' he asked, without looking at Paedur.

'Wherever you wish . . . captain,' the bard stressed the last word.

Maildun smiled grimly. He turned his head to look into the bard's eyes. 'Some day I will kill you,' he promised.

Paedur nodded. 'Would that that were possible,' he said feelingly.

The captain moved away, and walked down the length of the ship, shouting orders, sending the *Avenger* on, further into the Island Sea.

CHAPTER TWELVE

As the morning wore on, two islands slipped by in quick succession. With a stiff wind behind them, the *Avenger* skipped over the waves, making her difficult to control and dangerous to bring into shore, and, on Germane's advice, they bypassed them both.

The first island was walled round with a chest-high palisade of metal stakes that gleamed a ruddy copper in the sunlight. The island itself was tiny, no more than a rock, and, as they neared it, they became aware of a sibilant hissing emanating from it. Something moved on the ground behind the palisade, but they had almost passed the isle before the creature rose up on its hind legs.

It was man-shaped, but only vaguely so, having a squat, flattened head perched directly on its shoulders; two arms that reached to the level of its knees, and it stood on two stunted, bowed legs. It had a single eye set in the centre of its forehead, and long, curved talons on the end of its three fingers. It was completely hairless, and its skin, which resembled the underbelly of a fish, gleamed obscenely white. Its naked muscles rippled and flowed in an almost liquid fashion. It raised its long arms and screamed aloud when it saw the craft. Its cry was high-pitched, setting teeth on edge and sending shivers through the wooden spars. It screamed again and then stooped down to pick up flat chunks of razor-sharp flint, which it flung in the direction of the craft. Most fell short and splashed harmlessly into the sea, but a couple tore through the *Avenger's* sail and one ripped a chunk from the figurehead.

Maildun asked his young foster-brother to loose a sling shot at the creature, but the range was too great and the stone bounced off the metal palisade.

The Island of the Beast was still in sight when the second of the morning's islands rose up from the sea in a grey smudge. As they neared it they could see that it was covered by a low pall of smoke, out of which the tops of the trees rose indistinctly. The smoke seemed confined to ground level, and was shot through with bright arcs and streamers of flames, and yet the trees didn't seem to be on fire. Maildun had Germane bring the ship in as close to shore as possible, and as they sailed round the coast they saw that the smoke seemed to issue from vents in the soft, loamy soil, which also spat fire and flame at regular intervals. They could see pig-like creatures moving through the flames, bathing in them as mortal animals would in water.

Although the animals were unfamilar to the crew, the trees on the isle were similar to the apple trees of their homeland. They watched the pig-like creatures, their short-haired coats sparking and, in some cases, actually burning, striking the trees with their long hind paws, the blows serving to loosen the huge apples and drop them down into their midst.

Maildun would have sent some men ashore to gather some of the fruit, but the bard tossed a knotted length of rope onto the shore and they watched it burst into flame as soon as it struck the sands. Ruarc christened it the Island of Hell, and the *Avenger* sailed on.

The third island of the day appeared on the horizon as a sparkling point of light late in the afternoon, just as the sun was beginning to sink into the sea. The lookout cried 'land-ho' and Diurnan and Maildun joined the bard at the figurehead where he had remained since early morning.

The northerner shaded his blue eyes and squinted into the distance. 'What's reflecting the light?' he wondered aloud.

'Cliffs?' suggested Germane, joining them. 'I've watched the sunset turn the cliffs of southern Alba into blinding white walls.'

The bard shook his head briefly. 'Not cliffs,' he mumbled.

'What is it then?' Maildun demanded.

The bard looked over his shoulder at the captain, and then resumed staring towards the approaching isle. 'You must know, captain, that there are several Shadowlands which contain parts and portions – pockets, as it were – of the Island Sea. In some Shadowlands the islands themselves seem to move and change position; others serve to ensnare everything that comes within their range – including light, leaving them in perpetual night, and then there are still others which do the opposite . . .' He gestured towards the light. 'That isle could be one of those which is capable of reflecting back the light.' He shrugged. 'We must wait.'

The light changed as the sun sank down into the western ocean, shifting from a hard point of white to a softer, gentler, orange glow and thence to a pale, almost translucent cream. It blazed pink and gold briefly, and then the sun was gone and night fell. There was no slow twilight transition as in Erin and most of the northern islands of their own world – this was the swift suddenness of night that was usual in the warmer, southern latitudes.

With the onset of night, lights appeared on the isle – warm, gentle globes of brightness that seemed to strike a chord within most of the crew, filling them with an indescribable longing. Germane would have sailed in towards the island, but Diurnan cautioned him against it; he had a barbarian's instinctive distrust for something which seemed too welcoming.

Maildun's tiny cabin was in darkness, as the bard pushed open the door afer knocking and receiving no reply. He knew the captain was within and his strange senses told him that Maildun was awake. He stood in the open doorway and allowed his eyes to accustom themselves to the dark, and then his other, non-human senses took over, and he identified the captain easily enough, even in the total darkness. He was lying on his bunk with a bottle of ale held in the crook of one arm, and a naked sword in his hand.

'You can put the sword down, captain,' Paedur said softly, closing the door behind him.

He watched Maildun's expression change from anger to astonishment, to fear and then to loathing. The captain sat up, but he did not sheathe the sword. He looked in the direction of the bard's voice. 'You can see me, can't you? You are not truly human, are you, bard?'

'I have said that I am not,' Paedur agreed quietly.

'What are you then: god, demon, *sidhe*?'

'None of those. I am . . . I was a man, a mortal man, but circumstances changed that. Now I am more than mortal, but less than human.' There was a note of terrible loss in his voice, and Maildun shivered with the sound of it.

'You have powers?' he asked.

The bard laughed grimly. 'Aye, I have powers; powers which make me god-like on this world and your world. I can call up the elements and weld their forces to my will; I can command any man to do my bidding; I am faster, stronger, more powerful than most men. I can travel through the Shadowlands with ease.' He paused and then added bitterly. 'And the price I paid for all that was my humanity.'

Maildun shivered and he felt the hairs on his neck stand on end as his flesh crawled. He placed his sword on his bunk and drank deeply from the bottle. 'Do you eat or drink?' he asked.

'There is no need,' Paedur said regretfully.

'And you can see me now?' Maildun enquired in an awed whisper.

'I can see you clearly.'

'You sound as if you regret your powers.'

'Maildun,' Paedur said with a touch of pity in his voice, 'I am old, very old. I told you I knew your Christ. That was neither a lie nor an idle boast. I knew him. I watched him die on that grey, chill Sabbath eve.' His voice trailed away, and the only sound audible was the slapping of the waves against the side of the ship. 'I am immortal, Maildun. I do not regret my powers; they have enabled me to see much and experience even more. But I am tired now, and if you wish to know the truth, I long for death.'

Maildun stood up slowly. He picked up his sword and stretched it out before him in his right hand. The cabin was so small that it almost touched the bard's chest. He spread his legs and then wrapped his left hand around his right. 'Do you wish me to kill you, bard?' he asked quietly, formally.

Paedur laughed and shook his head. He touched the sword with his hook and the metal began to glow, illuminating the tiny cabin with a cold blue fire. Maildun gasped in surprise but held tightly to the sword. In the light the bard's colourless eyes blazed with a similar blue fire.

'You can take your sword and plunge it into my heart,' he said, 'but you will not – cannot – slay me.' The shadows under his face twisted and shifted, and gave his features an almost demonic cast. Maildun lowered the sword, immediately dousing the light. He heard the bard speak a word and the oil lamp flickered into life. Paedur remained standing by the door, smiling. 'I came here only to tell you that we are approaching the Isle of the Cat and Fort – or so it is called on the ancient charts.' He shrugged. 'But it seems I told you more than I intended.'

'Perhaps you should have told me so in the beginning,' Maildun suggested.

The bard nodded. 'Would you have believed me then, without having seen what you have seen, without having experienced what you have experienced?'

'I think not,' Maildun said doubtfully. 'Tell me about this isle,' he said.

'It is a place of refuge. It offers both solace and temptation.

109

Solace in the form of rest, food and wine; temptation in the form of jewels, gold, silver and marvellous weapons which are scattered about, unchained and unguarded. You may bring your crew ashore, captain, but you must ensure that they do not succumb to that temptation.'

Maildun nodded. 'I'll see to it.'

The bard nodded, and then turned to go.

'Wait!' Maildun called. 'Tell me one thing, if you will . . . ?'

'If I can.'

'What are you doing on this voyage?'

The bard paused before replying, and then he spoke slowly, picking his words with care. 'Like you, I am looking for something. But while you are looking for your father's murderers . . . I am seeking an end to my life.'

'You wish to die?'

Paedur nodded silently.

'And you hope to find your death here on the Island Sea?'

'Many ships have sailed the sea, or a portion of the sea, and come back with fragments from its history; yours will be the first voyage fully to explore the islands. Much of the magic of your world and mine still exists on these islands. The magical Tuatha De Danann came from them originally, as did the demon Formorians. When the De Danann retreated from the worlds of men, some came back to the Island Sea. They were the greatest magicians of their time: if any one remains, surely they would be able to help us . . . to help me?' It sounded almost like a plea, and Maildun could only nod and whisper, 'I hope so.'

The high white and silver walls of the fort changed quickly from drab grey to blinding light with the sunrise; it looked as if the stones were hollow and had been illuminated from within.

Maildun, Germane, Diurnan and Paedur stood by the prow and watched the changing colours of the Palace of Refuge. The fort was no taller than any chief's fort in Erin, but it had that indefinable stamp of age about it that told of its De Danann builders. The walls were constructed of white chalk blocks, each one perfectly square and symmetrical, and fitted together so closely that a knife blade would not fit between them. The roof had been sheathed with what looked like beaten silver, and the windows were arched and silled with the same material. A huge double gate was set facing out onto the low sandy beach, and both doors had been painted with white and silver.

Maildun, with Gussan, his foster-brother, Diurnan and Tolga,

one of the crew, set out in the larger of the *Avenger's* currachs for
the island when the sunrise had burned the light mist off the sea.

The sea was smooth and gentle, and the running tide carried
the small, light craft in onto the beach. Sand and gravel crunched
and scraped along its hardened leathers as it settled ungracefully
on the low beach.

Maildun and Diurnan splashed ashore, their weapons ready,
while Gussan stood by as Tolga tied up the craft.

They moved slowly up the gently sloping beach and stopped
before the high, painted and silvered doors. They were not
closed, and a tall mound of sand had grown up in the crack
between them where they were ajar.

Diurnan rested the side of his head against the wood and
listened, but, aside from the whispering of the sea on the beach
and the thudding of his own heartbeat, there was no other sound.
He straightened and waved the others back and then, his huge
war-axe held lightly in his right hand, he pushed against the left-
hand door.

The wood creaked and groaned and then, with a huge sigh that
dislodged a shower of sand down onto him, the door moved back
smoothly and thumped against the wall. The sound echoed down
the corridor, and took what seemed like an eternity to die away.
But there was no movement from within.

Diurnan moved forward lightly, his every sense alert, although
some instinct told him that the palace was empty. And yet,
hadn't lights burned there the previous night? He shrugged,
dismissing it as magic, something he could understand, but not
comprehend.

Maildun followed behind him, the heels of his boots ringing
sharply on the smooth stone flags. In the vicinity of the doorway
the flagstones were covered with a light dusting of sand, but once
beyond that they were smooth and polished. He breathed deeply,
savouring the air of the tall, arched corridor. Although it tasted
faintly of the sea, there was another odour that it took a moment
to define; he breathed it in again before identifying it: it was the
smell of burning wood and roasting meat. His stomach rumbled
loudly.

Diurnan turned round and grinned. 'And I thought I was
imagining it,' he said.

The corridor opened out into a huge circular room, and they
stopped at its threshold and looked around in amazement. The
walls, like the exterior, were painted white and composed of the
same regular blocks, but they were nearly invisible beneath

banners and standards, rows upon rows of weapons, spears, swords, both great and small, knives of all descriptions, battle-axes and slings, shields, helms and pieces of body armour. There were round and gleaming tables set along the walls, each of which were piled high with lengths of gold and silver, precious stones and rare cloths. One table held nothing but intricately worked goblets and tableware, and another nothing but torcs of all kinds.

The floor of the room was painted in squares of black and white, like the squares of a *fidchell* board, with the black squares inlaid with marble and the white with polished quartz.

In the centre of the floor was a huge circular table, piled high with steaming food and drink, the centre-piece of which was a whole roasted ox. There were thirteen place settings.

Maildun and Diurnan walked slowly round the table, while Tolga stood by the doorway, and Gussan fingered the heavy golden torcs, his weak eyes gleaming greedily.

'The food is hot,' Maildun said quietly, his voice dipping to a whisper, as he looked about.

'The mead looks fresh,' the northerner added, 'and that fruit still has this morning's dew upon it.'

'But who is it for?' Maildun wondered. 'Surely not for us?'

'There were lights last night,' Diurnan reminded him.

Maildun nodded. 'I know. And yet . . .' He paused. 'The bard told me that there would be food and drink, and solitude and rest, if we so desired on this isle . . .'

'There is another door here,' Diurnan said, moving round the table to a spot behind the high chair.

Maildun joined him, and together they approached the door-way. This led through into a second, smaller chamber. Once again the walls were white, and once again the floor was inlaid with black and white marble and crystal squares. Set onto each black square was a short quartz pillar, and jumping sedately from pillar to pillar was a small black and white cat. It paused as they entered the room, stared at them for a score of heartbeats, and then continued jumping from pillar to pillar in a seemingly random pattern.

Maildun waited, watching the cat, and then, when it landed on a black pillar quite close to him, he said softly, 'Is the food in the room beyond for us?'

The cat looked up at him, the pupils of its startlingly green eyes widening, and then it purred deep in its throat. Maildun glanced across at Diurnan and shrugged. 'I suppose it's for us,' he said.

They ate quickly and sparingly, and during the brief meal Maildun decided he would send the crew ashore in groups of twelve to eat and drink their fill. Diurnan would stay ashore and make sure they stole nothing.

As they were leaving Gussan paused by the tables which held the intricately worked torcs. He picked up one of the heavy, twisting coils of metal. He squinted across at Maildun as he slipped it up on his arm. 'I must have this,' he said, his sharp voice brooking no argument.

'*No!* The bard said that we must take nothing.'

'"The bard said, the bard said,"' Gussan mocked, 'and what do you say, brother? Surely a single torc will not be missed amongst all this lot?' He indicated the huge table overflowing with similar items.

Maildun hesitated and then Diurnan spoke. 'We have been treated with hospitality and kindness – for the first time on this accursed voyage – on this island, and I do not think we should repay that kindness with theft.'

Gussan's dark eyes narrowed. 'Theft? Are you calling me a thief,' he said stiffly, 'you, of all people, who come from a race of thieves . . .'

'Enough of this,' Maildun snapped, 'put it back, Gussan.'

His foster-brother grinned, showing his teeth in a tight smile, and then he slowly and deliberately slipped the torc up his forearm to his bicep. His left hand rested on the hilt of his sword.

Diurnan swung his battleaxe up on its leather thong, and then caught it just under its heavy head with his left hand. 'You can take it off your arm, or we can take off your arm,' he said pleasantly. He was about to say more when he felt something brush against his leg. He looked down and saw it was the small black and white cat. She was walking slowly and deliberately on her paws, her back arched. She moved up and spat at Gussan.

Diurnan laughed and then stooped to brush his huge hand against her upraised fur. 'Put it back, Gussan, this little lady doesn't like you taking her property.'

Gussan deliberately turned his back on his foster-brother and the northerner. He began searching through the gold. 'I think perhaps another to match . . .' he began.

There was a hiss, and Diurnan felt a brief flare of heat against his hand. And then it was as if a small ball of blue-white and red-black fire had taken off from the floor. The air crisped as it shot towards Gussan. Maildun managed to shout a warning, and his foster-brother's battle senses brought his sword half out of its

113

sheath, before the ball of fire punched through his chest in a fist-sized hole.

Gussan fell to the marbled floor, dragging a score or more of the torcs with him, the hole in his chest bubbling and hissing, charred white ribs and honeycombed lung clearly visible. His flesh took on a greyish hue and then, like wood ash, it began to flake away into a fine powdery dust. Within a matter of heartbeats, Gussan was nothing more than an oblong dusty shape on the floor, with only the gleam of gold showing through. The cat sat on the table above him and fastidiously licked her paws.

CHAPTER THIRTEEN

The grey ash floated on the water for a moment before dissipating on the waves. Maildun dropped another handful on the water and then emptied the small earthen container overboard. It was not perhaps an honourable burial, but it was the best he could do for his foster-brother. He rubbed his hands together, brushing away any flakes that remained, but no matter how hard he rubbed, he still felt as if they were coated with ash.

A hand fell on his shoulder and squeezed it tightly in sympathy. 'He is gone and you are not to blame,' Paedur said softly.

'I feel responsible,' Maildun replied tightly.

'He was warned not to touch the artifacts.'

Maildun shrugged. 'But it was such a small thing, a torc, he had many of them . . . it was not as if he needed it . . .' He shrugged again, realising that he was making excuses only to himself. He shook his head and looked to port at the diminishing island. 'He stole it, I know.'

It was now two days since his foster-brother's sudden death. Many of the crew had refused to go across to the island, fearing the tiny, furred guardian, and Germane and Diurnan had spent much of the time ferrying food and drink across to the ship from the isle to build up its depleted stores.

Maildun had gathered up his foster-brother's ashes and had initally thought of bringing them back to Erin, but had then reconsidered. It would be better if their father did not know how dishonourably his son had died. He wondered briefly if Gussan's soul would find its way to the Christian Heaven, or the ancient Underworld of his own race – or would it perhaps wander through some strange and alien limbo until the end of time? He looked over at the bard; he would know, but Maildun found he did not want to know the answer.

The *Avenger* sailed on, and by noon they had entered a small archipelago of islands, arrow-straight and pointing west to east. Ruarc immediately named them the Arrow Isles.

The first island in the group was small and almost perfectly circular. It was little more than a outcropping of rock – but it was completely enclosed by a low wall that burned orange and gold in the warm light. Another wall ran down the centre of the isle, dividing it in two.

There were about a dozen white sheep on the right-hand side of the wall, and the same number of black sheep on the left side.

Germane brought the craft in close to the shore and the entire crew lined the rail and watched the animals cropping the short, wiry grass that almost completely covered the isle. Diurnan was for taking a currach and going ashore, with the intention of butchering one of the animals for mutton, but the bard forestalled him. He asked for two light throwing spears and then handed them to the northerner.

'Put one on the right hand side of that brass wall,' he requested, 'and then throw the second into the left-hand side.of the garden.'

Diurnan nodded uncertainly, but threw the two spears in quick succession. They thudded into the ground on either side of the brass wall, and then those who had gathered to watch stared in amazement as the two spears began to change in colour. The spear on the right-hand side of the wall changed from the blade upwards, the heavy bronze head paling and lightening until it took on the colour of old bone, and then the wood itself changed to a stark whiteness. The spear on the left-hand side also changed colour, but this time to an absolute blackness.

Paedur smiled. 'Dare you walk onshore now?'

Diurnan shook his head and then Maildun suddenly gripped his arm and pointed. 'What's that?'

'That is the Keeper,' the bard said sombrely.

A huge creature had suddenly appeared on the island, seemingly rising up from an almost grave-like pit in the centre of the isle. He was tall, certainly taller than the *Avenger's* main mast, and completely black. He was clad in a crudely-shaped, rough cloak of animal skins that were totally white. He straddled the wall and stared out at the ship, and then he casually stooped down and lifted up a handful of the sheep in one long-fingered hand. He gently placed the animals on the left-hand side of the wall, and they immediately began to change colour, from white to black. And then the creature laughed, a shrill, womanish, high-pitched laugh that sent shivers through his listeners' spines.

Paedur etched a sign in the air before the creature and then spat into the water, and a dense fog suddenly rose up from the

116

waves and enshrouded the walled isle and its terrifying keeper. The bard shivered and then turned away.

Maildun gripped his arm and stared into his thin face. 'What in the name of God was that?' he demanded.

The bard glanced back in the direction of the isle, which was now completely covered by the fog, although elsewhere the sea remained clean and calm. 'That was the Keeper of Souls,' he whispered. 'You have just seen innocents condemned.'

The second island in the archipelago was distinguishable from the other, in that it rose from the water in a series of jagged peaks and was certainly the tallest they had thus far encountered, as well as the largest. A broad, gently-sloping, sandy beach rose up from the water's edge and disappeared into tall dunes, which in turn opened out into broad, open grasslands.

Germane and Diurnan went ashore in the currach. Maildun had protested, but the bard had said that the isle was not too dangerous, and the navigator pointed out that he wished to climb the mountain to survey the lie of the islands ahead of them, and the probable direction of the currents.

Diurnan dragged the light craft up high onto the beach while Germane stood by, his bow ready. The navigator saw the northerner stop and then stoop down, and he hurried over to him. Diurnan pointed to the ground. 'What do you make of that?'

Germane stooped over and then he straightened abruptly, wrinkling his nose in disgust. 'Dung!'

Diurnan laughed. 'Aye, dung! But what sort, eh?'

'I'm afraid I'm not a connoisseur of dung, my friend,' Germane said slyly. 'I lack your advantages.'

The northerner punched his friend in the arm playfully. 'It's pig dung; fresh too. Perhaps we'll have a little bacon for our evening meal?'

'This morning you said we might have a little mutton,' Germane reminded him.

The northerner sobered. 'Aye, well . . . we'll see.'

They made their way up through the dunes, coming across more evidence of pigs, and then they set out across the grasslands towards the mountains.

Diurnan saw them first. He stopped suddenly, his left hand raised, bringing Germane to a halt, his bow ready. The northerner pointed through the long grass towards a spot which stood out flesh-white against the green, and then he grinned and placed his finger across his lips. He bent down slowly, his eyes never leaving the spot of white ahead of him, and when he stood up again, he held a handful of stones, 'Be ready now,' he warned.

He threw the first of the stones beyond the white spot; it moved. He then threw another and another, and then he flung a handful into the air. There was a squeal, and then a scream, and then a small herd of white pigs burst through the long grass directly towards them. Germane saw one old boar with wickedly curving tusks, yellowed and stained with what looked like dried blood, come charging towards him, and he loosed an arrow. The bronze-tipped length of wood took the creature directly through one eye and it crashed to the ground almost at his feet, and he was fumbling for another arrow when he realised that all the creatures were gone. He looked round and found Diurnan standing over the bodies of two small sows, grinning hugely.

'We'll eat well tonight,' he announced proudly.

Germane prodded the boar by his feet. 'Tough eating I shouldn't wonder and,' he added with a grin, 'you're carrying this one back to the ship.'

They left the three dead animals in a heap and hoped they would be there when they returned. So far they had seen no large animals – or indeed any birds – on the island, and, unless the other boars were very hungry, they wouldn't touch the dead beasts.

The route to the mountain led through a rocky hinterland once they had passed beyond the grasslands. Soon the ground began to grow hot underfoot, and they passed steaming holes in the ground, and little gushing springs whose waters were warm to the touch. They continued climbing upwards, and now, when they looked back, they could see the sharp blueness of the sea with the black dot of the *Avenger* outlined against it.

They rounded a spur of rock and came upon a rapidly flowing river . . . and then they both stopped in amazement. Directly before them on the far side of the river was a giant man-like creature, similar to the one they had seen that morning, except that this one's skin colouring was a dark tan instead of completely black. Beyond him they could see a herd of enormous cows moving through the rocks.

The giant appeared to be sleeping, and Diurnan took a few steps forward and stood upon the edge of the river to stare open-mouthed at the creature. And then he yelped in pain and danced backwards, hopping on one foot, holding the other in his hands. He slumped to the ground and tore off his sandal. Germane stood

118

watching him in astonishment, but when he looked at Diurnan's right foot, he saw that the flesh was raw and puffed and the sole of his sandal was browned and blackened as if it had been burned. Germane looked at the river again. It certainly seemed to be no different from any other river except . . . for a high mountain river, it was flowing quite slowly. The navigator pulled an arrow from his quiver and dipped it into the water. The feathers on the shaft crisped and then the wood seared and blackened, and then the metal head bubbled and melted. Whatever it was, it wasn't water.

Diurnan stood, one hand resting on Germane's shoulder, his blistered and swollen right foot raised off the ground. His fingers dug painfully into the slim southerner's flesh. They stood watching the giant and the cows for a while and then they turned away, making their slow way towards the shore. Just as they were about to round the span of rock, Diurnan paused and looked back. His fingers tightened convulsively on Germane's shoulder.

'What is it?' the navigator demanded.

'Nothing; never mind. Just keep going.'

'Has the creature woken up?'

Diurnan shook his head silently.

'What then?'

Diurnan paused and rested his foot gingerly on the ground. He jerked his head back in the direction from which they had come. 'Those cows,' he said.

'Aye, what about them?'

'They were only calves!'

'Calves . . . ?' Germane repeated.

'And if that's the size of the calves, what of the cows or the bulls?'

Germane breathed deeply, absorbing the implications of what the northerner had said. 'What if the rest of the fauna on this isle is in the same proportion?' he wondered aloud.

Diurnan nodded.

'But the pigs . . .' Germane protested.

'I don't know,' Diurnan said, looking over his shoulder.

The two men set off for the shore as quickly as the northerner's injury would allow.

In Maildun's small cabin the bard bathed Diurnan's foot, which had now swollen to almost twice its size, and he applied a salve to the skin which had come up in ugly water blisters.

'The foot should be fine in the morning,' he said, squeezing the cork back into the small jar. 'Try not to walk on it until then.'

Diurnan nodded his thanks and, leaning back against the cabin wall, propped himself up with a spear that he was using as a crutch. 'Ach, but the damned stuff looked like water,' he said, more to himself. He shook his head. 'I should have known . . .'

Paedur nodded. 'You must learn to trust nothing in this Shadowland. You must remember that this is not your own world, and each island is different, unique in its own way. Some – a very few – are safe havens; most are deadly.'

'Even the safest havens have their guardians,' Maildun said bitterly, the memory of his foster-brother's death still fresh.

The bard nodded. 'Even so.' He straightened, his cloak settling about him, wrapping him in shadow. 'A different set of rules operates in this world; rules which are only broken with impunity. Your brother broke one of those rules, and he paid the price.'

'For taking a torc!'

'For taking a torc.'

'That wouldn't have happened in Erin. As a king's son he had a right . . .'

'A right to steal?' Paedur asked. 'He may have done so in Erin, but that will not be tolerated here. We take only what we need or what is given to us. If we are to leave this Shadowland, we must leave it with what we entered it with: no more, no less. Oh, we will lose men and goods upon the way, and so we will be able to take some things to balance that when we leave. But that balance must be maintained.' He paused, and then said in a gentler voice. 'And you must remember, Maildun, your brothers were warned not to accompany you. Your crew number was fixed by tradition and they broke that number.'

'Are you saying that none of my brothers will leave this world?' Maildun asked in a hushed whisper.

'I fear not,' the bard said sadly.

There was a long, uncomfortable pause while Maildun absorbed the news. Eventually Germane asked, to break the silence, 'What of the isles we passed this morn, bard?'

'The Isle of Sheep.' Paedur shrugged. 'For generations, scholars and philosophers have pondered upon the idea of the Shadowlands – for there are many – and their functions. Some were of the opinion that they were the mirrors of your own world, and that every deed done in the real world is repeated in one way or another in the Shadowlands. The deeds may not be repeated exactly, but rather symbolically. And what you saw this morning, as I said to the captain, were innocent souls condemned by chance . . .'

'But by what right . . . ?' Germane demanded.

'Does there have to be a right, a reason?'

'But condemned by chance,' Germane protested.

'What other way is there?' the bard asked. 'And would you tell me that it is different on your own world?' He held up his left arm with the silver hook shining ruddy in the light. 'Think before you answer me.'

'What of the giants?' Diurnan asked.

Paedur nodded. 'Aye; the folk of these isles are tall in stature. Their origin is supernatural. They have been banished to this Shadowland . . . for various reasons.'

'Are there any more to come?' the northerner asked.

Paedur nodded slowly. 'One, just one, but the most fearsome of all. Tomorrow we meet the Miller of Hell.'

CHAPTER FOURTEEN

They heard the low, grating rumbling long before they sighted the third island of the Arrow Isles. The sound throbbed through the chill pre-dawn air, making every piece of wood in the *Avenger* thrum and vibrate. The sea grew choppy and unpredictable, with sudden swells and cross-currents pulling and clutching at the longship.

Maildun ordered the crew to the oars and, with Diurnan calling the beat and Germane at the helm, they struggled to keep the craft on an even keel.

Maildun stood with the bard in the prow, one hand idly plucking splinters from the figurehead as he watched the low, flat isle appear out of the early morning sea. He could feel the vibrations booming through the wood beneath his fingers, and he was conscious that the bard held his hook a little away from his body, as if the metal were vibrating into the bone.

There was a touch of fire on the eastern horizon, and then the sun came up with a swiftness that never ceased to amaze him, although Germane assured him that it was common in some of the southern lands of their own world. With the passing of the twilight greyness, the entire eastern sky took on light and colour, bringing it alive, outlining the small isle in sharp relief.

From the distance it looked the smallest of the Arrow Isles, and even as the *Avenger* drew near it still managed to appear insignificant and nondescript. It seemed bare and barren, with a rough, stony beach rising up to small irregular hills. There was no sign of any vegetation, nor was there any sign of animal or bird life. The island seemed no more than a barren lump of dead rock, and might have been so – except for the continuous booming and vibrating that emanated from it.

The *Avenger* had now entered an almost circular area of white water that surrounded the isle, and Germane handed over the rudder to one of the crew and weaved his way down the ship to join Maildun and Paedur. 'It's madness to bring her in any closer,' he said, 'there's no telling what lies beneath the waters; we could be sailing into a reef.'

The captain looked at Paedur. 'Well?'

The bard stared out over the waves, his eyes squinting in the morning sunlight. He shook his head. 'I can see no rocks,' he said.

The navigator was about to protest that it was impossible to judge what lay beneath the foaming white water, when the bard turned to stare at him with his large, colourless eyes. 'There are no rocks,' he repeated.

Germane raised his small hands. 'I believe you.' He was about to turn away, but then he struck the wooden figurehead with his fist. 'There may be no rocks, but what happens if we're shaken apart before we reach that lump of stone.'

Maildun slapped the chipped wood of the ship's rail. 'We constructed this craft according to the druid's instructions, remember; we must be protected.'

Paedur smiled bitterly. 'Do you still place trust in a druid's magic although you worship the Christ?' he asked, before turning away without waiting for an answer.

The *Avenger* rode up onto the rocky beach with a scream of timbers and a rending of cracked leather. Oars snapped, sending men reeling, ribs, arms and jaws cracked with the whiplash. The craft staggered and then listed, toppling men and supplies down onto the beach or into the water. For a long while thereafter there was almost total silence, which was only broken by the occasional moans or cries of the injured.

Maildun awoke with the salt water slapping in his face. He had been thrown forward over the bow of the ship and down onto the rocky beach. He had been lucky; all he had were a few bruises and a sore head. He pushed himself to his feet, and then leaned against the side of the listing ship, while the world spun around him and the pounding in his head lessened and increased with a regular rhythm.

Stones rattled behind him and he spun round, his hand reaching for his knife, but the movement was too sudden and he felt his legs melt back into the ground.

Strong hands caught him before he crashed face-first onto the rocks, and then he was hauled up the beach to where others of his crew were lying, along with most of the supplies. He was eased to the throbbing ground – and it was the ground that was shaking, not himself, he realised – and then Diurnan squatted down beside him. The tall northerner's face was creased with worry, and one of his blue eyes was almost shut with an ugly, purpling bruise. 'How do you feel?' he asked.

'How do I look?'

Diurnan grinned. 'I hope you feel better than you look.'

'What happened?'

'A sudden wave . . .' Diurnan shrugged. 'It caught us from behind, threw us forward and up onto the beach. We were lucky.'

'*Lucky!*' Maildun sat up and groaned as his head throbbed.

The first mate nodded. 'Aye, lucky. A few bruises, broken bones and cuts, but no one dead. The bard is attending to the injuries now.' His eyes clouded as he looked down the beach to where the tall, dark-cloaked shape was bending over a prone figure, a dull blue witch-light shining along his hook. He looked back down at Maildun. 'Germane and I have been round the *Avenger*. She's damaged, but nothing a little time and some wood and skins won't fix.'

'And you?' Maildun asked.

Diurnan touched his swollen eye and winced. 'Ouch, I've had many a black eye, I'll recover. Germane cracked a rib, but the bard healed that, and both Colga and Ruarc are fine.'

'Help me up.' Maildun held out a hand and Diurnan hauled him to his feet. He staggered as the ground beneath his feet throbbed again. Diurnan nodded at his look. 'It's been like that since we landed; sometimes stronger, sometimes less so. Germane says it reminds him of the fire-mountains in his own land that sometimes tremble and rumble for months before blowing fire . . .'

Maildun caught the northerner's hesitation, and looked up sharply. 'But . . . ?'

Diurnan gently turned the captain round and pointed up the beach towards the low, rocky foothills. 'There is a huge pit – an abyss – beyond those hills. This isle may not be large, but it goes down to a tremendous depth. The sound seems to be coming from there.'

'What's down there?' Maildun asked.

'The Miller of Hell,' Paedur said, coming up silently behind them. He took Maildun's head in his strong, slim fingers and turned it roughly to and fro, and then he searched through the copper-red hair, probing his skull. His fingers came away with flakes of dried blood. 'You're lucky; you could have cracked your skull like an egg; your head will ache, but there's no damage done.'

'My crew . . . ?'

'I've healed the more serious injuries, but I'm loath to exhaust myself totally in healing; the minor injuries will have to wait.'

'Then how do we get off this island?' Maildun asked.

Paedur shook his head. 'We cannot; we need permission.'

'Permission?' The captain turned round and looked up towards the foothills. The bard nodded silently, and moved away.

Maildun ran his fingers through his beard. He shook his head and winced. 'I wouldn't like to . . .' he began.

'Nor would I,' Diurnan agreed, 'but if we need permission of some sort . . .'

'What's to stop us just sailing away?'

'It's going to take us at least two days to get the *Avenger* seaworthy again,' Diurnan said, 'and before that we need wood and leather. We are trapped here until then.'

Maildun nodded and sighed. 'Aye, then. Let us rest and eat; we'll pay the Miller our respects in a little while.'

From the top of the small hill, the ground sloped gently down into a rocky valley, the floor of which was far below sea-level. Although it was not long after noon, the valley was shrouded in shadow and it seemed likely that the sun never touched its floor.

A broad, well-worn pathway led down into the depths, disappearing in a thin white line into a huge, red-glowing cave mouth far below.

'I thought you said that this island was uninhabited,' Germane said to Paedur, pointing to the road.

'No one lives here but the Miller,' the bard said.

'Then who uses the path?' the navigator wondered.

'All mankind,' Paedur said, and set off down the bone-white road into the shadow.

Maildun, Germane and Diurnan shouldered their weapons and followed the bard. The road sloped gently downwards, meandering through little rocky valleys and gullies, crossing rock-strewn plains of burnt earth, and past tall pillars of stone winking and sparkling with multifaceted crystals in the light.

As they descended they felt the heat increase, and now the grinding and throbbing rose and fell in long, slow waves that rippled through the earth in billows, sometimes with enough force to send them tumbling to the ground. Once they were forced to stop, while a tall pillar of rock shook and swayed as the ground trembled violently, and then it gracefully crashed to the ground, sending jagged splinters of stone flying through the air. The ground trembled again, and the pile of rocks shook and rattled about until all trace of the standing stone had disappeared.

Soon the sunlight had dissipated into a grit-laden haze and, although it had been possible to see down into the valley from above, it was impossible to see up into the sky once within it. The four men wrapped their cloaks about their mouths and noses, squeezed their eyes shut against the sparkling dust, and plodded on.

The booming and terrible grinding was all around them now; it was part of them, within them. Speech was impossible, and they were deaf to everything save the sound of stone grinding on stone. Every bone in their bodies shook and vibrated, and the bard clutched his metal hook close to his chest, and his face was tight in agony as the metal strummed deep into the bone. Their progress was slow and painful, and soon it was an effort to keep going and the very act of putting one foot in front of the other was a strain. Time lost its meaning; they could have been walking through the valley for all eternity. And then there was silence.

More than silence: an absence of all sound.

The voices awoke Maildun. He lay on the dark, baked earth listening to the two voices nearby conversing in low, even tones. One was familiar; the other . . . the other seemed to be coming from a great distance, or from within a cave, and its booming, slightly echoing quality was somewhat muffled. He heard movement beside him and then a warm hand touched his forehead. 'Captain?'

Maildun's dark green eyes flickered open and took in Germane's worried face. The navigator raised his hand and placed an upraised finger across his lips. He tilted his head to one side – behind him.

The captain sat up slowly, wondering what was missing. His broad hands sank into the thin covering of pulverised stone that covered the ground, and then he suddenly knew what it was: the booming and grinding had ceased. He stood up carefully, feeling the rush of blood to his head. Black spots danced before his eyes and he squeezed them shut and shook his head. When he opened them again, he found he was looking straight into a huge cave mouth.

Memories began to trickle back. He could remember struggling towards the dark opening, following the bard. And then

Paedur had disappeared into the cave mouth and the booming had increased and . . . he remembered no more.

The cave mouth was huge; broad enough to fit the *Avenger* in lengthwise, and tall enough to allow her to clear it with room to spare. A huge wooden double door had been fitted across it at one time, but half of it was missing, and the monstrous hinges hung empty and rusted into barely recognisable lumps. The other door was charred and burnt, and frozen part-way open. Many of the shield-like rivets had disappeared, and the wood of the door was hacked and chipped and there was a huge length missing close to the ground.

Maildun took a step forward and then remembered Diurnan; the northerner had been just behind him before he fell. He turned unsteadily and found Germane kneeling on the ground beside his prone body. Even as he looked, Maildun saw the burly northerner raise his head and look groggily about. The navigator helped him to his feet and together they joined the captain.

Germane nodded towards the opening. 'The bard is within,' he said quietly, his voice sounding hoarse and raw. 'There is someone else there also; I've heard them talking.'

Maildun nodded and then winced as his stiffened neck muscles protested. He massaged the base of his neck and shoulders and twisted his head from side to side. 'I've heard them also.'

'What'll we do?' Diurnan asked. 'We still have our weapons . . .'

'But if the bard is within it should be reasonably safe,' Germane said.

'And if the bard is a demon sent to lure us into the pit?' Maildun asked, fingering the small cross he wore about his neck.

'He hasn't done so yet,' Diurnan said, 'and he's had plenty of opportunity.'

Maildun nodded reluctantly. 'We have no choice but to trust him.' He drew his sword, wincing as it rasped and grated with grit in the scabbard. 'We'll go in.'

The interior of the cave was warm and smoky, the air gritty and touched with a myriad different odours, some familiar – hauntingly so – others totally alien. From where they stood, just inside the shattered doorway, they could hear the two voices in the distance, and then the bard's voice rose in a laugh – one of the few times they had ever heard him express any sort of outward emotion.

They walked down the short length of the corridor. It turned sharply to the right, and then left, and then debouched into a

127

huge, circular room that was piled high with gold, silver, precious metals of all kinds; jewels, cut and uncut; bolts of cloth; weaponry of all ages and from many lands; armour; amphorae of wine . . . all the wealth of a world.

In the centre of this vast cavern was a huge grinding mill.

The bard appeared from behind the mill. He stopped when he saw the trio, and then beckoned them forward with his hand. He was smiling and his colourless eyes were sparkling, reflecting back the metal brightness and cloth patterns around him.

'You have recovered, I see,' he said softly.

'A little shaken, but otherwise . . .' Maildun began, and then stopped in amazement as another figure came round from behind the huge mill. He was a monstrous bear of a man, standing easily three times Diurnan's height, and broad in proportion. His skin was deeply tanned and covered in a fine, silky down, almost like fur. His face was broad and pleasant, and his eyes were wide and dark. He smiled, his teeth startlingly white and pointed, like a cat's.

'This is Maildun,' Paedur said, in a slightly singsong inflection. 'This is Germane, called the Navigator, and this is Diurnan Lenkard, the Northman, first mate aboard the *Avenger.*'

The giant nodded to each in turn, his moist eyes lingering briefly on each face, seemingly staring at and through them. *'I am Trecende,'* the giant said slowly, his voice booming in the vastness of the cavern, *'but it has been a long time since anyone has bothered to ask.'* His huge hand stroked the worn mill-stone. *'This is the Mill of Trecende.'* He smiled again, his pointed teeth now yellow in the light from the countless oil-lamps scattered about the room. *'I am sometimes known as the Miller of Hell.'* And then he laughed.

His laughter boomed around the cavern in a huge, rolling wave. Metal clanked and coins slipped from overturned casks with the vibrations, bolts of cloth hissed and rasped as they slid down the piled wealth on the floor, and the miller's laughter rocked loose a great pile of tiny gold coins that crashed to the ground with a musical clinking.

When the giant's laughter had abated, Maildun asked him, 'Why are you called the Miller of Hell.'

Trecende grinned broadly and squatted down beside his mill. *'Tell me,'* he asked Maildun, *'look around and tell me what you see.'*

Maildun looked surprised, but turned round and surveyed the cavern before turning back to the giant. 'I see gold and jewels, fine cups, wrought weapons, swords, spears, shields, torcs and

128

pins of fantastical workmanship, lengths of dyed wool in many colours . . .'

The giant held up his hand with its surprisingly small fingers, and then turned to Germane. '*And what do you see?*'

'I see bushels of coins, gold, silver, bronze and copper from many, many lands. I see silks from the far-eastern lands, and spices from the Orient. I see feathers and furs from the Southern Lands, manuscripts and maps from my own country . . .'

'*And you?*' Trecende turned to Diurnan. '*What do you see?*'

The northerner looked around, his eyes puzzled. He glanced at Maildun and Germane and then said slowly. 'I do not see what my companions see.' He pointed to one side. 'I see gold, aye, and silver also. I see good swords and shields, fine warm cloaks, good furs, salted meat, and fish also, amphorae of wine and crocks of mead . . .'

The miller grinned and then laughed aloud again, before turning to the bard. '*And tell me, Paedur Hook-Hand, what do you see?*'

The bard smiled. 'I can see all that my companions see . . . and I can also see that there is nothing here but stones.'

The miller nodded soberly. '*Aye, you would see the way of things.*' He turned back to the puzzled trio. '*You see what you wish to see,*' he explained. '*You see the wealth of your own world. But I take the wealth of your world, and the many worlds like it, and I grind it into dust!*' He slapped the mill suddenly and laughed uproariously.

'But why?' Germane asked, puzzled. 'And why should we each see different things, and why should the bard see only stones?'

The miller shrugged and lumbered away, and began piling the wealth of the world onto his mill.

'You see what you value most,' Paedur explained, watching the miller. 'You covet certain goods more than others, and that is why you see them here. It is all an illusion.'

'But why do you see only stones?' Germane wondered.

The bard smiled and his expression hardened. 'I see what is. I covet no goods. Wealth means nothing to me.' He turned away. 'Come; we must be gone. When the mill is filled, he will begin to grind – that is the sound we heard on our way here.'

'But why, Trecende?' Germane suddenly shouted. 'Why?'

The miller turned slowly, his muscular arms filled with wealth which differed according to the observer. '*Why?*' His broad face creased in a frown, and the pain in his soft eyes was terrifying. '*Because it is my doom; because it is my bane. This is my hell and I am the Miller of Hell; I grind the wealth of worlds into dust.'* And he turned away and disappeared into the depths of the cavern.

The three men stood in the huge cavern listening to the footsteps echoing up from the corridor, and then, as one, they turned round and made their way out into the dust-laden air.

It was evening by the time they returned to the beach. Some of the damage to the *Avenger* had been repaired, and the ship itself had been righted and now bobbed in the shallow waters just offshore. The huge leather sail was spread out over the beach and a score of men were busy with bone needles and gut repairing the rents and tears. Some of the gaping holes in the fabric of the craft had been repaired with patches which they had carried from Erin for that very purpose. The cracked beams had been taken out and replaced with beams from less essential parts of the ship, and the first mate reckoned that the *Avenger* might be seaworthy by the following evening.

Later that night, when the stars burned fiercely in the purple skies, the bard told the three men the tale of the Miller of Hell as they sat around a low, crackling fire.

'There was a time,' he began, 'when the old world, which is now gone, had not even risen. In that time, the gods appointed giant custodians to the Shadowlands; guardians to ensure that they did not stray too far from the path of right.'

'The Dwellers in Jotunheim,' Diurnan whispered.

'Aye; they ruled the Cold Wastes beyond Asgard, the World of the Gods and outside Midgard, the World of Men.' The bard's large eyes blinked, mirroring the flickering image of the fire. 'The mythologies of every race tell of these giants. The Greeks tell of the sons of Tartaros and Ge, and even your own race, Maildun, speaks of the feats of Finn mac Cumhail, the builder of the Giant's Causeway.

'But then the nature of the giants changed: they grew greedy and boastful, arrogant in their great strength and powers, and they began to take the world of men unto themselves.

'And chief amongst these was Trecende. As giants go, he was small in stature, but his strength was great and his cunning greater. He began to amass a vast amount of wealth, taking by force what he could not steal from the various worlds by stealth.

'And then the giants grew even more arrogant and attempted to storm the Heavens and usurp the gods, but they were defeated and cast down to the earth and abased. And the mythos of all races recalls the Wars of the Giants.

130

'The giants were set menial tasks; those who thought themselves the judges of worlds were set on tiny islands with naught but sheep to herd; those who amassed land were given a small herd of cows to watch; and those who had stolen were set to grind the wealth of worlds into dust: and this was the fate of Trecende.'

Sparks from the fire wheeled upwards into the heavens, spiralling in an intricate, lonely dance before sputtering away to dust.

Sound rumbled in the distance, and then rolled along the beach in a great wave, sending stones clattering down into the water. The Miller of Hell was at his mill.

CHAPTER FIFTEEN

Ruarc waited until the bard turned round and looked at him. He had been standing for some time, before Paedur turned from his constant scanning of the horizon and took notice of him. The bard pushed back the hood of his furred cloak with the point of his hook and paused, obviously waiting for Ruarc to say something.

The young man coughed in embarrassment, sudenly unwilling to face this formidable stranger. But then the bard smiled, suffusing his hard face with warmth and compassion. 'I don't bite,' he said gently, 'nor do I drink blood,' he added, 'no matter what the crew might think.'

Ruarc blushed. 'I never thought you did . . .' he stammered.

'But it would not surprise you if I did.' Paedur raised his hand, before he could reply. 'Why do you wish to see me?'

Ruarc stepped forward and unfolded a long, wide tube of supple leather. 'I have been attempting to make a chart of this sea . . .'

'The Island Sea?'

Ruarc nodded. 'The Island Sea. I have attempted to plot our course through the islands. See,' he pointed to a spot near the foot of the chart, which had been daubed in red juice. 'This is the Isle of Ants, and this is the Shaped Isle of Birds . . .' His finger moved slowly up the crude chart, pointing out the islands they had visited or passed.

Paedur nodded. 'You have done well; this is one of the best charts I have seen of this Shadowland. But what do you want from me?'

'I would like to know our route; what path are we following?'

Paedur looked at him for a moment and then smiled coldly. 'Route? Why, we are following no route at all; we are wandering aimlessly – if one discounts the hand of fate and the threads of the Pattern.'

'But surely . . . ?' Ruarc began in confusion.

The bard shook his head. 'We were thrown through to this region by the druid's spell. The gate we used is now closed; we must try to find another gate, a gate between the worlds which will bring us back to your world. Now, rather than wander hither and yon through the islands, I have elected to follow them in as straight a line as possible, east to west into the sunset. If you are looking for a route, a direction, then that is it. Hopefully it will bring us in contact with as many of the isles as possible, and perhaps with someone with enough power to throw us back to Erin's seas.'

Ruarc rolled up his chart carefully. There was a numb feeling in his chest and he had to resist the urge to shred the chart into pieces. 'And if we cannot find someone to show us the way back . . . ?' he whispered.

Paedur shook his head. 'Oh, there is little doubt but that we shall. This is a world rich in magic. Since its creation only the raw elemental forces have been worshipped; no gods rule here. The many gods of your world have had little use for it and have not yet leeched it of its magic.'

'But what of the Miller of Hell,' Ruarc protested, 'surely he did Satan's work?'

The bard smiled again and shook his head. 'Like the several sorts of wealth your foster-brother and his companions saw in the Mill of Trecende, the Miller's title, like much of this world, is an illusion. It is far easier for them to interpret his title as "Hell" rather than its true term; far easier for them to accept that he was consigning the wealth to the Dark Lord.'

Ruarc crumpled the chart in his strong hand, the leather snapping and cracking loudly. 'Then what was the truth?' he asked, looking straight into the bard's empty, reflective eyes. 'Was there any wealth . . . the gold . . . the silver . . . the precious stones . . . the weapons . . . ?'

Paedur turned aside, one eye catching the blue of the sea, the other remaining dark and in shadow. 'There was no wealth,' he said, 'there was nothing but stones. He was grinding stones, that is his bane: to grind stones for all eternity. He was a cunning and clever man, and now he grinds stones interminably.' Paedur nodded briefly at the younger man and turned away. Ruarc hesitated a moment, staring at the bard's tall figure before he too turned away.

A wind struck up as the evening rolled in, and it carried with it a wailing.

The bard heard it first, and broke off a story he was telling the crew about the coming of the Tuatha De Danann to Erin. He listened, his head tilted slightly to one side, and then he looked across at Diurnan and dipped his head towards the prow. The northerner nodded and slipped away, wondering what the bard had heard on the wind.

Maildun joined him at the prow and then Germane came up, saying that the currents had changed, a sure sign of land ahead.

There was a whisper of cloth and then the bard too joined the three men. 'There is land ahead.' He raised his hook. 'Listen.'

For a few moments they heard nothing, save the lull of the sea, and the snap of the wind against the sail. The wind gusted again, and then they all heard it: a thin, high keening, the sound of a soul in mortal terror or the very depths of despair.

'*Banshee!*' Maildun snapped and crossed himself.

Germane followed suit, but also fingered the small amulet he wore around his neck. He didn't truly believe in the *banshee* himself, but he did believe in the vampire, the blood-sucker, and he had heard enough about them on his travels to recognise the similarities between the two creatures.

'Listen again,' the bard commanded.

The wind was stronger now, and it also carried the faint, but unmistakable traces of humanity: sweat, urine and faeces.

'*Banshee,*' Maildun repeated, 'the cry of death.'

The bard shook his head in disgust. 'The *banshee* wails in Erin only; they are unknown in the Shadowlands.'

'Then what is that sound?' Maildun demanded.

'The Isle of the Damned,' Paedur said ominously, glancing across at the captain, and then he sketched a sign in the air with the point of his hook. 'I would advise that you avoid it,' he added.

'Impossible,' Germane said abruptly. 'The tide is flowing with us, and we are caught in a strong cross-current; we are being drawn in towards the island.'

'Use the oars,' Maildun snapped.

The navigator shook his head. 'Not yet; it is too soon. We do not know how far the current reaches; it might be a short band on one hand, and on the other it might stretch for some distance. Better not to tire the men out too soon. Let the current carry us in towards the isle,' he advised. 'Once close to the shore we should be able to row around the island and break free of the current.'

'Sound advice,' Diurnan agreed.

The bard nodded silently, and folded his hand and hook up into his sleeves.

The sounds grew clearer as they drew on. Towards midnight they seemed to strengthen, as if the hour brought additional terrors with it. And then, when the first glimpses of dawn touched the horizon, the cries died down to little more than a subdued whimpering.

The island rose out of the dawn like a low grey cloud. It was almost indistinguishable from the thunderheads that were massing on the northern and eastern horizon, almost obscuring the dawn. From the distance it looked uninhabited, but the intermittent wind still carried the stench of massed humanity and the occasional moaning.

The sun rose up behind the clouds, giving them weight and substance, making them appear all the more ominous. Shafts of butter-coloured light touched the sea, gilding the white-capped waves in gold, reflecting off the low black cliffs of the isle, sparkling in the ebon-coloured sand.

The island was black. Black sands rose onto black cliffs, which were capped with seared and withered vegetation. And, as the *Avenger* neared the isle, the watchers could see movement on the beach and along the cliff-tops. The shafts of sunlight moved again, picking out the tall figures that were also totally black and clad in long cloaks of raven feathers.

They were not the true dark-folk of the hot Southlands, Germane said, for they lacked the characteristic features and hair of the Southerners. The throng on the isle seemed to be a mixture of all races and nations, and there were some who had never walked the world of men either. And they were all weeping and in great distress.

'Why do they weep?' Colga, Maildun's eldest foster-brother asked, joining the small group gathered at the prow.

'It is the Isle of the Damned, brother,' Maildun answered him.

Colga stared across at the island, his brow furrowed. 'I thought damnation was fire and burning,' he said to the bard, almost accusingly.

Paedur shrugged. 'They may not be followers of the White Christ; they may not be damned by his faith.'

Colga's expression hardened, and his left hand touched the hilt of his knife. 'Careful, lest you blaspheme,' he warned coldly.

Maildun laid his hand on his foster-brother's arm. 'Pay him no heed, Colga, he is a faithless man, having no gods to worship and feeling that loss.' His eyes pleaded with the bard not to deny him.

Colga stared at Paedur, as if seeing him for the first time. Since the start of the voyage, Colga had preferred to work and eat and

135

sleep with the rest of the crew, finding companionship with men who were more like himself. He had avoided the bard at all costs, and always took care to cross himself and touch his amulet – a piece of the True Cross – as a protection against the Evil Eye.

'Demon-spawn, by the look of him,' he said finally. He turned his back on the bard and looked at his brother. 'Have a care lest he bewitch you,' he warned.

'Aye, I'm wary.'

Still with his back to the bard, Colga continued. 'He knows you are my foster-brother? And he knows I'll kill him if he brings you to any harm?'

Maildun nodded, but the bard said, 'I know; you need have no fears . . .'

Colga swung round, his knife coming free of its sheath with surprising ease and swiftness for such a big man. 'I'll not hold speech with demon-breed,' he snarled, the knife not a finger-span away from Paedur's throat, 'nor will I suffer them to address me.' He moved the knife slightly, allowing it to catch the light, throwing it into the bard's eyes. Paedur's eyes blazed golden with the reflected light, and Colga, startled, stumbled back and crossed himself.

'Demon-spawn,' he said again, his voice a little shaken.

The bard bowed and then turned away, making his way silently down the length of the deck, the crew falling silent as he passed, and then crossing themselves behind his back, or making the Sign of Horns to the Older Gods.

Colga turned back to his brother, but Maildun held up his hand. 'If you're going to ask me to rid ourselves of the bard, you are asking the impossible.'

'Ah, he has bewitched you!'

Maildun shook his head. 'He has not. But he is the only person who knows these islands in this . . . this world or Shadowland. We need him !'

'Faith in the Lord will carry us through and back to our own land,' Colga stated flatly.

'The White Christ is not worshipped here,' Diurnan said calmly. He had always found Maildun's eldest foster-brother's faith a little too fanatical and overpowering. Maildun's faith, although strong and firm, was not as fiercely protective as his brother's.

'The Lord is everywhere!' Colga glared at the tall northerner. 'Even here.' His right arm encompassed the *Avenger* and the sea, and then the stubby fingers pointed towards the isle. 'And there is the irrevocable evidence of that fact.'

Diurnan shook his head and turned away in disgust, unwilling to argue.

Colga turned and grasped Germane's forearm in a grip of iron. 'You must bring the *Avenger* in close to shore . . .'

The navigator shook his head. 'I won't risk the ship.' he stated flatly.

'As close as you dare then,' Colga growled. 'I wish to go ashore.'

'What madness is this, brother?' Maildun demanded.

'I am going ashore.'

Maildun shook his head. 'Impossible; we are sailing around this isle . . .'

'I am going ashore,' Colga repeated ominously.

'But why, brother. In the name of God, why?'

'They are the damned – even the demon-breed said so – but why have they been damned, and who damned them?' Colga's voice dropped to a murmur. 'Perhaps,' he continued slowly and his light brown eyes took on a flat and glassy stare, 'perhaps they have even been damned by the Lord' – he crossed himself rapidly – 'yes, yes; damned by the Lord and cast to this outer fringe of Hell.' He was nodding now, convinced by his own twisted logic. 'You can bring me in as close to the shore as you dare,' he said to Germane, 'or you can sail around the island, and I will be forced to jump overboard and swim for the shore,' he said to Maildun.

The captain nodded wearily. 'You would too, wouldn't you?'

Colga nodded, smiling broadly.

'Bring her in as close as you possibly can,' Maildun said to Germane.

The currach scraped up onto the beach, leaving a dark reddish-brown smear on the ebon sands. Colga splashed through the shallows and pulled his tiny craft high up onto the beach. Behind him the track in the sand began to change colour, rapidly turning back to ebon.

The watchers on board the *Avenger* saw the bulky warrior walk steadily up the beach, his footsteps leaving discoloured indentations in the sand. They saw him pause by the first group of people and watched as he sank to his knees.

Maildun shouted aloud, thinking he had been struck, but the bard laid his hand on his arm and said, 'Wait.'

They saw Colga come unsteadily to his feet, and begin tearing

137

off his clothing and weapons, and now he too was weeping. Someone brought him a ragged black cloak and he mingled with the Damned, distinguishable from them only by his lighter colouring. He moved away from the beach and disappeared from sight.

Maildun turned to the bard, his mouth opening in a question, but Paedur shook his head. 'He is lost; he will not return.'

'By Christ he will!' Maildun spat. He turned to Diurnan. 'Take two men with you and bring him back,' he commanded.

'If you go you will not return,' Paedur warned the northerner.

Diurnan hesitated, looking from Maildun to the bard and then across towards the island. And then he shook his head. 'I am not a coward, Maildun, but I will not go.'

'Germane?'

The navigator shook his head. 'I've no wish to throw my life away needlessly.'

The captain breathed deeply, attempting to stifle his growing anger, and the gnawing feeling of helplessness he felt. He had lost one brother, and now he was losing a second, and there was nothing he could do about it.

Ruarc came running up. 'What are we going to do?'

'I don't know if there is anything we can do,' Maildun said softly.

'We must! He is our brother!'

'I know, I know. But I don't want to lose any more men to that cursed isle.'

'So you're just going to leave him there to rot!' Ruarc shouted. 'And, now that you've got rid of Gussan and Colga, you'll get rid of me, and that'll leave your way clear to the throne . . .'

Maildun struck him backhanded, sending him sprawling onto the deck. He stood over his fallen brother, tight-lipped and ashen-faced, his red hair and beard almost bristling with rage. 'You are my brother,' he said slowly and distinctly, 'and only because you are my brother will I allow you to say that. But you will say it only once; there will be no second time . . .' he warned. He turned away, and pointed to the two nearest crewmen. 'Arm yourselves, and go ashore and bring back my brother.'

'Maildun . . .' Paedur said, a note of warning in his voice.

'Stay out of this,' the captain threatened. He stood by the port rail while the small currach was lowered into the choppy water, and then watched the two men strike out strongly for the shore. He then stood watching while they too were met by the Damned,

138

watched them throw down their weapons and tear off their jerkins, saw them wrapped in the raven feather cloaks, saw them disappear into the interior of the isle.

The crew of the *Avenger* were utterly silent and even the heartbeat of the sea seemed to dull and mute. Maildun leaned against the rail, his knuckles white against the wood, and it seemed now as if the wailing of the Damned changed a little and there was a new note, one almost of mockery and defiance, in it.

Paedur's silver hook touched the rail by his white-knuckled hands. 'There may be a way,' he said softly.

'To bring them back?'

'Not all of them,' the bard said cautiously, his eyes taking on the deep blue of the sea, and then changing to a deeper night shade as he looked across at the isle. 'Your brother is lost,' he said finally. 'He defied the druid; he was doomed before he set foot on board the *Avenger*. He has but fulfilled his destiny.'

'I will pray for his soul,' Maildun said numbly.

Paedur nodded. 'That is all you can do.'

'You said there might be a way to bring them back . . . ?'

'Choose four men; the strongest amongst the crew. Arm them and give them cloaks of pure wool. Before they set foot on the isle have them dip their cloaks into the salt water and then cover their mouths and noses. Have them make sure that the cloth is wet at all times. If they hurry they may be able to bring back the two crewmen.'

'Perhaps they might even be able to find my foster-brother?' Maildun suggested.

'Ach, but you are not listening to me,' Paedur snapped, as close to losing his temper as the captain had ever seen him. 'He is gone, lost – you will never find him.' His hook shot out and pointed towards the isle. 'The island is black – rocks, vegetation, sand, even the water. The inhabitants are black – all of them. And you will recall the Island of Sheep we passed but recently? You will recall what happened when the throwing spear touched the soil? This island is much the same, except that the process of discolouration is not quite so dramatic. Your brother will be indistinguishable from the Damned,' Paedur finished coldly, 'for now he, too, is damned.' He was about to turn away, but paused and nodded towards the lowering skies. 'You had best have your crew hurry; there is a storm about to break.'

The cries of the Damned rose in intensity as the wind picked up. Lightning flickered briefly across the skies in the distance, followed, a few moments later, by a long rumble of thunder.

Rain patterned along the beach, churning the black sand into a filthy, glutinous morass, and the four crewmen from the *Avenger* found themselves struggling through a sticky, tacky bog. As they disappeared up the beach, Germane had the crew take up the oars, for the current had shifted now and was pushing them offshore. The oars dipped and rose rhythmically, attempting to hold the craft steady, beating time while the tension mounted as there continued to be no sign of the crewmen.

Suddenly the bard pointed, his hook flashing in the dulling light. Maildun leaned over the rail, almost toppling into the water in his eagerness, straining to make out the moving figures on the black beach against the black cliffs.

Lightning crackled and a jagged streak came to earth on the beach, fusing the ebon sands into globules of glittering glass. But in that brief instant, when the world had been washed bone-white, Maildun had seen his four burly crewmen struggling down the beach with two white men in their grasp.

Lightning flared again, and then again, leeching the colour from every living thing, rendering the island even darker. The wind howled, and the voices of the Damned exulted in unison, their wailing assuming an almost rapturous intensity. Thunder rumbled like the laughter of a god and Diurnan shivered, the skald's tales of his youth about Thor coming back to him all too clearly. It was very easy to hear the Voice of the Thunder-Lord in that rumbling laugh.

The rain now redoubled in intensity, and sluiced across the decks, drumming on the polished wood and stretched hide, rattling and pinking off the metal shields and bucklers.

Maildun remained by the port rail, seemingly oblivious of the driving, ice-touched hail, intent on the currach which was now wallowing heavily in the heaving waves. Beside him the bard pulled up the hood of his long cloak and folded his hand and hook in his sleeves. The rain ran in twisting rivulets off his cloak as if it had been oiled.

Diurnan joined them and stood for a moment, watching the crew of the currach struggle against the swell, the wind and the rain. He turned away and joined Germane at the tiller, and, after a brief conversation, he walked down the deck, his strong, battle-toughened voice sending the men to the oars, calling the beat. The starboard oars lifted once and then dipped, lifted again and again, and slowly the *Avenger* turned, its bow pointing towards the shore. The navigator shouted a command, and Diurnan changed the beat, and now both sets of oars, starboard and port sides, dipped in unison and the longship slipped forward towards the tiny, struggling craft. They were rowing against the current, but the same current was also pushing the currach away from the island, although the wind had a tendency to draw it off to one side. Germane shouted again, and Diurnan stopped the beat, and the oars dipped and dipped again, threading water, while the hide craft bumped against the port side, and the shivering crew were hauled aboard and the currach pulled up.

The two crewmen who had briefly joined the ranks of the Damned seemed slightly dazed, almost as if they were waking from a drunken stupor, but the four men who had gone in search of them seemed unharmed. They told of a small valley behind the beach which teemed with humanity, all of the same dark colour, all clad in cloaks of ravens' feathers, and all wailing and crying aloud.

When the two crewmen had been revived, they were unable to tell a coherent story and, indeed, they never afterwards recalled much of their brief sojourn on the isle, merely that they wept because they 'knew', although they couldn't express in words what they knew.

Afterwards Maildun took the bard aside and asked him if he had any idea what made the islanders cry and moan.

Paedur shook his head. 'If I knew that, I too would be damned.'

'Is it . . . was it their knowledge which damned them, or did damnation bring that knowledge?' Maildun wondered.

'That is a question for philosophers,' Paedur said, 'and I am but a simple bard.'

Maildun snorted rudely and spat into the sea. There was a lull in the storm, and the sea and sky were now calm and clear, smelling and tasting clean after the odour from the isle.

'You are more than a bard,' Maildun said, with something approaching good humour, 'although I'll be damned if I know what you truly are.' He paused and then asked. 'Could you not guess why they were damned, or why they wailed, or what my crew knew?'

Paedur looked over at him, his eyes taking on the points of light from the sky, transferring them to the shadow of his face. 'I would guess that absolute knowledge is a damnation; I would guess that the Damned are omniscient and that their very omniscience damns them.' His forefinger and thumb formed a circle. 'Thus: absolute knowledge brings its own damnation.'

141

Maildun was silent then, staring down into the depths of the purple-black water. 'But Our Lord God is omniscient,' he said at last.

'Truly omniscient?'

'Truly.'

'Then he too is surely damned,' the bard said, turning away.

CHAPTER SIXTEEN

They sailed through the eye of the storm and back into the wind and rain. It lasted for the remainder of the day and well into the night. Once free of the Isle of the Damned, the huge leather sail was loosened and the *Avenger* rode before the wind, away from the cursed place.

In the storm's aftermath, Maildun walked the *Avenger's* shining decks, now sheened with silver from the star-bright skies. It would be easy to believe that he sailed the seas off Erin's coast, if it were not for those alien configurations and too-bright stars. A sudden thought struck him, and he paused, scanning the heavens: there was no moon, and he could not recall having seen one previously. Shaking his head, he resolved to ask the bard later.

A shadow detached itself from the main mast and stepped into his path. The captain paused, his left hand falling to his knife. 'Who is it?' he called.

The figure moved forward and Maildun recognised his foster-brother, Ruarc. The younger man hesitated, while Maildun waited patiently for him to make the first move. For a while the silence between them was unbroken, and the sounds of the sea seemed strangely magnified. Then Ruarc stepped forward and the pale starlight took his face, etched it into bone and shadow, and, for a moment, Maildun found himself looking at a skull.

'I'm sorry,' Ruarc said finally.

Maildun pulled him into his arms, and then held him as the younger man shook with sobs. 'I'm frightened,' he said between chattering teeth.

'I know, I know,' Maildun sighed.

'I don't want to die, and now Gussan and Colga are gone, I know the druid's warning is coming true.'

'Don't say that,' Maildun whispered, 'you're all I have left.'

'We only wanted to be with you. You were our brother, we couldn't let you sail off without us. We didn't think the curse . . .' His voice faltered again.

'We'll defeat it yet,' Maildun promised. 'The bard is powerful;

143

his gods are not our gods, but they are powerful in this world. I'll have him invoke them to protect you.'

'It won't work; no man, be he human or god, can escape his fate: even Cuchulain was bound by it.'

'The Hound knew what he was doing when he took up his arms on that fated day,' Maildun said. 'The druid told him then that, although he would be honoured and remembered for all eternity in Erin, his life would be brief and end violently.'

Ruarc pushed himself out of his brother's arms. 'Don't you see, Maildun, we too defied the druid. He said that if we accompanied you we would not return. And now Gussan is dead, slain by a demon in cat form, and Colga is damned.' There was a note of desperation in his voice that came close to outright panic. 'I don't want to die.'

'You won't; I'll protect you,' Maildun promised with a confidence he did not feel.

'What should I do?' Ruarc asked simply.

'Rest now – and pray,' Maildun answered numbly.

Germane stood with Diurnan by the figurehead and remarked that they always seemed to come upon the islands with the dawn, almost as if they had lain in wait overnight and popped up with the first light to trap and startle the voyagers.

Diurnan thought for a moment, and then remarked that perhaps the isles were evenly spaced, or the island had been visible for some time from the *Avenger*, but what with the night and no light to see her by . . .

'I thought the Viking had no sense of humour,' the dark southerner remarked sourly.

'I don't,' Diurnan replied, his face smooth and expressionless, 'all I was saying was . . .'

'Oh, I know what you were saying,' Germane said quickly, 'you're as pragmatic as any Gaul.'

'I'm not sure whether that's a compliment or not,' the northerner said with a smile.

'Nor am I.'

'But the island . . .' Diurnan reminded the navigator.

'Oh, aye.' He shaded his dark brown eyes with a slim, calloused hand and stared across the sparkling sea towards the island. 'Well, it's curious enough,' he began, 'flat, rising towards a small hillock in the exact centre, if I'm not mistaken. There is some sort of stone table in the centre . . .'

'A dolmen?' Diurnan interrupted.

Germane squinted again, trying to make sense of the shape through the glare of the rising sun on the sea. He could make out a flat table stone and the uprights . . . and then he realised that he was looking at it from one end. Now that he had it fixed in his mind's eye, he could visualise the tall dolmen of gleaming black stone in the centre of the isle.

'A dolmen,' he nodded. He squeezed his eyes shut and then opened them again, the glare beginning to leave after-images on his retina, confusing him. 'What are those lines?' he asked Diurnan.

The tall northerner shook his head slowly. 'I don't know; the island seems to be divided into four equal sections, and there seems to be something set in each division.' He shook his head. 'Better ask the bard.'

'What would you ask the bard?' Paedur wondered, joining them and leaning over the side of the craft, staring across at the approaching island. His mirror-like eyes took up the sun's silver-bright reflection from the sea and burned in his head like coins.

'Is yonder isle divided,' Diurnan asked, 'or do our eyes deceive us?'

Paedur straightened and pushed back the hood of his cloak with the point of his hook. The wind took his long, fine black hair and shook it loose, pulling it away from his face, revealing the fact that the lobe of his right ear was missing. Colour touched his normally pale cheeks and for once he seemed almost human. Almost.

He nodded towards the island. 'That is the Isle of the Elements: Earth, Air, Fire and Water. The island is divided by four walls, one of copper, another of silver, a third of gold and the fourth of crystal. Each part is guarded by a personification of that element: thus, a warrior in the first part, a queen in the second, a king, and a maiden.'

'And what is their function?' Germane wondered.

'Must they have a function?' the bard asked, turning to look at the navigator, the light dying from his eyes to be replaced by a muddy brown.

Germane shrugged uncomfortably. 'I thought everything had a function; so the philosophers say, do they not?'

'Philosophers have a tendency to see a function in everything; if they cannot see it immediately, then they are apt to create one. The island,' he nodded across the waves, 'is but an image which appeals to your upbringing and background. Were you to show the isle to someone with a different background and culture, he would more than likely see something similar – and yet different. The similarity lying in that most mythologies have fundamental similarities, the differences being in the interpretation of those fundamentals.'

'Like the Miller's treasure,' Diurnan said.

'Just so.'

They turned, as Maildun came up the deck and joined them. He looked across at the island and then back at the bard. 'Does the island hold anything for us?'

'Only a lesson and a mystery,' Paedur said, with a slight smile on his thin lips. 'I would not land on it though. Like the land of Tir na nOg, time flows differently on that isle.'

'It seems different though from all the other islands,' Maildun said shrewdly. 'It looks almost unreal.'

The bard nodded. 'It does not properly belong to this Shadow-land, but it is one of those places, like the Isle of Solitude, which are common to all the planes of existence. You can see the dolmen which links it with your world and all the other worlds.'

The *Avenger* had now moved in closer to the shore, and the island, with its four curiously ornate, low walls and the high chairs in the centre of each segment with their still, silent occupants, could clearly be seen.

'They look real enough,' Maildun said, gazing at the figure of the proud, regal man on the throne of gold, the matronly woman on the ornate seat of silver, the tall warrior on his bronze pedestal and the willowy young maid on a low stool of sparking crystal.

'Oh, they are real, but, as I've said, time flows differently for them. They are gods of the forces of Fire, Air, Earth and Water, but their bane is to be trapped in an eternal spiral of timelessness. Were you to watch them for an age, you might just see one of them moving but a fraction.'

'Is it possible to invoke them?' Germane asked. 'I once saw a shaman in the Gaulish Forests, a descendant of the Picts, I think, raise a storm spirit of wind and rain.'

'And you said the druid whose spell condemned us here raised the elements,' Diurnan said suddenly.

Paedur nodded. 'You, Germane, saw your shaman raise the *elementalis*, which is also what Archu's druid called down,' he added to the northerner. 'The *elementalis* are petty, minor spirits of the earth, air, fire and water. They lack the grandeur and power of the Major Forces, but, in their very pettiness, they can do much hurt and damage.'

'You said there was a lesson and a mystery here,' Maildun

reminded the bard. The captain leaned against the ship's rail, staring across at the island, idly wondering what the gold, silver, copper and crystal walls were worth and who had constructed them. He glanced over his shoulder at Paedur.

The bard smiled, his eyes lighting up with good humour. 'I think there would be many lessons to be learned from that isle,' he said almost wistfully. 'I would look at it and realise that the gods themselves are wont to move very slowly and deliberately on occasion.' He looked over at the captain and smiled again. 'Perhaps we should not expect too much of our gods, eh?'

Maildun frowned, but chose to ignore the barb. 'What is the mystery of the isle?' he asked slowly.

The *Avenger* had not passed the main bulk of the island and already a second isle could be seen behind it, lying quite close at hand.

Paedur stared back at the Isle of the Elements and said softly, 'I would wonder who – or what – had chained them there. And I would wonder what force – what god – the gods worship?'

The second island was small and almost completely circular, and seemed to be sheathed in silver. A high tower of shaped and polished stone stood on a slight hillock in the centre of the isle. The hillock was surrounded by water, which gushed upwards at regular intervals in tall spumes which almost topped the tower. Graceful bridges arched from the topmost windows of the tower down to the golden-sanded beach, which was the only part of the island that was still in its natural state and untouched by the metal.

'Surely that, like the last island, does not belong to this world,' Germane said in wonder, looking at the water fountaining upwards under the crystal bridges.

'Oh, it is,' Paedur nodded. 'I would think that it is the remainder of a pleasure garden of one of the satraps who ruled when this land was whole.'

'It looks unreal,' the navigator said softly.

'It's real enough,' the bard assured him. 'The pleasure gardens of *tLanteco Astis* were famed throughout the known world, and the vegetation which once adorned Babylon's crimson and ebon walls were but crude attempts to imitate them. The gardens were, in themselves, miniature worlds, with strange beasts and terrifying fauna. When this world sank, fragments of these gardens survived – which accounts somewhat for the many and varied lifeforms.'

147

They were now close enough to the island for the sparkling spray from the fountains to sprinkle across the *Avenger*. Diurnan ran his finger across the figurehead and tasted the droplets of water. 'It's pure,' he said in surprise.

'Is the island dangerous?' Maildun asked, staring in awe at the tall silver tower and the four crystal bridges.

Before Paedur could answer, the water round the tower rose in a seemingly solid sheet, erupting upwards with a great rush of sound, almost completely enveloping the conical cap. It surged for the space of a few long heartbeats, and then plummeted downwards again. The water crashed onto the silver pavement of the isle and splashed out across the sea and over the *Avenger* in a fine mist.

Almost as one, the crew keeled over where they stood, dropping to the deck in a death-like slumber. Paedur stood while Maildun, Germane and finally Diurnan slumped around him, and then, with his silver hook tingling with the residue of the magic, he too slipped into oblivion.

Consciousness returned to Maildun in slow stages, sound registering first, and then smell, followed by sensation. He knew he was lying on cold, smooth stone, and that he was at some height, for he could hear the wind whipping and cracking not far from him. He remained where he lay, unwilling to move and betray his alertness, exploring his surroundings as best he could.

He tested the air, and found it was sweet and sharp, full of sea-salt, but mingled with another, almost bitter odour, rather like wine which had soured in the skin. He felt the stone beneath his face; it was ice-cold and smooth against his cheek, and it too was tainted with the slightly bitter odour. He cracked his eyes open a fraction, peering through entangled lashes. But there was nothing before his face except a long stretch of polished floor – polished silver floor.

He knew where he was then: in the tower on the isle.

Maildun lay still, listening intently and, when he was satisfied he was alone, he raised his head and looked around. He was in a round chamber which, judging from its size, must be near the top of the tower. It was floored as he had suspected with silver, and the walls were covered with the same metal. As he rose shakily to his feet, countless red-bearded and red-haired warriors were reflected back at him from the walls and floor. The ceiling was quite low and he guessed that there must be another room above his head. There was but one window in the room and it

148

was close to the ceiling and slanted inwards, so that all he could see was an oblong of startlingly blue sky. He examined the floor carefully but, even with his experience of similar towers in Erin, could find no trace of the doorway he knew must be there.

Some time later the sun moved round and sent a long, slanting beam in through the window, lancing across the floor and bouncing off the polished walls, suffusing the chamber with light. Maildun began pacing then, conscious that time was passing, and he began to wonder what had happened to his ship and crew. He tried hard to remember, but he found he couldn't work out whether the bard had fallen before him or not. Surely the bard would not fall prey to the enchantment? But then, why hadn't the bard warned about the island? What if he didn't know?

Maildun continued pacing, and slowly the arc of sunlight moved round and the bar of light slid across the floor, crept up the smooth wall and then disappeared altogether. Night would fall soon, he knew. Germane had explained the swiftness with which night came down, but he still found it difficult to understand: in Erin there was a gradual twilight and then night crept slowly in, but in this world it was day and then night! He snapped his fingers, and then shivered; the sound seemed immeasurably lonely in this tiny room. He knelt on the floor then and tried to pray, but the phrases that the brown-robed father-confessor had taught him as a child seemed shallow and meaningless now: it was easy to believe there was no Jesus Christ on this world. He crossed himself quickly then: that was blasphemy.

Outside night fell, and the sky lit up again with the broad sheets and swirls of light that were the night stars. Maildun stood beneath his window and stared upwards, but the dim, distant and completely alien stars made him feel all the more alone. He continued pacing the floor, brooding on what had taken him to this world, wondering whether he would ever find his father's murderers. Already that intense burning and bile-like taste for revenge was gone. It was difficult to contemplate revenge, when all he was concerned about now was to return to Erin. His lust for vengeance had lost him two brothers and a lot of his crew, his friends, and he knew, deep in his heart, he knew, that if he ever sighted the rugged Cliffs of Moher again, Ruarc would not stand with him. He was tired now, tired of it all . . .

When he awoke the room was ablaze with light, and he cried out unconsciously, one hand attempting to shield his eyes. When his heart had settled and the vague phantoms which had haunted

149

his sleep had disappeared, he found he was staring at a young woman, of no more than ten and seven years, standing above a square opening in the floor. She held high a tall, flaming taper, and the shadows danced and flickered around the room, vying with the reflected light. Maildun rose slowly, suddenly ashamed of his startled outburst. In the torchlight he could see that the young woman was very pale – indeed, almost deathly so, although that might have been a trick of the light, and that her eyes were unnaturally large. She was clad in a simple brown homespun, shapeless and soiled with what looked like dried blood around the shoulders.

She stepped back from the opening in the floor and indicated that he was to go down. The light from the opening streamed upwards, turning her face into a mask, rendering it hideous.

Maildun walked the few steps to the opening and looked down. Beneath him a room blazed with countless burning candles, each one as thick as his arm, and the stench of burning fat and tallow that wafted upwards was almost palatable. He glanced across at the young woman, and once again she moved the torch in her hand, indicating that he was to go down. With a muttered prayer, he descended.

The room was slightly larger than the one he had occupied, and it too was sheathed with silver: floor, walls and ceiling, which served to magnify and reflect the light. The fat candles were set into niches in the walls and arranged in little clumps on the floor that he fancied the bard, or perhaps Germane, might be able to decipher, for they had the appearance of magic and the arcane about them.

He looked round the room, and then turned back to look up at his guide, but she was gone, and so was the ladder and the opening he had climbed down through. Since he hadn't heard her come down, he realised she must have stayed behind and pulled the ladder up after her.

Dismissing her for the moment, he walked round the room. The first things he noticed were four black doors, each one taller than a man, set into the walls. Round towers of this sort usually had only one door . . . and then he remembered the four crystal bridges that connected the tower to the beach: this must be part of them. He tried each door in turn, but they were locked and he could find no trace of any bolt or handle on his side. The doors were shaped from no material he knew. It was certainly not wood and it did not seem to be metal, but when he examined them closely he thought that they might have been slate or even coal –

if that were possible. He ran his broad hands down one; it was smooth and seemed almost oily to the touch. And then he remembered that, although there had seemed to be no opening in the floor above, the young girl had somehow managed to lock herself in, which meant that there had been a mechanism, only he had not found it. And might there not also be a similar hidden lock on this door?

He was on his knees, probing the base of the black door, when he heard a click, and saw reflected on the black surface that the door behind him was beginning to open . . .

He was moving almost before he realised it. He practically threw himself across the chamber towards the opening door. He stumbled through one of the arrangements of candles on the floor, burning his legs and slipping on the pooling grease. His momentum broken, he staggered through another design and then fell forward, sliding across the floor to come to a stop beside a pair of tiny feet in ornate metallic sandals.

Maildun looked up, past a silver-touched gown and into the amused gaze of the most beautiful woman he had ever seen in his life. One of the De Danann, the thought formed in his head, when he realised that she was speaking.

'Greetings, Maildun, son of Oilill Agach of the land of Erin. You honour my hearth.' Her voice was soft and gentle, a hint of an untraceable accent in it. 'Will you not rise?' She extended a small hand, with long, slender fingers, tipped with vermilion-painted nails. Maildun touched the fingers, expecting to find them cold, like stone, but instead they were warm and flesh. He rose to his feet, suddenly conscious of his soiled, salt-encrusted jerkin, fraying sandals and unkempt hair and beard.

He managed a stiff bow. 'I am your servant,' he said huskily, watching the woman while trying not to appear too obvious about it.

She was smaller than he had first thought, coming barely to his mid-chest. The first thing he noticed was her hair: a long and luxurious black mane that flowed down her back like a portion of the night. Two small braids looped above her ears, and these had been set with seed-pearls that winked like stars. Her face was almost triangular, coming down to a small, pointed chin that accentuated her high cheekbones and slightly slanted eyes. Her eyes were blue, a sharp, hard colour, like polished sapphires, and their very hardness and coldness took much from the beauty of her face.

She was clad in a shimmering gown of silver-tinged cloth that began low on her breasts and fell to her feet in graceful folds. Her arms were bare, but were wrapped around with finely-wrought torcs and wristlets.

Finally conscious that she was looking at him in some amusement, he bowed again to hide his sudden colouring, and then managed to stammer, 'I imagine you to be one of the *Sidhe*, like the maid, Niamh Golden-Hair, who took Oisin to the Land of the Ever Young.'

She shook her head gracefully, her thick black hair rustling together in secret whispers. 'I do not know this Niamh Golden-Hair, nor this Oisin. The Land of the Ever Young I am familiar with.' She paused, while she looked slowly and deliberately round the chamber, surveying the damage he had caused in his wild charge across the room, and then she turned back to Maildun. 'Was this Niamh Golden-Hair very beautiful?'

'She was reckoned to be the most beautiful woman in all the world, but . . .'

'But?' she pressed.

'But I do not think that there could be anyone more beautiful than you,' he said impulsively.

She nodded serenely and brushed past him, and then he wrinkled his nose, for, although she was perfumed, there was a bitter, acid-like stink about her.

'What is your name?' he asked.

The small woman turned, and her chilling eyes widened. 'I am called Leucosia in the world of men. I am the last of the Sirens.'

CHAPTER SEVENTEEN

'You say that almost as if you expect me to know you,' Maildun said slowly, as the small woman turned away from him. He saw her watching him in the reflection of the black door before her, and he saw her cold blue eyes contract to pinpoints before she turned to face him again. When he looked into her face, he found she was smiling.

'What?' she said in mock surprise, 'you have not heard of the Sirens. Truly?' she persisted when he shook his head. 'You do not know me, nor my sisters, Ligeia and Parthenope?'

'I don't know you, nor your sisters. Your names have a foreign touch to them though, and yet they are not strange enough to belong to this world.'

Leucosia shook her head and laughed, her teeth showing sharp and yellow-white in the candle light. 'No, I am not of this world; my world and yours are the same, but it is time that separates us. When I knew your homeland,' she added almost wistfully, 'it was called the *Insula Occidentalis*; the Western Isle at the Edge of the World.'

'You must be old then,' Maildun said carefully.

Leucosia nodded absently, looking round at the upset candles and grease smears on the polished silver floor. 'I am old,' she said finally.

'Older than the bard?' Maildun wondered softly.

The Siren looked up sharply, and the candle light took her eyes and faceted them into jewels. 'A bard?' she repeated quickly.

'A bard,' Maildun said, rubbing his sandaled foot in the wax on the floor, 'though not like the druids and ollavs of my own land. A man taller than I, and thin, with a long, sallow face and fine, dark hair. His eyes are mirrors and . . .'

'And there is a hook in place of his left hand,' Leucosia said coldly. 'Aye, I know your bard – Phemius.'

Maildun shook his head. 'He is called Paedur.'

Leucosia waved her hand. 'Names change, and all men change, all but that one. If he sails with you, beware him.'

'He has been a friend to me,' Maildun said quickly, 'he has guided us through this Shadowland, and with his help we will return to Erin.'

The Siren bent over gracefully and began to straighten the candles Maildun had knocked over. She looked up at him once and her smile was bitter, and aged her face, giving it an almost hawk-like appearance. 'He is a seeker of death,' she said. 'Immortal like myself, he seeks to end his life. Death follows him, but only touches those around him. My sisters and I once thought of him as Hades, the Lord of the Dead, or perhaps one of his sons; but he is no god.'

'And you?' Maildun asked. 'What are you?'

Leucosia straightened slowly, her gown hissing like steaming water. 'I am . . . what I am. A woman, and lonely.' She turned away from him and looked at the black door, and then touched it with her tiny hands, and immediately the image of the red-haired warrior shivered and vanished and was replaced by the picture of a longship on a stormy sea. 'Look; your coming was foretold, you were destined for me, Maildun, son of Oilill Agach.'

Maildun shook his head. 'That is impossible; I am seeking my father's murderers, I must sail on.'

The Siren's expression changed and hardened. 'This is what will happen if you sail on,' she said, and her painted nails rapped against the black door. The image changed, twisting and shifting, and now the longship rode a violent sea, with huge waves washing in over the mast. Tiny, ant-like figures were swept along the decks and disappeared into the rolling waves. The image shifted again, running with colours like oil on water, and now it showed a small, rocky isle with the wreck of the *Avenger* strewn along its beach. She tapped the door again and the colours flowed and disappeared. 'You need not be on that ship,' she said softly, 'you should stay here with me.'

'I am sailing with my crew on my ship, and you cannot stop me.'

She laughed then, a high, thin, almost musical laugh, – that lost its beauty somewhere and ended in a bird-like cackle. Maildun crossed the floor in three quick strides, gripped her wrists in his calloused hands and swung her round to face him. Her wrists were so small that his fingers overlapped and, for a moment, he felt as if he were holding a bird: small, delicate and fragile.

Leucosia looked up at him, and her hard blue eyes seemed almost vague and distant. 'You can have me if you wish,' she

154

said, in a voice that was little more than a whisper. 'I am giving myself to you.'

'I do not want you,' Maildun snapped, pushing her away from him, back against the door.

'Be not so hasty,' the Siren said, leaning back against the door and pushing the shimmering gown down to her waist. Against the black doorway the paleness of her skin was startling, and her nipples stood out against her tiny breasts like polished stones.

Maildun looked at her, and then he laughed slowly and deliberately. 'I am used to taking my pleasure with women,' he said, 'and not with girls.' He turned his back on her and kicked his way through a pattern of candles.

Her scream stopped him in his tracks. It began as a woman's cry of rage but ended on a different – unhuman – note. Reflected in the doorway in front of him, Maildun saw Leucosia's form change and warp, saw her hunch down as her legs and arms seemed drawn into her. Her features shifted and sharpened and, as he turned round, the creature that had been Leucosia rose up on huge, leathery wings that almost completely filled the room.

He staggered back as the wings buffeted him and, as the candle flames were tugged inwards before finally dying, he caught a glimpse of the Siren, the half-human, half-bird creature that had once haunted the coasts of ancient Greece. As the room plummeted into darkness, Maildun knew with an almost sickening certainty that this creature – and stories of the Morrigan, the Crow Goddess of Death of his own race, came back with sudden clarity – this creature would slay and eat him.

Leathery wings struck across his shoulders, sending him down to the greasy floor. He slid along the polished stones and heard the creature's pointed beak strike the stones. He continued rolling until he struck against the curve of the wall, with claws clicking and scratching in his wake.

The acid-bitter stench was stronger, and now he could identify it as the sour stench of a bird's nest that has been fouled often. He edged along the floor. In the absolute darkness he could see nothing, but he was unsure how strong the Siren's night sight was. His fingers touched the fat tube of a candle. As a weapon it was almost useless; he would have to ram it down her throat or plunge it into her eyes to be effective.

Claws clacked on the floor, and the leathery wings scraped harshly off the walls. In the brief instant he had seen them, the wings had seemed to resemble bat's wings, although these had a hooked spur at the tip of the longest 'finger'. If they were like a bat's, they might not be very powerful, and, if he could somehow manoeuvre himself round behind her, he might be able to throw himself . . .

Air parted and a claw struck, not a hand-span from his face, crushing a pile of candles to pulp. Maildun pushed himself to his feet, striking out with the candle in his hand, using it like a knife. It sank into soft, foul-smelling plumage and the creature screamed with high-pitched rage. Its huge wings beat off the walls, and the inrush of air drew Maildun forward and down. Claws struck at him in insensate fury, but by some miracle managed to miss him, sometimes by no more than a finger's width. He twisted beneath the Siren's wing, and came up behind the creature. He threw himself up and onto the bird-woman, one hand digging into her matted fur, the other attempting to draw back her small head. The Siren's wings closed together, meeting just above and behind his head in a sharp clap of sound. The blow stunned Maildun and he slid off her back into a pool of tacky beeswax.

Only a handful of heartbeats could have passed while he remained unconscious, and when he opened his eyes he found the Siren standing over him, her hooked and taloned claws pressing down onto his shoulders, her great wings rising and falling slowly. He saw her raise her head, saw the huge pointed beak preparing to descend . . . and in that instant wondered how he could see!

The Siren screamed, the cry more womanish than bird-like this time, and Maildun briefly caught the stench of burnt plumage and scorched flesh, before the fine black feathers about her head curled and burst into flame. Leucosia reared up and Maildun used the opportunity to thrust himself upwards also, toppling her off him. Her huge wings beat and her flailing claws caught him across the chest, lancing pain through his entire body. He staggered against the wall, fire and ice in his lungs with every breath he took and it was then that he saw the square opening in the ceiling and the pale, large-eyed face of the young girl who had led him down. She was kneeling above the opening, her torch poised to thrust again at the Siren.

Leucosia staggered around the circular room, her screams almost continuous now, as the fire ate through the flesh of her face and began to work downwards into the fur on her breast. Her thrashing wings only served to fan the flames, drawing them in and onto herself. She crashed blindly around the room, her claws striking out right and left as if she sought to take Maildun

156

with her into death. He threw himself to one side as the tip of her leathery wing scraped along the wall towards him, and crashed to the floor. The pain in his cracked ribs made him want to vomit, and startling spots of colour danced before his eyes. A shouted warning sent him rolling away as Leucosia lumbered past, and when he looked up he saw the small, gilded ladder being carefully lowered down rung by rung. He waited until the Siren, now a mass of flame, passed him again and then he leaped for it. His hooked fingers caught the bottom rung, ripping the ladder from the young girl's grasp, dragging it clattering to the silver floor. The blow to his chest almost robbed him of consciousness but, with one hand pressed close to his chest, he clawed his way upwards towards the opening.

In her pain, the Siren must have heard the crash of the falling ladder, and in a final attempt she flung herself across the room towards the sound. She missed it the first time, but her crisping wings touched one of the spars and the hook at its tip clung to it. Leucosia turned towards the ladder and began to transform into her human shape.

A small hand gripped Maildun's fingers and attempted to haul him up. The young woman's face before him shifted and changed in the firelight from below, and Maildun briefly imagined her to be someone he once knew. He paused on the topmost rung, shaking his head stupidly, trying to put a name to the face, only dimly aware of the throbbing in his chest and the ice-fire in his lungs. He saw the young woman's face moving, saw her mouth working, but all he could hear was the cracking of the fire below and the throbbing of his heart. She struck him across the face then, almost rocking him back down into the room below, but the pain and sudden vertigo snapped him back to reality.

He hauled himself up the last step and over the lip, into the room which had previously been his prison. The young girl went to drop the stone back into place, but Maildun touched her hand lightly and then looked down.

Leucosia had regained her human form, but not completely, for she still retained her great leathery wings. She climbed the ladder slowly, flames wreathing around her like serpents, tongues of flame darting upwards, singeing his curling hair, crisping his beard. For a single moment she was beautiful; it was as if the fire which had burned her bird-like body had not touched her human form, and was only now beginning to take hold. She screamed then, and vomited a streamer of flame. Maildun dropped the stone into place, and then tried not to listen

157

to the pounding and the screams which penetrated the silvered stones. They continued on for far longer than they should have done.

He looked across at the young girl now sitting huddled to one side of the room, the torch with which she had burnt the Siren still clutched in her hand like a sword.

Maildun moved slowly and painfully across the floor towards her, suddenly feeling all the cuts, bruises and burns, and the pain in his ribs making him nauseous. He gently prised the torch from her frozen fingers and then held it high, and looked at her properly.

When he looked into her large eyes he suddenly knew who she reminded him of, and he had to blink away the image which rose into his mind. For in that instant he had seen the face of his mother overlying that of this young girl. But the only similarity had been in their eyes, which were the same shade and carried the same expression, the same look of fear and innocence . . . and madness.

CHAPTER EIGHTEEN

Maildun awoke suddenly with the nightmare image of the bird-woman fresh behind his eyes. Without moving, he attempted to assess his situation. The silver-walled room was bright, heralding daybreak, and tendrils of white cloud drifted across the window. He was lying propped up against the wall directly across from the young woman who had saved him.

He sat up then, and winced in agony, the sudden movement tearing into his chest, and his sharp intake of breath burning through his lungs with an even colder pain. The young woman moved and murmured in her sleep, and Maildun took the opportunity to examine her in the wan, reflected light.

She could not have been called pretty and her too-pale skin, smoke-grey in the pale light, gave her a deathly appearance. There were bruises on her arms and legs, and her rough dress, which had hiked to above her knees, revealed that she was shockingly thin.

She opened her eyes.

They were as he remembered them, huge and dark, with neither expression nor intelligence in them. She looked at him for a score of heartbeats and then she smiled, exposing a row of tiny, perfectly white teeth – which had been filed to points. Something in his expression must have warned her, for she closed her mouth and, childlike, clapped both hands across it.

Maildun rose stiffly, his hand clasped to his side, taking care not to breathe deeply, and went and knelt by her side. He touched her hands, gently pulling them from her mouth, and then he smiled. Hesitantly, she smiled also, and he nodded. She spoke, mouthing words slowly and distinctly, but they were in a language he had never heard before, and the curious sounds sent a shiver tracing its way down his spine.

'Let's see about getting out of here,' he said slowly, not sure whether he was speaking to reassure the young woman or himself. 'How do you open this?' he asked, touching the stone in the floor.

Her dark eyes, a curious mixture of green and brown, flared in fear, and she shook her head from side to side, speaking rapidly in her musical tongue.

'I must,' Maildun said quietly. 'She is gone, gone, do you understand? The fire took her.' He pointed to the burnt-out torch that lay on the silver flagstones.

She continued shaking her head, but she slowly edged towards the opening, looking first to the torch, and once reaching out to touch Maildun's singed hair and beard. And then she chuckled, the sound shocking the young man with its very innocence and childishness. She reached past him and touched the stone twice, once at the topmost, left-hand edge and once at the bottom. She then pressed on its opposite side with the flat of her hand and it swivelled upwards. The young woman looked down into the room below – and fell back screaming!

Maildun grabbed the torch and swung it down through the opening at the sudden shape he saw there. Metal glittered and the torch snapped in two, and, in that moment, Maildun found himself looking down into the face of the bard.

Maildun watched as the island slipped down into the sea behind them, and breathed a sigh of relief. He touched his ribs, feeling the welts where the bard had worked his magic, but the pain was gone and his lung had been healed.

But he had changed; he stared into the star-bright water, and tried to work out how and why. The how was easy enough – any Christian youth exposed to this cursed world and its damned inhabitants and foul sorceries could not fail to change. He smiled wryly, remembering how he had thrilled to the tales of the ancients, of the coming of the various races from across the seas, and of how they had fought monsters, and the demon Fomors, to take the bright green land of Banba. A tale was a fine thing, but he found the reality somewhat different; he would rather listen to a tale than actually live one.

Why he had changed was a different matter. He had already endured enough in this Shadowland, seen much, heard more, certainly enough to change his mind, his opinions, and thoughts; but why should a brief stay – he had been told it had been a day and a night – in the Siren's tower change him so quickly? Surely it had not been the thought of death: that held no fears for him; indeed, he expected to die in battle, he had been trained for it from youth, and yet . . .

Was it that the Siren would have eaten him?

It was strange, but it was that thought above all others which

160

repulsed him, sent some part of his mind screaming. And yet his forefathers had taken a warrior's head in battle, and he had heard tales of human flesh-eaters before.

Was it that it was easy to talk of death and boast of meeting it bravely, and yet, when one faced death – death in the shape of a pointed beak and claws – that the reality was different? He shivered suddenly, dismissing the thought; better to leave such brooding to Germane or Paedur. He pulled his cloak tighter around his shoulders and stared into the foaming water.

The circular room was a shambles. Maildun tried to recall what it had looked like the previous night, when he had first come down the gilded ladder into its candlelit brightness. Everything was blackened now, with oily and greasy smears, and the air was foul. The silvered walls were gouged and in two places the actual stones had been almost ripped from the wall. The floor was a filthy mess of candle-wax, feathers and clumps of charred rag. But it wasn't until he looked at them closely that he realised that these rags were actually part of a body. He gagged and pushed his way to the open door, and then recoiled into Diurnan's arms, for, still clinging to the door frame, was Leucosia's severed hand. It had been torn off at the wrist and the stump seared and twisted into a claw with the heat, and Maildun had the brief nightmare image of the creature tearing at herself in her agony like any trapped animal.

Diurnan knocked the piece of flesh aside and thrust Maildun out through the doorway with the warning, 'Careful now, that crystal's wet and treacherous.'

The crystal bridge arched gracefully out over the miniature lake of fresh water, down to the beach. With the sunlight glistening off the water, it looked ethereal and insubstantial, but Maildun had no eyes for it, all he could see was the tall-masted outline of the *Avenger* rocking in the clear blue water below. He could see figures moving on the deck and faintly heard the cheers that rose up when he appeared.

He turned back to Diurnan. 'There is a girl . . .'

The northerner nodded. 'Aye, Germane is getting her.'

'She is mad,' Maildun said quickly, unaware that at that moment he looked quite mad himself. 'She speaks a strange tongue. She was a servant of the Siren bird-woman and saved me when . . .'

'Aye,' Diurnan nodded sympathetically, and almost casually struck Maildun a glancing blow with the haft of his battleaxe

161

across the back of his skull. The young man slumped noiselessly into the northerner's arms.

Germane, meanwhile, had climbed slowly up the ladder at the bard's insistence. 'The girl fears me,' he said softly. 'Your looks and size should reassure her.'

She screamed when the navigator's head appeared and shouted at him in her own language. He stopped and frowned and then glanced down at the bard. 'That language is familiar, very familiar . . . I wonder where she's from.'

'Just get her down,' Paedur said, slipping his hook into a fold in his cloak, lest he startle the girl again. He heard her cry out and found that he too could distinguish something familiar in her tongue.

He stood in the centre of the room listening to Germane speak reassuringly to her. There was something about this isle, some-thing about the smell, in particular, which brought back memories . . . but he was old, and his memories were many, and the particular one he was seeking remained elusive. He rubbed his booted foot in the candle grease and wondered what manner of creature Maildun had fought here. The hand on the door was human, but that proved nothing, and the candles seemed to indicate some form of arcane ceremony; there were feathers also; might that mean that birds had been sacrificed . . .?

The bard stepped back into the shadows while Germane coaxed the girl down the ladder and into the room. She was shivering with fright, her hands clasped before her in an attitude of prayer, and her lips were drawn back over her teeth. He looked again: her teeth had been filed into points in such a manner than the top set fitted nearly into the bottom.

Once down into the room, the young woman stopped and looked around uncertainly, and something like satisfaction seemed to creep into her face as she surveyed the destruction. Then she caught sight of the bard's tall, cloak-wrapped shape in the shadows and she screamed, and tried to free herself from Germane's arms. Paedur stepped into the light, slipping his hook free, allowing it to take and hold her attention long enough for him to touch her forehead and temples with the thumb and index finger of his right hand. Her eyes rolled in her head and she dropped into Germane's arms.

'Do your wounds trouble you?'

The bard's soft voice startled Maildun, jerking him from his reverie. Unconsciously, he touched his ribs. 'No . . . no, they're fine; there's no pain.'

The bard nodded silently. He was wrapped in his long black and purple cloak of fine hair, with the cowl pulled up over his head, leaving his face all but invisible.

'Do you want to tell me what happened?' he asked finally, when Maildun made no move to speak.

'Do I have to?'

'Of course not. If you would rather leave it until another time, if it is painful for you . . .' The bard straightened, but the captain touched his cloak, his fingers tingling.

'No, stay. I don't think there is anyone else who will understand or be able to answer my questions.'

'I will do what I can', Paedur said quietly, although Maildun thought he detected a note of caution in his voice.

'There was a woman on the isle,' the captain said softly, his voice little more than a whisper, 'a beautiful, beautiful woman; I would have said that she was one of the *Sidhe* folk.'

'Did she have a name?'

'She was called Leucosia . . .' Maildun said, and saw the bard stiffen, 'you know . . . knew her?'

'I knew someone of that name once,' Paedur said, 'but that was a long, long time ago . . .'

'She said she was old, old and immortal. She said that she was a Siren . . . and that she once knew a bard called Phemius.'

In the long silence that followed, the lapping of the water against the side of the *Avenger* seemed unnaturally loud, and the creak of the leather sail was clearly audible above the heartbeat of the sea. Eventually Paedur nodded, the movement barely visible in the fullness of his cowl.

'I knew a Leucosia once,' he said, 'a Siren as you say. A woman, but having the appearance of a young girl barely having achieved maturity. She was beautiful, very beautiful. I loved her in my own fashion, and I thought she loved me in return.' There was a pause and then the bard's voice hardened and took on a note of bitterness. 'I was old even then, but I had no longing for death at that time. I even contemplated taking a woman to wife.' He shook his head, and the captain could see the starlight dancing in the mirror of his eyes, as Paedur stared up into the heavens. 'She was a Siren, one of the last of a race that has long since passed into myth; a hybrid of woman and bird, having the lusts of one and the appetite of the other. She and her sisters would sing sailors to their doom, luring them onto rocks with their voices which were very beautiful. I thought her dead, long dead.' He laughed. 'Indeed, I didn't think of her at all.' And then

163

he shook his head. 'No, that isn't true, I thought of her when I grew tired and lonely. I thought her surely dead and did not mourn for her. But why, now that I know she is truly dead, why do I now feel sorrow?'

'Perhaps because of your love for her?' Maildun suggested.

'Human,' the bard said harshly. 'There are few emotions left to me now; I wasted them in my youth, what little I had left, that is, for in truth, I paid for my immortality with that part of man which makes him human: his emotions.'

'But you feel the pain of her loss.'

'Aye, and that is curious. Perhaps this Shadowland will bring me death after all.'

'The Siren said that death followed you, but left you untouched and took all around you.'

'The Siren did not lie.'

'She showed me an image too, of a ship wrecked in a storm and cast up on a beach, with all hands dead.'

'She showed you a possible future, which can differ greatly from the actual future.'

'I've found I do not want death,' Maildun said softly.

'Few men do.'

'I've found I do not want to bring death, either.'

'Some men labour a lifetime until they reach that conclusion.'

'I've also found I've no wish to continue on my quest for vengeance. Can we now return to Erin?'

'I'm afraid that is not possible; you know it is more than just a matter of retracing our steps. We can only go forward, encircle this Shadowland, and arrive at the point which is directly opposite that by which we entered.'

'How did she, Leucosia, come to be here? Even you did not know of her existence here.'

'I don't know.' The bard shook his head slowly, glancing back in the direction of the island.

'Are you not curious?' Maildun wondered.

'Some things it is better not knowing.' Paedur straightened. 'I came to talk to you, and I have done most of the talking again. It is a sure sign of an old man. I will leave you; you should try and rest, there is a long way to go still.'

'One last question, if I may. Who was Phemius?'

Paedur turned to look at him, and Maildun could only see the points of light that were his eyes, all else was in shadow. Even though he knew him, it was hard not to shudder in his presence. 'Phemius was Odysseus – whom men call Ulysses – bard.'

'Leucosia said she knew a bard called Phemius . . .'

The bard turned to look at him. 'Yes . . . ?'

'Were you Phemius?'

'Phemius had two hands,' Paedur said, turning away, his hook shining like a half-moon in the night.

The girl, who had been taken to the captain's cabin, did not reappear on deck until close to noon the following day. As if to herald her appearance, the lookout called out the presence of yet another isle.

She stood by the door, blinking in the sunlight, the pallor of her skin all the more pronounced now, her eyes seeming even more luminous. She clutched the doorframe with white-knuckled fingers, and her eyes darted to and fro like an animal seeking escape.

She was clad in some of Germane's clothes, he being the smallest of the crew, but even these were too big and hung loosely on her, giving her the appearance of a small boy dressed in his older brother's cast-offs.

The navigator saw her first, and moved quickly down the deck towards her. She smiled shyly when she saw him, but her filed and pointed teeth turned her face into a demon's mask. Germane bowed slightly, smoothly covering the shock and revulsion he knew must be visible on his face. He stood aside and indicated that she might walk before him towards the small group gathered in the stern of the ship. But her large eyes merely continued to regard him dully and without understanding. He took her arm then and led her, unresisting, towards Maildun, Diurnan and the bard.

'I think she is witless,' Germane said softly as they joined the small group.

Maildun nodded. 'I thought so.' He looked the girl straight in the face and smiled. He spoke slowly and distinctly. 'I would like to thank you for saving my life . . .' There was no reaction and he shook his head. 'She doesn't understand.' He glanced across at Paedur. 'Perhaps you could . . . ?'

The bard nodded briefly, but first he pulled off his cloak and wrapped it in a bundle around his hook. His black leather jerkin and leggings, like his furred cloak, seemed to absorb the light. With his hook concealed, he stepped in front of the girl. She looked at him incuriously, and then her eyes widened into an expression of absolute terror.

Paedur spoke to her then, using a score of different languages,

165

some of which seemed vaguely familiar to Germane, who was widely travelled, some of which were totally alien and utterly unhuman. But the girl only stared at him, her lips moving soundlessly.

'But she speaks,' Maildun said, 'she spoke to me, cried out a warning . . .'

'I think its you, Paedur,' Diurnan said carefully.

The bard nodded. 'I know; I seem to terrify her.'

'Why?' Maildun wondered.

'She might mistake me for someone,' he said, watching her carefully.

'Or something,' Germane added.

'Leucosia said she once thought that you were Hades,' Maildun said quietly. 'Might not this girl think you a creature from that mythology?'

'I am beginning to think that she is not from the Siren's world, nor of the world of men.'

'But she is human,' Germane protested. 'Do not dismiss her because she is different. I've travelled most of the known world; I know how people differ in their clothing, habits and colouring. Do not dismiss her because of her pallor or her teeth; I know of some tribes of the Southlands who do the same.'

'Navigator,' the bard said with a smile, 'you have sailed the seas of your world. I have sailed the seas of many worlds and times; there is little you can teach me of the races of man. She is not of the world of men. Look closely at her – her skin has been untouched by the sun; already it begins to burn and she has only been exposed for these few heartbeats. Look at her eyes, large, round, with no white and an enormous pupil, and see how she squints in the daylight, even though the sun is behind her. Her stature is small, but that in itself is not unusual. However, look at her teeth: made for flesh, fresh meat, not fruit and vegetables. She is not a creature of the earth . . . but,' he added slowly, 'she may be a creature from the earth.' He looked around. 'Do any of you know the Old Gaelic tongue? I would rather not speak to her again.'

'My foster-brother . . .' Maildun said quickly.

'Bring him here.'

As Diurnan moved away to find Ruarc, the bard continued, 'I think she is a creature of the barrows, a woman of your own lands, aye, but one of the race the Tuatha De Danann bred for their own uses when they returned to the secret places, the earthen caverns, when they left the world of men.' He looked up

166

as Diurnan returned with Ruarc. 'Speak to her in the Old Tongue of your race. Ask her name and her race.'

Ruarc looked at the young woman for a moment and then framed the questions in the ancient tongue of Erin. 'Who are you?'

'My name was Rathnait in the world of men,' she answered hesitantly, 'Rathne in the realm of the Shining Folk, and I had no name in the tower of the bird-witch.'

'You hailed from Erin?'

'I know of no land of that name,' she answered. 'My world was Banba, and my people were the People of the Goddess.'

'How did you come to be here in this world?'

'The Tuatha De Danann left the fields of men and retreated to the hidden fields. They took their most loyal servants with them, but for them to survive in the Great Earth Place, they changed them – into something less than human. I was once beautiful,' she said, her voice rising, 'and they turned me into this . . .' Her teeth clicked and locked together. 'And because they could not feed us, they sent us forth into the world of men each evening to feed.'

Ruarc took a deep breath, although he already had some indication of the answer to his next question. 'And what did you hunt?' he whispered.

Rathnait stared at him coldly, her eyes without expression, her voice, when she spoke, without inflection. 'Men called us *banshee*, and our prey was men.'

CHAPTER NINETEEN

There were voices on the wind.

At first there was just a vague murmuring, almost indistinguishable from the eternal sound of the sea, but as the *Avenger* approached the isle, the murmuring broke up into sounds and snatches of conversations, some distinguishable, others totally incomprehensible.

The island was small and dark, little more than a barren clump of stone, covered with what seemed like burnt and dead vegetation. However, as the wind and tide carried them closer, and the sounds of the voices became clearer, the watchers could see that the vegetation seemed to be shifting and moving. And, while it was composed almost entirely of a uniform dun colour, there were some speckles and splashes of colour shot through it, like too-bright flowers on dead grass.

It was Germane, with his sharp eyes, who made out what the vegetation was. 'They're birds; the island is covered with birds,' he said in wonder.

'But who speaks?' Diurnan wondered. 'I can see no one . . .'

'Neither can I,' the navigator said slowly, 'and yet the island is so small . . .' His voice trailed away as he squinted across the glittering waves towards the isle. 'There are only the birds,' he said in a whisper.

As the tide changed and the *Avenger* drifted in closer to the shore, Maildun, mindful of their earlier encounter with the birds that had attacked them, had Diurnan set the men to the oars in case they had to break free of the tide's pull.

Maildun watched the island, with its shifting carpet of feathers and claws, with a feeling of revulsion deep in his stomach; he doubted if he would ever be able to look at any winged creature again without feeling sick. At any moment he expected to see Leucosia rise up from amongst the birds, her leathery, almost translucent wings spread . . . He shook his head; the image of the Siren would haunt him to the end of his days.

'Are they birds, real birds?' he asked aloud, as the bard's long, thin shadow fell across him.

'Nothing is real in the Shadowlands,' Paedur said, leaning across the rail, and staring out towards the island.

'Are they really talking then?' Maildun persisted irritably.

'What do you hear?'

'I hear speech.'

'Recognisable speech?'

Maildun cocked his head, listening. 'Well . . . almost.'

'Almost, but not quite.' The bard smiled with something approaching good humour. 'And yet, if you were to listen long enough, you would swear by the White Christ that you heard the voices of your loved ones, your step father, your brothers. And if you were to ask any of the crew what they heard, then they would tell you the same, for they would have all heard the call, the cries, the pleadings, the laughter and the promises.'

'Why?' Maildun murmured.

'The Siren and her sisters shipwrecked crews using the same method,' Paedur said. 'There were few ships that escaped their attentions. Tell me,' he said suddenly, 'what would have happened if you had come upon this isle by night, or in a fog, and heard the voices of those you had left behind in Erin calling out to you?'

'We would have put into shore, I suppose,' Maildun said.

The bard nodded. 'Those birds are carnivorous.'

The captain started. 'But we're drifting in towards the isle!'

The bard held up his hand. 'Like the Sirens, they are not true birds; unlike the Sirens, their powers of flight are extremely limited. We can sail quite close to the beach without any real danger. However, if I might suggest that you station some men along the deck with spears and shields, in case any of the creature should prove venturesome. If they do, you might eat fowl this evening.'

Maildun hawked and spat into the sea. 'I doubt if I'll ever touch bird-flesh again.'

Paedur smiled again. 'I cannot say I blame you.'

However, the *Avenger* sailed around the Bird Isle without encountering any difficulties, although several of the crew would not take the bard or Maildun's word that there was nothing on the island except the creatures. The men swore they had heard the voices of their loved ones amongst all the others. Diurnan offered a currach to anyone who wanted to go ashore – but he also pointed out that the *Avenger* would not remain to pick them up. No one volunteered to set foot on the island.

169

Ruarc stood with Rathne in the stern of the ship as the evening drew in, and the ever-changing stars took up their positions in the eastern sky.

'My mistress often spoke to me of the stars,' Rathne said in the Old Tongue, the High Speech of the Tuatha De Danann sounding as soft and as liquid as the sea.

'I don't recognise any of these stars,' Ruarc said quietly, 'although the bard did name them for me. He gave them strange and warlike names, all except that one' – he pointed to the Pole Star – 'and that one I know.'

'The North Star,' Rathne said.

Ruarc nodded. 'It seems some things never change.'

'My mistress often told me stories of the stars,' the girl-woman said, 'she told me the tales of her gods and heroes, and how they came to be enshrined in the stars.' She looked back at Ruarc, her face grown powdery and indistinct in the deepening twilight. 'Tell me, do the Old Gods still hold sway in Banba?'

Ruarc shook his head. 'Those days are long gone. Some three hundred years ago Patrick, the son of a Roman and a follower of the Lord Jesus Christ, brought the New Faith to Erin.'

Rathne shook her head. 'So many changes; Banba is now Erin, and this Jesus Christ – such a strange name – is he a warrior or a king?'

The young man smiled and shook his head. 'No . . . well, not quite. You worshipped Angus Og, Morrigan, Danu and the Dagda?'

Rathne nodded. 'Aye, and more; most hailed from the De Danann people.'

'Well, much as you worshipped them, so too do we worship the Christ.'

'He is a warrior?' Rathne asked again.

Ruarc shook his head. 'He did not believe in violence.'

The *banshee* looked disbelieving. 'He is a magician then?'

'He had great powers, but I would not call Him a magician.'

'A craftsman?'

'His father was a worker in wood; I suppose He would have had some skill and training in that, but I don't know,' Ruarc confessed.

'But all the gods of my people were either warriors, magicians or craftsmen,' Rathne protested. 'What was your Lord Jesus Christ then?'

Ruarc tried to answer her, but found he could think of no suitable reply. In the end he said simply, 'He died for us,' but,

170

even as he said it, he knew the *banshee* would not understand. Perhaps she was an instrument of the Devil, sent to tempt him away from his faith. But, surprisingly, Rathne nodded, although the movement was almost invisible in the darkness. 'He gave his life for his people; he gave his blood so that the fields should be fertile and the crops tall and strong, the women and animals fruitful?'

Ruarc shook his head in frustration. She was missing the point. 'He gave His life so that we might live,' he said.

'Have I not said that already?' Rathne wondered.

'What are we going to do about the girl?' Maildun asked softly.

Cloth whispered as the bard shrugged. 'What do you wish to do with her?'

'We cannot take her back to Erin with us,' the captain said emphatically.

'Why not?' Paedur turned, the first of the night stars beginning to sparkle in his eyes.

'Because . . . well because . . .'

'She saved your life, Maildun,' Paedur reminded him. 'you owe her that – and what value do you place on your life?'

'I know, I know.' Maildun ran his fingers through his beard. It was still short and crinkled, and in some places burnt down to the flesh. 'I've already talked to Germane and Diurnan about this. They both gave me much the same advice.'

'Then why ask me? The decision must be yours; I cannot tell you to abandon her on the next isle, or to throw her overboard . . .'

Maildun raised his hands. 'I know. But we cannot take her home – that is, if we ever reach home,' he added, staring out over the night-purple sea.

'Oh, I think you'll reach home,' the bard said, and was about to turn away, when Maildun stopped him.

'A moment, if you will. Advise me . . . please.'

Paedur turned round and waited.

'She is a *banshee*,' the captain said, 'not a creature that wails for an unfortunate's coming death, but a . . . a creature that feeds on flesh and blood – human flesh and blood . . .'

'A vampire,' Paedur said, with a slight smile, showing his own teeth.

'A vampire. How can I be responsible for bringing her back to Erin's shores?' He paused and then said slowly, 'I think you

171

should know that I have sworn an oath to rid our land of all the creatures of darkness and evil should I ever return.'

'That might not be so easy,' the bard warned, 'the creatures of the night are a close-knit clan. The hunter oft becomes the hunted.' He shifted his position, the half-circle of his hook glittering briefly. 'My advice to you, Maildun, is to do nothing; perhaps the problem will be resolved before you reach Erin's shores.'

'Have we far to go still?'

'It is perhaps nearer than you think,' Paedur nodded then and melted into the darkness, leaving Maildun standing alone by the rail. Behind him he could hear the vague sounds of conversation as Ruarc and Rathne stood by the stern, talking together.

The morning brought bright sunshine, and land. At first the lookout cried, 'Land,' and then added, 'a continent surely.' But, as the sun rose up into the heavens, and washed the world with light and colour, the land mass ahead of them broke up into a score of islands, lying one behind the other, giving the appearance of a range of hills.

A stiff breeze struck up with the sunrise and the mainsail was unfurled, and the *Avenger* skipped across the sea towards the first island.

From the distance it looked almost barren, and as the ship closed with it, they saw no signs of life. They were about to pass it by when a small man came running down the beach, waving his arms and calling out to them. Even so, they would have continued around the isle, convinced that the capering figure was a trap, had not the wind carried his cries to them, and they found he was speaking in Irish.

Maildun and Diurnan rowed in to shore in the currach, while the *Avenger* rocked at anchor in the small natural bay on the windward side of the island. They splashed through the shallows, pulling the small craft up the beach behind them. Maildun had drawn his sword and Diurnan carried a long fishing gaff. They approached the figure cautiously, wary still of a trap. Suddenly he went to his knees in the wet sand, crossed himself and began to pray in a thin, high falsetto.

'What is it?' Diurnan asked. 'And how did he get here?'

'I'm damned if I know; shipwreck probably. Mad certainly.'

The figure leaped to his feet. He stood no taller than the captain's chest, and his naked arms and legs were unbelievably scrawny. His clothing consisted solely of his hair, which was

172

surprisingly thick, and was wound around his torso and waist like a white blanket.

'My prayers have been answered,' he said, his voice quavering, cracking and squeaking, as if it had not been used in centuries.

Maildun raised his sword and prevented the old man from approaching too closely. Diurnan moved round behind him, his cold blue eyes searching the dunes and clumps of rocks for signs of movement.

'Who – what! – are you?' Maildun demanded.

The old man's head bobbed up and down. His hair fell across his face and, coupled with his thick beard, almost completely enveloped him, leaving only his two eyes, which were bright green, peering through the thicket. 'I am Madoc, yes, yes, Madoc of the Land of Grace, of Erin.' He crossed himself quickly again. 'And you, you, who are you? A prayer surely, an answer to a prayer.'

Behind the old man, Diurnan shook his head, and Maildun sheathed his sword. 'I doubt if we are your prayer,' he said, smiling thoughtfully, 'but I am Maildun, and that is my ship, the *Avenger.*'

The old man danced about, his calloused bare feet clicking on the stones and sand like boot heels. 'Maildun . . . Maildun . . . *Avenger . . . Avenger,*' he chanted. 'Pray, pray, yes I will pray for you.'

'Who are you? What are you doing here?' Diurnan asked suddenly.

'Madoc. Madoc, yes, I am Madoc, of the Land of Erin,' the old man changed, his voice rising and falling disconcertingly. 'A traveller once, a sailor, a seeker of truths, a teller of tales, a wanderer, a bard, but a hermit now.'

'How did you come to this place?' Maildun asked.

'Why, but by water. I sailed, yes, sailed. Such a voyage, such a saga, such a tale; I will tell it, if you will . . . ?'

The old man looked so hopeful that Maildun was reluctant to deny him. 'I'm sorry,' he said, as gently as possible. 'Time . . .'

Madoc cackled, the sound close enough to a bird's cry to send shivers down the captain's spine. 'Time, time, there is no time in this world.' Abruptly, the glittering light died from his eyes and the old man slumped, his shoulders sagging. When he looked up, he brushed the hair away from his eyes, exposing as much of his face as possible. 'I cannot tell you how long it has been since I last set eyes on a human being,' he said quietly, his accent now cultured and gentle. 'Time means little in this place; I am inclined to think that it is Hell, but I believe the temperature in that region is somewhat warmer.' He smiled wanly. 'And so, perforce, I am left with the conclusion that this is some sort of half way place, a way-station on the road to damnation – or redemption,' he added with a grin. 'You must forgive my apparel; but the nights can be bitter, and one uses what God has given one.'

'You have been long in this Shadowland?' Maildun asked.

'So that is what you call it,' Madoc said softly, 'aye, and it is as good a name as any for it. I knew I had somehow left behind my own world, and I knew I was not yet dead – although I might have wished that it were so several times – and so I came to the conclusion that I have reached my . . . destiny?' He paused and then nodded. 'But you must forgive an old man; age dims the brain, and one finds oneself answering one's own questions. But yes, I have been long in the . . . Shadowland,' he paused and Maildun nodded, 'although it is impossible for me to reckon the exact length of time. But long enough to see those stars – they are not the stars I knew in my youth – shift slightly in their orbits. Long enough for me to reach this state.' He spread his arms.

'But what do you eat?' Maildun asked.

'Oh, there are fruit and nuts in season, and there are often fish cast up on the beach; an old man's fancy makes it seem as if these are gifts from the Divinity: scraps from his table, for which I am truly grateful.'

'Are you alone?'

Madoc shook his head and his eyes began to glitter again. 'Alone, alone, not alone, no man is ever alone. I have my god; he is my companion, and look, look . . .' He pointed to the small dun-coloured birds that perched in the branches of the stunted trees and bushes. 'These are my children. Ah, but you look, you look and you say, "he is mad", but these are my children, and my children's children and their children. For they come here, you know, they come here when they die, they come here in the form of birds, and they keep me company, for I never die; I age, but I never die, no, oh no, never die . . . never die . . .'

'Do you want to come with us?' Maildun asked gently.

Madoc shuddered, his entire body spasming. The madness died in his eyes. 'What would I do, where would I go? There is nothing for me back in Erin; my kin and kindred are dead and gone . . . and I must admit to a fear of death. Does that surprise you; that an age-old man who, in some ways, longs, wishes for, and sometimes even pleads for death, should fear the same

174

spectre? Perhaps, like Oisin returning from Tir na nOg – and I do not doubt its existence now – I too would age and yet linger on, a helpless child-man.' He smiled toothlessly, and shook his head. 'I will remain; I am happy here in the main. My meals are regular, and I am not alone.' He smiled. 'It is an old man's fancy to imagine that the birds you see here are the souls of my kindred. It is a harmless fancy and it gives me comfort.' He straightened and seemed to test the air, his nostrils flaring. 'Ah, but you must go, the wind will change shortly, and you must be away.'

'Has your exile taught you anything?' Diurnan asked.

'Many things, oh, many things, but I am old and my memory dies, yes, it does, and all that I have learned, I have forgotten, gone . . . lost . . . everything forgotten . . .'

Maildun and Diurnan left the old man and hurried down the beach. They rowed back to the *Avenger* in silence.

CHAPTER TWENTY

The clang of metal on metal was immediately followed by a huge red glow that lit up the sky above the island. There was another clang of metal striking metal, and again there was a rush of wind, followed by the roar of flames, which brightened even the noonday sky.

Maildun, standing in the prow of the ship with the bard, raised his hand, and Diurnan relayed the order and the oars paused. Germane handed the tiller over to one of the crew and came down the deck and, together, he and Diurnan joined the captain and Paedur beside the figurehead.

'What do you make of it?' Maildun asked the bard, but it was Diurnan who answered.

'I remember once coming over the hills close to my home; it was a hard, cold day with the sun low in the sky and everything was silent. And then the heavens were brightened and the sounds were much as they are now.' He grinned broadly. 'I thought the Thunderer had come for me, but it was only the smiths working their forges.'

Paedur nodded silently, and Maildun drummed his fist against the wood. 'Aye, that's the sound, a forge.'

The metallic clanging came again, only this time it stopped in mid-stroke and the bellows noise died. The silence was almost complete, for the wind had dropped and the sea was calm. There was a low, growling rumble and then, clearly and distinctly, they heard a huge voice speak in what Germane and Paedur recognised as the language of the Hellens.

'*They come brothers.*'

'*Close? Are they close?*' a second voice asked.

'*Near enough.*'

'*It is an age since we last dined on man-flesh,*' a third voice said. '*But let us be sure of our meal; let them approach.*'

Germane provided a rough translation, while the bard leaned over the edge of the craft, listening intently. He glanced back over his shoulder. 'Have your crew row us out of here,' he said, 'but keep the craft prow foremost to the isle. If they are what I

176

think they are, they will have difficulty in determining how close we are to the isle.'

Germane and Diurnan hurried down the decks; Diurnan ordered the men to the oars and impressed on them the need for absolute silence, and then, with Germane at the tiller, he began to call the beat, a strong, slow pull. With barely a ripple, and without a sound, the *Avenger* began to move away from the Smith's Isle.

'*How fare they?*'

'*They do not move.*'

'*Perhaps they are resting; puny man-flesh tires easily.*'

'*Soon brothers, soon.*'

There was a long pause and then the voices began again.

'*Now, brothers, now?*'

'*No, they remain . . .*' There was a pause. '*But they are moving away!*'

'*Zeus!*'

A figure, impossibly tall and broad, strode out from a cave on the island. Behind him the mouth of the cave glowed red and metal was hammered briefly and furiously, and then he was joined by two others. They were manlike but huge, clad in rough leather aprons and sandals, but otherwise naked, and they were covered with a thick, bristling hair. They had but one eye set in the centre of their foreheads. They roared, a mindless cry of rage, and then one drew back his arm and threw something that glowed and hissed as it flew through the air . . .

'ROW, DAMNN YOU, ROW,' Diurnan roared. He changed to a battle-beat, and the *Avenger* leaped away like a startled horse.

The glowing ingot of metal, a chunk bigger and broader than a man, fell into the sea, exploding in a shower of scalding steam and water, sending a wave washing in over the figurehead, drenching the bard and captain.

The second giant drew back his arm and threw also. His missile was longer and thinner, not unlike the main mast of the *Avenger*. It sizzled through the air, not a spear's length from the fleeing craft, and entered the water almost smoothly, only to erupt again in a great explosion of steam and boiling water.

The giants roared again, and the third twirled a long length of cord around his head several times before releasing it: it was a sling and its shot was red-hot. A score or more of crude spheres, bigger than a man's head, sped towards the *Avenger*.

'More speed!' Maildun shouted, but knowing that it was useless. Even a short run at battle-speed would exhaust the

177

hardiest Viking crew, and his men had been too long asea with poor food and insufficient water. However, Diurnan increased the beat fractionally and for a moment it seemed as if the *Avenger* would outrun the red-hot shot.

But now the one-eyed giants fired more shot after them, and there was a distant roar of sound as the bellows were worked to heat yet more sling-shot.

The first load scattered around the *Avenger* in a deadly hail, hissing and foaming into the sea in huge geysers of steam. One lump ripped through the sail before falling into the sea, but otherwise there was no damage.

But now the crew were exhausted, their arms and shoulders leaden, and the *Avenger* was beginning to drift on the waves.

The second load of sling-shot struck the *Avenger* fairly amidships. Luckily, it was smaller than the first load, barely a handful of glowing balls of metal. One piece glanced off the figurehead, sending Maildun and Paedur tumbling backwards to avoid it. It snapped off the snarling dragon-prow before falling into the sea. Another bounced off the deck, almost at Ruarc's feet. He felt the rush of heat, saw the ball bounce along the deck, like a stone skimmed across water, and then saw it roll almost lazily over the edge, leaving a seared and crazy trail behind it. Two more shots tore through the sail, the first starting a small fire which quickly extinguised itself, but the final shot ploughed straight into the deck, ripping through wood and tarred leather hides. The shot entered diagonally and exited almost directly below the tiller; the *Avenger* began taking on water and immediately began to wallow.

Three men threw themselves onto the ragged hole in the bottom of the craft, attempting to plug the opening with their bodies. Diurnan grabbed a pile of leather 'patches' and launched himself overboard, coming around and under the ship, feeling the chill rush of water past his face as he manoeuvred round to the hole. He spread the leather hides over the hole, and felt hands groping for them from the other side, holding onto them, and then he had to let go, to come round and up for air. The remainder of the crew seemed to be bailing when he surfaced; in that short space of time, the ship had taken on a surprisingly large amount of water. He shouted for a mallet and nails and, just before he dipped back into the water again, he saw another score of red-hot metal balls coming in towards the ship, and then he saw the bard raise his arms . . .

The glow from the shot turned the bard's eyes into glowing points of fire, transforming his face into a mask. He raised his

178

arms, tilted back his head and began to draw the lightning down to himself. The air was suddenly rank with ozone, and Maildun spat the foul taste into the water. And then the bard's hook began to glow. The twisted sigils cut into the flat blade burned with a blue-white tracery, and Paedur's voice, which had been low and muted, now rose in timbre and volume. He cried aloud, calling something, commanding something . . . and then he stopped, and folded his arms across his chest.

And just as the first of the sling-shot reached the stricken craft, his left hand moved – and lightning forked from his hook, and danced from ball to ball, crackling and sparking round each in a cacophony of light and sound. The balls shattered. Red hot pieces of shrapnel showered the deck, puncturing through wood, leather and flesh indiscriminately, but the damage they did to the *Avenger* was minimal and the wounds were minor in the main.

Paedur then raised his left arm, until it was directly above his head. Now the lightning danced from the tip of the silver hook and writhed down his arm, touching his face with white fire and ebon shadows, flowing from his dark cloak like water. He lowered his head for a moment, and when he raised it again his eyes were fire and ice like the lightning. And then he slowly lowered his arm, until it was pointing a little above the Isle of the Smiths.

There was a sound of tearing, as if a huge length of cloth had been rent from end to end. The lightning which leaped from the bard's hook seemed little more than a spark, but, by the time it reached the isle, it was a huge, ravening bolt of destruction. It seemed to linger only briefly by the three giants, before darting like some living creature into the dark maw of their smithy. And then it fed.

The tidal wave that followed the awesome detonation lifted the *Avenger* and carried her far.

'How do you feel?'

Paedur opened his eyes, and found himself staring into Maildun's concerned face. He sat up, wincing as every muscle in his body protested. Looking around, he found he was lying in the captain's tiny cabin, wrapped in his cloak. He swung his legs over the side of the cot and examined his hook; its silver was dulled and tarnished, the runes on the blade clogged with what looked like soot. He pulled round a corner of his cloak and began to clean the hook methodically. 'I've felt better,' he said finally.

'We thought we had lost you,' Maildun said slowly, sipping

from a beaker. 'When the island blew up, I was too busy trying to keep the *Avenger* afloat, trying to keep the men under control, trying to . . .' He shrugged. 'We almost lost Diurnan,' he added quietly. 'He had gone down to patch a hole close to the tiller; luckily he had just surfaced for air when the island exploded.' He grinned. 'I've never seen a man come up out of the water so fast. Apparently he saw something like it once in the Northlands, and knew what would happen.' He drank again. 'One of the men told me what happened to you. He said he saw you lying there with the lightning dancing round your body, sparking off everything metallic. When we eventually picked you up – when the lightning had died – we could find no heartbeat; we thought you were dead.'

Paedur smiled. 'It's not that easy to kill me, I'm afraid.'

'There was no heartbeat,' Maldun repeated, staring into his cup.

'It's very easy to miss a heartbeat,' Paedur said, concentrating on cleaning his hook.

'I've taken enough to know where to find it and when there is one – and when there isn't.'

Paedur raised his hand of flesh and blood. 'If you cut me, you'll find blood: no heart, no blood! I may have sacrificed many things when I purchased my immortality, but I do retain all the outward – and most of the inward – trappings of humanity: including my heart.' The bard continued polishing his hook, working the blackness out of the cracks and runes. He glanced over at Maildun. 'How fares the *Avenger*?'

The captain shrugged. 'There is a hole big enough for a man to climb through aft, but thanks to Diurnan it won't sink us – yet. The sail is being repaired at this very moment. There are a couple of large holes in it. When you destroyed the sling-shot and broke them up into all those slivers, they cut through the craft in many places, but most of the holes have been mended. Some of the crew were injured,' he added.

Paedur nodded, and raised his hook. 'When this is clean again, I'll do what I can.'

Maildun nodded his thanks. 'What we really need now is an island to beach on to repair properly that hole in the keel. The patchwork is fine, but it is only a temporary measure, and I'd not like to face a storm with it. Problem is,' Maildun continued, 'there don't seem to be any islands round here. I fear the explosion pushed us far. Germane says that the stars have changed also,' he added quietly.

The bard looked up sharply. 'Stars? How long have I lain here?'

'All of yesterday afternoon, last night, and the day is almost done now.'

The bard swore and, pulling his cloak about his shoulders, strode past the captain and out onto the deck.

Twilight wrapped the *Avenger* in a shroud, coating everything in a smoky tinge. The water had turned dark and vaguely ominous, and the first stars were beginning to shine in the skies above. There was the sound of flint, and then the first of the lightbowls sparked to life, but they only served to deepen the twilight into night.

The bard moved silently down the deck, his cloak billowing behind him like a huge pair of wings. Men still crossed themselves when he passed, or touched amulets and muttered prayers; although they had come to recognise that without him they would probably never reach Erin again, they still regarded him with fear and loathing. At the rudder, Paedur touched Germane's shoulder, startling him, and then moved away; the navigator followed him. They stood together in the stern of the craft, watching the first stars appear.

'They have changed,' Germane said softly, 'some, but not all.'

'You're sure?' the bard demanded.

'I'm sure. I know the stars of my own world like the creases on the palms of my hands: they are my livelihood, my guides. When we first came to this sea, I noted the stars, their shapes and their positions, and I'm convinced that some of these have moved, or disappeared altogether. Is that possible?'

Paedur nodded. 'It's possible. In the same way that the explosion of force threw us to this sea, so too the aftermath of the force that destroyed the Isle of the Smiths might have pushed us onto another sea.' He nodded towards the heavens. 'Let us wait and see.'

The stars appeared quickly, following the brief twilight, some singly, others in clumps or broad, almost gauzy washes of light. Some pulsed singly, others shone in colours and shades that had never been seen in the skies above Erin, or any other land.

'There!' The bard pointed skywards with his hook. 'The Pole Star; at least we have not moved too far from our own world.'

'That configuration is also familiar,' Germane pointed to a spiralling cluster of stars. 'Only it seems to have moved.'

Paedur followed the navigator's finger, and then he suddenly nodded and smiled. 'Aye.' He turned to face the southerner, and

181

the firebowls reflected in his eyes, turning them gold and bronze. 'We have merely shifted position on the Island Sea; luckily we remain in the same Shadowland – but in another part of it.'

'From the position of the Pole Star, I'd say we've moved north,' Germane said.

'Aye, we've moved northwards,' Paedur agreed.

'But there are no islands.'

'Oh, there are. There are isles aplenty. Sail on,' he advised, 'and on the morrow you will see the Ancient Cities of the Tuatha De Danann.'

CHAPTER TWENTY-ONE

In the pre-dawn light, the sea was the colour of fresh milk.

'I've seen mountain streams run this colour in spring,' Diurnan said, 'and sometimes out into the mouths of the fjords staining the sea, but never this far from land.'

'The water isn't cold,' Germane said quietly, 'and . . . and it doesn't look like water. It looks different.'

The sun came up, staining the horizon in shades of salmon and rose, tingeing the milk-water with blood, but as the sun rose into the heavens, it seemed to leech both the red and white colour from it, leaving it pure and clean. Soon the water grew ever clearer, until eventually the sea-bed, far, far below could be seen in perfect detail. The water lost all texture, lost every trace and tinge of colour, until it seemed as if the *Avenger* sailed through the skies and the crew looked down upon a land far below – but a land through which shoals of miniature fish darted and twisted, and long, darker creatures curled sinuously around rocks that were decorated with aeons of crustations and feathery growths.

The shadow of the longship moved sedately across the sea-floor, disturbing slumbering crabs, sending them scuttling for cover, and once they saw the sleek and deadly shape of a shark glide by, twisting as the ship's shadow passed over it, but then gliding on, its primitive brain unable to distinguish what had so briefly touched its consciousness.

The bard called it the Invisible Sea, and said that there was a substance in the water which purified and cleansed it of the impurities which usually allowed the water to reflect the sky which, in turn, coloured the sea. The water was pure, and to prove it, he had buckets lowered into the invisible waves, and the men drank their fill of the tepid, sparkling water.

As the day wore on the character of the sea began to change, and occasionally long streaks of pale colours, frighteningly akin to clouds, drifted by. In the late afternoon these clouds coalesced to form once again the milk-like covering which had so startled the navigator and Diurnan that morning.

The following morning the rising sun once again burned off the clouds, for they looked like nothing else, and turned the sea to glass. Only this time, instead of the natural sea-floor beneath the *Avenger*, a broad and paved road of white stones stretched into the distance.

Maildun stood by the destroyed prow of the longship and stared down onto the road. He felt a curious twisting in the pit of his stomach as he watched the *Avenger*'s shadow drift across the broad roadway, and vertigo touched his throat as the impression of flight was heightened by the absolute clarity of the sea below.

'The Long Road,' Paedur said softly, joining him, 'the road that once led – still leads! – to the Four Cities of Light, the cities of the Tuatha De Danann.'

'Have the cities sunk, then, like the world of *tLanteco Astis*?'

'Not quite,' the bard said. 'Originally these cities, – which you should see shortly – lay close to the borders of your own world, so close, indeed, that on a fine day, or a day when the mist was touched with the gold of the setting sun, their images might be painted across the skies briefly in shining mirages; thus they entered the mythology of your race.

'However, when the land that now forms the Island Sea sank beneath the waves, it sent ripples through the many Shadowlands, creating disturbances and distortions. Many of the Tuatha De Danann – who were not wholly human, but not quite gods – fled the Cities of Light and crossed the divide to your land, bringing with them many, many things, but principally the gifts of learning and healing.' Paedur gestured down towards the broad road. 'Some, however, remained, and although the sea rolled in on them, they yet managed to keep a certain part of their own Shadowland about their cities, and thus they survived, surrounded and covered by the waves, but yet safe and protected from its destruction by the power of their magic.

'In time – for this occurred when the Races of Man were still young – the residue of their magic seeped through the waves towards the sunlight, and so strong and powerful was that magic that it purified the waters, cleansing them of all dirt and residue, and leaving what you see now.' His hook swept out. 'You are sailing above the Land of the Last of the Tuatha De Danann; the first and last of the sons of men to do so,' he added with a wry smile.

The massive walls of the first city rose up out of the sea-bed like a colossal growth. They flowed upwards smoothly, the rocks

184

showing no crack or seam, gleaming bone-white in the afternoon sunlight.

'The White City of Muirias,' Paedur said.

Once beyond the towering walls, which almost scraped the *Avenger's* keel, they were over the ancient city itself. From their great height, they could see that it had been laid out in a series of concentric circles, and the dwellings themselves, which were squat, while the towers were almost unnaturally slender, were also circular. The many windows were circular too, and the doorways were arched. They could see evidence of broad rivers and fountains, the former almost indistinguishable from the streets, except that they were sword-straight, and the latter fantastically convoluted with intricate sculptures in the midst of the broad open spaces.

However, as they drifted over the centre of the city of Muirias, they passed a broad swathe of devastation which radiated outwards in long arms into the city. It was impossible to tell what it had once been – although it seemed likely that it had been a park of some description, although on a scale that dwarfed even the great forests of Erin.

A broad white road, almost twice the width of the road that led into the city, led away from it and into the north to where the walls of a second city could be seen, rising tall and golden from the sea-bed.

'Failias,' Paedur said, 'the City of Gold.' He pointed off the starboard bow. 'Yonder, you will find Finnias, the Silver City, and directly in our path lies the City of Bronze and Copper, Goirias.' He looked across at the captain. 'Give the order to bring us about, our route lies yonder . . .' He pointed off the port bow. 'And now we sail the Sea of Wonders.'

The afternoon shadows were just beginning to lengthen when the *Avenger's* slim, dark shadow glided over the massive brazen walls of Goirias. The sunlight gave it a warm, ruddy texture and the walls of the slim towers and squat, rounded dwellings glowed as if they had been fired from within. Like the White City of Muirias, which the bard said was sometimes known as the City of Bone, the buildings were round, as were the windows and doors. And, as they passed over the centre of the city, they saw that here too a huge area had been laid waste, as if it had been ravaged by fire.

'I thought you said that the last of the people of the goddess still lived,' Maildun said to Paedur, as they moved over the area of desolation.

'They live here still.'

'But I've seen no movement; the streets and gardens are empty.'

Paedur smiled grimly. He leaned over the side of the craft and looked down onto the City of Bronze and Copper. His eyes turned to coins. 'You won't,' he said softly, and Maildun heard the change in his voice, the resonance of a trained *ollav*, that told him that the bard was about to speak from his vast lore. 'You see before you a monument to the Tuatha De Danann: their abiding monument, their everlasting tomb. When the People of Danu called upon their powerful forces to encase their cities in pockets of magic, they stipulated that the Cities of Light should remain unchanged and unchanging for all eternity.

'And so they are; generations of men have risen and fallen, empires have come and faded, but still the cities remain. The inhabitants remain also, unchanged and unchanging – and that is their bane: they are trapped in a spell of their own making, a pocket of magic timelessness – of nothingness. Time does not exist for them, it has no meaning, and they are now as they were aeons ago. A warning to all who call upon the Old High Magic.'

Maildun looked down at the ruddy city and shivered suddenly. What a demise for a great civilisation; trapped for all eternity.

'Are they aware?'

'Aye, and that is the worst part of it. They are fully aware and alert.'

'It would be like being buried alive,' Maildun whispered, and automatically crossed himself, closing his eyes as he did so. When he looked down again, the warmth had seeped from the stone and it had taken on a blood-like hue. It reminded him now of a great open wound . . . He straightened abruptly, breathing in great gasps of salt sea air, cleansing his mouth of the sour taste that had flooded it. 'Full sail,' he called, 'I want to be away from this place by evening.'

'You have nothing to fear from it,' the bard said quietly.

'I would not sleep tonight if I knew that that was down below me. Could you not break the spell?' he asked suddenly.

Paedur shook his head. 'It is far beyond my meagre powers.'

'What will release them then?'

'Only time. If there is ever a violent cataclysm in this or one of the neighbouring Shadowlands, the shock wave might break the magical bonding. Unfortunately, the sea would just rush in and cover them. They are doomed.'

Maildun stood by the rail, gazing towards the horizon, refusing to look down at the city through the invisible water. He smiled at the thought: 'invisible water', he was becoming quite a philosopher in his old age.

The sun slipped towards the horizon, turning the eastern sky purple with approaching night. The water once again took on its milk-white staining, only now it was tinged with the crimson of the setting sun, and the shadow of the *Avenger* danced tall and thin across the water. He was about to turn away, when he saw the sudden sparkle of fire from something almost directly ahead. It was tall and reflective, but in the twilight details were blurred and difficult to distinguish. 'Lookout; what's that ahead?'

There was a moment's silence, and then the man answered. 'I'm not sure; an island certainly, a wall possibly.'

The navigator joined Maildun by the remains of the figurehead. He rubbed the heels of his hands into his eyes and then leaned forward, staring dead ahead. He shook his head slowly. 'I am unsure; it looks like an island with a wall round it. But the wall seems to be moving,' he added slowly.

'Paedur!' Maildun turned and shouted. As the bard joined them, he silently pointed ahead.

'It is the Island of Water, and it would be better if we passed it before full night.'

'A contradiction, surely?' Germane said softly, while Maildun shouted the order for the men to man the oars. 'An island of water?'

'Wait; watch,' Paedur said, folding his hand and hook into his sleeves, and dropping his chin onto his chest, so that the shadows took his face.

With the crack of the wind in the sail, and the steady beat of the oars, the *Avenger* passed the island with barely minutes to spare before full night fell. The wall, which the navigator had thought to be moving, turned out to be an almost continuous wave, which rose smoothly in a tall curve, taller than the *Avenger's* mast, and then foamed down onto the beach to disappear hissing and foaming into the sands. The flow of water was continuous, although of irregular height, and seemed completely to enclose the isle.

Torches moved behind the wall of water, and a huge, evil-smelling bonfire burned on the beach, just above the high-water mark. Shapes, that were only vaguely human, milled around behind the flames, and there were shouts and cries, mostly of fear and rage, audible above the crackle of the fire and the monotonous rumble of water.

An occasional spear or stone was thrown at the longship, but the wall of water robbed them of much of their force and they rattled harmlessly against the decks. The only real threat came when a score or more of large, round objects patterned onto the decks. Men scrambled for cover, breaking the rhythm of the oars, and the ship wallowed dangerously and drifted perilously close to the foaming water, before Diurnan managed to hustle the crew back to their benches and re-establish the beat.

When these objects were examined later, they were found to be about the size of a child's head, with three small indentations to one end, coming to a point of sorts at the other and covered in short, coarse hair.

Maildun, Germane and Diurnan had come to the conclusion that they were some sort of animal when the bard, with a touch of real humour in his eyes, took the ball and sliced through it with his hook exposing a pale and fleshy interior.

No one believed him when he said that it was a fruit.

CHAPTER TWENTY-TWO

'You said we were sailing the Sea of Wonders,' Maildun said, carefully running an oily rag down the length of his sword.

Paedur nodded silently. He was standing by the stern, beside Germane who had taken the tiller and Maildun, who was sitting cross-legged on the deck, cleaning his weapons.

'What is the Sea of Wonders?'

'The Sea of Wonders is that part of the Shadowland which is nearest to the other Shadowlands, and is thus infected by them and which, in turn, infects them. It is therefore part, and yet not part, of two – or more – Shadowlands.'

'A limbo?' Maildun asked, looking up.

'A limbo,' Paedur agreed, 'but not a place of nothingness; rather, it is an area – many days' sailing in either direction – which had the properties of both those regions, but without having the natural laws of either.'

'I didn't think natural laws held any sway in this world,' Germane said, smiling.

The bard looked shocked. 'But there must be something which holds this world together; the laws may differ – completely and radically in some cases – from the laws that prevail in your own world, but they are there, nonetheless. There are explanations for the curious phenomena we may encounter. We may not be able to discover those explanations, but they are there.'

'That island yester-eve,' Maildun said, 'why was it so import-ant that we pass it before nightfall? What is the explanation for that?'

Paedur grinned, his eyes taking up the blue of the sea and sky. 'In the evening, the wall of water round that island redoubles in force, sucking everything within a certain radius onto the shore. How else did you think the island came to be inhabited.'

'Why did the people seem to fear us?'

'I don't think they feared us. I think they were more enraged by the fact that we seemed to be escaping.'

'They were dangerous then?' Maildun asked.

'They were cannibals,' Paedur said softly, exposing his teeth in a feral smile.

Rathne touched Ruarc's arm lightly, so lightly at first that he did not notice it, and it wasn't until he saw his shipmates' expression change to one of loathing and disgust that he realised that someone was standing beside him.

Before he could say a word, she tugged at his arm, pulling him away towards the stern. 'Something to see,' was all she would say.

The *banshee* led Ruarc to the port side and then pointed across the waves with her long, slender hand. Her crimson-tipped nails caught and held his attention, and he had to make a conscious effort to follow her pointing fingers.

'Look, *see!*'

Ruarc squinted against the glare of the sunlight off the sea and followed the *banshee's* pointing fingers. At first he found the glare too bright for his eyes and he had to blink away the spots and sparkles of colour that danced across his vision. When he looked again, he still found it difficult to make sense of what he was seeing.

About a league off the port side of the vessel, the sea surged up out of the placid ocean in a smooth stream and arched over a tiny clump of rock, before smoothly rejoining the ocean on the far side of the isle without a ripple. Ruarc shook his head in wonder, and looked at Rathne. 'Is it not pretty?' she said, her voice and expression childlike, and, if it had not been for her needle-pointed teeth, she would have looked like any young women of Erin who had just been shown something strange and wonderful.

'Very pretty,' he mumbled. He turned and called out for his foster-brother. Rathne glanced at him curiously, her large eyes clouding with sudden tears. Her head bowed and then she turned away from him quickly.

'I've seen water spouting from the sea before,' Diurnan said to Maildun as they joined Ruarc, 'but I've never seen anything like that.' He nodded towards the arching water.

'No, it's not dangerous,' Paedur said, as Maildun turned to ask the question. 'It is curious, it is a wonder – part of the Sea of Wonders – nothing more.'

Maildun had Germane bring the *Avenger* round and they sailed as closely as possible to the tiny clump of stone with its arch of water. The air grew damp as they approached, and the arch began to glitter with tiny, spectacular rainbows as the light refracted through the droplets. They sailed through the strait between the rock and the descending water, their mast just scraping through beneath it. Fish darted through the water, moving swiftly from left to right with long strands of seaweed rippling in their wake. Diurnan prodded the smooth arch of water with his spear and managed to gaff some small fish. It was indeed, as the bard had said, a wonder.

'What will you do with Rathne when we reach Erin?' Ruarc asked his foster-brother later that evening.

'If we reach Erin,' Maildun reminded him softly.

'Well?'

'Why do you ask?' Maildun finished his drink and looked into his foster-brother's tired eyes. Maildun sat on the edge of the cot in his tiny cabin, with Ruarc standing before him, unwilling to sit down.

'I'm just curious,' he said defensively.

'Are you sure that's the only reason?' Maildun asked softly. He leaned forward, his hair and beard turning blood-red in the torchlight, and jabbed a finger at Ruarc. 'Remember what she is,' he said quietly. 'Remember what her appetites are.'

Ruarc shook his head. 'I cannot believe she would eat human flesh, drink human blood.'

Maildun smiled humourlessly. 'I'm no bard, and I'm sure Paedur would tell the tale better than I, but you know enough about the habits of the *banshee* to know what she is.'

'*Banshees* cry a warning of death to certain families,' Ruarc said coldly, 'nothing more.'

Maildun suddenly spat in disgust. 'Ach, you know better than that; that is a tale put about by those priests who refuse to accept the evidence that our ancestors ate their dead.'

'That's not true.'

'Ruarc, you know it is,' his foster-brother said gently, 'you have heard our father tell of the creatures that came forth at night to haunt the battlefields and feast upon the dead. You know our father and uncles have taken heads in battle.'

'But Rathne . . .'

'Rathne is a *banshee*, a woman of the *sidhe*, not a true De Danann certainly, but changed by their magic so that she is no longer human. Have you ever seen her eat?' he asked suddenly.

Ruarc shook his head. 'Never, but nor have I ever seen the bard eat,' he said defiantly.

Maildun nodded. 'I know. The bard is not human, and I'm not

191

sure whether he is a god or a devil, but he means us no harm, and I don't think he will pose a threat to us should we return to Erin.'

'And you think Rathne will?' Ruarc demanded.

'I would not like to think of her prowling the night in search of corpses,' Maildun whispered. His gaze caught and held his brother's. 'And what happens if she cannot find a fresh corpse; would there come a time when she would first have to kill and then feed?'

'She wouldn't!'

Maildun shook his head. 'I wish I were so sure, but no matter what your feelings for her are, you must realise that she can never be let loose in Erin.'

'You won't kill her,' Ruarc warned.

'Why not?' Maildun asked softly.

'I . . . I won't let you.'

His foster-brother stood up slowly. He was a head taller than Ruarc and muscled in proportion. He shook his head. 'Do you love her?'

Ruarc hesitated and then he too shook his head. 'No . . . yes . . . I don't know.'

Maildun suddenly struck him across the face with the flat and then the back of his hand, the sudden blow sending him rocking back on his heels against the door. 'I spoke to you before about threatening my authority. You're infatuated by the first woman you've seen in months – and never mind that she's a flesh-eater.'

Ruarc held the back of his hand to his bleeding lip. His eyes were small and dark, filled with loathing and hatred. 'At least my tastes run to women, brother!' he spat. He was gone before Maildun could react.

The captain closed the door and then stood leaning back against it, his arms folded across his chest. He was losing his brother, he knew. He had seen how he behaved when the cursed *banshee* was near; aye, and she encouraged it too. He shook his head, swearing silently, ruing the day he had taken her on board. Aye, she may have saved his life, but what would be her price: his brother?

Maildun pulled his cloak round his shoulders, blew out the small lightbowl and then stepped out on deck. The wind had freshened steadily since nightfall, and the leather sail cracked and strained, and the sheets hummed. The sky was beginning to cloud over with long bands of shifting clouds obscuring the brilliant stars and streaks of light. The waves were choppy and, from where he stood, he could see Germane and Diurnan standing by the rudder, their cloaks held tightly around them.

There was a storm brewing.

The *Avenger* was silent save for the muffled snores of the sleeping crew, and the occasional slapping of the waves against the tarred sides. A light burned beside Germane, throwing his face into shadow and picking out Diurnan's pale hair and beard, but aside from that there was no one else visibly moving – although he felt sure that at least some of the crew must be alert and awake. Maildun walked down the length of the deck, suddenly feeling very alone and weary. Whatever motivation he had had for this mission of vengeance was gone; now, he only felt the exhaustion and the desire to return to Erin. 'Vengeance is the Lord's' – well, the Lord could take his revenge on Archu, the Hound of Slaughter; he wanted none of it.

He leaned against the mast and stared up through the ropes and sail into the star-strewn heaven. With their reflections cast into the water, it was easy to believe that they sailed the heavens, like the De Danann of old, who had sailed through the air to Banba. He watched the encroaching clouds swallow their bright-ness and light, and felt chilled.

'Imagine lifetimes spent feeling as you are feeling.' A shadow moved beside him, and he recognised the bard's furred cloak. He had the cowl pulled up over his head and round his face, and his arms were tucked into the wide sleeves: if death ever wore a human form, Maildun realised, then he was looking at it.

'I am weary of it all, bard,' he said softly.

'With you, it will pass,' Paedur murmured, 'with most humans, it passes. It is part of human nature to be optimistic; I lost that optimism generations ago.'

'How will it end?'

'For you, or for me?' Paedur asked, standing close enough to the captain for him to smell the faint traces of spice and sandalwood from the bard's cloak.

'For both.'

'You are sailing upon a myth – and sailing into your own legend; in times to come men will speak of the Voyage of Maildun.'

'And you?'

Cloth rustled as the bard shrugged. 'I will continue.'

'If you seek death so ardently, could you not kill yourself?'

193

'It was once prophesied that my death would be both wonderful and tragic – and supernatural. I doubt if I will die by mortal hand. I will continue.'

Maildun nodded, not trusting himself to speak. After a silence that began to lengthen uncomfortably, he said, 'There's a storm coming.'

'It will pass us; for some reason, storms do not blow on the Sea of Wonders. However, we'll soon be beyond its reach and back into the Island Sea proper.'

'How soon?'

'We should sight the pillars with first light; once past them, we are back into the Sea.'

CHAPTER TWENTY-THREE

The pillar was a testament: a testament to raw power, to massive, untamed, elemental force and power. It rose up from the sea into the heavens, tall, straight and proud. It took the morning light and its gleaming surface was washed in salmon and rose, touched with gold, and then, as the sun cleared the horizon, shaded back to its original silver colouration.

And as the *Avenger* closed on the towering pillar, they could see that it was indeed fashioned from solid silver.

It was octagonal, the sides being longer than the entire length of the *Avenger*. It disappeared down into the depths of the ocean and straight up into the vault of the heavens, joining them with a silver bar. The metal was smooth and polished, except for an area about a sword's length in height at the level of the *Avenger's* decks, which was covered in an arcane design which Germane said reminded him of some writings he had seen which originated in the lands far to the east. This area, which was indented from the rest of the column, was covered with a fine silver mesh of superb workmanship.

'But what is it?' Maildun asked, looking upwards to where the pillar disappeared into the clouds with no sign of tapering.

'Yggdrasill,' Diurnan said softly, 'the World Tree.' He caught Maildun's curious look and continued. 'The tree which holds this world together, having its roots in the earth and its branches in the heavens, encompassing the world.'

'Must you label it?' the bard asked. 'Can you not admire it for what it is?'

'And just what is it?' the captain asked.

'A wonder?' Paedur suggested.

'Can you read the script?' Germane asked him, pointing to the arcane runes.

The bard hesitated a fraction too long. 'I cannot.'

'Are you sure?' Germane murmured quietly, for his ears only.

'There are some things I might not like to read.' The bard's eyes glowed silver from the pillar.

Diurnan reached out to touch the column. The metal felt slick and slightly warm to his touch, and he ran his blunt fingers over the delicate silver mesh longingly. He looked over his shoulder at Maildun. 'You realise that when we return to Erin, no one will believe us?'

'Paedur?'

'The column is self-perpetuating,' the bard said. 'Take some of it and it will only repair itself. I don't think it will miss a handful.'

Diurnan nodded and pulled out his knife. With the rocking of the *Avenger*, it was difficult to concentrate on any one piece of metal, and when he finally did find a handhold in the mesh, his knife blade blunted as he attempted to saw through the hair-fine silver. Eventually the bard leaned over and, with his silver hook, sliced through a small patch and let it fall into the northerner's hand. The sea lifted the craft then in a smooth swell that carried it away from the pillar, and pushed them towards the second pillar that lay about a half day's sail beyond the first.

They heard the voice almost immediately. It was a sound, a sound of incredible strength and power, but unquestionably a voice, and coming from the top of the pillar. The words were indistinguishable, the language impossible, and on occasion it fell so low that the timbers of the *Avenger* groaned and threatened to fall apart, and the crew could feel the bass vibrations in their bones. It continued in a long chant or incantation, the voice rising and falling as the clouds twisted and swirled round the top of the pillar, seemingly changing direction and shape at the voice's command. Strangely, no one at any time felt in any danger; such was the power and force of that voice, that surely it would not pay any attention to the craft which must have seemed puny – if, indeed, it was even visible – to the owner of the voice.

The bard refused to name the speaker, saying that it was better not to name such creatures, because there was power and magic in names and lest, by the very act of naming them, they would be called down; and there were some creatures and beings, he added, that even the very gods themselves did not disturb.

'We were wondering whether it might be some sort of sickness,' Germane said to Maildun.

'How many of the crew have you checked?'

The navigator leaned against the stump of the figurehead, as the longship swayed slightly on the smooth sea. 'Most of them; they all report symptoms of disorientation, dizziness, a sense of . . . unreality, of not belonging to anything!'

Diurnan nodded. 'I've felt it too.'

Maildun ran his fingers through his beard. 'So have I, I think. A feeling of loss?'

Germane nodded. 'Disassociation. Events seeming to slip out of their sequence. I once breathed in the fumes of a certain plant which had the same effect,' he added.

The captain turned to Diurnan. 'Will you go and find the bard?'

Rathne curled up in a ball and held her head. She could no longer think clearly; time was twisting and flowing together. She could remember her time in the forts of Banba clearly now, and the palaces of the Tuatha De Danann. She could see the blue-white fire of their magic clearly again, felt the skin-tingling change come over her: felt the hunger. The hunger was strong now.

It had been a long time since she had eaten. Leucosia had not treated her well, but she had fed her, and she hadn't eaten since Maildun had slain the Siren . . . when she had helped Maildun slay the Siren, she corrected herself. She was as much to blame.

She had played her part well, played it to perfection. The ship, when she first saw it, although it was strange and new, was undoubtedly from her own world: for her it meant the answer to a prayer. If only she could get on board and return to her own world – anywhere on her own world – she could make her way back to Banba: home. She had to get onto that ship – no matter what the cost. And she had, but she was paying the price now . . .

She felt the hunger rise up and take her.

'The disorientation will pass,' Paedur explained. 'Remember, this sea is part of two disparate Shadowlands; you are feeling the effects of both of these worlds.' He nodded towards the approaching island. 'Once beyond that pillar, we shall be back in the Island Sea. The disassociation you are feeling is a side-effect of moving further away from your own world. If we were to remain a little longer in the Sea of Wonders, the effects would be permanent.'

Maildun looked up in understanding. 'That is why those unlucky folk who return from the Otherworld are mad?'

'Not mad, but lost. One does not emerge from a Shadowland unchanged. Sometimes it is possible to gain something, all too often one loses, and it is very easy to lose one's soul, or identity.'

Maildun nodded. He glanced across at Diurnan. 'Put the men

to the oars, let us pass that isle as quickly as possible and be gone from this cursed place.'

In her eyes he was no longer a man. What feeling she had had for him had disappeared in the ravening lust for food, for fresh, warm meat and blood. She reached out for him, her fingers hooking into claws . . .

Instinct warned Ruarc. He turned, his eyes lighting into a smile when he saw the young woman . . . and the smile froze on his face as he noted her glazed, wild-eyed expression and bared teeth. He stared at her stupidly for a moment, and then her nails raked across his face, stripping flesh in four long ribbons, narrowly missing his eye. He screamed aloud and stumbled backwards, both hands going to his torn face. Rathne licked her bloody fingers and then threw herself forward, her weight bearing the young man to the deck. The hunger would soon be satisfied.

Paedur reacted first to Ruarc's terrified scream. He turned, his eyes widening as he saw the young man struggling beneath the frenzied girl.

Germane cursed and plucked a small throwing knife from his belt, pulled his arm back, but Maildun knocked it to one side, before dashing across the deck towards the *banshee*.

Rathne pounded Ruarc's head against the deck, and his body relaxed beneath her. She swallowed her scalding saliva, and then looked up in time to see Maildun and Paedur bearing down on her. She moved with surprising speed, pulling Ruarc's knife free and lunging upwards, at the captain. The knife struck Maildun's belt and twisted from her hand, but the blow winded him. Her straightened fingers then drove upwards into his throat as he bent double, sending him reeling back, gagging.

She jabbed pointed fingers towards Paedur's eyes, hissing like a wild cat. He caught her left hand in his right and pulled her in towards him – and deftly cut her throat with his hook. There was little blood and she crumpled almost weightlessly to the deck.

Diurnan almost crashed into the bard as he came running up, a long fishing-gaff held in both hands. He eyed the corpse dispassionately, before kicking her in the ribs, turning the body over. Her torn throat gaped obscenely. He nodded at the bard. 'Effective; not the first time you've done that, I'll wager.'

'It solves a lot of problems,' Paedur said, turning away to kneel by Maildun's side. The captain had risen to a sitting position, but he was still coughing and there was a greenish tinge to his face. 'Is she . . .?'

The bard's eyes flickered across to the body. 'Dead.'

'Ruarc?'

The bard looked over his shoulder. Germane and Diurnan were helping the young man to his feet. He looked dazed and frightened, and the tears in his flesh stood out sharply against the whiteness of his skin. 'A sore head and a cut face,' Paedur said, 'he'll live.' He looked back at Maildun. 'You're lucky; a little higher and that knife would have gutted you, a little harder and that blow to the throat would have killed you.'

The captain rubbed his throat carefully. Rathne's fingermarks were clearly outlined against the livid flesh. 'I feel like I've drunk bad mead.' He held up his arm and Paedur hauled him to his feet.

Ruarc shook himself free of Germane's and Diurnan's hands. He walked round the corpse and stood before his foster-brother. He was trembling violently and looked as if he were resisting the urge to be sick. 'You've had your wish,' he whispered, 'and I hate you.'

'She was about to tear your throat out,' Paedur said quietly.

Ruarc struck out at the bard, but Paedur caught and held the young man's arm, and pushed it down. Ruarc spat at him and then his eyes rolled in his head and he slumped to the deck, unconscious.

CHAPTER TWENTY-FOUR

Maildun christened the island *Aonchos*, which in the old Gaelic tongue meant One-Foot, and Germane and Diurnan argued whether it was indeed an island or a pillar. In all the sights they had encountered on the Island Sea and the Sea of Wonders, it certainly ranked among the strangest.

A pillar rose out of the water to about the height of the *Avenger's* mast. It was squat and massive, with each of the four sides being longer than the length of the *Avenger*. The pillar was surmounted by a perfectly circular disc, which had been fashioned into a miniature island, complete with sandy beach giving onto a smooth, grassy plain, and rising to a small range of low hills in the centre. From the distance they could see a series of low white buildings, and there was evidence that one of the fields had recently been ploughed. However, no smoke rose from the dwellings and they saw no sign of movement.

Germane brought the *Avenger* in as close to the pillar and island as was possible. The pillar was of metal but, whereas the previous pillar had been of unblemished silver, this was rusted and corroded in places, stained with the evidence of many long years spent in water.

Looking upwards, they could see that the island itself seemed to be constructed of metal, and they could see great rectangles of dulled metal held together by massive bolts. There was a steady dripping of water beneath the isle and the sea itself about the pillar was fouled and streaked with rainbow-hued liquid, and dead fish floated belly-upwards in the murk.

They had sailed part way round the pillar when they came upon the door. Germane's dark eyes spotted it first, noticing it because it stood out as being in better repair and cleaner than the rest of the metal. It was set almost flush with the sides of the pillar and there was no sign of a handle or lock. Diurnan hammered on the metal with the flat of his sword, but even though the metal rang and echoed, there were no sounds of movement within and the island and pillar – which they took to be hollow – seemed to be deserted.

Eventually they sailed away without finding out anything about the island. It was another of the unfathomable mysteries of the Sea of Wonders.

And so they quit the region between the Shadowlands and sailed back into the Island Sea proper, once more to continue on their quest. A quest which, Maildun reflected, had changed dramatically, although it still remained a search, but now the object of their search was differenct. The captain shook his head and pressed his fingers to his eyes; such thoughts were alien to him, and then he shrugged, putting them down to the passing region of limbo and its disturbing effects.

At first they took the shadow on the horizon to be a storm brewing, but as the day passed and they closed with it, it became clear that they were sailing towards a land mass. It was impossible to say whether it was an island or something larger: it was certainly the largest area of land they had yet encountered on the Island Sea. It stretched north to south in an almost unbroken line, with a jagged, splinter-tooth range of mountains running down along it. With the setting sun behind them, they watched the many rivers and lakes turn blood-red and gold in the light, and a spectacular rainbow arched across a broad band of whiteness, which Diurnan announced must be a waterfall – although if it was visible from that distance, it was certainly larger than any he had ever seen before.

After some discussion with Germane and Paedur, Maildun had Diurnan stagger the crew in night-shifts and, with the *Avenger* running before a full sail, he put them to the oars so that, by the time the false dawn brightened the sky to the east and paled the stars, the broad, gleaming shoreline of the island-continent was visible. He then ordered the anchor dropped, and they bobbed offshore until full dawn and sun-shine, to await the coming day.

The bard called out for Maildun just before the hunting horns sounded. Maildun, Germane and Diurnan joined the bard by the port side, as the long procession rode down onto the beach and spread out in a complete half-circle close to the water's edge.

There were two score or more warriors, clad in polished leathers, brightly-hued cloaks about their shoulders and riding squat, shaggy beasts that had a touch too much of the goat about them to be truly called horses. The warriors were armed with tall, leaf-bladed spears and carried a short sword or long knife strapped across their stomachs.

201

In the half-circle, surrounded by the warriors, stood a dozen young girls. They were alike to a startling degree, but they were not twins – although, with their long, pale gold hair and wide eyes and strong cheekbones, it would have been difficult to tell them apart from the distance. They were clad in long gowns of dyed wool, and there were gold torcs about their wrists and throats.

One, slightly taller than the others, stepped forward and beckoned to them.

Maildun looked across at the bard. 'Well?'

Paedur hesitated, and then he shook his head. 'I must admit to knowing nothing about this isle. I get no feeling of a trap about it and yet . . .'

'*Yet?*'

'Yet it doesn't feel right.' He nodded towards the isle. 'They could have let us land and then ambushed us. They could of course have sent out the maidens and kept the warriors hidden – and yet they didn't. I am just wondering why.'

'Might not the warriors be the maidens' guards?' Germane asked. 'I've seen some girls in the warm southern lands walk around the towns followed by a guard with a drawn sword.'

Paedur nodded. 'It's possible. We don't know what beasts roam the isle.'

'We'll go over,' Maildun said decisively. 'Not all of us; you and I, Paedur.'

'And what if it is a trap?' Diurnan demanded.

Maildun smiled with his old good humour. 'Then you'll just have to come over and get us, won't you?'

'Is it not foolish to risk both of you?' the navigator asked. 'The crew follow you, not me, not Diurnan, and without Paedur to guide us we will be truly lost.'

'He is right,' the bard murmured.

Maildun nodded stubbornly. 'Even so, you and I are going across,' he said. 'With your powers we should be able to avoid any trouble.'

'I wouldn't place too much faith in my magic,' the bard said with a smile, 'it has the unfortunate attribute of not working when you most need it.'

'I'll take that risk.'

'Welcome, Maildun, son of Oilill Agach; you have been long expected.' The young woman crossed her hands across her breasts and bowed deeply, her thick hair of pale gold whispering forward across her face.

202

'It seems I am expected everywhere on this world,' the captain remarked with a wry smile.

'Why, all know of the Voyage of Maildun the Wanderer,' the young woman said in her slightly accented voice, her russet eyes opening wide.

'Even with a little magic, intimations of the future are possible,' the bard said quietly, 'and you must remember that time flows differently here.'

The young woman smiled again, although this time a little less warmly. 'Just so, Paedur Hook-Hand; even your coming was foretold.'

Paedur touched the Bardic Sigil on his left shoulder with the tips of his first and third fingers and bowed slightly. 'I am honoured to think that my presence should have appeared in your foretellings.'

'Should we not be honoured that the Wandering Bard has chosen to visit our poor island?'

'It was not by choice,' Paedur said shortly, and the young woman's expression hardened. Her gaze held his for a heartbeat and then dropped, and she busied herself with the sleeve of her gown. She then looked over at Maildun. 'My mistress, Ranume, Queen of the Isle, bids you welcome, and commands me to invite you and your crew to a feast of welcome in your honour which will take place at sunset. She further bids me tell you,' she continued, seeing the captain look round at the silent warriors, 'that no harm will come to you or your men on this isle, for there is a *geasa* on us all to prevent bloodshed and avoid violence.'

Maildun looked pointedly at the weapons that the warriors carried.

'These men are an honour guard,' the young woman continued, 'there are no dangerous beasts on this isle, and its flora is both tranquil and placid. Here all life lives in harmony, and death is all but unknown to us.' She glanced sharply at the bard before looking back at Maildun. 'You and your crew will join us?'

'We will be honoured to.' He turned to Paedur. 'Why don't you return to the *Avenger* and tell Germane to bring her in as close to the shore as possible. One other thing, have Diurnan ensure that the men are armed with nothing longer than their eating knives when they're coming ashore.'

'And where are you going now?' Paedur asked.

'I will present myself to the queen.'

'Alone? Do you think that's wise?'

203

'You heard this young woman . . .'

'Do you usually believe everything you hear so easily?' Paedur demanded.

'I trust her,' Maildun hissed.

'*I do not.*'

Maildun's hand rested on the hilt of his knife. 'I think you are wrong this time,' he said, smiling pleasantly, conscious that the young woman was looking at them.

'Have you ever known me to be wrong?' the bard asked, in little more than a whisper, and then he turned away and climbed back into the currach. Standing tall in the small, round craft, he raised his left arm, and allowed the sunlight to touch his hook. The currach shifted easily on the swell and drifted out – against the current and tide – back towards the *Avenger*.

Maildun stood on the beach watching him leave, a tiny doubt beginning to creep into his composure. A few heartbeats ago he had been sure that the island was perfectly safe and that the woman was telling the truth, but now . . . He frowned, trying to grasp the elusive thought. A feather-light touch brushed his arm and he found himself looking into the wide, russet eyes of the woman, and all doubts vanished. Surely this island was Paradise?

'It's a trap, I'm convinced of it.'

'Well, where's Maildun gone, if it's a trap and, more to the point, why did you let him go?' Diurnan demanded.

'And what would you have had me do?' Paedur snapped, 'crack him across the skull and make a run for the boat?'

'What are we going to do now?' Germane asked reasonably.

'Get him back, of course,' Diurnan began, but the navigator held up his hand. 'Why did you let him go in the first place?' he asked the bard.

'Two reasons; to lull suspicion – and we must be careful,' he added, 'for my reputation seems to be not unknown – and, secondly, to enable me to return here without having to fight my way out, to warn you.'

'And what do we do now?' The navigator repeated his earlier question.

The bard pointed across to the island to a point where something sparkled and glinted in the sunlight. 'It's my guess that that is the palace. It's not far enough from the shore to prevent any great difficulties should we have to fight our way out and, despite what that young woman said, those warriors have been battle-trained in some war. They sat those beasts with perfect ease and, although they were all armed with the same weapons, they had made enough personal modifications to them to speak of their being professionals.'

'Would they know how large our crew is?' Diurnan wondered, shading his eyes with his hand and trying to gauge the distance from the beach to the palace.

'Not precisely, but I'm sure they could guess to a close enough number – that is, if Maildun doesn't tell them in all innocence.'

'Is that likely?' Diurnan asked.

The bard shrugged. 'He accepted what she told him without question; he might.'

'Did she cast a spell on him?' Germane asked.

Again the bard shrugged. 'I'm not sure; I doubt it.' He raised his hook slightly. 'I can usually tell when a spell is being worked. No, I think it was more a natural property of the island itself.'

'But surely that means that if we set foot on the island that same property will entrap us?' Germane asked.

'You will have been forewarned; that should help.'

'And if it doesn't?'

The bard turned towards the island and considered. 'It is a large island and, if the spell is being cast by one person, they will find it difficult to maintain over too great a distance on so many. It will soon falter, and even if it didn't, no spell is powerful enough to hold you for all eternity; even Oisin grew weary of the delights of Tir na nOg.'

Germane brought the *Avenger* in as close to the shore as he dared. The bay was wide and shallow, and they ground to a halt in the soft sands roughly a dozen oar lengths from the beach.

Diurnan had briefed the crew on what to expect and what he expected of them, and then the bard had warned them of the dangers of accepting the island and all it presented without questioning. He illustrated his warning with brief anecdotes of an almost sentient island which thrived on human flesh.

Diurnan stood beside the bard, as the men slid down the ropes into the shallow water and began wading towards the shore. 'We could disobey the captain,' the northerner said, almost reluctantly.

Paedur nodded silently, his clear, reflective eyes watching the water turn from blue to mud as the sand was churned up in the crew's wake.

'We could go ashore tonight, you and I, and carry him back – by force, if need be.'

205

Again the bard nodded.

'Well, why don't we!' Diurnan demanded desperately. 'Why are we standing here, allowing the entire crew to follow the captain onto an island which you believe may have ensorcelled him?'

'Man has always had a need to see his folly through,' the bard said, with a grim smile. 'Let him experience the island with all its treacherous delights. The island – and, indeed, this whole voyage – are part of his destiny; it is not within your or my power to deny that destiny.' He paused, and then nodded towards the shore. 'Go with them, watch over them, guard Maildun.'

'But what about you . . . ?' Diurnan protested.

Paedur shook his head. 'The island is not for me; I will remain with the ship. I will be here when I am needed.'

The northerner opened his mouth, but the bard raised his hook, forestalling him. 'Go now . . . and, Diurnan,' he added softly, 'be wary; I sense something terribly wrong with that island.'

CHAPTER TWENTY-FIVE

The column of men came out of the forest and into the clearing – and stopped in amazement, looking up at the structure that rose up out of the green sward before them.

One of the honour guard swung his goatish mount round in a tight circle and pointed across the clearing with his spear. 'The Palace of Ranume, Queen of the Isle,' he announced, his accent thick and guttural. 'Aye, your captain is within,' he said, as Diurnan pushed his way through the gasping crew.

'Safe?' the northerner demanded.

The guard glared down from the back of his mount. 'Aye, you were told no harm would come to you on this isle; we keep our word.'

'Aye.' Diurnan sounded unconvinced. He looked round and caught Germane looking over at him. He nodded briefly, and the southerner raised his hand, and called the crew forward. Diurnan remained standing by the side of the winding, paved track, chivvying along the stragglers, and looking up at the towering palace.

Although, if it was a palace, it was like nothing he had ever seen before.

The walls rose from the grass in tall, thin columns, like the gilded trunks of some metallic trees. They towered to an impossible height and their crests burned gold and bronze in the waning sunlight. The walls were also no thicker than the northerner's middle finger, and in some places there were cracks and openings which enabled him to see into the interior of the palace. There were no gates.

Beyond the walls, within the palace, the forest had been allowed to grow almost unmolested, and only the many branching paths and tracks of white stone indicated that it was indeed under the influence of man. Tall bushes lined the paths, in place of corridors and walls. Spreading branches had been fashioned into the roofs of compartments, and many-hued bushes formed living tapestries and hangings.

The honour guard led the crew of the *Avenger* down along the main track and out onto a broad, white-paved area which was completely surrounded by closely planted trees. In the centre of this glade was a smooth, grassy hillock rising up out of the white stone like a miniature island in itself. There was a marvellously carved and worked stone throne on the top of the hillock, and seated on the throne was a stunningly beautiful woman. Standing beside her, one hand resting casually on the stone, was Maildun.

Diurnan marched up to the foot of the hillock and rested one booted foot on the polished white step, He looked up at the captain, deliberately ignoring the woman. 'Are you unharmed?'

Maildun looked surprised. 'Of course I'm unharmed.' He frowned. 'Did the bard not tell you what transpired?'

'He did.'

'Then surely he passed on the queen's promise?'

'He did.' The northerner shrugged uncomfortably under both the captain's and the queen's stare. 'Do not blame me for being cautious,' he said.

Maildun smiled. 'Of course not; one does not expect civilised behaviour from a barbarian.'

Germane's fingers closed in warning on Diurnan's wrist. Maildun stepped forward and held out his hand. The queen placed her small fingers in his and rose slowly. She was a surprisingly tall woman, even taller than Diurnan, who stood head and shoulders taller than most men. Her hair was the colour of ripe wheat and flowed down her back in a thick mane. Two braids framed her face. Her eyes were huge and russet-coloured tending to red, like an animal's in torchlight.

The queen was clad in a short gown of pale green which was hemmed with a band of gold. A slim gold belt encircled her small waist and she wore hoops through her ears to match. She wore brass sandals.

She smiled, exposing tiny, perfectly white teeth, but the smile never reached her eyes. 'I am Ranume,' she said loudly, her voice accented, but pleasantly so. 'This is my domain, and I bid you all welcome.' She paused and the crew cheered uncertainly. 'Your coming had been foretold, and everything is prepared.' She raised her hand, and scores of the almost identical young women appeared from behind the throne. 'These are my daughters; they will take you to your rooms, where you will find fresh clothing, and they will conduct you to the warm-water streams. They will be your constant companions during your stay here. When you have rested and refreshed yourselves, you may return here for a night of feasting.' She bowed and the crew cheered again, this time more forcefully. The young women moved out from behind the throne and took their places beside each of the crew.

'You are all welcome to Paradise,' Ranume said, and then she turned away, Maildun following her.

Diurnan stepped back and found himself looking into the wide russet eyes of one of the queen's daughters. She was almost identical to the woman standing beside Germane and the rest of the bemused crew.

'What is your name?' he asked gruffly, suddenly conscious of his grubby appearance, and aware that it had been some time since had had last bathed.

'I am Rine,' she said simply, staring intently at him. 'I am to serve you in all things.'

'In all things?'

'Your will is my will,' she said.

Diurnan jerked his head towards the throne. 'Where has the captain been taken?'

Rine looked surprised. 'Your captain has been taken nowhere. He is the chosen of the queen; he is her companion.'

A sudden thought struck the northerner. 'You are a daughter of Ranume?'

'We are all the daughters of Ranume, Queen of the Isle.'

'How old are you, Rine?'

The young woman frowned. 'I do not know what you mean,' she said at last.

Diurnan glanced across at Germane, but the southerner was busy plying his companion with questions also. 'I mean,' he said, 'how many summers have you seen?'

Rine shook her corn-coloured hair and smiled slightly. 'Summers?'

Diurnan frowned. 'Does the weather ever change here, Rine?'

'This is Paradise,' Rine said seriously, her wide eyes clouding, 'nothing ever changes. All was, all is, all shall be.' She reached out and touched his arm. 'Come, you must bathe, rest; there will be feasting this night, and every night hereafter.'

But Diurnan refused to be moved. 'How many sisters have you, Rine?'

She laughed then, a brittle, almost childish sound. 'Why, as many as need be,' she said, turning away and making her way round the grass mound and out through a gap in the hedge behind the throne. Diurnan swore to his wild northern gods, and then he hurried after her.

The feasting began just after sunset and continued on long into the night. It was held in a huge circle that was enclosed by tall, sweet-smelling bushes, whose leaves – as many of the revellers and their companions discovered that night – made a soft and comfortable bed. The food was plentiful and varied, and ranged from thin broths to thick meats and strange tart and sour sweetmeats. There was wine and mead aplenty, and another plain, almost water-like drink that burned like fire going down and exploded in the stomach.

The food was served in large metallic bowls and the drink in short-stemmed, chunky goblets. There were no tables and the men sat or sprawled on the warm, scented, cropped turf.

Maildun, with Ranume on his arm, wandered through the feasting crewmen, laughing and joking with some, and ignoring others. He walked past both Germane and Diurnan without seeming to see them, and then disappeared into the shadows with the queen.

Diurnan attempted to question the navigator, but he found that Rine was always at his side and Germane's companion, Rane, seemed intent upon clinging to the dark southerner with equal fervour.

The following day, Maildun awoke Diurnan and Germane, disentangling them from the arms of their companions, and suggested that they explore the island.

'Where's the queen?' Diurnan asked, pulling his tunic over his head.

The captain waved his hand. His eyes seemed distant and occasionally he stopped in mid-sentence and his mind seemed to wander. 'Oh, she attends to matters of state. She must adjudicate on some points of law.'

Germane looked at Diurnan. 'I thought there was no danger on this isle.'

'There's not,' Maildun said indignantly.

'But there must be crime, if she needs must judge a case,' Diurnan said quickly.

The captain gazed from one to the other, and then he smiled thinly. 'I'm sure it is but a minor matter. Come.' He slipped his arm round both their shoulders – which was completely out of character, for he was usually the most reticent of men – and drew them through an opening in the hedge and onto one of the white-paved tracks.

There seemed to be no buildings on the Isle of Paradise, nothing that could be directly attributed to the hand of man.

Even the golden walls of the palace had a natural look to them, and Maildun explained that they were indeed tree trunks, but imported from one of the far-distant islands, carried there by one of the vessels that sailed between the worlds. The queen's throne, for example, although at first glance it seemed to be a remarkable example of the mason and master-carver's art, took on a crude and altogether different appearance in the hard light of morning, and now looked nothing more than a chunk of stone that bore a natural resemblance to a seat. The glyphs and runes had melted into imperfections and blotches in the stone itself. The only things which one could say with any degree of certainty were the work of man, were the pathways. However, Maildun said that they were the work of a huge species of slug which had crawled these islands in olden times – the white tracks were its slimed trail, now hardened by time and polished by the elements to their present condition.

And the pale-haired, russet-eyed young women were everywhere.

When Germane asked the captain how it was that the queen could have had so many daughters and still retain her looks and beauty, Maildun had looked puzzled and his eyes had darted quickly around, as if seeking assistance from behind the trees and bushes, but when none had been forthcoming, he had shaken his head and murmured that he didn't know.

Rine and Rane came for Diurnan and Germane later that afternoon, and took them away to bathe, eat and make love, and then later on that night there was another feast. The following day, Maildun came again for his companions and they walked the Isle of Paradise.

And thus it continued.

Diurnan opened his eyes at the touch, and found himself locking up into a long, thin face, and two eyes which were perfect mirrors. He closed his eyes again. Something cold and pointed touched his cheek, gouging painfully into his flesh – and the pain brought memories.

'*Paedur!*'

'It seems my warning was in vain,' the bard said softly, 'but then it looks as if you had other things on your mind.' He smiled down at the sleeping form of Rine.

'The warning . . .' Diurnan said slowly, rolling out from beneath a blanket of woven leaves.

'The warning. To watch and question . . .'

211

'Aye,' the northerner nodded vigorously, 'to question, to question everything.' He shrugged. 'Well, we were just settling in, allaying their suspicions for a few days . . .'

'Diurnan, do you know how long you have been here?'

Something in the bard's voice stopped the northerner cold. He looked up, his boot still in his hand, 'How long?' he whispered.

'Half a year as you would measure time!'

'But that's . . .'

Paedur smiled. 'Impossible?' He shook his head. 'No, I fear it is not impossible. Now, you dress yourself quickly and awaken the men. We must make haste; the queen will breed soon.' He raised his hook, forestalling questions. 'I will answer everything later. Now go.'

'And you?'

'I am going to find Maildun.'

The bard wandered through the gardens of the Isle of Paradise, following instinct that had been honed by ages, seeking Maildun and Ranume. With his unhuman senses he looked at the singular growths and saw the ruins they concealed, the huge scars in the earth that they covered and the vast burial grounds that they sheltered. The Old Magic was strong here; he felt it tingling in his missing hand, felt it burn along his arm, saw the runes in his hook begin to sparkle with arcane life, tasted the tartness of it on the air, experienced the Power.

And he suddenly knew it would be possible for him to find death here.

He rounded a tall copse of trees that concealed crumbling statuary and came upon the queen's 'bedchamber'. It was an almost circular opening, completely enclosed on three sides by high, closely-knit bushes, and topped with the spreading branches of the surrounding trees. A small, round pool was set in the middle of the opening and beside it was a bundle of woven blankets. Paedur could see bright red hair over the top of the leaf-woven blankets.

There was movement from the water and the bard melted back into the shadows. Ranume rose up out of the water in a smooth, almost effortless leap. She padded silently across the velvet grass and stood above Maildun. With the heel of her right foot, she kicked out at him.

'Maildun?' Her voice was very soft, like the whisper of a blade coming out of its sheath. 'Maildun?' She folded her arms beneath her breasts, and waited.

The young man opened his eyes, rolled over and looked up at

212

the queen. Still semi-conscious, he watched the almost green light trickle down her glistening body, turning her shining blonde hair to jade.

'Maildun.' Ranume moved, and droplets of water dripped from her pouting breasts and fell across his face. He reached out slowly to touch them, felt the moisture beneath his fingers and face; experienced the sensations with an almost childlike wonder. The Isle of Paradise had taught him many things, but primarily it had taught him to experience. It had brought him truly alive.

He threw back the blanket and rose slowly to his feet to stand swaying slightly before the queen. Ranume reached out and ran her fingers through the hair on his chest and across his flat stomach. He watched her lazily, gazing calmly into her wide eyes, although his body began to respond.

'It is time, Maildun.' Ranume smiled, her face hardening into a mask. She raised her arm and pointed towards the pool. 'Wash; you must purify yourself before we join in sacred union. Wash!'

Maildun continued to gaze into her face for a few heartbeats, and then turned slowly and walked across to the pool. Ranume watched him for a moment and then she turned away.

Maildun walked towards the pool. He could feel each individual hair on his head and body shift as he walked, he could feel the play of his muscles as he moved . . .

There was movement, a blur of darkness and then something hard hit him low in the stomach, doubling him over. He felt the pain.

Paedur swung his hook round and cracked the captain across the side of the head, and then stooped and allowed the crumpling body to drape itself across his shoulder. He turned then and ran, ignoring the queen's outraged screams.

The guard appeared from behind the trunk of an ancient oak, dragging his sword free, surprise mingling with hate on his dark face. Paedur slashed at him without breaking stride, and his razor-sharp hook sliced through gleaming leather and flesh, leaving the warrior clutching his throat and chest.

The bard allowed his usually dormant additional senses to come into being, and the forest immediately took on a thousand incandescent hues, as the living flora and moving fauna took on colours and shapes, and registers of heat and sound. He was conscious of the cold-white anger and rage of Ranume moving fast behind him. To his left there was a column of warriors, the crimson of their controlled rage blanketing out the softer shades of the life around them. Before and to his right the confused

213

milling of the *Avenger's* awakening crew reflected like oil on water. A flash of crimson, and a guard stepped out into the middle of the path before him, broad-headed spear levelled. With no time to call up his magic, the bard simply rushed at him, trusting to his speed and reflexes to carry him through. The guard lunged, and Paedur, burdened with Maildun, barely managed to elude the beaten bronze head. He chopped with his hook, severing the spear-head and then, swivelling on one foot, kicked upwards with the other, catching the guard beneath the chin. His teeth clicked together and his eyes rolled in his head.

The bard burst into the clearing and was immediately surrounded by the *Avenger's* crew. Diurnan took the captain from his shoulder and hoisted him onto his own. The men shuffled around uncertainly for a few moments and then, with the bard's commands ringing in their ears, set out at a stiff pace for the shore, Diurnan leading, with Paedur to the rear.

Afterwards, Diurnan could never recall how they actually reached the beach. He would tell a confused tale of leading the men along the white track, while behind them the very air itself burned and crisped with strange traceries of light. Some things did remain clearly in his mind though: the screams of the dying . . . Ranume's incomprehensible shouting . . . and the almost musical chiming as one of the tree-like silver towers of the palace toppled gracefully down into the forest.

Once they reached the beach, the crew began to shake off the stultifying effects of the island, and dived into the water with a will, striking out for the *Avenger*, fear spurring them on. Germane, who had almost recovered, helped Diurnan carry the awakened Maildun out to the ship, and the bard was the last man off the beach, as he dodged two warriors on their goatish mounts. When he did take to the water a few moments later, he left one creature disembowelled and the second rider looking at the stump of his arm, his expression blank and shocked.

There was no wind and so the men took to the oars, pulling the *Avenger* strongly away from the cursed isle. They had almost rounded a headway when Ranume appeared on the cliffs. She was clad in a scarlet gown, and in the afternoon light it looked as if she burned.

Maildun stood by the rail and watched her, his eyes beginning to glaze. He was still dazed and wandered around like a man awakening from a long dream – or a man without his soul.

'*Maildun!*' Ranume's voice shivered on the air, and, almost as

214

one, the men rested on their oars and the ship started drifting in towards the isle.

'*Maildun*, return, my love.'

Maildun reached out across the waves, his eyes filled with longing.

'*Maildun!*' Something glittered in the air, like a long, irregular sliver of light stretching from the queen's upraised hand. The captain reached out and plucked something from the air: a silver thread.

'Return, my love.'

The *Avenger* heeled and almost overturned. Against the tide, it turned of its own accord, and began to move in towards the shore.

Diurnan's huge hands closed over the captain's forcing his fingers apart. Paedur ran up behind the struggling pair and struck Maildun in the small of the back, sending him to his knees. The captain released the thread, and the *Avenger* immediately began to wallow. Diurnan roared the beat and Germane brought her about.

They had almost rounded a second headway when the craft lurched violently, sending men sprawling to the decks, dragging the oars into the air. There was a scream of triumph from the shore and Ranume raised both hands high as if in offering. Thin filaments of light fluttered between her fingers, like a web. Her hands moved, and the *Avenger* once again turned in towards the shore.

Paedur raced down the deck, his mirror-flat eyes searching for the thread that must be connecting the ship to Ranume. Maildun was still unconscious, with Diurnan standing over him, and the remainder of the crew were struggling to row the craft free of the witch-queen's pull. He stopped, his face hardening into a mask; there was one person he had not checked yet . . .

Ruarc screamed in surprise as the bard's iron-hard fingers closed on his shoulder, and squeezed. The pain was excruciating and drove him to his knees, the silver thread falling from his numb fingers. Paedur swore in a sibilant tongue; Ruarc's hatred for his brother would kill them all yet. He shifted his hold on Ruarc, moving it from shoulder to neck, and then slammed him face down into the deck.

The thread, almost hair-thin and invisible except when the sunlight touched it, whispered down the deck, the crew scrambling to avoid it.

'*Maildun!*'

Ranume's cry brought the captain awake. His eyes shifted and focused, and then settled on the silver thread slithering past his face. He reached out for it . . .

Paedur's hook bit down into the deck between his outstretched fingers and the silver filament. For a moment Maildun saw the angular runes in almost painfully sharp relief, saw tiny sparkles of light touch them. 'Touch it and I'll take your hand off at the wrist!' The bard's voice chilled Maildun with its total inhumanity. He looked up, and saw the thin, angular face transformed into a death's mask, saw his own distorted reflection in the mirror-like eyes.

The bard looked up and away, and nodded. 'Away now; we are free of her; thrice called, thrice failed.'

Diurnan called the beat and the *Avenger* pulled from the Isle of Paradise, running as if from a storm.

CHAPTER TWENTY-SIX

'And it never occurred to you to question how the queen could have such a large number of almost identical daughters and still retain her youth?' Paedur asked, leaning over the edge of the craft, staring down into the night-black water. The sky was overcast and, with only the lights at stern and bow, the bard was barely visible.

'Rine said that she had as many sisters "as need be",' Diurnan said slowly. 'I wondered what she meant then and I was going to ask her, but somehow it didn't seem so important.'

'Nothing seemed important,' Maildun said quietly. Since they had passed beyond the influence of the Isle of Paradise, the captain had kept very much to himself, for he seemed to hold himself responsible for allowing the entire crew to become trapped on the isle.

'That is the nature of the isle,' Paedur said. 'It promises eternal comfort – but at a price.'

'What is the price?' Maildun asked.

Paedur smiled, his teeth suddenly white in the darkness. 'The price for your crew would have been eternal boredom, and the eventual loss of themselves. The price for you would have been death.'

'But the queen said . . .'

Cloth rustled as the bard nodded. 'Aye, the queen said many things; do not believe the word of kings, priests or gods,' he said with a touch of irony in his voice, 'for their word is law, and the law is liable to change.' He shrugged again. 'The queen was an inhuman . . .'

'No,' Maildun protested, 'she was perfectly human.'

'Outwardly.'

'A lamia?' Germane asked quietly.

'Not quite; Ranume was more of the tribe of Empusae, the vampire-demons.'

'Her sandals!' Germane said suddenly, 'I knew there was something about them. I wondered why, when there was a surfeit of riches everywhere, she would choose to wear brass sandals.'

'Yes; she was one of Hecate's daughters.' The bard turned towards Maildun. 'She would have used you to satisfy her lusts and then, when you were satiated, she would have torn out your throat and drunk your blood. The empusae can conceive but once a year – and this was her time.' The bard's voice changed slightly. 'You would have fathered a tribe of female demons.'

'May God have mercy on me,' Maildun whispered to himself.

The following morning brought an island; a small, thickly wooded isle with an ancient volcanic cone crowning it. Birds that were almost familiar rose wheeling overhead, and the whole island seemed so natural that it reinforced the pangs of homesickness which had begun to infect even the hardiest sailor.

Maildun would have passed it by, but Paedur had been curiously insistent that they land, and in the end the captain had acceded to his wishes and both Diurnan and the bard had gone ashore in the currach.

'It smells natural enough,' Diurnan said, breathing deeply. He glanced across at the bard, suddenly anxious. 'It is, isn't it?'

Paedur nodded, pushing back his hood with the point of his hook, allowing his long hair to blow in the breeze. 'It is both natural and safe. The only dangers here are the usual ones of any isle.'

'The dangers of any normal isle, or the dangers peculiar to this cursed sea?' the northerner asked, shifting his battleaxe on his shoulder.

'A normal isle,' Paedur said, moving quickly up the beach and into the fringes of the trees. 'We are close enough to your home world now, Diurnan close indeed.'

'Why did you insist that we land here?'

Paedur pointed into the forest. 'I'm looking for something.' He looked back at the northerner. 'You've noticed how Maildun has been behaving . . . ?'

'Aye, I fear for his sanity.'

'Was he ever completely sane?' the bard asked gently. 'Would a sane man have undertaken this voyage?'

Diurnan shrugged uncomfortably. 'In a similar situation I might have done so myself.'

'Truly?'

They pushed their way through the tall undergrowth and into the forest proper, while Diurnan considered his answer. At last he shook his head. 'No, I don't think I would.' He shrugged. 'When I was younger, perhaps. But the world is changing now –

or perhaps I'm just getting old. I saw my father slain before my eyes: I knew his slayer, but I didn't kill him – he was a bigger, stronger, better and more experienced fighter than I was. I rejoiced later when I discovered he had fallen from his vessel and drowned, pulled down by the weight of the spoils he was wearing. It was a fitting death. I saw my mother grow old bearing a dozen children, barely half of whom survived. But I never felt the need to avenge her; she had lived her life, fulfilled her destiny.'

'Just so. But that is not Maildun's way. He originally wanted revenge on a father he never knew, and now he wants revenge on his father's murderers – and by doing so will make himself no better than they.' The bard grunted and pointed, and then moved quickly off to one side. 'And yet, if you ask,' he called back over his shoulder, 'he will tell you he is seeking revenge for his mother's destruction.'

'Aye,' Diurnan nodded, hurrying after the tall, dark shape of the bard. 'Paedur, what are you doing?'

'Collecting some fruit.'

'*Fruit*! What for?'

'Why, for Maildun, of course!'

'What is it?' Maildun asked, gingerly taking the large, rough-skinned globe from Paedur's hand.

'It is unique to the Island Sea; it has the qualities of crushed and fermented grapes, and the texture of honey.' He handed Maildun a goblet and then, holding the fruit over the cup, sliced through it with his hook. A thick, red ichor bled from the fruit into the goblet, immediately emitting a heady odour. Maildun breathed deeply. 'Aye, honey.'

'Drink!' the bard commanded, 'all of it and in one swallow, mind,' he added.

Maildun looked into the half cup of blood-like fluid uncertainly.

'Don't look at it,' Paedur advised. 'Just close your eyes and drink.'

Maildun, refusing to close his eyes, stared into the distance and then lifted the goblet and swallowed its contents. He handed the empty cup back to the bard, his eyes rolled in his head and he collapsed onto the deck with a sigh.

Paedur breathed in the heady odours from the cup and wrinkled his nose. 'Perhaps we should have diluted it somewhat.'

Maildun remained unconscious for the remainder of the day,

through the night and on into the second day. He moaned and twitched in his sleep, and once he laughed in high good humour. When he awoke towards evening on the second day, he smiled for the first time in weeks and immediately asked for more.

'Dreamfruit,' Paedur explained to Diurnan and Germane later that day, as the crew carefully drained their rations of the diluted fruit. 'The liquor brings pleasant dreams, makes all things seem possible, dissipates worries and concerns.'

'It sounds almost dangerous,' Germane said, sniffing carefully at the cup of watered-down liquid he held in his hand.

'Oh, it is. Use it more than twice or three times in your lifetime and you will become addicted. Soon, nothing will matter but the fruit; it will become your food and drink. You can die of thirst beside a stream or starve to death beside a laden table.' He pointed towards the crewmen who were beginning to sample the liquid. 'When they sleep, I will cast the remainder overboard. But as for now,' he added, 'join them, drink a little, and I will tell you such a tale that will set your imagination afire and bring you dreams beyond comparison!'

The lookout's warning came just as the bard felt the first tingling in his hook. The crew lined the port rail and stared up into the heavens, squinting into the sunlight, trying to make out the shape that beat slowly across the skies.

Germane squinted against the glare and shaded his eyes. 'It's a bird,' he said in awe, 'but it's bigger than any bird I've ever seen before.' He closed his eyes and looked again. 'It must be a roc, A *chamroch*.'

The bard's hand suddenly closed on Diurnan's arm. 'Follow it!' He called the navigator and Maildun. 'Follow it . . .'

'Why?' Maildun demanded, 'look at its size; it could lift us out of the water.'

'It leads us home,' Paedur snapped.

The roc flew steadily on into the afternoon, its huge wings beating a down-draught that disturbed the waves even from its great height. The *Avenger* raced before a stiffening breeze, and with Diurnan calling a battle-beat, the oarsmen sent the light craft skipping across the water.

Towards late afternoon the huge bird dropped lower in the sky and headed for a tumbling bank of cloud that lined the horizon. With that special silence, even at sea, that the night brings on, they could hear the creature's wings beating powerfully, but at the same time they also became aware of a rasping, soughing sound, as of the wind through tall grass, and once the roc gave a short cry, which was almost like that of an old man, coughing.

'It's dying,' Paedur said quietly to Diurnan as they stood before the shattered figurehead and watched the bird slip lower in the skies.

'Is it old?'

'Old? Aye, it is old, even as I measure time, it is old. It has probably seen empires rise and fall,' he added bitterly.

'To be long-lived . . .' Diurnan said wistfully. 'To be able to achieve all that one wished.'

Paedur grinned crookedly. 'One achieves all that rather quickly, and after that . . .' He shrugged. 'You would probably end up like me – seeking death on an enchanted ocean.'

Diurnan shook his head. 'I think I might enjoy being long-lived.'

'You recall the tale I told you yester-eve of the coming of the Partholonians to Banba?'

'I recall it.'

'You recall that Delgrade, once-queen of that people, still lives . . . ?'

'Until the end of time, you said.'

'Would you truly wish that then, Diurnan?' the bard asked. 'To be alone, truly alone, your race, your family, everyone you knew, dead and dust?'

'But I could put my experience to use . . .'

Paedur laughed, one of the few times the northerner could remember hearing him express any real emotion. 'You remind me of myself, when I first gained the gift of life immortal. My ideas were as high and as pure as yours. However, I've found that humans fear what is not like them; like me, you would end up being loathed and despised.'

Diurnan nodded a little doubtfully, and then he shrugged. 'I doubt if I'll ever get the opportunity in any case.'

Paedur glanced at him curiously, before turning away.

The morning light showed that the roc was now even lower in the skies, and that the band of cloud on the horizon had resolved into an island, covered in a rich green sward. There was a tall construction of white stone that stood out sharply against the greenery, which was set in the centre of an area of barren earth. As the *Avenger* neared the shore – for it had become apparent that the creature was heading towards the island – they were able to make out that the isle was covered with a huge flock of sheep, and that the area of white they had seen was a large beehive construction in the shape of a church . . . a church of Erin!

Maildun stood leaning over the remnants of the figurehead, staring in amazement at the church. It was a sight he had never thought to see again, and only the figure of the dying *chamroch* destroyed the illusion that he was looking at an isle off the coast of Erin.

'It's not your homeland,' Paedur said quietly.

'But that's a church . . .'

The bard joined the captain by the rail. He nodded towards the huge, bronze-winged creature. 'And that?' he asked. 'No,' he shook his head, 'that may be a church of Erin, but this is still not your world.'

'Well then, where are we – what is that place?'

'My experience of the Island Sea does not extend this far, and beyond its name I can tell you little. That is known as the Monk's Isle, though an older account calls it the Isle of Life.'

The captain remained staring out towards the island, seemingly lost in thought, chewing absently on the corners of his moustache. 'We'll land,' he said decisively.

The bard remained silent, while Maildun turned away, calling for a currach to be prepared and shouting for Diurnan.

The sea was calm and, with the northerner pulling strongly at the oars, the small, light craft skipped across the water towards the rocky beach. Maildun leaped out as the first stones grated beneath the hull, and scrambled up the beach, sword in hand, while Diurnan dragged the craft up beyond the high-water mark.

The two men stood together warily, their weapons ready. The northerner grinned crookedly. 'This reminds me of that island we first landed on – the one with the giant ants.'

Maildun grimaced. He shifted his longsword from left to right hand and loosened the knife in his belt, before nodding to a thin, winding track that led up from the beach towards the church-building. 'Well, someone lives here, at any rate.'

'Something?' Diurnan suggested.

Maildun snorted rudely and then moved quickly up along the worn pathway.

The track led up along the beach, avoiding the many rock-pools, and across the blasted and barren landscape that surrounded the church. The rocks were scarred and in some cases seemed to have been melted by intense heat. And what was perhaps even more frightening was the fact that this area of crushed and powdered rock only continued for a certain distance in any one direction from the church, and beyond this area of desolation the rest of the isle seemed to be richly fertile.

The church itself was a tall, beehive-shaped building of flat stones piled – seemingly at random – one atop the other. However, both Maildun and Diurnan knew that such buildings, although cold and draughty, were amazingly sturdy and some, on Erin's wild western shores, had withstood many years of storm battering. The church was surmounted by a gleaming brazen cross and had been constructed of white stone, which made it stand out starkly against the drabness of the surrounding rocks.

A shadow moved in the darkened doorway of the church and Maildun raised his sword. 'Come out!'

'Put down your sword, Maildun, son of Oilill Agach, your fear comes not from me, but from yourself.' An old man stepped out of the doorway and stood regarding the two men, with no evidence of surprise or fear on his thin face. He was small and wizened, and stood with his hair and beard almost reaching to the ground. Beneath his covering of hair he seemed to be naked, with scrawny bones protruding like sticks, but his voice and eyes were bright and good-humoured.

Diurnan circled the old man and then darted into the church. He reappeared a few moments later, and silently shook his head.

Maildun sheathed his sword with a click. 'Who are you?' he asked the old man.

'I am Marcus, once a brother in the monastery of Clonfert, in Erin. My abbot was . . .'

'Brendan the Voyager!' Maildun exclaimed.

The old man nodded, pleased. 'The same; it is gratifying to see that his name has not been forgotten.'

'I thought his voyage a myth, a story for winter's evenings,' Maildun said quietly.

'What will your voyage become, Maildun the Wanderer?' Marcus asked, his toothless mouth opening in a wide grin. 'Come, come with me; let me show you my island.' He stretched out his hands to either side. 'Ah, but see how an old man becomes proud and vain: let me show you this island, God's Island,' he amended.

'How did you come here?' Diurnan asked, as the old man turned away and took the track that led round and beyond the church.

Marcus glanced over his shoulder and his expression sobered. 'Ach, but when I think back on it, it makes me angry at my own stupidity. It was our own fault – this way! – and there is no one to blame . . .'

'Why don't you start at the beginning?' Maildun suggested gently.

Marcus stopped and turned round. His constantly mobile face had changed to a concern that was almost comical. 'Ach, but you must forgive me; when you've lived alone as long as I have with no one but the sheep to talk to, it's very easy to forget that one's own story, although of inestimable importance to oneself, would mean nothing to strangers.'

'You are an educated man, then?' Maildun asked.

Marcus nodded proudly. 'I am. My family were vintners, suppliers to most of the Middle Sea coasts. I was educated in the best schools, and sent to Erin to finish my education, with my two younger brothers, to the holy man, Brendan.' He turned round again and continued on up the track. The ground had been constantly rising, and now the white church lay a little below them and they could see the top of the *Avenger's* mast over the church.

'When my brothers and I learned that Brendan was to sail into the sunset seeking the Isle of Paradise, we resolved to join him. However, the number had been set at twelve of the brothers and Brendan, and there was neither room nor want for three additional men. However,' he flashed a quick, toothless grin over his shoulder, 'that did not prevent us from joining him.' He shrugged his bony shoulders. 'Nor did it prevent us from dying: that was our payment.' He stopped and turned round again. 'You can see just about all the island from here,' he said, pointing downwards. 'I see you've sailed from the east; well, we sailed from the west and encountered the island you will meet with soon, the Isle of Fire. We were passing by it, praying for the souls we saw trapped thereon, when I was suddenly hoisted aloft by a creature of flame. The brothers prayed for me, and Brendan blessed me; perhaps it would have been a little more useful if they had attempted to pull me down.' He shrugged. 'The contemplative life does not lead one to swiftness of thought or action. They thought I was being carried to my destruction, as my two brothers had been destroyed before me, for our crime of unsettling Brendan's holy number of twelve plus one. I wasn't, as you can see.' Marcus smiled again. 'I was carried here and dropped into that lake down there.' He pointed off to one side to where a broad sheet of water glistened in the mid-morning light.

'I have passed my time by building a church to the Christ Jesus here on this foresaken isle . . .' and here his smile faded.

'What's wrong?' Maildun asked.

Marcus looked at the captain with something like pain in his eyes. 'This was completely green when I first came to it. That . . .' he pointed towards the church and the area of desolation around it, 'only occurred when the church was built and consecrated to the Christ Saviour.'

'Perhaps this island had been dedicated to a different god,' Diurnan suggested, 'and now he wars with the White Christ for the land.'

The old man nodded slowly. 'Perhaps; indeed, I fear you are correct.'

'We followed a huge bird here . . .' Maildun began.

'Ah, yes, the roc!' Marcus turned and pointed towards the lake. 'You will find it down by the lakeside. It has been here before . . . well, perhaps it is the same one, although it could be another – although I doubt if there could be two such. Sometimes it is accompanied by griffins, sometimes by eagles.'

'But why does it come here?' Diurnan asked.

Marcus smiled slightly. 'Why, but to renew its youth. This is the Isle of Life.'

The roc was huge. It lay on the rough, sandy beach by the lakeside, its gold-pinioned wings spread, and each span was longer than the length of the *Avenger*. Seen close to, its feathers had a metallic lustre to them, as if they were bronze or copper. The creature was facing away from the two men, so they could see nothing of its head or claws. They could hear its breath wheezing and rattling, and it sounded like an old man dying of the chest sickness.

There were birds sweeping in and darting around its head, and it wasn't until one alighted close to Maildun and Diurnan to preen the roc's tail feathers, that the northerner recognized them for the prized golden eagles. And there were a score of them, preening and picking the lice from the huge bird.

As the sun drifted down towards the horizon and the shadows lengthened, the host of eagles rose up in one body and the setting sun took their plumage and turned them into balls of molten fire as they circled around the stricken bird. Their harsh cries echoed on the evening air and, almost in return, the roc croaked back at them, its voice pitifully weak, but still retaining elements of its awesome power and majesty.

And then it moved.

Maildun and Diurnan saw a claw that resembled forged and reforged iron appear from beneath its massive body and plunge into the earth, sinking into the turf. The leg muscles tensed and the roc lurched forward towards the water. A second claw appeared and gouged a series of scarred cuts in the earth as it pushed the creature even nearer the lakeside. Its wings rose and beat feebly, the down-draught flattening the small bushes and hurtling both men to the ground. The roc rose briefly and then fell again, splashing into the shallows. With a sudden surge of strength, its two claws dug deep into the soft earth, its wings beat and beat again, and the roc lifted and then settled onto the lake. With an almost human sign of contentment, it sank beneath the waves.

Maildun stood up from behind the concealment of some bushes and would have walked down to the water's edge, had not Diurnan gripped his arm and pointed into the heavens. The captain looked up and saw the host of eagles descending towards the lake, thick, leafy branches clutched in their taloned claws. When they were above the spot where the roc had disappeared, they allowed their burdens to drop into the rippling water. Most of the branches sank immediately, but a few remained afloat, and the two watchers saw that these resembled the branches from a holly bush, and came complete with serrated leaves and clusters of red berries. Most of the berries seemed to split when they reached the water, and soon a thin red veneer coated the surface of the lake. Gradually the discolouration spread, until the water burned blood-red in the waning light.

There was a disturbance out in the centre of the lake, a bubbling which turned the red water to bloody froth. The disturbance increased until the entire lake was in motion, with crimson and pink waves splashing onto the lakeside.

And, in an explosion of sound, the roc reappeared. Not the tired and sickened bird that had sunk beneath the waters, but a young, vibrant, majestic creature from the very depths of legend. Its massive wings held it aloft just above the surface of the lake, their powerful beating sending water high into the heavens, the same water that fertilised the isle. It swivelled its elegant head and two huge, whirling golden orbs regarded the cowering men for what seemed like an eternity. Its horned beak opened and they caught a glimpse of a flickering pink tongue and a raw, open gullet, and then it called, its cry shattering the twilight silence with a sound that had not been heard for a thousand years or more.

It rose, slowly and majestically, restored to the prime of its youth. It circled the island once, twice, and then it turned away towards the setting sun, its train of eagles diminished by its size to mites.

It seemed a long time afterwards that Diurnan moved. He shook off the spell of the roc's rising from the bloody waters of the lake and stepped forward, away from the bushes. Maildun reached for him, but the northerner shook off his hand.

'Where are you going? We must be gone.'

'Not yet,' Diurnan said, 'there is something I must do.' He walked down the scarred and torn turf towards the water.

'*Diurnan?*' Maildun demanded.

'The waters renewed the roc's life . . .' He turned to the captain and his eyes blazed. 'Might they not renew mine, grant me eternal life?'

'You fool!' the captain snapped. 'And what if the roc cleansed itself of its poisons in the water; what will happen to you if you bathe in those poisons?'

'Everything has its risks and its price,' Diurnan said, allowing his axe to fall to the grass, and then running forward and throwing himself into the water in a long, shallow dive.

CHAPTER TWENTY-SEVEN

'But I feel no different,' Diurnan said softly to Paedur later that night, as they stood beneath the main mast watching the bulk of the Isle of Life disappear below the horizon.

The bard's teeth flashed in a smile. 'Oh, but you won't. You will never feel any differently than you did this afternoon. You are now immortal – no, perhaps not wholly immortal, but long-lived certainly; long-lived enough perhaps to regret this day.'

Diurnan shook his head. 'Oh, I doubt that,' he said confidently. 'It is a dream come true.'

'Take care then lest that dream turn into a nightmare,' Paedur said, turning away and disappearing into the night.

Diurnan leaned back against the mast and stared up into the heavens. He watched the strange configurations and sweeps of gauzy light, and found that they looked brighter, sharper, than they had before. The colours were more distinct and he could distinguish subtle variations of colour in the sheets of stars. It was very easy to imagine that they were alive.

'How do you feel?'

Diurnan turned and found himself looking into the captain's hard green eyes . . . and then he wondered how he could perceive their colour in the dark. And even as that thought came to him, he realised that it was not truly night – not for him! Like the bard, he now had sight in the dark.

'I . . . I'm feeling fine,' he said slowly, as the realisation sunk in; it was the first true revelation of his change.

'I thought the water might be poisoned,' Maildun said softly, as the two men moved away from the mast and made their way down the length of the ship.

'I wasn't really thinking clearly at the time', Diurnan admitted, 'all I thought about was the fact that I might renew my youth . . .'

'Perhaps it was just as well that it didn't work.'

The northerner hesitated. 'Aye, perhaps.'

'I doubt if you would have been truly happy,' the captain

continued, reaching the stern and leaning over the side to stare down into the black water. 'Would he, Germane?'

The navigator glanced over, his face, in the light of a small, guttering fish-oil lamp, impassive. 'I doubt it,' he said cautiously.

'Aye,' Maildun nodded. 'The bard tells us that he is immortal – and I've no reason to doubt him – but he sails with us seeking death. Leucosia the Siren was also a seeker of death. No, Diurnan, immortality is a curse; you should thank God you did not achieve it.'

Diurnan grunted non-committally. Something prevented him from telling Maildun that he had indeed achieved life immortal, but Germane, he suspected, knew.

'The bard says we are near home,' the navigator remarked changing the subject.

Maildun nodded. 'Aye, but he also admits that he knows little about this part of the Island Sea.'

'The old hermit said we would soon come to an island of fire,' Diurnan said, recalling Marcus' words.

'Then let us hope it is soon; I am wearied of this voyage,' Maildun said softly.

'And what of your revenge?' Diurnan asked.

With his new sight, the northerner saw the captain's face tighten with pain, saw him crossing himself. 'God has seen fit to punish me for attempting to usurp his place. I once mocked him and said that vengeance was mine – he has taught me otherwise.'

'And Archu, the Hound of Slaughter?'

Maildun shrugged. 'He means nothing to me now.'

The wind, gusting from offshore, carried with it the sounds of laughter and the stench of blood.

Paedur joined Maildun by the rail and they looked across towards the almost flat island. Even from the distance they could see the vast number of people moving about, and they saw the flash of weapons rising and falling.

'Avoid it,' Paedur advised.

Maildun nodded. 'Aye, but I'm curious; they seem to be fighting and yet there is the sound of laughter.'

'Ask Diurnan and he will tell you tales of the berserkers; warriors who ran naked into battle, howling with maniacal laughter. Avoid the isle,' he repeated.

Maildun shook his head; his hair, which, at the start of the voyage, had been startlingly red, was now shot through with silver, and there were lines around his eyes and mouth. 'No, we will pass close to.' He turned and stared into the bard's eyes, his own distorted reflection staring back at him. 'You see, I have come to the realisation that this voyage was . . . *ordained* for me.'

'Ordained?'

The captain nodded. 'Ordained. By God.'

The bard examined his hook closely. When he looked up his eyes were flat and expressionless. 'I would prefer destiny or some such phrase. My experience with gods is that they have little time or use for man.'

'No, no, no. It is the will of God. This is my penance.'

Paedur nodded cautiously. 'As you will, then.'

Maildun smiled. 'Aye, as I will, as God wills. We will pass close to that isle, perhaps there is a lesson there for us.'

'Should we not be pressing on?' Paedur asked. 'We are not far from your world now – I can feel it.'

'The island first.'

The island was almost flat and roughly rectangular in shape. It rose straight up out of the water like the plateau of a sunken land. There were no cliffs or beach and there seemed to be no vegetation of any sort. The island was filled with thousands of milling people, seemingly drawn from every race and time. They were engaged in a battle of sorts, although even when one was dealt a mortal blow and fell to the ground, as soon as his slayer had moved on he rose to his feet again and continued to fight.

And everyone was laughing.

The carnage was frightening, and seeing the dead rising to fight again was even more so, but the laughter was hideous. It was high-pitched and grated along the spine, setting the teeth on edge, and it was truly insane.

And then there were the faces. Germane saw them first, just a glimpse, a fleeting glimpse of a figure that had looked terrifyingly like his long-dead father. When he looked again the small, dark-haired man with the matched short swords was gone, but there was another, a taller, wild-haired, ebon-skinned woman he had known and loved in the port of Alexandria – but she was dead too, dead of the plague that had swept through the port in his absence. And then suddenly, everywhere he looked, he saw faces and people he had once known: his dead brother, who had drowned beyond the Pillars of Hercules; his sister, who had married well, and then died in childbirth; his mother . . . but he had not seen his mother in years, and though he had not thought of it, he reckoned that she must be dead now . . .

Iron-hard fingers bit into his shoulder muscles and spun him round. He looked into the bard's face, saw his pained expression mirrored in his flat eyes. 'It is all an illusion,' Paedur said coldly, 'an illusion intended to trap you.' His voice was low and controlled, commanding and powerful.

'But there are people there I know . . . knew . . .'

'Illusion.' The bard placed the flat of his hook against the navigator's cheek, and Germane winced at its other-worldly chill. 'See it for what it truly is.'

Germane looked across at the isle again. The writhing, deadly dance went on, but the figures were all strangers. There was no one he knew. It had all been an illusion, but, as he looked along the deck, he saw that all the crew were under the same spell – all except two.

One was Diurnan who, like the bard, was moving steadily down the deck, shaking the men out of their trances, forcing them to see the island for what is was, and the other was Ruarc, Maildun's foster-brother. And he was attempting to lower a currach into the water.

Germane shouted and ran across the deck towards him. They only had two of the small craft left, and one was in poor repair. Ruarc's face contorted into a mask of rage and he swung at the navigator with the currach's flat oar. Germane threw himself down to the deck, feeling the oar pass through his hair. He frantically rolled to one side as Ruarc chopped down with the blade of the oar. Ruarc set his shoulder under the light craft and, with a final effort, heaved it overboard. The vessel splashed and shipped some water before righting itself, and then the waves took it and batted it against the *Avenger's* port side. Ruarc took one final swing at Germane, and then threw himself into the water beside it. He scrambled into the boat, almost overturning it in his haste, and then he used the oar to push himself away from the *Avenger*. Once free of the craft, the tide took his light craft and carried him in towards the shore.

Diurnan ran up to Germane, a throwing spear in his hand. He hauled the slim navigator to his feet, took a stance and drew back his arm. Germane laid his hand on the northerner's arm and shook his head. 'Let him go, Diurnan, I'm unhurt.'

'He would have killed you!'

'He's mad,' Germane said softly, watching Paedur drag a raving Maildun from the rail and club him to the deck with the flat of his hook. 'I'm beginning to think it runs in the family – related or otherwise.'

The tide carried the currach in towards the shore, and threw it

231

against the cliffs that rose straight up out of the water. The currach shuddered, but the seemingly frail craft was amazingly resilient and bounced back, before the tide lifted it again and forced it in on the cliffs. Ruarc was ready the second time and, at the height of the wave, threw himself forward and up onto the cliff. His fingers scrabbled for a hold as the water fell away, and then he pushed himself up onto the flat plateau. He ran into the crowd, and his voice could be heard above the maniacal laughter, 'Colga . . . Gussan . . . Colga!' He reached for a tall warrior, and then screamed aloud as the face that turned towards him was nothing more than a skull. He screamed again as the creature drove a crude sword into his stomach, and fell to the bloody stones. When his assailant had moved on, the creature that had once been Ruarc opened his eyes. His mouth moved and the scream bubbling in his throat turned to laughter, hideous, demented laughter.

'I saw my brothers, and a man whose face was as familiar as my own; I saw my father.'

'Illusion, all an illusion,' Paedur said gently. 'If you had seen them in their true guises, you would have seen little more than skeletal figures.'

Maildun swung his legs off his cot and rested his elbows on his knees before cradling his head in his hands. 'But I saw my father,' he insisted. 'Even though I've never seen the man, I knew him.'

The bard nodded, his eyes burning golden in the light from the oil-lamp. 'Aye, in all probability you did see your father.'

Maildun looked up and smiled slightly, something of his old good-humour showing in his pained eyes. 'I told you the island was there for a reason. I told you I felt the hand of God in all this,' he said proudly.

'Maildun,' the bard said quietly, 'Ruarc took one of the currachs and rowed to the isle.'

The captain's face hardened, and he rose shakily to his feet. 'Well, why hasn't a party gone over for him?' he demanded.

'Maildun, we left that isle behind us some hours ago now.'

'And Ruarc, you left Ruarc there?'

'The isle induces a special madness – he was lost the moment he set foot on its stones.'

'But you could have prevented him from going,' Maildun raged.

'Germane tried; Ruarc almost killed him for it.'

Abruptly Maildun slumped back down onto his thin pallet. 'So they are all gone: Gussan, Colga and now little Ruarc.' He looked over at the dark shape of the bard, and there were tears in his eyes and his haggard face looked even more aged. 'For years I looked on them as my brothers. Colga was our leader, and then Gussan and I were nearly of an age; Ruarc was the youngest, the handsomest, the quickest, and now they are all gone.'

'They knew the druid's warning, and yet they chose to follow you of their own free will because they loved you – you will always have that.'

Maildun nodded wearily. 'I know, but that won't bring them back.'

The door to the tiny cabin opened and Diurnan stuck his head in. He looked from Maildun to the bard, and then back to the captain. 'You had better come now, Maildun; the sky is afire.'

CHAPTER TWENTY-EIGHT

'I've heard tell of something like it,' Germane said, as Diurnan rejoined him with the bard and Maildun close behind. They stood in the prow while the navigator shaded his eyes and looked towards the horizon, which was aflame with a shimmering curtain of fire, paling even the night stars.

Diurnan nodded. 'Aye, so have I.'

Germane looked over his shoulder at Maildun. 'I've heard tales of the Ghost Lights in the Northern Seas, beyond Thule; this would seem to be something similar.'

Diurnan shook his head. 'Not this; the Ghost Lights are soft, shifting bands of colours, like a curtain across the skies . . .' He stopped, suddenly embarrassed by his own eloquence. 'These lights are too harsh,' he finished.

Germane considered. 'I don't know. It looks as if the entire world is afire.'

'Fire!' Maildun looked round at the northerner. 'What did the hermit say of an island of fire?'

Diurnan swore. 'Of course; he said an island of fire lay in our path.' He nodded towards the horizon. 'That must be it.'

Maildun ran his fingers through his beard. 'Probably an outpost of Hell,' he muttered, turning away.

The dawn light paled the lurid fire, but the island itself, when it rose in a mass of flame over the horizon, did indeed seem like an outpost of Hell.

It was a broad, flat disc shape, but beyond that they could see nothing, for it was walled in by towering sheets of flame that seemed to be revolving slowly around the isle. The flame was completely silent, nor was there any sign of smoke, and where it touched the water there was no steam or hissing.

'Another illusion?' Maildun asked bitterly as they neared the isle.

Paedur shook his head doubtfully. 'I don't think so. The wind is behind us, and onshore. Another few lengths, though, and we'll know whether it's real or not.'

And they were barely two ship lengths from the isle when they

234

felt the first pricklings of heat. Soon it had become almost unbearable, a furnace blast that beat at flesh and made metal too hot to touch.

There was a sudden flash of green on the island – and then it was gone.

'What was that!'

Paedur rubbed his hook reflectively. 'It looked like a gate – an opening – of some sort in that wall of fire.'

'And that sudden flash of green?'

'Grasslands,' the bard said slowly, 'it looked like a stretch of rolling green grasslands.' His voice was hushed in wonder.

Maildun half turned. 'Germane, bring her in closer.'

The navigator shouted something, but his words were lost on the now quickening breeze. He handed the steering oar over to one of the crew and hurried down the deck to where Maildun and Paedur were standing. Diurnan joined them.

'We dare not go any closer,' Germane protested.

'We must, we must.' Maildun's voice was soft and almost distant as he gazed intently at the island.

Germane looked to the bard for support, but the bard too seemed entranced by the island.

'The heat is too much,' Germane continued, looking at Diurnan. 'If we continue, we stand the risk of setting the sail aflame.'

'He's right,' Diurnan said loudly, trying to break the spell that seemed to have enthralled both Maildun and the bard. 'I've men sluicing the deck at this moment to try and keep us cool, but it's not good enough. It's madness to continue,' he snapped angrily.

Maildun nodded slowly. 'Aye, madness.'

Diurnan turned to Germane. 'Take us away from . . .'

The door in the fire opened again.

There was indeed a rolling green grassland beyond the wall of fire. A meadowland hauntingly reminiscent of Erin's pastures, and it stretched back into gentle hills, which in turn rose into purpling mountains which, though they should have been visible above the top of the fire, were not. There was a flicker of colour – and the fire rolled around again as the gate shifted.

The spell of the meadowland hidden behind the wall of fire kept the four men still and silent, waiting and watching for the next opening.

The door opened.

And now there were figures moving behind the fire, seemingly

untouched and unconcerned by the heat. They were tall, attenuated figures, ethereally beautiful, with hair the colour of gold
thread. Their features were perhaps a little too thin and sharp to
be human, and their eyes a little too large and too bright in their
faces. Their garments were of the finest cloth and they carried
goblets and platters of gold.

The gate closed, but the image remained of the feasting folk.

'The People of the Goddess,' Paedur whispered softly, almost
to himself.

'The Tuatha De Danann?' Maildun asked.

Paedur nodded slowly. 'The Tuatha De Danann.' He turned
away from the island and wiped the edge of his cloak across his
face. His hand was trembling. 'The island reeks of powerful
magic,' he said slowly, 'I find it enervating.' He looked at the
captain. 'I think it would be wise for us to move on.' He jerked
his thumb back at the isle. 'We have not registered on their
consciousness yet, but, if we did, I doubt they would even give a
second thought to swatting us like an insect.'

'I thought you sought death?' Diurnan asked, half-seriously.

'True death, aye,' Paedur nodded, 'but the De Danann offer
only an everlasting limbo, a half-life. They would suck you dry
and leave your drained husk to perform the most menial tasks
like an imbecile. Even their magic wall feeds upon the life forces
of those of the Race of Man whom they took into captivity with
them.'

'The *banshee*?' Maildun asked.

'No, not the *banshee*. The *banshee* was a woman of your world
who went into the barrows with them, but was changed by them
to exist where there would be neither food nor drink for her;
those slaves on the isle are merely life-forces to be used and
drained to fuel their magic. And that is why the longer we linger
here, the more noticeable our own seeping life-forces will
become: soon we would have neither the will nor the strength to
escape their pull.'

Maildun nodded. 'It does indeed seem like an outpost of Hell.'
He nodded to Germane and Diurnan. 'Take us away from here.'

Paedur looked at the island for a last time and then deliberately
turned away when the gate reappeared. 'I think even your
Christian Hell would be preferable to a living death as a slave to
the People of the Goddess.'

'Why did they leave Erin?' Maildun wondered aloud.

'Their time was done; the Age of Gods had passed and the
Time of Man was at hand. All things of creation have their

appointed times and durations, and theirs had run its course. All things end.'

'Even men?'

Paedur nodded. 'Especially man.'

With the Isle of Fire now behind them, and the wind full in their sail, the *Avenger* skipped along at a steady rate. The crew worked more willingly and with a lighter heart than they had for a long time, and even raised their voices in a bawdy sea-shanty without Diurnan's urging.

'They know we near their homeland,' Paedur said to Germane, as the navigator eased the longship around to catch the breeze.

'I know; it's almost as if I feel . . . lighter, somehow.'

Paedur smiled, one eye reflecting the blue of the sky and the other the dun of the sail. 'You are, for you are re-entering the transition between the two planes; there is a region of "greyness" that belongs to neither.'

'Like the Sea of Wonders?'

Paedur shook his head. 'Not quite. The sea was a separate entity existing inside another entity; naturally the distortion and disassociation was more severe. Here we are gradually moving from one plane to another.'

'Towards the opening left by Archu's druid?'

Paedur shook his head. 'No; when we were tossed northward, we lost any chance we had of ever reaching that opening.'

'But we are heading towards a gateway?'

Paedur nodded. 'Aye, we are heading towards the Gate in the Arch, the first – or last – sight on the Island Sea.' He held up his hook and would say nothing more except one word. 'Wait.'

The colossal arch that rose from the evening sea was the colour of bone and, with the sun sinking down behind it, it glowed the colour of old ivory. It took the form of two broad uprights rising straight up from the sea and topped by a broad, flat archway. The stonework was entirely covered with tiny, ornate and detailed pictograms cut in bas-relief.

'It reminds me of the great henges in the Land of the Britons that are sacred to the druids,' Germane said as they neared the archway.

The bard looked from Germane to the archway, his eyes taking on the rose and ivory colouring. 'Aye, they served the same function once,' he said quietly. 'They are the doorways between the worlds.'

'A doorway?' Maildun asked, joining them by the rail.

237

'A doorway connecting the planes of existence,' Paedur explained.

'But we didn't come through a doorway when we arrived in this world,' Maildun protested.

The bard shook his head. 'Ah, but we did. Such things,' he nodded towards the archway, 'are but conveniences; any proficient person can move at will through the veil between the worlds. Archu's druid's ability, coupled with his sudden and violent death, created the rent in the fabric of the worlds and pushed us through. The rent would take a long time to heal – centuries of your time perhaps. But this is a doorway, and the doorways are permanently open, and yet they usually have a guardian, someone who controls the access from one plane to another.' He suddenly pointed with his hook. 'And there is the Guardian of the Gate.'

There was a man standing atop the broad, upright beam of stone. With the sun behind him, his features and age were impossible to distinguish and his overlong hair, beard and the long ragged robe he wore flapped and blew in a breeze that didn't touch the *Avenger's* sails.

Diurnan called the order and the oars lifted, and then dipped again slowly, merely holding the longship in place before the archway and just beyond its attenuated shadow.

Maildun and Paedur stood at the prow and stared up at the shadowed figure, and the captain glanced nervously at the bard before cupping his hands around his mouth and calling up to the man. 'We seek passage through the Gate of the Arch, back to the land of Erin.'

The small man remained standing atop the arch, staring silently downwards.

'I am Maildun, captain of the *Avenger* . . .' Maildun began again.

'Your name, your lineage and your voyage are known to me.' The voice, though rasping with seeming ill-use, was strong and forceful. 'Why should I grant you leave to journey between the worlds, Maildun, son of Oilill Agach?'

Maildun glanced quickly at the bard and then up again at the figure on the rock. 'I . . . we have been long avoyaging, we wish to return home.' He paused and then added, 'Is Erin truly beyond the archway?'

'Banba lies through the gate,' the figure said, 'and know that I once hailed from the Isle of Torach, which lies off Banba's north and western shores.'

238

'You are from Erin . . . Banba?' Maildun asked, puzzled.

'I am. I was. It is many years since I breathed the sweet air of my homeland.'

'Then how did you come to be here, and what is your name?' Maildun asked, but the bard reached over and touched his arm lightly. 'Be careful; he might not wish to answer and your questions might anger him.'

The figure laughed. 'Nay, his questions do not anger me. It has been long since anyone took the time to ask me such questions.'

The sun had dipped down behind the archway, and rose and salmon light silhouetted the figure in blood and shadow. The tall shadows of the uprights stretched out on either side of the *Avenger*, and a breeze, warm and touched with the smell of damp earth, blew through the gate.

'My name is . . .' The figure paused and then seemed to shrug. 'My name is of no account. I am the Guardian of the Gate; I have been so for longer than I can remember, and thus I will remain until the end of time, or until this gateway is closed. I was a monk in Banba once, when the faith was newly come to the land, but I betrayed that faith and stole from my brothers and the followers of the faith. I grew prideful, and, resolving to flee the monastic life, loaded up a currach with all my worldy goods and set sail for the warm southern lands where there is forever sun and warmth. I was . . . trapped.' The figure paused, as the sun sank down behind him in a welter of blood and fire, and the sky blazed briefly before plunging into darkness. Overhead the alien night stars blazed and wheeled across the sky – but through the archway the hard and brilliant points of familiar stars sparkled into life.

'My greed trapped me,' the Guardian continued. 'And to save myself, I was forced to abandon my wealth and cast it into the sea. I was told it would be returned to its owners,' he added drily. 'As punishment, I spent many years on a tiny barren rock that drifted across the seas of its own accord. I ate when fish were cast up onto my rock. I drank when it rained.'

'And how came you here?' Maildun asked quietly.

'My floating rock carried me through the gate,' he said simply. 'The old Guardian of the Gate was waiting for me. He was an old, old man then, and he had guarded the gate since the dawning of the world. He informed me that my punishment was to assume his task; henceforth I would be the Guardian of the Gate – my penance to stand here, on the edge of my own world, but unable to return to it.'

'Will you let us through?' Paedur asked suddenly, his powerful voice carrying clearly through the night silence.

'If I were a mean and spiteful man, Paedur Hook-hand, envying your return to your . . . my . . . world, I would say no. But I am not a mean and spiteful man,' he added quietly. 'And I doubt if I could stop you if you wish to travel on; could I, bard? However,' he continued, without waiting for an answer, 'you may travel through with my blessing.'

'I thank you for that,' Maildun said.

The Guardian laughed. 'Do not thank me; thank your God, for he has brought you through the Island Sea, although surely you deserved and invited death on more than one occasion. Your bard will tell you how often the Island Sea has been traversed.'

'It has never been successfully traversed,' Paedur said quietly and the Guardian continued.

'You are destined to meet with your sworn enemy, Maildun. When you encounter Archu, the Hound of Slaughter, bear in mind God's mercy towards you.

'You, Paedur Hook-Hand, are destined to continue your wandering. Perhaps it is mere capriciousness, but those who willingly seek death rarely find it.

'And you, Diurnan Lenkard, enjoy and utilise your gift, learn from this bard its dangers, and avoid them.

'Your destiny, Germane, has been all but fulfilled. You have sailed beyond the world of men; fulfil your destiny now and create a record for future generations to read and learn from.'

The Guardian rose and spread his arms, and the barest glimmer of white fire danced across his chest, momentarily highlighting his face, illuminating . . . a skull.

'The Gate of the Arch opens; sail on and complete the Voyage of Maildun.'

CHAPTER TWENTY-NINE

There were no dramatic changes as the *Avenger* sailed through the Gate of the Arch, the tip of its mast barely clearing the cross-beam. Indeed, the only sign of their transition was that the configurations of the stars changed from the sweeping bands of light and cloud to the singular brilliance of the more familiar stars of the skies above Erin.

'We're home,' Maildun said in a whisper, as if unable to believe it. He looked across at the bard for confirmation.

Paedur nodded, folding his arms into his sleeves. 'You will sight Erin with the dawn.'

'No mighty magic, no winds, gales, thunder and lightning?' Diurnan asked with a smile.

'Not necessary. The druid's death brought that on.'

'And the Gate?'

'What gate?' Paedur asked, stars dancing in his eyes.

The northerner turned around and pointed, 'That . . .'

The Gate was gone.

The *Avenger* passed a small island in the early hours of the morning. Compared with what they had witnessed, it was unremarkable, barely a ragged chunk of stone, white-streaked and lichened. Scores of gulls and gannets rose and whirled briefly above the rock before settling down again. One bird, however, hung on narrow, outspread wings above it and then it slowly circled the *Avenger*, before setting off on the port side, its narrow wings beating slowly and strongly.

Germane shaded his eyes; the bird was difficult to distinguish against the lightening sky, but he thought he knew the shape. 'It's a falcon,' he said at last, and looked at Diurnan. The northerner nodded silently.

'Well then . . . it can only be going to one place,' Maildun said softly.

The sky lightened gradually, unlike the sudden mornings of the Shadowland, and the sun came up in a smearing of colours across the eastern skies, tinting the drabness with light, washing

241

the grey from the waves. There was land on the horizon, a narrow band of blackness with the night stars still sparkling above it. But, even as they watched, the cliffs began to glow with colour and took on shape and definition.

The *Avenger* had returned to Erin.

In the still night, the trained voice carried across the waves in a powerful rendition of one of Cucuhulain's feats.

Maildun shivered, recalling the bard who had cast them forth onto the Island Sea; he too had been recounting one of the tales of the Setanta.

'All things come full circle,' Paedur said quietly, standing beside him. 'Thus you return to Archu's fort, and now you fulfil your destiny. Remember the Guardian of the Gate,' he advised, turning away and rejoining Germane and Diurnan as they armed themselves and made ready the last remaining currach.

The song finished and voices raised in cheers and laughter and then called for more. Light lanced out from the squat fort and darted down the beach in a long, yellow bar as the door was opened. A voice that was little more than a rasp cursed loudly, and the door was hastily slammed shut.

With Maildun and Diurnan at the oars, the small currach skipped silently across the water in towards the shore. The tide was high and brought them up almost to the foot of the low dunes. The voices were clearer now, and they could smell the odours of freshly cooked meat, mingled with the warm earthiness of a smoking fire on the air.

The fort was a large, round building of wood and thatch, surrounded by a tall palisade of sharpened, fire-hardened stakes. However, the palisade had been allowed to fall into disrepair, and the four men moved through it without hindrance. The building itself was surrounded by a scattering of smaller outhouses, with nets hung to dry to one side and the stench of rotten fish mingling with the odours of offal. The fort had two doors, one to the front and one to the rear, and two small, square windows had been cut into the sides.

Maildun positioned himself at the main door, while the bard moved away to the rear, flitting like a wraith across the muddy ground. Germane and Diurnan positioned themselves by the windows.

The minstrel's voice rose to a crescendo and, in the silence that followed before the applause, Maildun kicked in the door, his

242

blow sending the rotten wood across the earthen floor, scattering sparks and cinders from the fire in the centre of the room.

'I am Maildun, son of Oilill Agach,' he announced.

There were twenty or more men in the fort, along with a score of women and a scattering of servants. Their clothing had clearly seen better times, and the stench of unwashed humanity was almost overpowering in the confines of the building. Maildun, however, had eyes only for one person.

Archu, the Hound of Slaughter, rose from his honour-seat directly facing the door. He was a tall man, though now stopped by age, and his hair was silver-grey. He had once been muscular, but that had now run to fat, and his paunch hung over his belt. His square face was seamed and lined, and his light blue eyes were hard and bitter. He grinned, and the scar on his neck where his throat had once been inexpertly cut moved like a second mouth. 'Maildun . . . Maildun.' He shook his head in wonder.

Maildun pulled his sword free and held it up before his face with both hands. 'I have come for you, Archu,' he said coldly.

The reiver folded his hands across his broad chest, and then a wickedly curved hook crept around his throat. 'If you were to continue holding that knife,' Paedur whispered, 'I might be forced to slit your throat – and properly this time.'

Archu stiffened and dropped the knife he had slid from a sheath sewn into the back of his belt. 'Be still,' he commanded his men, sensing the gathering tension and the slow movements towards weapons. His eyes widened slightly as Germane and Diurnan joined their captain, one with a nocked and ready bow, and the other with a huge, double-headed, battleaxe.

'I should kill you, Archu,' Maildun said, his voice beginning to tremble with emotion.

The reiver nodded and then winced as the bard's hook bit into his throat. 'It would be what I would do if I were in your place.'

'I should butcher you, as you did my father.' Maildun advanced slowly, his sword held out before him. 'You do remember my father?'

Archu grimaced, the lines on his face deepening. 'I remember your father – and he was never worthy of a son like you.' His voice grated, little more than a croak. 'He knew little of honour. He would not have done the same for you, you know that, don't you?'

'I know little about my father – and the little I know, I don't care for,' Maildun's voice faltered.

'Perhaps what you know is enough; he was neither a good nor

243

honourable man.' Archu smiled crookedly. 'I should talk! I am not a good man – not as they define good in these modern times – but I am a man of honour.' He said this proudly, straightening himself almost unconsciously.

'Honour!' Maildun spat and, stepping forward, placed the tip of his sword against Archu's throat; along the line of his scar. The bard withdrew his hook and stepped back, but for one moment his eyes caught and held the captain's, and Maildun had a brief glimpse of a figure with a face he did not recognise reflected in the flat mirror eyes. 'Honour! What do you know of honour?' he demanded. 'You bled my father like a pig and then burned him in the House of God.'

Archu raised his head as the sword bit deeper into his throat. He swallowed hard and the raw scar worked like a mouth. 'I gave him the chance of fair and single combat – he refused. He slew one of the priests of that church with the holy cross taken from the altar.'

'You're lying,' Maildun screamed, and swung his sword round for a decapitating blow. Archu continued to regard him evenly, his watery eyes unflinching even in death. The sword came down – and stopped barely a finger's breadth from the reiver's throat. 'You're lying,' Maildun said, and looked to the bard for confirmation.

Paedur stepped away from the wall and raised his head. His eyes took in the firelight and blazed red and gold in his face. 'He does not lie,' he said simply, and then dipped his head, extinguishing the fire in his eyes.

Maildun regarded him dumbly for a score of heartbeats, his sword still quivering at Archu's throat. And then it dropped and Maildun fell to his knees beside it, his hands frozen on the quillons. His shoulders heaved in silent sobs.

Archu knelt down stiffly beside him. He reached out and touched the young man on the shoulder. 'I regret slaying your father,' he said hoarsely, 'not for his sake, but for yours.' His grip tightened. 'I would have given much to have had a son like you who held honour in such high esteem – even misplaced honour.' He looked up and found one of his servants. 'Bring food and drink,' he commanded. 'Our honoured guests have travelled far and both hunger and thirst . . .'

Maildun raised his head. 'We cannot . . .' he began.

'Why not?' Archu asked.

Maildun looked first at him and then up at the bard. And then he shook his head. 'I can think of no reason why I should not dine with you,' he said finally, rising to his feet. He reached down and helped the older man up. 'No reason at all.'

'And your companions?' Archu wondered.

Maildun turned and looked at Germane and Diurnan, now beginning to lower their weapons. 'Let it end here, old friends,' he said.

'Does it end here, Maildun?' Paedur asked from the shadows.

Maildun turned and looked over Archu's shoulder at the tall, shadowed figure of the bard. 'It ends here.'

'And vengeance?'

'"*Vengeance is mine, saith the Lord*"' Maildun quoted, '"*forgive those who have sinned against you, as you would be forgiven.*"' He looked away from the bard and over to Archu. 'I would ask your forgiveness,' he said simply.

'And I yours.'

'Then it is ended,' Paedur whispered.

Even the brightest lamp eventually dims, and a vengeance like that of Maildun could not be long sustained against the trials and dangers of the Sea of Islands. The Word of the Lord carried him through much tribulation and pain, and he, recognising the Lord's justice and mercy, chose to exercise clemency in turn.

He returned to Erin after an absence of three years and seven months, and eventually took to the contemplative life where he passed the remainder of his days.

Germane, who had been called the navigator, took to the sea only once thereafter, but found it dull and uninspiring after the magic and mystery of the otherworld, and it is he who was responsible for the fashioning of this tale.

Of the blond northerner and the shadowed bard there is naught known. Both immortal, they visited Ard Macha briefly, where Diurnan left the silver mesh he had cut from the Silver Pillar as proof of the voyage, and then they set off to wander the known world. Perhaps they wander still.

Aed the Fair, Bard of Erin.

BIBLIOGRAPHY

The following is a select bibliography of works dealing with the Voyage of Maildun. However, works relating to the Voyage of Saint Brendan, the Voyage of Bran and the Voyage of the Ui Corrai's Boat are of related interest.

Best & Meyer: *Immram Curaig Mailediun*. (Anecdota from Irish Manuscripts, 1907)

Lady Gregory: *The Voyage of Maeldune*. (A Book of Saints & Wonders, 1906 & 1907)

Hamel: *Immram Curaig Mail Duin*. (Immrama, 1941)

– On the text of *Immram Curaig Mailduin*. (Etudes Celtique, 1938)

Joyce: *The Voyage of Maildun*. (Old Celtic Romances, 1879)

O'Growney: *Imomramh curaigh Maele Dhuin*. (Gaelic Journal, 1891–1892)

Stokes: *The Voyage of Mael Duin*. (Revue Celtique, 1888–1889).

The manuscript of this work was prepared on an ICL PC15 computer, using Word Star software, courtesy of POS Systems, and Fred Hanna (Booksellers) Ltd., Dublin.

Warner Books now offers an exciting range of quality titles by both established and new authors which can be ordered from the following address:
Little, Brown and Company (UK) Limited,
Cash Sales Department,
P.O. Box 11,
Falmouth,
Cornwall TR10 9EN.

Alternatively you may fax your order to the above address. Fax No. 0326 376423.

Payments can be made as follows: cheque, postal order (payable to Little, Brown and Company) or by credit cards, Visa/Access. Do not send cash or currency. UK customers and B.F.P.O. please allow £1.00 for postage and packing for the first book, plus 50p for the second book, plus 30p for each additional book up to a maximum charge of £3.00 (7 books plus).

Overseas customers including Ireland, please allow £2.00 for the first book plus £1.00 for the second book, plus 50p for each additional book.

NAME (Block Letters) ....

ADDRESS ....

....

☐ I enclose my remittance for _____

☐ I wish to pay by Access/Visa Card

Number ☐☐☐☐☐☐☐☐☐☐☐☐☐☐☐☐

Card Expiry Date ☐☐☐☐